hog-dogging

n. 1. a (blood) sport in which trained dogs corner (wild) pigs; 2. showing off; hot-dogging. (from Doubletongued.org Dictionary)

On a crash course:

Former Deputy Billy Lafitte The hog. A no-good, dangerous, shit-for-brains traitor

Special Agent Franklin Rome The law. A man willing to blackmail and bribe his fellow lawmen into helping him ferret Lafitte out of hiding, in order to do what the too-lax government wouldn't let him do back in Yellow Medicine county, just months ago. Billy's end will justify Rome's means.

Desiree Rome The wife. She's already nearly sacrificed her marriage to Rome once for Lafitte. She won't let it happen again.

Ginny Lafitte The bait. Squeeze a man's unstable ex-wife and watch her overprotective former love appear from thin air to stand by his family.

Steel God The backup. Leader of a cult-like biker club, God's got Billy's back. He gives the fugitive a turquoise motorcycle and fifty extra pounds of muscle.

Kristal The ride-along. Billy's biker gang version of Lady Macbeth.

Perry & Fawn The dangerous fools. Paint-huffing, knife-wielding rednecks who get tangled up in shit they don't understand.

Colleen The wildcard. A broken-hearted, vengeful woman just as hot for Lafitte's blood as Rome is. If she gets to Billy first, there won't be much leftover.

Will the desolate prairies of southwestern Minnesota survive this collision?

Hogdoggin'

a novel by
Anthony Neil Smith

BLEAK
HOUSE
BOOKS

Published by
BLEAK HOUSE BOOKS
a division of Big Earth Publishing
923 Williamson St.
Madison, WI 53703
www.bleakhousebooks.com

Printed in the United States of America
12 11 10 09   1 2 3 4 5 6 7 8 9 10

978-1-60648-024-3 (hardback)
978-1-60648-025-0 (paperback)
978-1-60648-026-7 (evidence collection)

This one's for Tang and Lorna

(The cats)

One

STEEL GOD said "Fuckin' guilty."

Made a lump in Billy Lafitte's throat, made his stomach twist the way you would a dirty rag. And he wasn't even the guy Steel God was talking about.

The guy Steel God judged guilty was called Red Gator. He'd come from New Orleans, so no matter what he'd done, Lafitte felt bad for him. Couple of Southern exiles in the middle of South Dakota making do in ways they had probably never expected, finding replacement families and lovers after realizing they'd never see the real thing again.

Well, Lafitte realized it. He'd fucked up, and no matter how much bile he had to swallow to stand there with Steel God's biker clan as his Sergeant At Arms, it made awful but righteous sense. Red Gator hadn't seen it that way. He'd made a stupid mistake of blowing a trade-off on purpose in order to get picked up and try to work a deal that put him back together with his dying sister and estranged kids while bringing down every last one of his fellow riders. Guess he didn't think the others would find out and short circuit his grand scheme.

Some stood, others sat, in a circle around Red, who was tied by wire to a kitchen chair out back of a half-burned farm house.

Fourteen of them that evening, a fire going on a jury-rigged barbecue grill, a split oil drum welded together, hot enough to keep the crisp frost of late fall off their faces even ten feet away. Red heard the verdict and dropped his jaw, strained forward.

He said, "It's not right! I wouldn't have told them anything real. They would've chased down a dead end. I'd never roll on you, God."

Steel God was reclining on a tree trunk, bottle of beer in one hand, cigar in the other. Damn thing wasn't even lit. The tree had been struck by lightning, caught the house on fire. Abandoned, but still a few undamaged rooms, so the clan took them over for a spell. Steel God listened to Red beg without batting an eye.

"You need to believe me. These guys," Red motioned with his head to the right. At the guys. At Lafitte. "They're feeding you bad intel because I know what they've got planned for you. I can tell you shit, man, you wouldn't believe." He scooted the chair closer. A couple of guys moved to stop him, but Steel God waved them off. Red could get an inch away and still not hurt Steel God. That's how he got the name Steel God—tough motherfucker. Beyond tough.

And yeah, Lafitte knew some of the guys were talking mutiny. Talking about going back to the Outlaws instead of sticking with Steel God's dream of a new society in the wilderness, new power. Maybe Steel God's people came across as cultish because of that, but Lafitte liked the man's dream. Angels or Outlaws, always fighting, getting corrupt enough that they'd forgotten why they rode together in the first place. Dealing meth, that was just a way to keep the family together. Let it become the whole enchilada and down you go. The Outlaws were "one-percenters", the few who ate, slept, and drank the gang life. But Steel God was one of an even smaller number. He'd grown weary of the wars with the other groups, of the hypocrisy, of the wheel spinning. The fucking drugs, Jesus, too many users among the merchants. He was done with that. Steel God would've preferred to drop the drugs shit altogether as soon as his people could make it on their own, live off the land. And he wanted the women to feel like a real part of the gang, not just sex toys. He could give a shit if you rode a Harley or not, as long as it was a bike you were passionate about. A couple of the boys even had jacked-up Yamahas and Kawasakis.

Over the past few years, Steel God slowly, quietly, seceded from the Outlaws until he was on the cusp of a peaceful transition. Then some reps from the larger clan came calling, tried to convince him to stay. Within an hour, three of the four Outlaws were dead and the survivor was forced to ride back home with a broken leg and a message. In the year since, they'd left Steel God alone, but in his ten months on board Lafitte had seen the signs that the enemies were just waiting for the perfect moment, and probably for a signal from the inside.

So this handful of mutineers was sowing discord amongst the family, and Lafitte's woman had told him about it. Lafitte had told Steel God, who had told his enforcer they'd keep it quiet for the time being.

Red was wrong about Lafitte. He would never turn on Steel God. He didn't want to lead, didn't want any spotlights shining in his face. Someone would recognize him. A certain someone who had shot down the only woman Lafitte thought could ever take the place of his ex-wife. Lafitte's only real ambitions extended to finally getting over his moral crisis and killing that fucker.

Until then, Lafitte didn't mind creeping around in Steel God's shadow one bit. Problem was Steel God himself had already decided that should he give up the ghost — the only choice was Lafitte or nobody. It was hard to argue with that.

Red Gator kept spilling his shit, enough to keep Steel God interested without giving away too much as to be completely useless. But he already was. Steel God was only letting him speak so as to scare those pussy-assed mutineers. Steel God lifted his beer to his lips, long pull, then grinned. Hard to see his lips through the thick coal black mustache and beard. He grunted, turned his face to the mutineers, of course standing all together. Dumbasses couldn't even work out how that looked.

"That true, fellas? You going to jump ship?"

They tittered, all nervous. "Naw, man, naw."

A few others laughed, too. The women of those guys laid it on too thick. Sun was going down and no one could see each other's faces as well, only by flame light, full of shadows. Steel God's laugh was rough like sandpaper, loud like Jimmy Page's guitar. Everyone laughed when Steel God laughed. He sat up.

"You…you going to bring down the Steel God?" Bellowed. It echoed back from the low clouds. He stood and chunked his beer bottle at the mutineers. They scattered, watched it fall amongst them and bust to pieces on hard dirt. Steel God stepped over to Red, who was a tad more relaxed in his chair now, and put his hand on the man's shoulder. Red's hands must've been numb. God knows Lafitte tied the wire tight enough.

"Jesus, Red, you've come down with diarrhea of the mouth now? If it's that easy for you to spill on your own clan here, why should I believe you wouldn't do the same to me?"

Oh, that got him. The shadows on his face changed. Red said, "Honest, God, you've got to. When have I ever? Why?"

"Red, do you think that lawyer who came for you was a public defender? Didn't you know that's our man? And I don't pay our man to let him make deals that betray me. As soon as he sat down, he tells me, there you go. The first thing you said." Steel God turned to face the group, said it to them even though they all knew the words. "*'I'll give up the big man for a free ride.'*"

Another round of laughing. Hee-hawing. Kneeslapping. Beer spitting. Lafitte just wanted to get it over with, get out of the wind. Disposing of Red Gator was his responsibility. He was already thinking of how to do it—knife across the throat. No, no, quiet but messy. Didn't want to attract the animals too soon. Had to be a gunshot, something like a .22 in the head. Bury him out in the wasted corn field, hope it was deep enough. It would be hard digging. Lafitte would have to recruit the mutineers. Anytime he was able to sidestep killing, he did. Tired of bodies. Didn't mind inflicting pain, though. Especially if it worked.

First things first. Time for the main event.

Steel God nodded at Lafitte, who stepped over to the barbecue pit, lifted the sledgehammer that was leaning against it. The wooden handle had been warmed by the fire. Made the wind all that much colder to Lafitte as he carried the hammer to Steel God. The big man dropped the unlit cigar, lifted the sledgehammer as if it were a helium balloon. Lafitte had never seen Steel God struggle with anything except a bad cough, leftover from his smoking days. Somehow Lafitte guessed Steel God could will himself to beat cancer, too, if that's what it was. No cough in sight that night. Just a giant with a huge hammer.

He told Lafitte, "Put him on the trunk."

The circle tittered some more, mostly the women, but they'd all seen it coming. No use fooling about it, think it was all just a scare tactic. Steel God hadn't kept his new club together this long because of his compassion. You played straight with him, he played straight with you.

Red Gator could hardly suck in breath as Lafitte and another guy named Fry, meth skinny but fast and vicious, loosed him from the chair and led him to the tree trunk. The circle closed in. Darker still. Lafitte's vision danced with squiggles, flashing greens, adjusted slowly. Red Gator's teeth chattered loud enough for all to hear.

"Stretch him out."

The wail started then. Red Gator let out a *Noooo! Please! Noooo!*

Poor guy. But it had been all their asses on the line because of this whiny prick. Punishment had to fit the crime. Lafitte grabbed Red's forearms, Fry got his legs. They pulled him taut on his back across the smooth surface of the trunk. He thrashed, pulled, but wasn't going anywhere. For a small guy, Fry was all muscle, tight like ropes that hold barges to their docks. Lafitte had never been a slouch, but Steel God had started him on anabolic steroids to make sure he always had the edge. The smell of Red's fear-sweat was like sulfur.

The circle, closer still. It parted like the Red Sea as Steel God finally made his way up front, then closed behind him. Hammer hanging at his side.

He said, "It's your words that got you in trouble. So let's see about taking them from you. Forever."

Lafitte had talked it over with Steel God. The punishment was only symbolic. Pulverize the snitch's jaw and teeth. Turn it to mush. Lafitte would still have to shoot the guy later. The only difference was the message behind it. Maybe someone can steel themselves for a gunshot. The shame of the punishment, though, in front of your woman, your friends, your brothers…that crushed a man's soul.

"Any last words, partner? Anything you need to say?"

Red's chattering teeth almost did him in. Whimpering now. "I'm sorry. I'm so sorry. God, please, I'm sorry. I…I'm just…sorry."

Steel God shook his head. "Ah, what a waste. You could've at least called me a goddamned son of a bitch. Because if you're looking for forgiveness, you've come to the wrong priest."

With that, Steel God hefted the hammer, made a clockwise windmill to get the feel for it. Double-gripped it, brought it up, back, then *down down down* on Red. Missed his jaw and instead crushed his throat.

Red's head, mouth gaping, lolled around on the trunk. Awful fucking noise scraping up through his windpipe, what was left of it. Chalkboard scratch, strangled duck, a bandsaw drowning. Lafitte winced. He was glad he hadn't seen it in the bright light of day. The circle seemed to whimper, this man gasping and grating for air that came like ice cream through a straw.

"Aw, shit," Steel God said. He let out a long sigh, the visible cloud of it hanging in the air over the trunk. Lafitte and Fry held tight to Red, violently shaking head to toe.

Steel God hefted the sledgehammer again. That was a surprise to Lafitte. He pulled his head back, still feeling the swipe of the hammer, maybe a couple of inches from his nose, as Steel God slammed it home on Red Gator's face. The scraping noises stopped. Lafitte wouldn't have to shoot anyone after all. Their usually merciless leader had finished the job for him.

Lafitte wondered if that second hammer strike, coming too close for comfort, was a hint of warning, too. Maybe Steel God really thought Lafitte was in on the mutiny. Not a good sign.

Steel God gazed down on what was left of Red Gator. Maybe he looked sad. Even though Red was a traitor, Lafitte was sure that Steel God understood the impulse. He needed to be taken out, but now they were a man down. The other clans would hear about it soon enough. The mutineers would grow restless, reckless. If it all fell apart, Lafitte wasn't looking for another front in his personal war. He might as well be as dead as Red.

Steel God dropped the hammer. Nodded at Lafitte. "Put him in the ground."

Then he grabbed one of his women and headed towards the farm house.

HOURS LATER, Lafitte spread himself facedown across the mattress in the upstairs room next door to Steel God's. Only one wall was slightly scorched. Looked like it had been a little girls room, with pastel yellow walls, some cobwebbed stuffed critters, and a fancy twin bed. He was sore, the dig draining his energy. He'd recruited two guys—one a mutineer and the other not, so he wouldn't have to hear bullshit about how Steel God had really crossed the line this time, etc. etc.—but neither one was digging as hard and fast as Lafitte.

His "old lady" sat beside him, her leg propped under as she slid his briefs down so the elastic stretched across the bottom of his ass. Kristal poked the small needle into the meat and plunged. Lafitte grunted. He would never get used to it. Not having much effect on his balls yet, but he didn't really care anymore. Sex was something to do, helped pass the time or get the steam out. Maybe twice a week, enough for Lafitte. Not like he would be falling in love.

Kristal, so pale her skin was see-thru in the right light—was a better friend than she was a lay. Twenty-three, nothing fancy about her until she dolled up in make-up. Limp brown hair hung past her shoulders. Plain skinny, not leaning either way. Couldn't suck cock to save her life. She only really satisfied him when she was on her knees, her ass sticking up in the air. In other words, nothing like Drew. She'd been tall, smart, and shy except when she gothed up to play bass with her psychobilly band. She'd been a substantial woman, built like an Amazon. Their one night together had brought him to his knees, literally, begging to do whatever it would take to please her. Had she lived, instead of being killed by a rogue Homeland Security agent as she accidentally pointed an unloaded shotgun in his direction, then this foray into the biker club never would've happened. Didn't matter where he would've hid then, as long as Drew was with him.

Even with that one big mark against her, Lafitte still liked talking to Kristal, though. Found out she'd quit meth cold turkey after her last man in the gang died in a shootout. She planned on leaving eventually to attend community college, maybe become an X-ray tech like her Aunt Jess. She knew how to get all the dirt on the mutiny and any other gossip without coming across like a snitch, even if that's exactly what she was, feeding info to Lafitte and thus to Steel God. Kristal was smarter than she should be, a high school dropout who could barely point out where she was on a map of the world, but someone had taught her well about other things along the way.

Even if the sex wasn't much to smile about, Lafitte did love the way she felt against him at night or on the back of his chopper. Nice heat. Nice smell.

Kristal pulled the needle out, swabbed Lafitte's ass cheek, and ran her hand over his back. She said, "You don't need these."

"He'll know if I stop."

"Maybe not. I think he's missing more than we realize."

Lafitte looked at her over his shoulder. "I don't like the sound of that."

"Fuck you." She slapped his ass, yanked up the briefs, nearly giving him a wedgie. "I'm on his side, is why I'm saying it. We need to keep an eye, help him out."

"So what's he missing?"

Kristal reached back for the dusty quilt at the foot of the bed, motioned with her hip for him to give her room. She covered them in the quilt and spooned tight against Lafitte. "The coup is coming from the women. Those guys just like pussy and fighting. It's the women who want some changes."

"And you think God doesn't know about that?"

A stretch of silence, then, "Does he?"

Yeah, Lafitte would be the one to know. Unless, of course, Kristal had been feeding him less than she should have. Maybe because she was in on it. Sneaky. He said, "Tell me who's leading the pack."

"Just so happens the one he chose tonight."

Lafitte remembered—she was the redhead, Anastasia. Been around a while, met up with her in Pierre, former mama in a Mongol chapter. Probably in her mid-thirties. Steel God had taken an instant liking, but he made the woman work her way up the ladder. He wanted to see if she really had what he needed or if she'd bounce out at the next big town. Turned out she was a tough bitch and a half. Raked some eyes the first time Steel God's eighteen-year-old fling of the week stared her down.

And that's who Steel God was sleeping with right then and there.

Lafitte sat up, feeling like a slack ass. If Steel God went down this soon, the rest would take it out on Lafitte. He went to throw off the quilt, but Kristal's hand pressed against his chest. His heart beat way harder than it should've. She hissed *Shhhhhh* and patted and eased him back against the mattress.

"She's not going to do anything tonight. It'll be a while. And I'm not all that sure she's wrong."

What he'd been waiting for. Kristal playing both sides, which made perfect sense. It wasn't his place to squeal on her for that. Steel God even admired her for it, told Lafitte when he first signed on that smart people were valuable out in the wilderness. They're interested enough in surviving to know who to stand with: "Good way to check the clan's temperature. Just watch the smart people, who they're talking to, all that."

She rubbed her leg against his stomach, laid her head on his chest. "Listen, I'm saying he's like the old king from *Lord of the Rings*. You see that?"

"Fantasy shit. Not my thing."

"Well this old king got under the spell of a bad advisor, sent by the evil wizard? It turned him all comalike, making him depend on this bad advisor even over his own children. So then the hero busts in and chases off the weasel, which makes the old king young again. See?"

What the hell was she talking about? "Keep going."

"God can't hack it anymore. He needs people he can trust to help keep him safe, but what if he's too stubborn to see that? What if he had a hero to chase away the cobwebs in his head and convince him to let someone else take over? It'll have to happen eventually anyway."

Yeah, Kristal was smart, all right. A goddamned politician. The problem with her plan was that it assumed the men of the clan would feel okay with something like that. These guys relied on the old ways, the law of the jungle—when the alpha male got too old to fend off the young lions, they took over by force and banished the old fart, left him to fend off the scavengers on his own.

He said, "How did you know he was sick?"

She stopped whatever she was about to say. "Oh my god. Sick, like *sick* sick?"

"Come on, really. Who told you? Who else knows?"

"Honest, I had no idea. I swear. Swear. To. God." Held up her hand. Her left. Like that meant anything.

Looked at the door first. You never knew who was listening. The club was like a family, true enough, and like any family, you couldn't trust any of these goddamned fuckers with your secrets. Better off taking out an ad in the paper.

"I'm telling you, strictly confidential, right?"

Her eyes lit up. Bad sign. Too late to worry now. "Promise."

"It's his lungs. I'm thinking either emphysema or a tumor. Probably tumor. And he's been hiding it a long time."

"Holy shit." She sat up, let the quilt fall off her breasts. Lafitte imagined Drew in the same situation. She would've held the quilt up. She would've made sure the subject at hand got more attention than her tits. Still, Kristal was freaked, started rocking back and forth. "I had no idea. Oh shit. Oh god."

Lafitte huffed, waited her out. Hard to tell where the feeling ended and the drama began.

She calmed down, and he said, "You know, he told me because he knows it's going to kill him. I think he'd rather be taken out by one of his own, one of us, than to let this shit take him out. Gone with a whimper instead of a bang."

"How long has he got?"

Lafitte took her by the shoulder, eased her back down and pulled the quilt up to her neck. "It would take a doctor for that, and you know good and damned well…" Gave her a squeeze. "I'm betting it's far enough along that it's an act of will to stay as strong as he is. And he'll keep it going until he's satisfied the club's in good hands."

"Your hands?"

Took him a while to say, "Maybe."

She cozied up tight again. "So, what do we do? Point out that maybe he needs more help than he used to? Be a little over-protective?"

"And he'll crack my skull. Especially if he thinks *you* know."

"No, he's smarter than that. He's going to wonder, sure. But you're a rock. We just give him what he wants, but in the background, start moving you up faster, so you'll have more day to day control, so—"

"Kristal?"

"Yeah?"

"Why don't you just leave? Don't you plan on leaving anyway?"

She lifted her chin. "Are you trying to get rid of me?"

"Jesus, come on. No, not that. All this sounds so complicated. What do you get out of it?"

She squirmed, made sexy little noises. Lafitte's ass throbbed where she'd poked the needle, the cold and the exhaustion getting to him. Kristal said, "Well, it would be nice to ride with the leader of the clan, you know? Be nice to."

Lafitte grinned. That old song *Leader of the Pack* spun through his head. Those old gangs, nice and clean like in the Brando movie. Yeah, so much less complicated back then. He liked Kristal like this, scheming. A lost cause and a bad idea, but still scheming none the less. Reminded him of a friend back in Minnesota, young woman Kristal's age. A woman who died to protect Lafitte. She was killed by a Homeland Security agent. Lafitte had a chance to take that guy out. One trigger squeeze and a pointblank shot. But he couldn't do it. Maybe next time.

He liked Kristal enough that night to stroke his hand down to her hip, ease it under the waistband of her skirt. Was going to suggest more when he heard something. Not really heard so much as sensed. Like a mosquito, or was it a bee? Buzzing, definitely.

"You hear that?"

Kristal said, "Hm?" She covered his hand with hers, urged him on.

"No, there's something." Stopped, started again. "Hear it?"

"It's like a cell phone on vibrate. Have you got a cell phone?"

He sure as hell did. A thin little number he kept in the pockets of his jeans. Only two people had the number, and in the eighteen months since one of those people had handed the thing over to him, it had never rung. Until right then.

He was out of bed, the world not at all cold anymore, scrounging for his jeans in the moonlight. Kristal sat up and bunched the quilt around her shoulders.

"You never told me you had a cell phone," she said.

"I never use it."

"Then why do you have it?"

He found his jeans. The buzzing had stopped. He freed it from the pocket. The message light was on. He flipped it open, scrolled for missed calls. Only one, and it was from Layla, the dispatcher at the sheriff's department he had worked in before making his life a total mess. Only she and the sheriff could call him, and only in an emergency. A specific emergency, really.

"Who was it?" Kristal said.

"Someone telling me to come home."

TWO

MAYBE the weather down South was nicer, the food as fine as he'd always heard, and maybe the money was sweet, but it was still the worst promotion ever. Luckily Franklin Rome had been able to pick his own purgatory—New Orleans—but he knew good and well that his being pulled back into the FBI from Homeland Security after the beating he took from Billy Lafitte in Minnesota was meant as punishment, regardless of the fancy title "Assistant Liaison for Domestic Terrorism" and the office that was larger than the shotgun house he was renting on the edge of the French Quarter.

Not just the beating, but the fact that he got carried away in pursuing Lafitte at the expense of other leads. His gut told him he was on the right track. Lafitte was the key. No matter how the Bureau twisted the evidence to make it look otherwise, even after the little band of wannabe terrorists, once captured, said Lafitte was definitely not one of their members, Rome still had that gut feeling he trusted more than his own senses. After all, a good magician can fool you. Rome was tired of getting fooled.

When the "promotion" came, Rome saw the sleight of hand in that, too. No way they could demote or dismiss one of their top black agents without a lot of scrutiny and politics coming into play. So they promoted him and offered him a choice of locales, as long as none of them were Minnesota or Washington D.C. Fine, sure, that was part of the game he signed up to play. His turn at bat, he chose New Orleans. They asked why. He said he loved jazz. Said his wife would love the restaurants. Turned out she loved the abundant rum and the drag shows more, still punishing Rome for running off to Minnesota while leaving her bored in Washington D.C., and then for backhanding her—once—after he'd returned to her constant complaints. He'd tried to apologize, desperate to repair the damage, but she ignored him and kept on sipping Hurricanes.

The truth: Rome chose New Orleans because Lafitte's ex-wife lived in Mobile, Alabama, only a few hours drive east. If anything would bring that traitorous fucker out of hiding, it would be putting some pressure on the Missus. It worked wonders the first time he'd tried it on Lafitte in an interrogation room back in Minnesota.

Rome was driving over to her place to have a one-on-one now that his hand-picked agents had made first contact after a few months of research, trying to find an airtight way to bring her in on this without tripping the alarm of the watchdogs. Even the appearance of him taking another shot at Lafitte might get him "promoted" even further. Maybe questioning the ex-wife, Ginny, would ruffle some fur, but he was sure they'd minded their dots and crosses. He found the case through the back door—Lafitte and his partner, Paul Asimov, had been suspected of killing a gang leader back before Katrina, but there was no body, no evidence. It was as if the banger just vanished. Another cold case, and Rome had recruited some go-getters he manipulated into loyalty, pretending he had no idea about the connection to Lafitte, then asking his people to chase leads on the down-low.

So far, so good. Green pines all along the interstate, much more lush than the Midwestern prairie. And the balmy weather lasted right on through most of the fall, so the whole thing was working out much better than he had expected.

His cell phone rang. His right-hand man, Agent McKeown. Rome answered, "Yes?"

"Sir, I've just received a call from our source up North. He thinks they've started trying to reach our subject, probably last night."

"Fine, good news. Any details?"

"Apparently they weren't able to get him on the phone. Had to leave a message."

"And we didn't get the number?"

"Not yet."

Rome had figured it out. After the yahoos in Yellow Medicine County had squealed to D.C. about what Rome was doing with Lafitte, they let the bastard go. First thing Lafitte did was scout out where Rome was staying and nearly kill him. Whatever it was that kept Lafitte from pulling the trigger—attack of conscience or Hand of God—Rome hoped it meant his way was the right way.

Then the brass yanked the reins, ordered him to cease and desist. But what they couldn't do was keep a young deputy who had FBI dreams from talking to Rome.

"So who tipped them off down here?"

"Not sure, sir. If I had to guess, I'd say the wife's mother. I think she's always kept a channel open, because of the kids."

"You can go at a moment's notice if needed, right?"

McKeown paused. "Won't that look suspicious?"

"Plenty of cover. I've got it all worked out."

"We could wait for him to come down here."

The agent's protests bugged Rome. Or maybe McKeown was asking for all the details because he was recording Rome, looking to make his mark in the Bureau that way.

Rome said, "Agent McKeown, you *do* remember why we're doing this, correct? And you do remember why I chose you?"

That quieted McKeown. Rome thought he heard a *beep* on the other side. Maybe the agent turning off his recorder. "Sure, always."

"You watch, and then you follow. I want to know where he is every second of his trip down here, who helps him, what sorts of hotels he stays in at night. That makes sense, right?"

"Yes sir."

"I'll be with his wife. Try not to call unless it's urgent." Rome hung up. Sniffed. Little pissant wanted to play games? Rome had discovered that McKeown was having an affair with a federal judge's wife. Some May-December action, as she had twenty-one years on him, but she'd spent most of those years in gyms and spas, it looked like. The judge was growing suspicious, put a private eye on his wife's trail. The private eye took his photos, as pornographic as anything behind the counter at your corner convenience store, but then tried to extort the wife. McKeown went to shit, drinking way too much and threatening to blow his career by going after the PI.

So the agent confided in Rome, who had been looking for a few people he could trust to help him out with his "hobby". No problem, Rome told the guy. I'll clear that right up *if...*

Long story short: the PI ended up with a broken jaw, a camera in pieces, and a promise from Rome that if the PI said or hinted or even thought of telling anyone about the judge's wife, he'd end up lost in the system, moving from prison to prison, a man without a name. And damned if it didn't work.

Yeah, McKeown. Don't forget who saved your ass.

In Minnesota, something like this would've depressed Rome, having to worry about your right-hand man flipping you off. But down South with the sun filtering through pine needles, he felt energized, kind of like Superman. McKeown? No match at all.

ROME ARRIVED at Ginny Lafitte's apartment complex in Mobile, found the right building, and climbed out of the car. He looked up to see her waiting outside on the second floor balcony. She stood with arms crossed tight, lips pressed tight. Rome read the body language—scared and angry all rolled into one. Pretty much the proper response to having a couple of Feds show up at your house and tell you they're investigating the possibility that your ex-husband killed a man when he was on the police force in

Gulfport, Mississippi, and that if you, Ms. Lafitte, know anything about this and haven't spoken up, well, we hope we don't have to pursue charges.

Angry and scared were good, Rome thought. Both made people say things they otherwise wouldn't. Plus, he was going hoping that she'd hold a grudge over Lafitte getting her older brother killed. Sheriff Graham Hoeck had been kind enough to give the disgraced Lafitte a job as one of his deputies after the post-hurricane debacle. Lafitte ended up pulling him into his personal vendetta against the few grassroots Islamic terrorists whom Rome swore had recruited Lafitte. Hoeck died in a cheap hotel room in Detroit, blown up by a suicide bomber. Lafitte and his girlfriend, in the same room at the time, came out barely scratched. Sure, he had nothing to do with it. The official record reflected that Lafitte had tried to save Hoeck. Rome knew better, and hoped Ginny Lafitte did, too.

He buttoned his suitcoat and made his way up the walkway, up the stairs, until he stood face to face with Ginny Laffite, her arms still self-hugging, probably giving herself bruises. He held out his hand. She unlatched, shook it.

Rome smiled. "Thanks for agreeing to see me. And I'm sorry about the way my fellow agents approached you. Really, there wasn't any need for threats. No, I'm sure we can handle this pretty quickly and painlessly." Waited a moment, then added, "I'm sorry for the loss of your brother. I worked with him briefly. He was a first-rate lawman."

She nodded, flicked her eyes around. If she didn't know about the gangbanger Billy shot, she sure as hell knew something else that would be worthwhile to him. She wore her hair back, a few strands spitting out here and there. He could tell why she didn't style it. Her hand was shaking like she was a human jackhammer. Bags under her eyes. Probably a nice looking Southern belle on any other occasion. Today she was doing her best to look washed-out and nervous. Why else would she wear an Auburn University hoodie sweatshirt when the temp here in October was still damn near eighty?

"Come on in," she said, then she turned for the door to her apartment, tried to get a grip on the knob. Her fingers slipped off. She tried again, yanked her hand back like she'd been shocked. Cradled her finger. "Damn. Broke a nail."

Rome grinned, made a reassuring hum, then reached for the door. "Let me get that for you."

Three

STEEL GOD wanted to get out of the farm house around sunrise before anyone noticed they were there. He'd chosen this place wisely, secluded from the closest neighbors by long stretches of barren field bordered by windbreaks of trees that still hadn't lost all their leaves yet. He had his people leave two at a time at thirty minute intervals and told them they'd meet at sundown. He also told them they needed to push their hogs for a mile before starting them up. Some pissed and griped, but in the end they did as they were told.

Lafitte waited, not sure how to tell God or Kristal, not sure they would understand. If they didn't understand, he was prepared to fight his way out. The message had been simple: *Your family. Call now.* He couldn't call back, not without giving away the game to whoever might be looking for him.

He'd already infuriated Kristal, turning into a typical biker instead of his usual friendly self when she asked why he had a cell phone, and if he was still a cop, and why wouldn't he answer her. He had said, "If you need to know, I'll tell you."

"I think you tell me now or I go tell God."

He knuckled her. Split the skin near her eye. Not much. Her face glowed red where he'd struck. The rest of it boiled. Those eyes, man, he was afraid to fall asleep.

But what the hell else could he do? He took her by the wrist, bent down, whispered, "I don't need you. If need be, I can get rid of you tonight and no one would ask any questions. Or if they did, not out loud. You want to know? You earn my goddamned trust." Tightened his grip. She yelped. "But if you *ever* threaten to squeal on me again just because *you* aren't in the know, I'll do things to you worse than what we watched happen to Red Gator. Do you understand me?"

Kristal breathed in sharply through her nose, but she finally nodded. He let go of her wrist, leaving an angry red tattoo. Like she'd just watched Bruce Banner turn into the Hulk, not even a glimmer of the man she'd trusted.

Lafitte hated himself for saying it, and it was much more likely he'd just let her off at a small town somewhere way the hell off the major roads and tell her to get gone, go find a better life. Too smart to be this stupid. It might not matter anyway. He'd be far down the road by nightfall and she could tell Steel God whatever the fuck she wanted, since Lafitte was going to tell him first.

Before falling asleep, Kristal had rolled back towards him, draped a leg over and rubbed his crotch with her thigh. "You might as well fuck me one last time, because you ain't getting any of this ever again."

Whatever. He told her, "I can't get it up. Go to sleep."

Next morning, Kristal was quiet but not exactly angry. She asked how he slept, asked if they could stop for a bowl of chili somewhere today.

Lafitte waited until he had dressed. He checked the cell phone again. Another message, same as the first. Kristal watched him put it back into his pocket. Not a word.

"Babe, you need to ride with someone else today. I think Richie Rich is free, pretty harmless." He was a new kid in the group, a five-foot-three trust fund baby with a temper. Real name was Trey Baum, and he'd gotten kicked out of his fraternity at San Francisco state, came looking to join a biker gang. Steel God rescued him from some Mongols who would've kicked his teeth out, broken his legs, but he let the kid fight off a couple and take some blows first. Tough little bastard. Richie didn't have an old lady, and since Steel God had elevated the status of women, he couldn't force anyone to sleep with him. A couple of young broads had their eyes on him, but they loved watching him squirm too much to give him release. If Kristal rode with Richie, it would make those bitches snap to attention. Consider it a favor. A parting gift.

Kristal's lips parted, hung open for a moment. Eyes got wider. "You mean…wait, I was mad last night is all. Better now."

"Maybe so, but I think I need to ride alone this time. Clear my head. Might help you too."

"I'm not the one hiding a cell phone."

He turned his head to her, his finger to his lips. Then, "You want to stay with me? I mean, over the long haul?"

She nodded. "I'd like to, yeah. You're usually…nice to me. You listen to me. But last night, I'd never seen that from you. Like some sorta Jekyll and Hyde thing."

Lafitte sighed. Kristal was right, and she was smart. She'd be on top of this, find out what it was about the phone that set him off. She'd plant some seeds among some of the women, who would then whisper in their men's ears. Those men would come for him and pry the secret out with fists and boots.

He told her, "I've got some stuff back home to deal with. The phone is a signal that I'd better deal with it now instead of later. I need to tell Steel God, so I want you to go on ahead just in case."

"Why didn't you say that in the first place?"

"No one's business. I don't unpack my baggage here, and I don't truck none of the club's baggage out. Two separate rooms with a thick wall between them."

Kristal stood from the bed, wearing only her panties, and slinked over to him, something she must've picked up from soap operas. Her hand glided across his back, and then she was hugging him from behind. Every bit felt phony to Lafitte. Like Steel God had said: read the temperature.

She said, "You'll be back? I feel safer with you, the way things have been going lately."

Maybe too smart for her own good. Lafitte turned in her arms, held her closer. "Just a few days, that's all." Thinking if she got caught as a mutineer, there went her happy ending. A voice in the back of his mind called out to take her along.

She wouldn't have it. He knew. Girl was ambitious. Besides, he didn't want an entire biker cult following him across the country. Maybe she'd work on Richie. That's who Lafitte planned on suggesting to Steel God as his replacement anyway. Young, loyal, strong. They would make a cute couple, and maybe he'd have a better shot than Lafitte at convincing Kristal to abandon the coup plans and wait her turn as the head guy's old lady.

He kissed her gently. "Be a good girl while I'm gone."

She grinned. "Tight as a nun."

FRY TOOK Lafitte aside at the gathering in the farmhouse before they rode, all sharing a quiet moment for Red Gator— who he had been before, not what he had become. After, as couples kept each other warm, Fry pulled Lafitte over to the hallway and whispered, "That did me in last night."

Easy to tell Fry hadn't slept. Maybe in days. He shouldn't even be on a bike, let along the hundreds of miles they'd need to ride.

"Did what in?"

"You know." Shifty eyed. "The *coup*."

"Yeah, okay. I can't believe you guys were serious."

"Does he know about all of us? About you?"

Lafitte grinned. "You think I'd have survived til morning if he had?" Not adding, Especially since I'm his hand-picked successor.

Fry's whispers upped to hissing. "You've got to let us know if, if, *that*, you know, that trunk thing, is what he has in store for us, right? Give us a day's head start or something?"

"Sure, man. Got your back." Lafitte knew that God wasn't ready to kill anyone else. If people wanted to leave, they could leave. A lot less messy that way. Red Gator's public execution was enough to keep the howling down through the Spring, at least.

Fry clamped his hand on Lafitte's shoulder, gave him a long hard stare, then, "My man. Solid."

Lafitte watched Fry fidget his way into the crowded living room, Steel God calling out the order in which they were to leave, when and where they would rendezvous, and what the plan was with colder weather sweeping in like this. Some of the mutineers might still be harboring sore feelings and delusions of grandeur, but one look at them all this morning, decked out in their jackets, the demon-winged sledgehammer patch on back proclaiming in gothic stitching *Steel Army MC*. Proud fuckers, in awe of the man like he was Jesus rose again.

STEEL GOD almost surely noticed when Kristal rode out with Richie Rich, but he kept it to himself until nearly everyone had left. It was early afternoon by then, two more couples having left, leaving God and his Sergeant-at-Arms alone. Steel God was between old ladies, his last having died of lupus months before Lafitte entered the picture, and no one knew if he was looking or not. The big man had been riding solo since, although with Anastasia spending more and more nights in his bed, Lafitte wondered how long before she was up there with him.

God and Lafitte sat on their choppers, stared at the horizon across the backfield, Red Gator's final resting place, at least until the soil is turned over by the tractors in the Spring, scattering what was left of him.

Steel God said, "Lover's spat?"

Lafitte let out a breath through his nose. "Something like that."

"She's trouble, ain't she? Smart one."

"You told me smart was good."

"No, I told you it's good to recognize smart. I didn't say let it suck your cock."

Steel God laughed, slapped Lafitte's shoulder. Lafitte cleared his throat.

When the laughs died down to rumbles in Steel God's throat, Lafitte said, "Something's come up. I've got to leave."

The big man lowered his chin to his chest. Belched silently. Then, "Fuck off."

"No, I'm serious."

"So am I. You said you wanted a new life. I gave it to you."

Lafitte couldn't argue that. He ran his hand across the hog's motor, the chopper a gift once Steel God was convinced he needed a new enforcer. The previous one got the message and split, headed for the Hell's Angels. The bike had been built for Steel God by his brother. A bulky thing, all chrome and a weird, almost aqua blue. Thick-wheeled. Sounded like a dragon. Then Steel God found out his brother had been wired up by local police when he delivered it to God for his birthday. So the bike ended up in a barn for the past three years, and no one heard from the brother again. Steel God gave the bike to Lafitte, gave him a jacket, too. Made him start shooting the steroids, though. Handed over plenty of rough work—guys skimming off cash or product, customers trying to cheat, couple of guys beating on their women for no good reason. Had to pay for the haul somehow.

"I can't let this one alone," Lafitte said. He kept his eyes on the ground beside his bike. "If I do, it'll haunt me. I'll drink myself to death, if I don't eat my gun first."

Steel God tugged his aviator glasses down so he could peer over the top, motioned for Lafitte to meet his eyes. Lafitte did. Ten seconds. Fifteen. Twenty.

"No. Have to say no, Billy." He'd never found a nickname for Lafitte. Said his name already sounded enough like a pirate. "Let's start pushing."

Steel God dismounted, held his handlebars, and pushed off for the road. A few steps on, he looked back. Lafitte straddling his hog, shoulders slumped. Not even thinking of moving.

"Come on, Billy. We can talk later."

Lafitte shook his head. "Can't. I've got to go."

"Thought we were done with that."

"I've got two kids." Lafitte didn't want to say that. Not to this thug. Lafitte was as loyal as possible out here in the wasteland, but it felt like role-playing in some fantasy world while waiting to get back to his real life. Didn't matter that the people he hurt bled real blood and begged for real mercy. Just actors playing victims the same way he was playing assassin. Nothing would tie him to any of this, even while he kept his own name, since what happened in the clan stayed in the clan. Talking about his real life with this…this cold-blooded killer, this egomaniac, and probably the most trustworthy friend he'd had in years, felt way bad.

But what else could he do? "Two kids and a wife. Ex-wife, but to me, you know. Look, something's happened. I need to find out what."

Couldn't lift his chin. He'd argued with Steel God before. He'd convinced the man several times not to kill someone when being smart was the better play. When he'd lost, he played the loyal soldier, did his job clean and quick. This was different. No more acting.

Lafitte waited. No answer. Kept waiting. Still nothing but bird calls and echoes. He finally looked up and found that Steel God was turned away, bike still pointed towards the road.

Lafitte said, "I'm not asking."

Steel God kicked his stand down and spun, started fast towards Lafitte. Stone-faced, one track mind. Lafitte reflexed backwards, forgot he was on a bike, nearly fell. Dismounted and let the chopper go as he scrambled for the Glock pistol his boss had given him.

Got hold, yanked it out, and lifted it in time to stop Steel God's advance. Maybe two feet between them. Steel God could've swiped the gun out of Lafitte's hand. Others had pointed guns at the big guy before and ended up with broken fingers and soiled pants after Steel God was through with them. But Lafitte did it and stopped his boss cold.

Steel God crossed his arms. "You know what this means, right?"

Lafitte swallowed hard. Tasted brass. "Means I go home and you go wherever it is you go."

Head shake. "Not that easy, Billy."

"It has to be."

"Goddamn it, I trusted you. I don't have time to start over with someone else, man."

Lafitte cleared his throat again. Maybe killing Steel God was his ticket back to respectability anyway. Could help forgive a lot. He gave up on the old cop's habit of keeping his index finger rigid along the side of the pistol, instead slipping it inside the trigger guard slowly so Steel God got the picture.

The big guy grinned, took a step back. He sniffed the air. Billy got a whiff, too. Somewhere, a plant was firing up the soybeans. Steel God said, "I always thought it smelled like ass during the fall here. You're the one that told me it was more like peanut butter. Captain Crunch, you said. I like that attitude. So…just take a vacation. Like a couple weeks. I can handle two weeks."

"I'm not coming back."

God was getting red-faced. "Who the fuck's going to do your job, then?"

"I like the Rich kid. I trust him." Lafitte's mouth was dry. He figured there was no use hiding his fear. "I wouldn't lead you wrong."

That got Steel God barking laughter. "That's why your woman rode off with him? You handing her off like some inheritance? Naughty, naughty." Shook his finger. Lafitte flinched.

Flinched hard.

The pistol bucked, but Lafitte had swung it up, above Steel God's chest, over his shoulder. He'd never seen the big man shrink, but there it was. He squeezed his eyes shut and crouched down, hands jerked up over his ears.

Fuck, Lafitte thought. *It's him that's scared of me.*

He recovered, got the gun low, this time getting a bead on Steel God's forehead while the man stayed low and brought his hands to his knees. Turned his face to Lafitte's. No anger. Mostly the puffy cheeks and rough grin reminded Lafitte of his father, when they'd gone fishing. When Lafitte had finally been able to catch one and get it off the line himself without any help.

Lafitte motioned with the pistol. "Up. You need to get out of here before someone checks out who was shooting."

Steel God nodded. Grunted. Then said, "I need a hand. Knees aren't what they used to be."

Lafitte thought about Steel God yanking him down, stripping the gun away, doing him in without a second to blink. The man looked tired, though. Squinched up with pain. Lafitte switched the gun to his left hand, reached out with his right. Steel God took hold, grunted himself up. Kept the grip tight a few moments more, Lafitte almost ready to fight for release when the big man let go.

They passed a couple of head nods, backed away from each other. Lafitte realized he'd dropped the gun arm, aiming at the ground.

Steel God noticed too, pointed and kind of laughed, not so loud. Shrugged and said, "So it goes."

"I'm sorry, but..." But what? It's his goddamned family. Lafitte hated that, thinking he even owed the guy an apology. "I've got to go."

Steel God turned to his bike, mounted up. No need to walk it out anymore. He was about to kick off when he looked over his shoulder, said, "You remember how to get in touch with Momma, right?"

Lafitte remembered. First couple of days with the crew, Steel God made him memorize a phone number. He said it was in case any one of his people got in trouble, got lost, got separated from the others. He'd drilled it into all the new members' heads. After Red Gator was arrested, Steel God gathered everyone up and gave them a new number, but said that they'd reach the same person as the last one—his own mother. Lafitte had never called, although he was tempted once or twice, if only to take a listen. He had no idea who would be on the other end, but the idea that Steel God had a mother still alive, and that she took messages for him, just plain silly.

Still, Lafitte rattled off those ten replacement digits soon as Steel God asked. The big man said, "If you finish with your business and change your mind about coming back, give Momma a call. Ask about Hugh. Ask her how Hugh's doing. Tell her you'd love for Hugh to drop in for a visit. She'll let you know what to do."

"Really?"

"Let's say about a month, okay? If you haven't asked about Hugh in a month, then I guess you meeting him wasn't meant to be."

Steel God kicked off and the chopper roared. He throttled high and long before saluting Lafitte like a Marine, sliced his hand down, lifted his middle finger and shook it hard. Big grin, big tobacco-stained teeth, and he was gone.

Lafitte waved away the kicked-up dirt cloud and tried to keep a bead on Steel God, but he had disappeared at the front of his dust wake.

Lafitte's stomach surged, burned bitter up his throat, and he doubled-over, spewing vomit across the ground. Dipped to his knees, let it keep coming, gasping for breath in-between. But the vomiting wasn't so bad. He was happy to do it. Hell, he was surprised to even be alive.

Four

THE PHONE RANG ONCE, then again. Rome thought his wife would pick it up as usual. The third ring, he shouted, "Honey?"

"Fuck you!"

Already slurring her words and it wasn't even noon. He'd promised to go with her to some shops on Magazine Street, but one file led to another and another, and he'd wasted two hours. Desiree hadn't said a word about it, of course. No, just sat in the kitchen with a bottle of local rum and a two liter of Coca Cola. Maybe Rome wouldn't have lost track of time if she'd sent up a reminder. But she wanted it this way, leaving it all on his shoulders while she stood back, arms crossed, not offering to bear any of it. What the fuck did she expect? You can't heal a partnership without any goddamned *partnership*.

"Fine, honey." The fourth ring cut off as the answering machine took over, the dial tone buzzing over the electronic greeting. Ten seconds later, Rome's cell buzzed. McKeown.

Rome started with, "Why'd you even call the house if you were going to call the cell anyway?"

"Sorry. Forgot."

"You have something for me? Some reason to interrupt my day off?" As if that meant anything, really.

"No word from up North, sir. No contact yet. This is about the wife's story."

Rome turned to the window, stared out at the courtyard he shared with several other shotgun houses. "Go on."

"Looks like it checks out enough that you can up the pressure. Nothing official, but the local noise has the banger's brother on the lookout for Lafitte. No one believes Asimov pulled the trigger. They don't think he was quite that hard-assed."

Interesting. Ginny Lafitte hadn't come right out and said it, but Rome got the feeling she was hinting at Billy carrying a lot more dirt than first expected. The woman was on the verge of a nervous breakdown, too. All the better to hang her out as bait. As long as Rome could keep his grip tight without crushing her fragile state of mind, he'd get a second shot at Lafitte and do it right this time.

"Maybe I can talk to the brother, then. Is he part of the gang?"

"No, he's clean. A grieving brother, but not beyond seeking justice on his own, I'd say."

"Call me if you hear anything else." Then he remembered his wife seething downstairs. "Leave a message on the cell. If Lafitte shows up, text me. Otherwise, I'll be in touch later this afternoon."

"Sir?"

"Busy. Promises to keep." Flipped it closed.

More staring. He couldn't get Ginny Lafitte out of his head. At first, she had seemed shaky, ready to crumble in little more than a stiff wind. As they settled to talk in her dining room, her daughter Savannah playing with a noisy handheld computer game, teaching math or something, although the kid punched buttons randomly instead of waiting for the full questions, Ginny took on a serene, possibly drugged, countenance. Like Elizabeth Taylor, but spacier.

"Please understand," she told Rome. "It wasn't about falling out of love. Maybe it's been too long to still be that sort of love, you know…"

She just stopped. Her head dipped, eyes went to a spot on the table. Rome cleared his throat. That didn't help. He said, "I know."

Ginny blinked a few times. "I won't do anything to hurt him."

"Mrs. Lafitte—"

"No. Please. Don't." A grin. "Ginny's fine."

I don't think so. "We're in better shape to help him than he would be on his own."

With that, she lifted her head, chin high, looked down her nose at him. "That's pretty damn scary to imagine, can't you see?"

It went downhill from there, but at least she talked. Damn it, if only to spite Rome, Ginny Lafitte spilled a few things she would probably regret later. Oh yeah, if she was willing to go that far on her own, Rome was certainly ready to push her off the cliff.

Except that as soon as he thought it, he felt kind of sick.

DOWNSTAIRS a few minutes later, Rome clasped on his watch and walked into the kitchen. Desiree was at the kitchen table, chin on her palm, elbow holding her up. Her other hand was curled around a glass, half-full of rum and cherry cola. Jesus, he'd even promised her a stop at Red Fish Grill, where they made Desiree's favorite hurricane, and that still wasn't enough to restrain her.

"I'm ready when you are," Rome said.

Barely registered him. "Whatever."

"I even told him not to bother me while we're out."

"Oh, that's right? I rate a full two or three hours away from the cell phone? I'm supposed to feel special?"

Not even looking at him. Rotating her glass slowly on the table, no coaster. A really fucking expensive table she'd demanded they buy from an antique dealer in the Quarter their first few weeks in town. Since then, she'd burned it with cigarettes, scraped it with knives, and left interlocking water circles all over.

Rome sighed. "I've been looking forward to this. I like to see you happy."

"Let me finish this first." Lifted her glass, finally looked up at him. She saw the cell phone clipped to his belt. "I thought you said—"

He had it off before she finished the sentence. "Habit. That's all. Look, I'm putting it on the bar here. See?"

Desiree rolled her eyes, turned back and hunched over the drink. Rome took a coaster from the bar, stepped over to the table and dropped it next to her glass. He lifted the glass, placed it on the coaster. Desiree reached for it as soon as his fingers cleared the rim. Slung the rum and cola and ice across his crotch before setting the glass back on the table, not on the coaster.

"Goddamn it, Dee! Sometimes…" Rome sucked breath and dripped on the stone tiles.

"Sometimes what?" She stood and faced him, crossed her arms. "Sometimes you want to hit me again, right? You do, don't you?"

"I didn't say that." But yeah, he did. That was the fucking point of all this, right? He'd come home from Minnesota to a frigid wife who second-guessed his choices, rode him hard— figuratively, if not in the bedroom. So she crossed the line one night and he wailed on her. Never had before. Bruised her cheek and arms. Raised a knot on her back. And after, when she locked herself in the bathroom and called their lawyer—she knew it was pointless to call the cops on a big Fed—he wished he could take that hour back. He cried, said he needed help. She didn't care.

But Desiree didn't leave, didn't file. Demanded counseling, then treated it like a joke, telling the counselor everything she knew the woman wanted to hear. Never bothered to go through with any of the homework, or date nights, or "good fighting". To humiliate him, that was the only reason she'd stayed. To humiliate, drain, and push Rome to another outburst so she could keep running a tab. Desiree was going to slow roast his rep, his manhood, and this marriage. But he kept trying. God knows he kept fucking trying.

Rome wiped his hand across the wet spot, only succeeded in getting his palm as wet as his pants. He took her in, still barely a wrinkle at forty-six. Glowing skin, a smooth dark caramel, her hair styled expensively. Eyes narrowed. Lips wet when angry. When she realized he was checking her out, Desiree kicked her chair at him.

"Think I can't defend myself? Like I'm weak and need you to protect me? Is that it?"

"I'm not going to hit you."

"You mean *again*."

"I mean ever."

Her purple dress hung above her knee. She wore sandals, nails painted rose. He remembered nights of foot massages, leg rubs, toesucking, pussy licking, hard fucking. Not lately. Only once in the last six months when she called him into the shower that morning, ravenous. Bit his lips when they kissed. She bent over and grabbed the sink while he took her from behind, water from the shower soaking the bathroom floor. They fucked all slippery until she came. Rome was so surprised he came right behind her. After a few moments of post-coital relaxation, rubbing his hands over her perfect hourglass curves, she pulled away, said, "I've got to clean up. You'll be late to work." Not a word about it later, when he called to see how she was doing. Tried to bring it up. Desiree said, "Don't. I'm picking up Chinese tonight. If you're late, I'm not waiting for you."

He wanted her again right there in the kitchen, his cock growing hard despite the cold chill of wet khaki. Getting a good look at her eyes for the first time in weeks. Willing her, sending out a silent *Fuck me, fuck me, fuck me* and when she didn't budge, he said, "I need you."

Her anger faded quickly, but her blinks and frown told him it wasn't happening. It made him burn even more. *Fuck this, just fuck her. Take her. She's your wife, man.*

Desiree stepped over, retrieved her chair, and sat again. Lifted her empty glass and placed it on the coaster. "You'd better go change. Hurry up. We might miss a good deal."

Rome's hard-on shrunk fast. He really needed to pee. He clipped his phone back onto his belt and retreated to the bedroom, imagining himself bound to the bed while next to him, Desiree stood wearing a large rubber strap-on, rubbing it across his face. Every few seconds, Dee would whip Rome across his chest with a frayed electric cord, cutting and stinging and she told him to watch and learn "what it takes, baby! This is what it takes!"

Yeah, that's what she was doing to him. Just a flitting thought, Rome told himself. Nobody ever got hurt from thinking. Besides, he was the one with the gun in this house.

Five

BILLY LAFITTE rolled back into Yellow Medicine County eighteen months after he'd left, a day after leaving Steel God. All it took was passing through a small town with yard gnomes surrounding the welcome sign to remind Lafitte of all he hated about this fucking state.

At the Sheriff's Department in Pale Falls, he sat in the lot on his hog a few extra minutes. Bad memories associated with this joint. He had been a deputy for two years before all hell broke loose thanks to a ghost from the past sticking his nose in where it didn't belong. Goddamn, you expect some peace and quiet in the middle of rural-fucking-Minnesota.

Lafitte dismounted, his ass numb where it wasn't aching. He kneaded some blood back into it before dusting off his chaps and jacket. Freed his skull from the helmet and got a better, non-bug splattered view of the small pale-red brick building that almost re-sembled a school, except for the extra cop squad cars out front. Looked like they'd been able to buy a couple more since he'd last been here. Dodge Chargers. Why the hell did they need that much horsepower?

The light of day had gone dark blue as the sun set, and the fluorescents in the parking lot were buzzing, charging up. Lafitte first thought about giving it until morning, seeing as neither the Sheriff or Layla would probably still be around when they could be at home on the back deck in front of a smoking chimney. The simple things. Seemed quaint, funny. Lafitte had once wished for a life without so much drama, but even after everything that happened the previous year and a half, Lafitte realized he was more of a drama fag than he'd ever imagined, just with guns.

It was worth it to check the station first anyway. That had been the plan they'd laid out a long time back when Lafitte had sneaked back into town days after beating the shit out of Agent Rome, the man who had shot Drew, then had the nerve to brag about it, throw down some photos of her on the slab. But he couldn't seal the deal, couldn't squeeze the trigger. After it looked like Lafitte had slipped the net, he circled around, found the Sheriff. The man was highly pissed, having let Lafitte go to save him from a life in solitary lockdown, mistakenly considered a terrorist by Rome. So what's the first thing Lafitte did? Almost kill a Fed? Not smart. Not at all.

Still, Sheriff Tordsen had believed Lafitte deserved a second chance. More like his fifth, sixth. Like he was some kind of prodigal son, although Lafitte couldn't understand why anyone would feel that way about him. Tordsen had given him a cell phone, told him they should only be in touch in case of an emergency, or if something came up that would give Lafitte an above-ground life again. Of course, he couldn't help himself—started calling Ginny's mom down in Alabama, demanding forgiveness over getting Graham killed. It wasn't his fault, but if not for Lafitte's gung ho bullshit, Graham would've stayed safe and sound back in Yellow Medicine County. A couple of weeks of frost from the bitch, he gave up. Didn't call anyone else. Waited for word, either some peace and quiet or some heavy motherfucking shit.

Too bad when the phone finally rang, it was the latter.

Lafitte took the steps to the front doors cautiously, trying not to burst in. His heart thumped double-time and he'd been spinning every possible emergency scenario in his head while on the road. Ginny dead, kids dead, Ham or Savannah, either, both, kids hurt, Ginny hurt, one of them needing a kidney, deep coma, jail, fire, bankruptcy, although her folks would help in those last few cases, so probably not those, which got him back on kids dead—accident? Murdered? Why would it be murder? Abduction? Some pedophile swiped them after school?

Lafitte had picked up a four-pack of Rolaids and kept thumbing them down to hold back the acid threatening to flood his system, make him puke, break his heart. Two more as he reached for the door, opened, stepped inside.

Much the same—wood paneling, a U of desks with Layla's the bottom center, right outside the Sheriff's office. Flat-screen monitors on every desk had replaced the dinosaur bricks. Filing cabinets, folding tables, a few well-tended potted plants. Lafitte avoided looking at the door leading to the interrogation room and holding cells. Only three deputies in the room, all of them turning to stare at him. He had forgotten that he looked like a biker. He *was* a biker.

A woman on the phone, Lafitte remembered her, hired only a few months before he'd left. Another man on his way to the back paused, then kept going. Must not have caught that it was Lafitte, but Lafitte clearly remembered the man as one of many who had stood outside this very building and spit and thrown beer cans at him, chanted *Traitor*.

"Can I help you with something?" It was the other deputy, walking over to Lafitte, hands loose and at the ready. Yeah, scary biker. Gonna walk into a sheriff's office and cause trouble. Sure. Shame, because he'd sort of been friends with this guy. Name was Nate, and he'd been fishing with Lafitte, been out to the house for steaks and beer. He'd been a young one at the department, just a stringy farm kid, but he'd beefed up this past year. A near military buzzcut on his scalp. Lots of confidence, and suspicion, in his voice. Bad sign. He was turning into a stern one.

Lafitte grinned, couldn't help himself.

"Excuse me, did you hear? Can I help you?" The closer Nate got, Lafitte could tell he was seeing though the hair and beard and muscle, figuring it out.

Lafitte extended his hand. "Deputy."

"Holy shit." Nate reached out without thinking. The handshake was quick, Nate pulling away when it really hit him. "Billy."

"You weren't expecting me?"

A step back. "I'd heard, maybe. You don't look the same at all."

Lafitte wanted to rub his hand through Nate's buzz and tease him, but the kid's eyes, there was something off there. Could be this wasn't all on the up and up.

"Sheriff's not in?"

Kid said, "Little late for that. You missed him by an hour."

"You in charge?"

That got a grin out of Nate. "A little. Heading up nights while we're short staffed. We even hired Colleen, remember her? From Marshall?"

"Hey, hey." She had been a new officer on a nearby larger town's force, and Lafitte had pushed Nate in her direction, talked the boy into hooking up with her. "You two still, you know, all right?"

Nate pulled in his bottom lip while nodding. He said, "Going good, really good."

The kid was still fidgety, fists on his hips, then off, then on, trying to look like he didn't want to grab his pistol, but there it was.

Lafitte held his wrists out. "What? Are you going to arrest me?"

"Hey, man, don't."

"You're a bit jumpy."

"Well," Nate crossed his arms. Biceps tightened. Lafitte was impressed. *Look at the little guy, all grown up. And I could still rip him in two*. Nate shrugged. "What did you expect? Okay, you're not a traitor, but *shit*, all the shit you actually did."

Lafitte cleared his throat, glanced away. New girl sneaked glances at him, flushed when he caught her. Like that would ever happen. He wasn't there to make friends or mend fences.

Nate said, "So...you're into bikes now?"

"Layla's out too, I guess."

"Yeah. You want to call her? Feel free to use the phone."

Nate stepped over to a desk, picked up a receiver. Lafitte's stomach fluttered, like the deputy seemed too eager to help.

"That's fine. I'm up against the clock here. Do you know what's going on? Everyone okay?"

"Far as I know. Like I said, I had an idea you might be headed back, but I don't have any details."

Lafitte's needle jumped and he knew the kid's heartbeat would be racing if he checked his pulse. He'd need several more years of practice and a teacher like Lafitte to serve the bullshit smooth as butter.

"I've got to go. Sheriff's probably expecting me."

"You want a ride? I can come with."

Lafitte lifted his helmet. "I prefer not. But if you don't mind straddling the hog and holding my chest—"

"I'm good, thanks."

Lafitte winked. He made for the exit, snugging on his helmet as he shouldered the door open and stepped into the night.

THE SON of a bitch wasn't out the door three minutes before Deputy Nate had Agent McKeown on the line.

"He's here, and he's changed."

"What does that mean?"

"He's ripped, like a bodybuilder or something. Like a bouncer. Long rock band hair. He's on a motorcycle."

It sounded like McKeown was writing all this down. "Did you see the bike?"

"Oh, yeah, as he was pulling away. Looked like a custom job, like those on TV. And it was weird colored, like turquoise."

More scribbling noise. "What about logos? Was he wearing a jacket?"

"Yeah, leather jacket. You mean what brand was it? I don't know."

"No, no, I mean art. On the back of it."

Nate remembered. He thought it looked pretty fucking cool. "A sledgehammer, with wicked spiky demon wings on the shaft. It said *Steel Army*."

"Good, that's good."

More scribbling, then some tapping. What, was McKeown on to something? Looking up the sledgehammer on the web? A good thirty seconds or so passed quietly except for tapping.

Nate said, "So what do I do?"

"Huh?"

"Now that he's here, what's next? I can follow him out to the Sheriff's house and wait for your people. He's alone and looks pretty tired."

McKeown sighed. The rumble tickled Nate's ear. "I thought I told you."

"Pretty sure you didn't."

"Don't do anything. We're on the case. Everything's going according to plan."

"I don't get it. He's here. We've got him. I can do this."

"Hey, wait, slow down." Kind of laughed through that. "We know you're eager, all that. Believe me, you've done enough to convince us. Sit tight now, and we'll work out the details for getting you on board here."

Nate sat down, spun back and forth in the office chair. Felt like a hall monitor instead of a cop. "Listen to me, though. Billy's no idiot. Once the sheriff gives him the lay of the land, he'll be in the wind."

"I appreciate your insight, Deputy," McKeown emphasizing *Dep-u-Tee* like that, like nails on a chalkboard to Nate. "In the future, we'll make use of your skills. Right now, just trust that we've got it under control, okay?"

A few more *Okays* and *Alrights* and the conversation was over. Nate slouching back into the office chair, back and forth, arms limp in his lap.

Sure, fine, the Feds had a plan. Of course they did. The whole point of Nate wanting to join up was seeing how those guys had it all together the last time they came after Lafitte. It wasn't a job where you had to wait and see what trouble the locals could stumble across or which dumbasses were setting up meth labs and blowing themselves up. The Feds knew who they were after and they had a plan to scoop him up.

Maybe last time they missed the mark, okay, but at least they had tried. To think the new sheriff and Layla had given Lafitte some help after he'd gotten so many people killed, including the old sheriff, a man Nate had respected like a father almost, it made his stomach turn. Stoked his anger. Then he saw what Lafitte had done to Agent Rome. Broke into the man's house and beat him bloody. Welped-up face, swollen ear, couple of broken bones in his hand. No way. Rome didn't deserve that for doing his job.

He would never admit it to anyone but Colleen, but it was pretty awesome to see a man face real danger like that and survive. Forget sitting around the station, sitting around in squads, never really feeling the adrenaline rush that he had expected from the job anyway. If he had to, Nate would take a punch, but not without dishing out some serious hurt on the bad guys along the way.

He told himself, Get real. Them telling you to stay put? That's another test. And wasn't there a subtext? McKeown couldn't come out and say it—*I can't give you orders while you're on duty for the Sheriff.* Yeah, maybe we're not too clear on the laws about that, but it sounds right. You can take off a few hours early, get Jorgenson to cover for you. Plus, Colleen's off tonight.

He rolled the chair forward, grabbed the phone, and dialed Colleen's cell.

She answered, "Hello there, baby."

"Sweetie, you want to have some fun?"

Six

"HE'S THERE, and I think he'll be on his way towards us within a couple of hours."

Rome took in a deep breath as McKeown told him. He was ready. "You think he'll take the interstate?"

"Yes, and we have someone ready to pull in behind him at Watertown and then again at Sioux Falls. But if he tries the back-roads, we've got an eye on him in town, too."

"They need to keep their distance."

"Absolutely, I understand. It won't be hard to keep up with him, though. He's on a turquoise motorcycle."

"What?"

"Turns out it's someone we've had an eye on but didn't know about the connection. He's joined a motorcycle club, this cult run by a real badass named Steel God. Looks like Lafitte's the new enforcer we've been hearing about."

With that, Rome couldn't help but let the grin wrinkle up his face. "Well, how about that? You know, if there's a way to frame this so it's kind of, you know, a coincidence…"

"We were after Steel God and it just so happened…"

"Good work, Agent McKeown. Very promising. Anything else?"

"I don't *think* so."

Killed the grin. "Explain."

"Seems our eager beaver deputy, the one who wants to join up? I just got some vibes off him like he might get in our way trying to impress us."

Goddamn it. Rome regretted making those promises. At the time, though, this kid coming to him and wanting to help, perfect timing. All Rome did was set out the best encouragement, promising Nate a fast track, and he bit hard.

Rome said, "Look, you know, he's fine. Keep him safe, don't let Lafitte get hold of him. We don't want him bleeding everything he knows."

He hung up, went back into the living room where he'd been watching a news report on something called "Hogdogging", a new backwoods sport in which Pit Bulls or Rotts were put into a pen with a mostly helpless hog. The dogs would rip into the pig, and all the people had themselves a grand time watching the carnage. He stood behind his recliner as the shaky video on the screen blurred out the faces of the spectators and the action, but he had a good idea.

Desiree sat on the sofa, legs curled up under her, reading the paper. A take-home daiquiri in her hand they'd picked up on the way home. Without looking up she said, "Do we really have to watch this?"

"I'm waiting for the weather."

"There is such a thing as the Weather Channel. On all day long." She turned the page. Must be giving her husband a break, holding back on the scorn. Didn't matter. Her sharpest barb couldn't pierce his good mood tonight. Everything going smoothly with Lafitte. He'd drive over for another talk with Ginny Lafitte in the morning, make sure to tighten the net just so.

Rome took a long look at his wife. He was thinking that by the time she'd finished that Rum Splash, she'd be plenty buzzed enough to maybe feel like fooling around. He didn't know why this night would be any different from the plenty of others she'd been drunk. Sometimes she would tease but then shut him down at the last moment, daring him to press further. Tonight, though, in this mood, he needed *something* from her. He thought back to the image from earlier, rubber cock jutting out from its leather harness around her hip, electrical cord slapping the palm of her hand.

He said, "I think we've caught a break in the case. Things might take a turn for the better."

"Mm hm." She kept reading.

"Enough to get us moved anywhere we want. Have you got any dream destinations in mind?"

Shrug. "Here's as good as any."

"Come on. Can't you see I'm trying?"

Finally got her to look at him. "Oh, I can see that. And you'd better keep trying too."

"What the hell else do you want from me? I'm wearing myself out."

Desiree folded the paper, set it aside, and untangled her legs. She scooted to the edge of the couch. "You still haven't gotten it. It's not about you and how tired you are. It's not about making a list and checking it off. It's about *me* being ready to forgive *you* because I feel you've really changed. Not some sort of process, none of that shit." Stabbed her finger towards him. "*I* say when it's okay, and if that takes until your goddamned deathbed, you'd better be happy about it."

Rome shook his head. Jesus, she was hot when she was hot, and it pissed him off that much more. He thought he knew her, but this wall she'd built between them, that's all he ever talked to anymore. The wall. He was feeling the wall grow thicker, another layer, feeling himself slipping farther out of reach. "Dee, babe, I...why haven't you left? Is that what you want?"

She sucked in a sharp breath through her teeth before laughing. "You'd like that, right? You can hit me and then get rid of me and start over on someone else."

He was pacing, mixing up Desiree's voice with the growling attack dogs on TV. A quick glimpse. Three dogs on one hog.

"It was only that one time. A couple times."

"But it's always been there, hasn't it? Think of all the temper tantrums you've gotten to take out on criminals instead of me. All the times you raised your voice louder than necessary. And now I see how frustrated you get when I shoot down whatever acts of penance you lay down before me. It's still there."

"That's taking it too far."

"The best way to starve a fire is to take away its energy."

Rome thought, *But you're feeding it.* His throat was thick, his whole body throbbing with his heartbeat. He walked over to the couch, reached out for Dee. "Stand up."

"You've lost your mind." She tried to look away.

"Just stand up, I said." A little louder.

She lifted her head, mouth open, no words coming. Another ten seconds. She stood.

Face to face, maybe a foot between them. Rome looked his wife over top to bottom to top again. About to fucking explode.

He said, "I want you to slap me."

"What?"

"You want to know what it feels like? Do it. Slap my face. Give it a hard one."

She stepped back and planted her hands on her hips, dropped her chin. Posed with attitude. "Uh huh. I see what's going on. I slap you, you can claim self-defense and lay hands on me. Not going to happen. I'm a lawman's wife, remember?"

"Babe, no. I promise, not one finger. Seriously, give me a hard one."

She flexed her left hand fingers. Tapped her foot. "I can't. We're not the same, Franklin."

"Bullshit. You say it's always been in me? Even more in you. The difference is you like to draw it out in little games, being all passive-aggressive. You ain't fooling anyone. It's as if you'd raked my eyes with your claws."

"You wish."

"*Yes,* I fucking well wish! Now do you want to be a bitch or do you want to hit me? I'll bet you've dreamed about it. Hit me, you cunt!"

She did. Short fuse. He barely saw it coming, and it came hard. Left hand high on his cheek. A nail caught his skin, nicked it. He closed his eyes on impact and saw a bright flash, then green, then he opened them and inhaled like he'd been underwater too long.

Dee's devil mask dissolved. "Oh, Jesus, you're bleeding."

"It's fine, it's nothing. Do that again."

She looked scared, more so than after the backhand that had started them down this road in the first place. He swiped at the blood from where she'd sliced him.

Rome said, "Don't make me say something worse. Just one more time."

The volume between both of them was swelling. The TV had moved on to really loud commercials.

"What the hell is wrong with you?"

"Goddamn it, I *love* you, Dee!"

Another slap. Screaming *No*. And another slap after that. Another. Then her nails scraped across his scalp as she grabbed the back of his neck and pulled him towards her. A vicious kiss, all teeth and lips. Smothering the breath between them, daring one or the other to break away.

She finally pushed him off. "You motherfucker, I think I've got it now."

"Think so?"

"That's what you want?"

"I want you."

TV commercial: loud arthritis medicine. Then loud soup commercial.

Desiree sat on the couch again, lifting her skirt as she did, knees high. "Take off my panties."

Rome got on his knees and crawled between her legs, pulled her panties down and off quickly. The pungent smell—sweat and sex and his wife—hit him full on. He hadn't seen her pussy in so long, wanted to take a long look, but Desiree slapped him again then forced his head into her lap.

"You know what to do, and don't come up for air until I let you."

He said, "Yes, babe."

"Don't talk."

Rome did as instructed, the cut on his face stinging as her wet thighs rubbed against it. Every now and then she'd push harder, smack him across the back, or call him a dog, a bastard, a motherfucking sicko, a piece of shit, but told him he'd better not stop.

And he didn't stop. And he was happy with the pain. And he was going to use Ginny Lafitte to help catch her ex-husband. And he was going to crawl on his hands and knees if that's what it took to win back his wife.

Seven

LAFITTE eased the rumbling chopper up Sheriff George Tordsen's gravel driveway, almost too steep. He scolded himself. Not even stopping to think this might all be a trap. Not thinking to try Tordsen's house first before stopping at the station. Not *calling* first, for God's sake.

Not even considering the path behind him becoming clogged with squad cars as soon as he dismounted. Funny, really, to think that the two things a man will lose all common sense for are his family and sex. Like an instinctual drive to make kids with any piece of tail that offers it up for you, then jump into volcanoes if it would save the little monsters.

Not to mention Ginny. Didn't matter that they'd now been divorced more than a couple of years and hadn't spoken since before he'd moved to Minnesota in the aftermath of Katrina.

After last year's spectacular flame out, though, he'd come to see things differently. Especially after his months with Steel God. Like it or not, Lafitte was a bad man who did bad stuff because he couldn't help it. Maybe he felt shitty about it most nights, but that didn't stop him from plowing on.

No one waited in Tordsen's front yard for him. The only vehicles other than his own were the Sheriff's official SUV and his wife's Outback. They lived on a bluff overlooking part of the Minnesota River Valley. Plenty of dense trees and jagged hills here, but out behind the house was a devastating drop into a sea of sawgrass, weeds, and a trickle of creek feeding into the river. Lafitte sat on the bike and revved, waited, not sure what to do. Came so far for what, exactly?

Tordsen must've heard the rumble. Hard to ignore. He stepped outside onto the front porch, leaned against a railing and crossed his arms. Lafitte let the noise go on another minute, not waving or smiling or anything like that, before cutting the engine and easing off the hog. He pulled off his helmet. His ears were hot and swelled. His temples throbbed. No wonder most guys in the gang never bothered with helmets.

Lafitte started towards Tordsen slowly.

The sheriff said, "Could've called first."

"I was just thinking that myself."

"Let me guess. You stopped by the station, too."

"That's why you're top dog in the county."

Tordsen loosened up and came down to meet Lafitte, shook his hand, then pulled him in for a quick pat on the back.

"Come on in for a beer."

Lafitte followed Tordsen inside, passed through the living room where Mrs. Tordsen sat in an overstuffed chair, a notebook computer on her lap, typing away. She took in the visitor over glasses perched low on her nose. Lafitte nodded and kept on. Didn't need any small talk. Wished he could've skipped this part too. Tordsen had been a friend when Lafitte really needed one, but that sort of generosity came with a price. You can't have someone save you and then expect to ever see them as anything other than a savior, which makes you resent them, which makes you freeze them out. It was easier to be hated.

In the kitchen, Tordsen handed a bottle of Coors Light to Lafitte, and they leaned their backsides against opposite countertops. Lafitte thought the sheriff looked thinner, more pale. He hadn't shaved in a couple days, at least. They took long sips of beer and waited for the other to speak.

Tordsen went first. "Nate holding down the station?"

"Yep. All grown up."

"Well, he's got his head in the clouds. He never forgave you, been bucking my authority since day one, but never to my face. I'd guess that he's already dropped the dime on you. Rome found the kid's sweet spot, offered him help getting on with the bureau."

Lafitte grunted. "He bought it?"

"Hook and line. I had to hear it from other deputies, of course. So I'm saying your cover's probably blown already."

"So Rome's still around?"

The sheriff took a sip, held it in his cheek before swallowing. Looked to Lafitte like it hurt. Tordsen said, "Not around here. They yanked him quick. Goddamn, son, you did a number on him."

"He's lucky considering the number he did on me."

"Anyway, they promoted him, but it was more to avoid a lawsuit than anything real. They made him promise to leave your case alone."

"Did it work?"

Tordsen held out his hand, waved it *so-so*. "Not exactly. We weren't sure you got the message. It was worth a try, though."

"I got it."

"Guess you won't have a chance to see Layla. I could call her now if you—"

"I'm not here for a reunion." Lafitte dropped his head. He knew what was next.

"Sure, I understand all that. I've just been thinking maybe we handled it wrong, and since you're here again, you know. We can work at it. Better than running."

Hanging with Steel God hadn't felt like running. Lafitte felt like he had sold his soul, but it was slightly more comfortable than looking over his shoulder every five miles.

He said, "Afraid not."

Tordsen sighed. Another long sip. Half through he gagged, dripped some beer. Pounded his chest. The cough was bad. His wife shouted from the next room, "Everything okay in there?"

The sheriff's pounding eased to palm pats and all scratchy he said, "Fine, I'm fine. Wrong windpipe. That's all."

Lafitte let the man breathe a few moments. Tordsen tried to stop the coughs, cleared his throat, squinted painfully each time.

"What have they done to you, George?"

Tordsen shook his head. One more clearing of the throat, turned and spat in the sink. "I did this to myself, letting this heartburn get out of control. The store brand stuff didn't help, but now it's just crazy. I got the doctor to prescribe something stronger. It doesn't work."

"Jesus."

"Burning holes in my esophagus. I'm going to Sioux Falls for tests next week. They'll figure out something."

Lafitte knew it was because of him. The Feds had made Tordsen's life a living hell, and the odds were against him getting re-elected. He would probably get pushed into retirement, barely enough to maintain. His wife would have to keep working as a teacher until the day she died. Tordsen's rep was shattered, his health going downhill, all because he'd stood up for Lafitte. Hadn't buckled at all. Lafitte might've hated him less if he had.

"I'm sorry." Lafitte stared at the floor. Tordsen kept quiet, probably expecting more. He wasn't going to get it.

"It's okay. Like I said, it's all on me. Should take better care of myself."

He left the rest unsaid, but there: *Easier to do if you turn yourself in.*

They had both thought this would blow over in six months. Turned out the Feds were persistent, if stupid. Lafitte had hid in plain sight for over a year. Really changed his mind about government conspiracy theories—not these guys. No, too power hungry, selfish, and absolutely unable to put themselves in the shoes of a wanted man. Local cops could teach them a thing or two about that, if they gave a shit. Better to keep those sorts of trade secrets safe at home.

Lafitte drained the beer, wiped his mustache with the back of his hand, and said, "Listen, George. Don't take this the wrong way—"

"Yeah, sure, I know. You want to get to your family, I know. They're all okay, nobody's hurt or anything."

The ache in Lafitte's shoulders eased up for the first time in two days.

"But it's not good. They tell me Ginny isn't all there in the head anymore, really shaken up over Graham. Probably not what you want to hear, but she blames you."

Lafitte tapped his fingers on the empty beer bottle. He had hoped Ginny would have heard the truth about what happened. But what were the odds, really? It looked bad no matter what color paint you slapped on it.

The sheriff kept on. "Your son's a handful, I hear. Pretty tough on the playground."

"Good. Want him that way."

"Ginny doesn't. She couldn't take it, sent him over to her folks' house to stay. It's been about a month now since she's seen him. Says he reminds her too much of you."

Lafitte squeezed his eyes shut. The last he saw Ham, barely out of his toddler years. Sweet kid. Squeezed tighter. No tears, not anymore. Turn them into something else, take it out on some other son of a bitch, but don't let Tordsen see you cry. "Sounds like a winner."

"I think they're close to taking your little girl, too."

There it was, the anger. Opened his eyes and slapped the bottle down hard on the counter. Paced. "Well, goddamn, has anybody thought about *helping* Ginny? Instead of taking our kids away and leaving her alone to do god knows what?"

"Hey, I'm only the messenger."

Lafitte got in Tordsen's face. "That's the easy out, ain't it? Bet her parents would say the same thing."

"You're really lucky your mother-in-law bothered telling us at all. Why the hell else would she call unless she thought you could help?"

"Because it's a fucking trap is why!"

Tordsen placed his fingertips on Lafitte's chest and pushed him back, nice and easy, a good two feet. "In my home, a little respect."

Lafitte paced some more, slowing finally and mumbling, "Yeah, sorry, my bad."

Tordsen stepped in his path. "You might not be too far off, and that's where Rome comes back in. The bastard's supposed to be forbidden to touch your case, but he got himself sent off to New Orleans. And guess who he's talking to?"

"I don't understand."

"Rome can't touch your Minnesota case, so he's found a way to sneak around on some old accusations that you and your partner killed some gang leader before you came up here. He's already talked to the in-laws and Ginny. That's what got Mrs. Hoeck on board, him threatening to hold Ginny accountable somehow. If you ever told her anything about it—"

"I didn't."

Tordsen looked Lafitte square in the eyes. "I was going to say I don't need to know if you had anything to do with it or not, but I guess you just answered that. Jesus, son, you make it hard to help you."

"I don't remember asking for all this. You're the one who let me out of jail."

"You're right, I did."

"Thanks for the beer." Lafitte started for the door.

Tordsen followed, waited until they were on the porch to say, "That's it?"

Lafitte was already off the steps, climbing onto the chopper. "What the fuck else is there? The only reason she called is to keep Ginny from going to jail. She thought I might be stupid enough to turn myself in if I knew about it."

"Are you?"

He hadn't thought that far ahead. If Rome had some sort of profiler on his team, that guy would say an arrogant ex-cop with a huge ego who's out for vengeance would come charging in like a one man army. And he'd be right. The one thing they wouldn't expect would be for him to blend into the background noise of America again. Only a callous asshole who was concerned about his own skin would go that route. He could do that, right? Give Steel God's number a call and limp back to the fold. Drink his ex-wife and the two kids he barely knew out of his head. Pretend to be the type of guy he used to lord over, cut deals with, or beat at every pissing contest because he was the one with cuffs swinging from his belt.

Sure.

"Nope. But I'm stupid enough to try something worse." Lafitte lifted his helmet as high as his scalp before saying, "Fuck it" and tossing it into Tordsen's yard. He got the bike going and took off.

EiGht

"**OO, OO**, there he goes," Colleen said. She had the binoculars.

"Yeah, I see him. Hold on." Not that they needed the specs. Nate was right beside her and could see Lafitte's weird blue bike and the dust trail it kicked up. They were parked on the other side of the river in Colleen's Corolla, the backseat cluttered with a few shotguns, several pistols, stun guns, and a whole lot of ammo. She'd showed up within five minutes of Nate's call, ready to go in her skintight jeans and long-sleeved Gretchen Wilson T-shirt, sneakers, hair pulled tight into a braid tucked into her collar. Oh baby. It got Nate heated up, but she brought him back down.

She'd said, "You staying in uniform?"

So he worked on changing out of his uniform in the cramped car, finally into street clothes, barn jacket, and Wolverine boots.

Got his boot tied a few moments after she shouted out. They watched Lafitte's bike rumble downhill until it took the turn out of sight. They knew he only had one way out.

"So…" Colleen's hands gripped the wheel at eleven and one. "We take him?"

Nate slipped a mag into his 9mm. "I don't know. I don't want to fuck up the FBI job, but…I don't know."

"Baby, if you're the one who catches Billy, they can't keep you out. You'll be a hero."

"We both will."

She grinned, put the car in gear. "I'm in it for the fun."

Colleen was a tough chick, built like a tank all over, god-damned ass that wouldn't quit. Nate had fallen hard because they both got jazzed by guns and action flicks, plus she was a farm girl who loved horses. Just what Nate's mom had hoped he'd find. She decided on being a cop after a couple of guys had attempted to rape her at a party her freshman year of college. She nailed one in the crotch and nearly broke the other's arm. Never wanted to feel looked at *that way* again, though.

Nate had never looked at her like that. Nate worshipped her.

"You're right," he told her. "Let's take him."

She jerked the car into Drive and started to go but then slammed the brakes, slid to a stop.

Nate pushed himself back from the dash, rubbed where his forehead had taken a shot. "Baby?"

Colleen grabbed his shirt and pulled him across the cup-holder and emergency brake for a deep hard kiss, her teeth clacking his, little bites on his lips. Then she let go, hands back at eleven and one.

She said, "This is going to be cool."

Nine

DESIREE leaned straight-armed against the bathroom sink and examined her reflection—flimsy silk wraparound loose at the waist, stark naked beneath, a sheen of sweat glistening, *yes, glistening*, and that little grin she couldn't shake. It made her laugh. Then she inhaled deeply and felt the muscles in her legs cramping ever so slightly from what had happened between her and Franklin.

She'd slapped the shit out of him and he wanted more, so she had done it again, and then he went down on her while she barked at him, called him awful, terrible, but true names. After she came hard, Desiree got up and grabbed Franklin by the collar, trailing him behind her to the bedroom, where she shoved him to his knees. He took it, no complaints, kept saying, *Whatever my baby wants*, and she saw the erection in his pants. Painful, pressing against the zipper. She sat on the edge of the bed, reached her foot over and rubbed the fabric covering his cock. Heavy breathing, moaning, and then she slipped her toes under his balls…and kicked them.

Franklin did her proud. He gritted his teeth and said *Whatever my baby wants* again. She pulled her foot away and grabbed his balls with one hand, squeezed tight.

"Baby wants you to suffer. Baby wants you to bleed."

"Whatever my baby wants." Strained.

Oh god, now that did it for her. She slapped him across the face one last time and then said, "Get your fucking cock out. But keep your clothes on."

She teased him another twenty minutes, stripping slowly, demanding he not touch his throbbing cock, sometime coming over to him and threatening to claw his eyes if he didn't watch her dance without music in front of him, touching herself while she weaved and kicked and squatted. And when she was dripping wet, she let her husband fuck her.

The memory sent her giggling again. Desiree couldn't look at herself, too embarrassed. Retreated to the toilet seat, leaned across to turn the bathwater on. A long hot soak. Time to think. Maybe she had been too rough on him all this time, but she had believed when the time came, she would know when to forgive. Her own mother had told her that if she wasn't going to leave him—which is exactly what she should have done, Mom thought, after he laid one finger on her, and Desiree had actually been leaning that way most days—she needed to break him into a thousand pieces, absolutely *destroy* him, then build him back one at the time like a jigsaw puzzle. But no one had told her how much more gratifying it felt to tear him down rather than give him any encouragement or hope or even a clue. Whatever this was tonight, though, she could live with that.

When Franklin had finished and Desiree laid beside him, her head on his chest, she still wasn't quite sure what to make of it. Gave him more grief to drive the point home: "It doesn't change a thing yet, mister, but it's sure as hell a sign of hope." And him: "I deserve everything you can dish out. Don't back down, please."

They talked more after that, Franklin opening up about what he was doing to help the FBI with the Lafitte investigation. Desiree had thought he was forbidden to work on the case, but Franklin said the Bureau changed its mind. After all, who knew Lafitte better than Rome, right? She warned him to be careful, knowing what had happened before.

"I'm insulated this time, not out there on the front lines. I won't even see him. Not even face to face until we're in court."

"His wife's really that gone?"

"I don't know. Looks more like a show to me. But even better, apparently Lafitte's got this cell phone, supposed to be one-way only, in case someone needs to reach him. But this moron ends up using it to harass his mother-in-law. Telling her he wasn't responsible for killing her son. What's she do? She keeps him on the line. She writes down the number. She handed us a goldmine."

Maybe it was meant to seem honest, but Desiree had known him too long. Franklin was holding something back. About his involvement in the case? About the ex-wife?

Frail white single mother? Put pressure in the right places…

Desiree wanted to dig, but then his goddamned cell phone rang. Felt to her like it was set to "Hypnotize". Franklin was out of bed, nearly running to the office to catch it. So she decided to take a bath.

As the tub filled, she poured in some moisturizing lavender-tinged crystals. How far could this go? She would have to look it up on the web. How would Franklin react to a whip? Or maybe she could tie him up. It had never occurred to her before. People who did those sort of things were freaks and sickos. Normal married couples, in spite of ups and downs, still needed tenderness and romance. If that was all true, then why the hell did the idea of Franklin tied wrists and ankles to the bed while she struck him on the thighs and chest with a leather strap make her tingle again? She closed her eyes. Her hand slipped between her legs…

Goddamn it, this wasn't right. It couldn't be. Franklin was up to something. She checked the water level, eased the stream off to a trickle, then went to find her husband.

His voice became more clear as she climbed the carpeted stairs to the second floor where Franklin kept his office. "But you cooled him down? I'll…yeah, I'll talk to him tomorrow. No, I'm keeping my word to him."

Desiree crept up the last step, stood outside the door so he couldn't see her. Sounded like more on Lafitte, though. Routine. Of course.

"Listen, I'll talk to Mrs. Lafitte again tomorrow. She's…well, oh yeah, I know. Could if I wanted to. You never can tell if that sort of thing will help the case though. Make her trust me more, perhaps."

Desiree looked down at her right hand. It had balled into a fist and was shaking wildly. She held it down, eased back down the stairs. Even with only one side of the conversation, it sounded like what it sounded like. Could be anything. Yeah, sure. Well, what did you expect? Freeze out a man for so long, you think he's not going to build another fire?

But what about tonight? With me?

Two fires are better than one, honey.

She backtracked into the bathroom and ramped up the hot water until it was like a hot springs. She let her wraparound fall to the floor, stepped into the tub, one foot—*way too hot*—bit her tongue. Second foot. Take the heat, the pain. Take it.

Just got Franklin back. I'm not letting him go again.

She sank her body into the tub, plunged her head under the water, the heat stinging but then easing off, every muscle relaxing, the grin creeping back to Desiree's lips as she resurfaced.

She thought, My man, and I'll keep him on a leash if that's what it takes.

Ten

OPEN ROAD. 212 was a long two-lane stretch through farm country that intersected I-29 in South Dakota, about forty miles west. Lafitte figured on stopping only when he was truly tired, like blacking out tired. Wanted to get as far South as Kansas City if he could. Eight hours, seven if he kept at top speed. He'd pulled all-nighters with Steel God before, helped by smoking some crank, plus the extra testosterone from the steroids. Probably wouldn't be using those anymore, but he'd need to do something to keep the new hard mass from melting to blubber.

Along this stretch, wind gusts rocked the bike and Lafitte fought to keep the thing straight. Crows on the road pecking at flattened rabbits flapped and lifted, hovering in Lafitte's path before curling up and away like a shot. The sun had faded and everything left and right and straight ahead was gray.

He thought through what Tordsen had told him, about Rome using his family on that old gangbanger case. Nothing to worry about—the body had never been found and the only eye-witness, Lafitte's partner, was dead. All Ginny could do was assume, so whatever Rome thought he had would come up a dead end. Lafitte was guessing this wasn't about the gangbanger, not even about the law, but rather about flushing an enemy out of hiding. Rome was telling his people one thing, but it dawned on Lafitte that once he showed his face, Rome had his own private idea of what would occur between them.

Fuck it. Lafitte had made his choice. He'd find out one way or the other now.

Without the helmet, the wind screamed in his ears like white noise, perfect fit with the flat fields, dead deer on the shoulders, leafless trees in small clumps. Summer in those parts fooled everyone like an ugly chick in good make-up. Once washed clean, you get a good look at what you'd really gone to bed with, made promises to, planted your seed in, and then you were stuck. Lafitte wondered, if he survived, whether or not he would return North, swallow his bile and try to mend things with Steel God, or go the other way and see if Tordsen would be willing to take on a "new face" in the department, new name and backstory and all that. No one would raise a finger if he kept his head down, grinded it out. Looking around at this purgatory landscape, he'd prefer to take his chances with Louisiana, Texas, maybe even farther South into Mexico, some modern day cowboy. Damned chopper was pretty much a horse, right? But that aqua blue shit would have to go. Lafitte was thinking a gray the color of storm clouds.

He heard the whine a mile or so back, thought it was a four-wheeler or some little hatchback. But then it got louder, coming up fast. Lafitte glanced at his mirrors. A riceburner coupe almost on top of him. Kids, probably. Let them pass.

Closer still, on his tail. Another glance in the mirror, maybe the passenger a bit familiar. The road was straight and clear. Lafitte hoped they would pass quickly, end the gnawing in his stomach.

They gunned it, pulled into the left lane, pulled slowly abreast of Lafitte. He turned his head. Staring right into the face of Deputy Nate, his thick little gal pal at the wheel. The boy had a rock hard face, but Colleen looked giddy. Nate kept his hands down, Lafitte guessing they were full of guns.

The car passed, swerved into the right hand lane, slammed on brakes. Lafitte took a wild swerve, hard left, clipped the rear bumper hard with his leg—*God...DAMN, that took off skin.* He stayed on the bike, but the car was already back at his side. Trying to ram him. Lafitte checked the lane ahead. A bend towards the right coming up. He couldn't see around it. He sped up, launched himself ahead of Colleen's car and tried to pull away. Leg throbbed like a son of a bitch. He couldn't get to his pistol while on the bike. Stupid, lack of foresight. Plain dumb.

The car gunned again, this time not bothering to pass. She waited until Lafitte was into the curve before bumping him, like she wanted to try a PIT maneuver, send him off sideways. Instead, she caught the open tire, stutter-stopped it as Lafitte went over the handlebars, wishing he hadn't dumped that fucking helmet in Tordsen's yard. The bike twisted and bounced off the front of Colleen's car, cratering the front grill. She careened left, popped a tire, and flipped. Scraped across the road on her hood.

The pavement was coming up for Lafitte's face. He turned his body hard, landed on his ass, tumbled off the shoulder into the ditch. Everything burned, ached. He found his hands, flexed them, then moved his legs around. Lucky motherfucker.

Lafitte checked back towards the road before trying to push himself up. He had to shout *Fuck* a few times in order to get himself off the ground and moving again, but he did it. Nothing felt broken. He checked the leg that had smashed into Colleen's bumper. Cut right through his jeans. Not pretty, probably needed stitches. He wasn't getting any stitches, so best to just find some rubbing alcohol or something, clean it as best he could. The rest of his shin was bruised real bad. It hurt to take steps, but he didn't have a choice. Staggered back towards the bike off in the grass. He lifted it. Crushed pipe, another shorn away. Lost a couple spokes. Dents, bruises, maybe a crack in the frame, but he couldn't see it clearly enough right now. Dazed.

Shit. It was all he had to drive.

Colleen's car was upside down and leaking gas. Both still inside. He took a long gaze both ways down the road, figuring it might be a few minutes before anyone else would make the scene and give them a hand.

"Unbelievable." Lafitte started towards the car. He picked up Colleen's voice within a few feet, talking to someone.

"Please hurry. I…I think he might kill us. Oh god, please. Can't you hear me?"

Lafitte eased himself into a crouch at her door. Her window was pebbled but still there. She was talking on a cell phone. Turned to him, then away in a flash.

"He's right outside, please. Oh god."

Lafitte shook his head, crashed his hand through the window. Colleen screamed. He grabbed her cell phone, brought it out and tossed it off into the ditch.

"Jesus, I'm not going to hurt you. You guys need to get out."

"I don't. I don't…I can't…" She was hyperventilating.

Lafitte looked across her to Nate. He was hanging upside down like Colleen, but out cold, his chin dangling, blood dripping off in strings. His nose was a bloody mess. Lafitte scuttled around the front to Nate's door. Window gone, frame fucked so he couldn't open the door. He reached in, checked to see if the kid was breathing. Yeah, still something there. Lafitte slapped Nate's face. Tried again. That roused him. Nate coughed, spit blood. Lafitte noticed the guns all over the roof below them. He pulled out his pistol and spoke loudly, firmly.

"Colleen, undo your belt and climb out your window. Nate. Nate? Can you hear me?"

Rattling breath, more coughing, but he was getting better. "Yeah."

"Undo your seatbelt. Easy. Then get out of this thing as fast as you can. But if you grab one of these guns and try anything on me, I'll shoot you in the face. Understand?"

A nod.

"I need to hear it."

"Yeah, I got it. Colleen's okay?"

"She's fine. You're both going to be fine. But you've got to get out of the car."

The smell of the gasoline was getting to Lafitte. Colleen flopped down with a grunt.

"Good girl, but don't touch those fucking guns. Get out, hands held high, and move way up front so I can see you."

A pick-up truck passed by, tapped its brake lights, slowed to nothing, the three guys in the cab gawking. Lafitte stood and showed them the gun and expected one of two things—they'd puff up and bring out their own guns, or they'd get gone.

They got gone. Pedal to the metal.

Lafitte had been distracted. Colleen was out of the way, hands high, mighty pissed off. Then there was the thump from Nate. Then a scramble. Lafitte couldn't get *No* off his lips fast enough, as Nate poked his arms and shoulders out, revolver and pistol, suddenly going *Pop pop*.

Lafitte did a quick step towards the back out of aim's way. "What did I tell you? What the fuck did I tell you?"

Colleen came running up to help Nate. Lafitte fired a warning shot over her shoulder, sent her scurrying. Yelling *Cocksucker murdering traitor bastard*. Fine with Lafitte, as long as she stayed out of the way.

Lafitte trained his gun on Nate's head and shoulders as they pushed farther out of the car. "Drop the guns and get out before the car catches fire!"

Nate twisted toward Lafitte's voice and stuck out the revolver, got a shot off. Lafitte dropped to his knees, in the clear, and took aim. *Just the arm. Just his arm.*

He fired.

Maybe it did get his arm. It got something. Nate screamed awful bad and his pistol hand fired involuntarily into the road. Damn thing scraped across the road and the gasoline and lit up like shock and awe. Colleen tried to get close, got pushed back when the flames whipped and scorched her. Lafitte shielded his eyes with his arm and saw Nate, flaming arms and head flapping around, piercing scream. Lafitte started towards him. Okay, some bad burns. They could survive that. Maybe wrap his leather jacket around one arm and reach for the poor kid.

Another couple of feet and Lafitte would've had him, but then the fire got to the open ammo spilled in the car, setting off rounds all over. A slug pinged the frame near Lafitte's head. Another dug into the ground right behind his boot. Then through the back window. Lafitte got up and ran as best he could and dove for the ground. Covered his head. An eternity, it seemed, of *pops* and *pings*, then it was over. Lafitte crawled up. No more noise from Nate, now engulfed. Flesh bubbling, smoking. Lafitte went *Aw, goddamn*. If he had only put down the fucking guns. If Lafitte hadn't been distracted, he could've dragged him out, slapped them both unconscious, and gone on his way. Just two kids playing cops and robbers, no matter if Nate had thrown in with the Feds, he didn't deserve this. *Goddamn.*

Lafitte looked for Colleen, found her on the other side of the road. He limped towards her. She looked alright. Her arms too red, maybe. Some cuts on her face and neck, but all small time.

Before he got across the road, she was already reaching for her back, pulling out a sleek .380, gripping it tight with both hands. She was breathing hard, tears streaming, but solid and in control. "Get on the ground."

"I'm sorry, Colleen. It's his own fault. I never—"

"I don't want to hear anything except you dropping to your knees. Hands behind your head."

Lafitte didn't think she would shoot. He hadn't gotten to know her so well, but guessed from the last few minutes, watching her react to Nate, she could be a badass but probably wasn't up for seeing another death right away. He kept coming closer to her.

"Goddamn it, I said *down!*"

Lafitte kept his hand out, open. Said, "I can't do that. You know damn well I don't deserve it."

"Oh yes you do." Sniffly, on the edge of stuttering. "N-Nate. You shot Nate."

"I wasn't trying to *kill* him. He was shooting at me!"

"I swear to God, I'm not letting you get away. Get on the ground. The Sheriff was wrong. You should've been hanged. Hanged and castrated and your body left for the dogs."

Lafitte stopped walking. No use trying to talk sense to the girl. He didn't have the time. Instead he dropped his hands, shook his head.

"I'm getting on that bike, if it still runs right, and getting myself out of here. If it doesn't run right, I'm going to commandeer the next vehicle that drives by. One of these options is better for you than the other, since I can't have you trying to arrest me while I'm waiting for a ride. Stop pretending to be hard and cry for your boyfriend." Lafitte nodded his head towards the fire, Nate's husk. "I don't care how bad you hate me, you'd better remember this is your fault. I was minding my own business, young lady."

He let a moment hang between them, and he knew she was trying to catch all that blame in a bucket and sling it right back at him. Searching for a profound slap in the face. But she couldn't argue with him. It was eating her up.

Lafitte turned for the bike, took a couple steps. Heard her behind him.

"Wait, you listen to me. You have to listen!"

"Not how it works."

The voice breaking more. *"It's not fair!"*

Ignored her. He waited for the shot, and when it came he flinched but didn't worry. Without a doubt she'd shot it straight into the sky.

Then she screamed, maybe some words in there, but mostly just ear shrieking that spread fast across the fields and scared birds out of trees.

He mounted the hog, cranked it. Looked up to see Colleen on her knees, face buried in her hands, the little gun hanging on her finger. It slipped off and fell into the grass and all you had left was her crying. It was hard crying, backed with fire and venom and if Lafitte were to wait another minute, the fire would get the better of her and she'd come up shooting.

The hog missed at first, then fought through the sputter and came alive. Roaring back. Behind Lafitte, the first wavering of sirens. He didn't have time to do a test jag. He got on his way fast, mental fingers crossed that the frame wouldn't snap in two once his speed topped eighty. Like he would get far now with an aqua blue chopper anyway. All he needed was enough of a head start to hide the bike somewhere and pick up another ride. And that was just to get him started.

LAFITTE SPED AWAY leaving Nate to his pyre and Colleen angry about breaking down. She glanced over at the flames, could make out Nate's head if she concentrated, but once it was in focus, she regretted trying. She sniffed back phlegm and tears—*Jesus, the smell. Burning flesh and gasoline.* The sirens were louder now and she damn well didn't want to get caught crying. Pretty much a career ender, and Nate wouldn't have wanted it that way.

What was the point of sticking around Yellow Medicine County, though, without Nate? She only took the job so they could be together as he started to blaze his own exit towards the FBI. Other boyfriends, you know, they liked that Colleen knew how to handle a gun but felt that dating a cop somehow fucked up the power dynamics. A man didn't need to check himself at the door for his woman. They would always answer a tad too late, maybe a fraction of a second, enough so that she knew they were watching every goddamned word.

Most other cops? Dating them was also a chore, the macho thick as musk. Always something to prove. Jesus, she wanted a relationship, not a competition.

Nate, sweet Nate. A gentleman. Her best friend. They liked the same stuff on their pizzas. Nearly thought the same thoughts. Now he had burned away because they tried to do the right thing. She should've shot first. Should've stayed in the car, made a plan.

Or at the very least, goddamn it, *should've shot that son of a bitch Lafitte.*

She stood. Sirens loud at gut-level now, the lights flashing not far away. No tears. Colleen took a deep breath. She was going to tell the story that got her free the quickest, because after that she was going to hunt that motherfucker down and slice him from his balls to his neck.

Eleven

ROME HATED the meetings worst of all. Men in ties sitting around sterile conference rooms, too much paper piled on the table, thinking they were making a difference by sharing what they knew about whatever the hell was in the mix that week. This one, some illegal immigration cases, referred to the FBI over terrorist concerns, and some drug-running out in the Gulf. Plus a couple of sightings of men from the Wanted list. Not to mention budgets, stats, and subcommittee assignments.

Hot air. The air conditioner was barely able to keep up with it all. Rome just sat, doodled. Thought about how to approach Ginny Lafitte later that afternoon. With her ex flushed out, it was time to turn the screws.

Rome was hardly necessary in the meetings. Every now and then they'd make use of his "expertise" for some small point about hierarchy, customs, and how previously foiled terror plots added to the bank of knowledge for the next attempt. But he wasn't an active participant in any case any more. They wanted to keep an eye on him. The agent he reported to had said, "It's required of you to attend meetings several times a week. You are an invaluable source of intelligence and experience for our agents." Translated: *We've got you, boy. Don't try anything funny again.*

It made Rome's "secret project" that much more dangerous.

Agent Williams went on and on about a proposed sting operation along the border with Texas to deter terrorists looking to sneak in across the Southern border. Sure, sure, issue of national security, blah, blah, blah. Rome was doodling his wife as a pissed-off huntress, with Rome subservient on all fours at her command. Just another idea for role-playing, should he ever grow the nerve to ask her.

Last night's hard fucking let off much of the steam between them, a surprise to both. This morning, she burned his toast, made weak coffee, and then demanded he crawl under the table in his suit to make her happy. That was hot. No relief for him, though. Desiree told him, "None for you until I say so, you worm. Don't even *think* of touching yourself, either. I'll know. You have to hold back." That alone had kept him daydreaming and semi-rigid all morning.

He didn't even notice the meeting had been adjourned until other agents rustled papers, started in on cell phones, and stood to leave. Rome cleared his throat and looked out the third story window, catching a glimpse of the Superdome, back in operation after being trashed during Katrina several years ago. Some had said, after the horrors that occurred when it was being used as a shelter, there was no way it could ever be seen as a place for entertainment again. Money won out, though, and there it was, home of the Saints and all the big arena tours.

"Agent Rome?" A voice from the other end of the table. Rome blinked, turned to it. Agent Stoudemire, Rome's "superior" supposedly, although Rome had originally been told he was "reins free" down here, reporting only to Washington. Lasted about three weeks. Stoudemire wasn't anything but a pencil-pushing accountant, more or less. "Franklin?"

Rome realized he hadn't responded. Jesus, don't screw it up. He had to play the game to avoid prying eyes. He turned his legal pad face down in his lap. "Sorry, Shane. Didn't get much sleep last night."

A smirk. "Pretty busy, eh? Maybe Desiree was keeping you up? I know that look, man."

The fucker winked at Rome. Rome imagined Stoudemire with Desiree. Desiree sucking the man's cock but watching her husband while she did it. Rome imagined punching Stoudemire's teeth out. He imagined Stoudemire in a motorcycle jacket. "What's on your mind, Shane?"

Stoudemire had walked down to Rome's end of the table, sat on it so he could face Rome, still deep in the chair. Classic intimidation technique.

"Well, we've been worried about you lately. I'd been meaning to ask how you're adjusting after being here a while and all, but things get in the way. You understand."

"Sure." *Split lips, bloody mouth, spitting his own teeth.*

"Exactly. Still, I know this is a big change for you, not being out in the field. Having to show these young guns how to do it right. I was the same way. Missed the action."

You know damned well the action made you piss your pants. Eager to fly a desk. "Hey, when it's time, it's time. At least I can get to all the things I'd wanted to do but couldn't because of the job."

Stoudemire grinned. It was one of those lies impossible to call anyone on. The only reason to join the FBI was the action, the power, and the chance to be in the know. All those things you suspected about the government? Mostly true, except now you were the one dishing out "I can't answer that, ma'am." It was all over now, and you were either like Rome or you were like Stoudemire—kicking and screaming as they carried you off the battlefield, or gladly sipping brandy and studying maps back at the Colonel's tent. Everyone assumed you would want the latter, so it was hard to look a man in the face after he's given the number one cliché "off into the sunset" answer and say, "What a sack of shit."

Stoudemire's way: "Good to hear. We'll have to compare notes on that sometime. I've got a fishing camp up around False River, if you happen to like that sort of thing."

Rome pulled the fakest smile he could. "Sounds like fun. Desiree and I like to travel a lot, though. I'll have to see if we can fit it in."

"Do your disappearances recently have anything to do with this travel?"

Oh, yeah, walked right into that one. Someone had been paying attention after all. Either that or he had a team member who needed some reminding about which had more leverage—the bosses or "What Rome knows".

"Disappear?" Rome laughed. "Like a magic trick? I've always got my phone with me."

"Still, you should make sure you're seen around the office more often. Don't want people here getting ideas. Plus, you've put some miles on the company car."

Shrugged. "Okay, I admit, it was personal use. Desiree and I were thinking, you know, maybe a beach house. Neither one of us has been to the beach much. Trying to find the right place at the right price."

Stoudemire stood, clapped Rome on the shoulder, then stepped over to the window, taking in the view. "You tried Gulf Shores yet? It's actually Alabama, if you can believe that, not as crowded as Pensacola."

"That's a good tip. Thanks much."

"You know, next time you're in Mobile, might as well keep driving south."

Stoudemire looked back over his shoulder after saying it. Rome was impressed, all this passive-aggressive buddy shit. Stoudemire had brass ones. Not quite telling Rome to cease and desist, not getting anything official on the record. A little nudge was all.

Rome shifted. One leg over the other. "Okay."

"What do you think of Mobile? Know anyone over that way?"

"Not really."

"Oh?" Eyebrows. "So, just out driving?"

Rome let out a breath. "Don't take this the wrong way, but that's pretty nosey."

"Not on company time. Like I said, it would be a good idea to be seen around here. We don't want people getting ideas."

Rome got out of the chair, tugged his suit coat straight. "I'll take the bus."

"I'm sorry?"

"If the car is the problem, I'll take the bus instead. Really surprised, Shane. I didn't know there was a curfew on me. This is something I should discuss with the home office, to make sure everyone's on the same page."

"Now wait—"

"And when I do," Rome stepped close behind the man, his face a reflection over Stoudemire's shoulder. "I'll make sure to leave out your own shortcomings, just between us guys. You know. Quote: 'Next thing you know, one whiff of misunderstanding and they'll give him my job.' Unquote."

Stoudemire stiffened. "That's a damned lie. I never said anything like that."

"Shane, buddy, hey. I didn't accuse you of anything, did I? All I'm saying is that if it was said, and someone happened to have sworn affidavits from more than two people who heard someone say that, along with a few more demeaning things—"

The man spun on Rome. Finger in his face. "You. You think threats are going to help you here? What's worse? Some guys in private conversation simply raising a few thoughtful points about job security, or you sticking your hand in forbidden cookie jars?"

Rome grinned. "First, those conversations? Not private on company time in a company office. Second, to answer your question, both. Both are equally worse in the government's eyes. After they discipline me for an internal matter, guess what gets the big headlines?" Rome spanned his hand across the air. "RACISM PLAGUES NEW ORLEANS BRANCH OF THE FBI. Yeah. Good for a Pulitzer, I'd say."

Stoudemire paled. Dude was sweating. Rome backed off.

"Your call, Shane. Either keep quiet and let me step in my own dog shit down the line, or put in the complaint and feel real good about yourself when you're out looking for a job. Maybe a consultant gig. I hear those pay pretty well for very little work."

Clapped the man on the shoulder, same thing Shane had done to him. "Thanks for the tip on Gulf Shores, though. I'll let you know how it turns out."

STOUDEMIRE wouldn't talk. Even if the threat itself wasn't enough to keep him quiet, Rome guessed guys like Shane would understand why he was still after Lafitte, and would be glad when Rome dragged the bastard in. It was more likely Stoudemire wanted a piece of the glory should Rome succeed.

No, what bugged Rome more as he made the drive over to Mobile again that afternoon, light rain keeping the wipers busy while much darker clouds and bold streaks of lightning were churning a few miles offshore, was how Stoudemire figured it out. Maybe it began with a good guess, but he wouldn't have brought it up unless he had confirmation.

Rome's team was pretty much under his thumb, the only wild card being McKeown. The smartest of them. He'd most likely already planned a way to come out on top in spite of Rome's nasty little secrets file. Hell, he'd be the type to admit to it, take his hit, and still have more on Rome than even Stoudemire. So if McKeown went up the chain, it must've been because he didn't trust Rome to keep his word.

Yeah, a very smart little prick. He had it nailed. Rome had no intention of bringing Lafitte to "justice". The whole charade of going through the back channels, looking for a solid case, building a team, all of that was to get Lafitte out of hiding. And, what do you know, it fucking worked. Next, Rome needed the man to keep coming, hell bent, exhausted, not thinking straight, right into Rome's trap. The traitor would disappear somewhere in northern Alabama, and Rome would rant and rave at his team for "losing the subject" before quietly letting them off the hook, sworn to secrecy.

Looked like McKeown wasn't going to let it happen. Or that's what he thought. Rome had covered more bases than necessary just in case. The problem with trusting other agents was that they were other agents. Simple. People paid to figure out problems, impress bosses, and look good in a suit.

As Rome pulled off the interstate and turned towards Ginny Lafitte's apartment, he added a new item to his mental "to do" list: End McKeown right after ending Billy Lafitte. Didn't matter what happened after. For Rome, there was no after. Only an end.

GINNY WOULDN'T sit down. She looked older and paler than the last time they'd talked. She started talking and pacing as soon as he stepped in the door. He followed her into the living room, sat on the couch and winked at Savannah playing on the floor. The child looked up at him with a blank expression before she giggled and destroyed the Lego house she'd built. Started over.

With Ginny's first words, Rome knew McKeown had been working two fronts.

"I hear Billy's mixed up with a motorcycle gang, right?"

Rome cleared his throat. "Only a rumor at this point."

"It sounded like more than that. You won't need my testimony anymore, that's what I mean. That other thing's not as much a slam dunk as the gang thing."

Goddamn it.

"I don't know where you heard that—"

"Oh, no, don't do that. Please don't."

Rome leaned forward, elbows on his spread knees. He looked down at the carpet, thick with lint and juice-box spills. Hadn't been vacuumed in a long time. "Our discussions are still of major importance. Two cases are better than one, so if we can convict on both—"

"But you can't. I'm only giving you hearsay and guesses."

"You can talk about his character, and about him getting dismissed from the police department in Gulfport."

Ginny shook her head fast like she was cold, slid her hands up and down her bare arms. Rome saw goosepimples. The apartment felt pretty warm to him.

"I won't do that. I don't think you can do that in court anyway."

McKeown had been feeding her a steady diet of the shit. She was seeing light at the end of the tunnel.

Rome pushed himself off the couch. She stopped pacing, chewed her thumbnail.

He said, "Your ex-husband is on his way down."

She got frightened deer eyes. "Billy?"

"As we speak. Now, do you trust that he's coming to *save* you or just dropping in for a visit with the kids?"

More thumbnail chewing. A dot of blood on her chin. "Does he…know…about what we've talked about?"

He stepped over to her, eased her thumb from between her lips. Blood pooled and ran down from where she'd bit through the skin. Cupping Ginny's hand, Rome guided her to the kitchen, ran cool water over her fingers. He spoke softly.

"I realize my colleagues might have told you about our new information, and they're mostly right from the legal perspective. Me, however, I'm thinking about your family, your safety. They're thinking about the law, but there's more going on than that, and I'm the one to trust."

"Okay."

"Do you have a place you can go tonight? Your parents?"

Ginny was transfixed by the running water. Rome prompted her again. She pulled her hand away, held it tightly in her other.

"No, not there. *He's* over there. He'll be there."

"You mean Ham?"

"He'll be there."

Rome nodded, said, "Ham." Then waited, watched. Ginny was panicked, swallowing hard, exhaling loudly through her nose.

Finally, Rome said, "You come with me tonight."

She brightened. "Okay."

Rome smiled at her. "Okay."

TWELVE

THE NEXT TOWN was barely there—a railside grain loading station, a couple of gas stations, one bar, and a burger shack. Lafitte had driven the bike hard and it stayed together. He kept the light off. It was finally dark enough to pretty much stay invisible unless they were really looking hard. Lafitte needed to get rid of the bike in order to truly blend in.

There were some kids in the parking lot of the burger shack, two cars and a truck at the edge of the road, the kids sitting on the lowered tailgate. A handful of farm kids with nothing else to do. Four guys, three girls. Someone was the odd man out.

They watched Lafitte watching them as he slowed, waited for another car to pass the opposite way, then pulled into the lot. Eased up to the burger shack, dismounted and headed towards the order window. The wind had ripped at the wound on his leg the whole time, and walking on it again sent new shockwaves through his nerves. He bit down hard on each step, tried not to show weakness. Quick glance back. Those kids were still looking. Good. This might work better than his first plan.

He ordered a Dr. Pepper, took it and sat on top of the weathered wooden picnic table and didn't particularly look in any one direction, although he was taking in the scene with those teenagers. One girl looked older, on the heavy side, wore too much lip gloss. She was probably the reason the others had beer to drink. Not like it was a secret to the guy running the off-sale, more like a technicality. The older farm girl must've been in her mid-twenties, but she was still hanging around sixteen-year-olds. Yeah, Lafitte knew the type. She'd be coming onto him soon.

The others—two white guys in jeans and hip-hop sneakers, their "going out" clothes. Caps askew, hair underneath cut close to the scalp. Probably one of them owned the late-eighties station wagon, worth a couple thousand bucks at most. A black guy, Timberwolves jacket, didn't look like he was from around here. He was the one driving the tricked-out Nissan. Another guy seemed to be the joker, trying to get the girls' attention by pulling stupid stunts, grossing them out with snot rockets and farts.

The younger girls, both white, one way skinny, not filling out the short denim skirt she wore, and the other packing just the right amount of dough, low-riding jeans, baring her midriff. Didn't matter. When the boys outnumbered the girls, the girls were all pretty enough.

The black guy and skinny girl were obviously a couple. Lafitte wondered if he was really friendly with the group, or if they tolerated him for the girl's sake. Small town farming community, Lutheran, old-fashioned. Lafitte counted them out because he didn't want to cause any jealousy, stress, whatever. If he played nice with that guy, the others would turn him in for spite.

Looked like the truck belonged to the older girl. She was the one who reached in for cigarettes, spun up the volume on some pop bullshit, one of those Idol winners. She lit a cigarette and watched Lafitte through the fog she puffed out, like it was a two-way mirror.

These boys were admiring the bike, though, trying to build the courage to come talk to Lafitte about it, show how much they knew from watching the chopper shows on TV. Elbowing each other.

"You go."

"Fuck you. I'll go when I'm ready."

"Sure. It ain't even all that. What's up with the color?"

Took a few minutes, but the two hip-hop wannabes broke off and strolled over. Seemed like the skinny girl and her boyfriend were happy to have time to themselves. They slipped into the backseat of the boyfriend's car. The decent-enough girl and goof boy were off in their own world, giggling, whatever.

Both guys were built about the same. Helping Dad or Stepdad in the fields packed on muscle, but after the harvest it started going to flab until spring. Hands in pockets, they approached the motorcycle, nodded at Lafitte. He gave a slow-motion nod in return.

"This okay?" one guy asked. He wore a thick flannel shirt over a Corona T-shirt.

"Just look. No touch."

"We're cool. No worries."

They circled. Squatted. Reached out once, but remembered they shouldn't. The one guy, wearing glasses and a Vikings shirt, looked over at Lafitte.

"You build this yourself?"

Not going to lie to them. "No. It was a gift."

"Man, if it weren't fucked up like it is, that would be worth a lot."

"It's still worth a lot."

"What's up with the color?"

Lafitte lifted the can of Dr. Pepper to his lips. Wanted to slow these kids down. Like jiggling the bait in front of a fish, you couldn't give the rod a jerk until the fish was on and running.

Lafitte said, "You don't like blue?"

"Weird blue."

"Color's a color. That one didn't bother me so much."

The older girl had been waiting to see if Lafitte was game for company. Soon she was coming over. Jeans too tight, one hand shoved in the top of a pocket while the other held a cigarette. Leather strappy sandals, a couple of straps broken. Toenails bright pink. She didn't stop at the bike. Went right up to the table and hopped on beside Lafitte.

"Nice bike. Pretty."

"It's a chopper."

She rolled her eyes. "It *does* have two wheels, right? I'm just messing with you."

Blonde hair, permed, bunched on her head like a shrub. Stretchy green top barely able to hold her breasts in. But she pulled it off well. Lafitte liked that, this woman's confidence making her sexy. She was used to being the big fish in a small pond around here. It was all an act, though. A while ago under different circumstances, Lafitte would've called her on acting confident enough to fuck strangers and teenagers, but scared that anywhere else in the world she'd get spit out half-chewed. Right then, though, he would rather use it to get what he wanted.

"Want one?" She held out the cigs. The blend of smoke and whatever supermarket perfume she wore made Lafitte want to sneeze.

He shook his head. "No thanks. What are you guys up to?"

"Same as always. You passing through?"

One of the guys spoke up about the same time. "This an ICI frame?"

To the guys, "I don't know." To the blonde, "All dried out. Needed a drink."

"Got some High Life Light in the truck if you want one."

He grinned. "Sounds nice."

The other bike admirer said, "You don't know who made the frame?"

"Dude, these pipes are done for." The boys crossed their arms. "They're all fucked."

Time to move. "Not so fucked. It runs. It's good. When's the last time you've seen a chopper like that in person?"

"Oh, I've seen them. Plenty."

"Jesus, Wesley, you have not," the blonde said, then laughing. She lowered her voice. "Too proud to admit they're local boys."

"Shut up," Wesley said.

"You never know where you might see a bike, though."

"True that." She nodded.

Lafitte looked away, another sip. Drink almost gone. The blonde shrieked.

"What happened to your *leg*?"

All the kids were interested then. The pain had dulled some, but Lafitte couldn't go much longer on his own. He needed a break.

"Let's just say I had a bad afternoon."

The blonde said, "Can I?" and reached her hand towards his leg. He didn't answer. She laid her fingers softly above it and leaned in for a closer look. Careful, nice touch. Maybe she was a nurse or training to be one. Nah, thought Lafitte. Probably just dealt with machinery accidents on the farm.

"You need stitches."

He shook his head. "It'll heal. Just need to clean it once I get where I'm going tonight."

She brought her hand up, looking for a shake. "I'm Fawn."

Sure, why not a shake. "Nice to meet you. Pretty name."

"My dad was a hunter. My first name is Mona, after my great-grandmother. And you are?"

Whatever name occurred to him first. "Kyle."

"If you want, I can carry you over to the ER in Watertown. Should only take about a half hour to get there."

"No, please. I'll be fine."

"That's not fine."

The joker and the other girl had drifted over by then. Mumbling to each other. Lafitte heard the girl call the kid "Goof". He saw green and purple dots around the kid's nostrils, where he'd been sniffing permanent markers.

He said to Lafitte, "Shit, man, you already had one crash today, and now you want another one with this trash?" Gave Fawn a hip-hop once over.

She gritted her teeth and seethed, "*Goof!*"

"Just saying, right? Never know when she might whip out her blade, cut your balls off."

"*Goof!*" Took a slash at him with her nails. He jumped clear. She went after him, the boy dodging and weaving.

Lafitte pointed to the car. "Whose wagon?"

The guy in the glasses raised his hand, then remembered he wasn't in school, brought it down quickly. His friends laughed.

"That's mine."

"Runs good?"

"Gets me where I need to go. More power than you'd expect out of her."

Lafitte nodded.

Fawn had given up on the huffer kid, who was taunting from across the road, and came back to the table. "Really, though, it's no trouble for me to give you a ride."

Lafitte said to the wagon owner, "What's your name?"

"Ben."

"Okay, Ben. You like that bike?"

Trying to play it cool. "It's a'ight. Needs new paint, new pipes."

The other kid. "Aw man, you stole this hog, didn't you?"

Great. Now they were all excited. Lafitte held up his palms. "Hey, hold up. I said someone gave it to me."

"Yeah? Who?"

Goof, circling closer, said, "Show us the registration!"

"Don't even know how to ride it, all smashed and shit."

Lafitte stood. That shut them all up. He turned to Fawn and said, "You got anything stronger than High Life?"

"Some Bacardi in the truck. Some Diet Coke." She reclined on the table some, her arms propping her up, dangling her sandaled foot. Lafitte had said the right thing. He guessed any of a hundred things would be the right thing. Dismissed the kid's warning, seeing as how there was no way to hide a blade in jeans that tight.

"Fuck the Coke. Give me some rum."

He followed her to the truck while the other kids hung around the bike. They knew the signals, knew when it was time to let the couples have some private time, or as much as possible in a parking lot. Closer, Lafitte heard some muffled new style R&B and groans from the Nissan. Tinted windows. Smart man.

Fawn opened her passenger door, perched half-in half-out, reached into the narrow space behind the seat and pulled out a paper bag. "Need a cup?"

"You mind if I take it from the bottle?"

Big grin. Fawn wasn't intimidated, not one bit. Had to take what she could get in the middle of nowhere. She'd probably let her high school principal go down on her, fucked plenty of married men, and hooked up with crank dealers if the mood was right. Would get her killed if she kept on like that, either by a beating, a disease, or suffocating after passing out face down and ass-up in some creep's back seat. She unscrewed the top and handed the bottle over.

Lafitte took a swig. Long time since he'd had any. Sweet, more like the red wine he used to drink before joining up with Steel God, then switching to mostly beer and cheap noxious whiskey. The rum switched on immediately, staving off the chill, numbing his mouth, his skin, the throbbing leg. Sweet, yes, sweet Jesus, what a cure.

He handed the bottle back to Fawn with a big rush of hot breath. She took it and tried to drink it like he did, giving up quickly and coughing, covering her hand with her mouth. Said, "Whoa, wow. I'm pretty tough, but I think I'll need some pop to smooth it out."

Lafitte hiked his wounded leg up on the rail. "Splash a little of that down there."

"You kidding?"

"Better than nothing right now."

"I said I could take you. I'm trying to be nice."

He caught her look, all pissy now. Like she wasn't good enough for him.

Lafitte said, "Look, I'll take that ride, sure. But we've got to go my way, understand?"

"Don't get greedy. I'm not stupid."

He looked through the windshield of the truck, saw the goof and the bike boys quickly turn away. "You trust those kids?"

Fawn got lost. "What do you mean? To turn me in? I'm just having fun, that's all. I only give them beer, not the hard stuff."

Yeah, sure. "That's none of my business. They obviously appreciate that. What about me, though? Think they'll talk?"

"Should they?"

Lafitte nodded, spat on the ground. "Wouldn't you?"

"Depends."

"Exactly. Now, it's not like I'm married to that bike or anything, and it's worth more damaged than your three rides put together, see?"

"If you say so."

Lafitte was on a roll. Smiling, feeling like a deputy again, charming his mark so that the details lined up in his favor. "I do. I say so, Fawn. And all I wanted when I pulled in here tonight was a quick Dr. Pepper before getting as far away as I could get in one night."

She was on the hook. She was running. "Hey, you don't have to tell me. I've been there."

"Right, you know. Even better would be if I could get rid of that bike, too. And I'm guessing Ben, if I were to trade him the bike for the wagon, would be cool about it and keep his mouth shut, right? Same as his friends. Same as you."

Fawn bobbed her head and licked her lips. Brave chick. "Oh, I think I'm going to need something extra to keep me quiet. I don't think I'm asking much, do you?"

He smiled, a big one. "I don't think I've heard the question yet."

She curled her index finger—*come closer.*

He eased in, thinking she wanted a kiss. And their lips did touch, yeah, just a peck, before he felt her hand slide across his thigh, her lips dodge left, and she whispered, "If you're holding, I'll trade you your ticket out of here for a piece of it. Ice? Weed?"

"A piece?"

"Whatever it's worth to you. Hundred bucks? Two? A good trade to keep us all happy."

"That wasn't what I expected you to say."

Fawn pushed him away half a foot but kept her hand on his chest. "Man, I don't trade *that* for anything. That I do only when I want to. And you have to work hard to make me want to."

Keep telling yourself that. "I didn't mean anything."

"No, I just wanted you to know."

"Got it."

"That's my final offer."

Lafitte heard the groans from the Nissan next to them getting louder. He looked over his shoulder, thought he caught the glimpse of the driver's eye, watching him and Fawn. Or really just Fawn. Funny, he was slapping skin with the skinny girl in the backseat but really had it hard for Fawn. Lafitte understood. She was like a snake charmer, knew the right notes.

He said, "One more thing."

She let him in close again. "What?"

"You come along with me until I get where I'm going. We'll see if I've worked hard enough by then."

She tipped the rum bottle up, took a long pull. Was a natural at it. Lafitte chuckled, thought, why, you lying bitch.

AFTER THE BIKER and Fawn left in the wagon, the gang didn't know what to do with themselves or Ben's new chopper. Even skinny Lana and her boyfriend C. T. got dressed and ventured out once they heard the wagon leave.

Wesley said, "We've got to give it a ride around town, man. That would be the balls."

Ben said. "You heard what he said. I've got to get it out of sight for a while."

"And get rid of that gay color." Goof, coming down off his marker buzz.

"It's not *gay*. It's, like, a show color. You know, it looks good on TV."

"Whatever. You've got to de-faggotize the hog, dude."

"De-faggotize!" That got Rochelle laughing. Goof had been

working her all night, trying to pop that "friend" bubble around her, but no go. He had at least wanted a hook-up if she would get drunk enough, but everything came crashing down after the biker showed up. No play. Motherfucker.

Lana said, "How are you going to explain this to your dad?"

"I don't know. It's not like he should care. I only paid four hundred for the wagon."

Goof slapped at imaginary bug bites on his legs. He wore khaki shorts even though the air was frosty. He said, "How about when it starts snowing? What'll you do then?"

"I told you I don't know. *God.* I mean, look at this. Fix it up, I can sell it for a lot of money and buy a new car."

Wesley grabbed the handlebars. "But right now, we need to take it for a ride!"

Ben grabbed the bars, shoved Wesley aside. Wesley tried to mount the chopper from the other side. Goof enjoyed this, watching Ben and Wesley fight about it. He had something else going in the back of his mind, though. This biker, willing to trade a fucking sweet bike for an old Cutlass station-wagon, didn't seem right. And he was hurting bad from that gash on his leg. They all had to know he was in trouble and in a hurry. Guy like that, what would he be worth?

Goof turned to Rochelle. "Let me use your phone."

She was about to hand it over when she pulled back, left him hanging. "You're not calling the cops, are you? We promised Fawn we wouldn't turn him in."

"Aw, come on. I'm not."

"Swear?"

"I'm not going to turn him in, bitch. Let me use the phone."

She crossed her arms. "Uh uh. No one talks like that to me."

Goof reared back on her. She flinched, stuck her hands out to shield her face. Goof plucked the phone from her loose fingers.

"Thanks." He ran about twenty feet away and managed to dial his uncle before Rochelle got to him and started beating his back. "Yo, Uncle Perry. Hey! No, forget the noise. If you want to make some big money, meet me at the burger shack. No, I'm not shitting you. I promise."

UNCLE PERRY pulled up in less than five minutes in his souped-up Mustang, one of those boxy ones from the 80's. Fucker was *loud*. Goof had made a half-assed peace with Rochelle by then, even though she was pissed and he'd probably ended whatever chance he thought he had with her. Tough tits. With the money he and his Uncle would split off the biker, he'd be moving up. Maybe even that junior chick who'd moved there from India. She was smoking.

Goof ran over to the Mustang, knowing the gang would figure out what was up. Heard one behind him say, "Shit. The Huffer Boys are going to fuck everything to hell."

"Goddamn Goof."

He didn't care. That's what they always said about him. And then he'd do a pitch perfect *Saturday Night Live* routine come Monday morning and have them all in his corner again. The class spaz had more pull than you'd think.

Hopped into the front seat. Uncle Perry had spun the volume down on the new Ozzy CD. The inside of the 'Stang was skeletal. A fine CD player and controls for the nitrous, hard-assed seats. Uncle Perry always looked like he'd just woken up. Red-rimmed eyes, three or four days of beard stubble. Goof had never known him to have a full beard or be clean shaven, always in the middle. He smelled like old sweat, cat piss, and paint. The paint made sense. He huffed the stuff, and that was where Goof had learned to do the markers. Perry leaned over to look out Goof's window. As usual, his permanent gold-stained upper lip and nose reflected the light like a mirror.

"Guy left that bike with Ben, you said?"

"Honest to God. He's in bad shape, went off with Fawn."

Perry grunted. He knew Fawn better than he wanted to. Had

to let her keep a bunch of his shit after they broke up because she had threatened to spill on all his under-the-table dealing if he didn't let her. Also, she was stone cold nuts. Cunt thought she was hotter stuff than she was. But Perry couldn't argue. She sucked cock like she'd gotten a degree in it.

"That's a good bike," Perry said. "I heard it on the scanner, they're looking for a guy on an aqua blue bike who was involved in a big wreck east of here. The FBI's looking for him, too."

"Fucking cool!" Goof was all fidgety. "He's in Ben's old wagon."

Perry sucked his bottom lip a moment. "You said he's injured, right? Alone with Fawn and injured?"

"Well, duh. Maybe she'll leave something for the scavengers. Don't you still have that gun?"

Some guy had tried to pay back a loan from Perry with an H&K semi-auto, but he didn't want it. Reminded him too much of what sort of lifestyle he was trying to avoid—the kind that got you dead quick. But, hey, it was the gun or nothing. Perry fired the thing off in the woods until the clip was empty and then tried to pawn it. Six pawn shops wouldn't touch it. So the damn thing was laying under his seat, unloaded and good for nothing except a threat.

"C'mon, Uncle Perry. I want in on this. Give me a break, man. I get half."

The kid had been a shit from the moment he could bite. His older sister's kid, only eight years difference between Goof and Perry. If there really was any money in tracking down the biker asshole, he'd toss a few bucks at his nephew, but half? What was the kid going to do? Annoy the guy into submission?

"Fine, ride along. But don't fuck it up. You fuck it up, deal's off."

"Says you."

"Yeah, says me." Perry reached under the seat and brought out the useless H&K, then turned his steel gray eyes to Goof. "You're sure it's only him and Fawn? No surprises, right?"

Thirteen

McKeown had this way about him, could sense a shift in the air or something. Couldn't call it paranoia since he was right so often. This time he sensed Rome had figured him out. Confirmed when he tried raising Ginny Lafitte on her cell phone and got nothing but the answering machine five times in two hours. All it meant was that he had to get Rome moving faster, put him and Billy Lafitte in the same room together, take plenty of photos of whatever ungodly beating happened, and then pull the men apart right before one of them killed the other. McKeown was certain Rome would want it up close and personal, and that he'd rather give Lafitte a chance as a man rather than take potshots while he was tied up. Franklin Rome had something to prove and was using FBI resources to help do it.

Joshua McKeown was happy to let him run with it, documenting every piece, until it added up to enough to help get himself promoted in spite of past *incidents*. Had to go and waste time with that fucking cougar. Hard not to remember how she made him feel, though, the hate and the ecstasy stirred into one drink. As bitter as the iced coffee he now sipped while sitting on a front window stool at a coffee shop in Memphis, the street lights flickering on and the strip lighting up bulb by bulb. His third iced coffee. Couldn't raise Ginny, didn't want to raise Rome yet. He was most likely the only one on the team who knew about the wreck in Minnesota, the fire that had killed Nate, Mr. Jr. Agent himself. Shit. He'd warned the guy, hadn't he? Was there any way to have expressed "Leave him alone" more strongly?

Three iced coffees. A leg that wouldn't stop bouncing. At least the good thing about doing his job from Memphis the last two months was that he could dress down in jeans and a pullover polo, some Reebok hiking sneakers. He could sit here at this window and make his calls and run next door for good tamales, down the block for BBQ, and anywhere on the strip for blues or good alt-country. He'd met a bass player from a tight bar band a couple of weeks ago, guy named Alexander, and they'd hit it off pretty good despite McKeown lying about his job. Told Alex he was an entertainment lawyer in town to help with paperwork setting up a new indie record label. Not the best choice, he thought, since Alex of course wanted to follow that lead, see if McKeown had an in there, a nudge towards the band's set, at least. Should've told him something boring, like "systems analyst."

It had been a fast two weeks. What he hadn't expected, although maybe he'd kind of suspected a few times in the past without acting on it, was what he was feeling for Alex. McKeown had fucked some cougars, thrown himself into a few college orgies and law school MMF threesomes, things getting hazy those nights, waking up naked with God knew how many hands on him, men and women. So, yeah, he had "experimented" and such. But to be truly bi? Just out and out desperately wanting to suck Alex's cock after only a few late nights out drinking, seeing bands, hitting Waffle House at three a.m. and trading stories, although McKeown's were all made up?

Yeah, he knew Alex was gay. He was only a friend, right? But then it seemed things were getting…uncomfortably close. Maybe Alex leaned in for a good night bro-hug and lingered too long. Maybe when McKeown clapped his hand over Alex's leg and left it there, to see what would happen. Shit, with women it was easy. With an orgy it was easier—you didn't *ask*, you just *did*. With

Alex, though, this was moving towards, well, McKeown had no idea. He was feeling bad because he'd lied about who he really was to protect himself from that psycho Rome.

Rome. Now there was a man who knew how to use leverage. Already had McKeown wrapped around his little finger, so he thought, with this judge's wife thing. But if Rome knew McKeown was bi? He'd threaten to swing open the closet door and flick on the light, expose him to his colleagues, friends, family, past lovers. So McKeown proceeded carefully, but it was getting to them both, like those few times where it seemed Alex was getting impatient, trying to set up those moments where a kiss comes naturally and then, you know, things from there go pretty fast. Thinking about it made his balls hurt. McKeown glanced around the coffee shop, adjusted his jeans as best he could. His throat got thick. This wasn't lust. If all he felt was lust then he could easily pick up the hippie coffee girl with the dreads. Looked like she'd take it up the ass. Or that art gallery curator he'd flirted with, another older woman. Or any number of college coeds at the bars past midnight, or even venturing into the gay dance clubs, inviting a slab of beef into the restroom.

Lust was easy. Always had been. But what he felt for Alex, this was full-on desire. Jesus. He'd never been in, like, a "real" dating situation with a man before.

He cleared his throat and thought about calling Ginny Lafitte one more time. No, wait. Go around her, go back to her mother.

She picked up on the third ring.

"Mrs. Hoeck, it's Agent McKeown again. Sorry to bother you."

"Oh, it's no fuss." She didn't mean it. "Is there something I can do for you?"

"Well, I've been trying to reach your daughter for a while now, and she's not answering. I was hoping you might have an idea."

"I assumed all of you people kept in touch. She called Agent Rome, I believe. Is he your superior?"

McKeown rubbed his hand on the leg that wouldn't stop bouncing. "I'm working with him on this matter. It's urgent I get in touch, though. Do you know of another way besides her cell phone?"

"She has it with her, I know. She called not long ago."

"Did she tell you where she was?"

A hum at Mrs. Hoeck's end. "Is that fair for me to say? I mean, aren't you supposed to respect her privacy?"

"When it comes to her safety and the safety of her children, I believe she won't mind if we have to put that aside, don't you agree?"

"But she told Agent Rome—"

"And I'll call him as soon as we're done. But, please."

A sigh. "I don't like Agent Rome. I don't like what this is doing to Ginny. But at least I know him. I barely know you at all."

Damn it, what happened to the good old days, right after 9/11, when people *respected* your ass if you were a Fed? McKeown recited his ID number, his full name, date of birth, and then Rome's number. "And that's the best I can do. Now, ma'am, it's urgent. File a complaint later if you have to, but think about Ginny first. We're talking about the man who killed your son."

"Billy?" Her voice shook. "You didn't say it had to do—"

"I'm sorry, I'm sorry, it's…not what you think. I shouldn't have said that." He squeezed his eyes shut. Wondered about the job prospects for a fired FBI agent. "I'm begging you."

The pause was so long, he thought she might have hung up, but then Mrs. Hoeck cleared her throat. "Ginny took her daughter to the aquarium in New Orleans. Just overnight, a getaway after all the stress she's been under." Then, shaky. "What about Billy? They found him?"

McKeown thought, *Rome has her.* "I'm sure she's fine. It's better if the team is on the same page, that's all. Agent Rome must've gotten busy. Again, sorry to bother you."

He gave her a few more soothing lines before hanging up and staring out into the street, brighter under the streetlights than it had been fifteen minutes ago in the fading sun.

Said under his breath, "What has he done?"

Flipped open the phone, dialed, waited.

Rome answered, "What?"

"Listen, something's come up in Minnesota, but I can't find Ginny Lafitte. Do you have any idea?"

"You called her cell?"

Of course he called her fucking cell. "No answer. It's urgent."

"What happened in Minnesota?"

"Where's Ginny?"

Quiet. McKeown glanced over to see Alex pushing through the front doors, coming over. McKeown stood, held up a hand. Mouthed, *Sorry. Work.*

Alex nodded, stepped past McKeown, running his hand up his arm as he did. The way he smelled, man. Spicy, almost. McKeown liked it, took in a deep breath. "Do you even know where she is?"

ROME SMILED. He kept his voice curt. "I think you should have more faith in me, Agent McKeown. Of course I know where she is. She told me. And she's being protected. That's all you need to know at this time. Understood?"

"That doesn't make much sense, sir."

"Yeah, well, it's natural to feel that way when you're not in the loop. Everyone has his or her own place in this operation, and yours is what it is."

Rome was driving home after stashing Ginny and Savannah in a really nice hotel down in the Quarter. He told them not to leave, took her cell phone along with him. Told her to only pick up the room phone. When they were hungry, they should put in an order with the concierge and he would pick up anything they liked, deliver it to the room. Then he flashed his ID downstairs, made the arrangements from that end. Big on two points: 1) "Don't let her leave. That's vital." 2) "No one sees her except you and your staff. Absolutely no one else."

He would let her call her mother once a day until this was over. She would never be in any real danger if things worked out according to the plans that were carved in cement inside his head. Now that he had flushed McKeown out, he would have to proceed along one of his detours, but they were built in.

Unless…

"So tell me what happened in Minnesota."

McKeown said, "We've got a problem."

Rome listened, stomach gnawing at him as McKeown described the wreck, what happened to Nate, what Colleen told the State Troopers on the scene. Topped by the mental image of a wounded Lafitte riding off on a damaged bike. Rome didn't like it. The man was like an animal—more dangerous when hurt, capable of anything.

"And we didn't plan for this?"

"We didn't know that little prick deputy had it in him."

"Jesus, who do you think he learned it from?" Rome shook his head. He turned the corner and pulled to the curb, only five minutes from home but not wanting to carry the workload in to Desiree that night. "Any bright ideas?"

"The Highway Patrol is manning the border, trying to close a net on him. Nothing yet."

"You think he'll keep coming south though, right?"

"There's no reason to think otherwise. All this did was slow him down."

"We can pick up the trail, then."

"That's my conclusion."

Rome looked at his watch. He had promised to be home fifteen minutes ago for dinner. Desiree was going to be pissed, and in a bad way. "What if the Troopers find him first?"

McKeown's sigh rattled Rome's speaker. "I don't have a real in with those guys. Pretty hardcore. We'll have to cross our fingers."

"Not *one* goddamn Trooper?"

"I'll see what I can do."

"Better." Rome hung up.

Five more minutes to the house. Everything went to hell if Lafitte got caught. Shit, shit, shit. Rome would be cut out. McKeown would appreciate the irony. Not a question anymore:

the guy had to go. Rome had the photos at home, could send them out first thing in the morning. It would be a surprise attack. Sink McKeown and full steam ahead.

But only if Lafitte escaped the net. Rome was forced to root for the fucker.

Rome banged his palm hard on the steering wheel, bit the inside of his cheek to keep from shouting. The palm pulsed. Damn thing would bruise, swell. He opened and closed his fingers gingerly.

Enough stress for the evening. Lafitte had made it almost a year and a half under the radar so far and knew how cops thought. Safe bet. Rome could go home, relax, wake up to better news.

He pulled into the driveway. Reached for his briefcase from the passenger seat, but his hand was aching. He left the case and climbed out, hoped Desiree was still in a forgiving mood. He had a great excuse, just one he couldn't tell her. So, "lost track of time" it would have to be.

The front door was unlocked. Rome closed it and stood for a moment. No TV, no stereo, no trace of Desiree's voice talking on the phone to her sister. Not a good sign. Maybe she'd packed up and left. Right when things were getting back on track, too. Could be Rome sent her over the edge on this one.

The lights were on, though. Plus that unlocked door. Hey, what if...?

He eased his pistol out of its holster, gritting his teeth as his swollen palm touched the cold metal. He could barely lift it. Finally got it in his other hand. Not a great left-handed shooter, but at this range he wouldn't need to be.

Rome was about to sweep through the kitchen when he heard her voice from the bedroom. "Franklin? Is that you sneaking around?"

She didn't sound distressed, just her usual level of pissed.

"Sorry. I tried to hurry."

"Come in here. We need to talk."

There it was. The tension in Rome's shoulders pulled harder. He tried to slip the gun back into its holster with the wrong hand, fumbled and nearly dropped it. Instead, he set it on the table in the foyer next to his keys. All he'd wanted was to come home, re-heat a plate of whatever Chinese she had ordered for delivery, and maybe hope for another round of what had happened the night before. Strike all that now. What he wanted most right then was a massage.

Hand cupped around the back of his neck, kneading, Rome shuffled to the bedroom ready to apologize for anything and everything. Total passivity. Play it slack. Man, his neck was *tight*.

Rome stopped in the door of the bedroom. The first thing he noticed was the scent from all those candles. Must've been ten or more, a blend of orange and mango and peach. Desiree had done some shopping. Not just the candles. His wife was standing at the foot of the bed in red thigh highs, stiletto boots, wearing an outfit made of little leather straps, barely wide enough for her nipples. A studded collar around her neck. She was slapping a short leather whip lightly on her ass.

"Baby," Rome said. It caught in his throat.

She snarled her lips. "Twenty minutes late means twenty min-utes of pain, mister. Now get over here and bend over this bed."

It was as if his neck hadn't been aching at all. "Yes ma'am."

Fourteen

LAFITTE LET FAWN DRIVE, let her choose the station on the ancient radio. She went with rock. It wasn't good rock, just loud. In the passenger seat, Lafitte couldn't help but doze off. Fawn smoked another cigarette and kept her window cracked enough for the smoke to roll out. The car was freezing, and Lafitte wasn't able to hear half of what she was saying. What he did catch was how she was talking about her ex-guys, things they did that she hated. Some memorable nights at parties. "You *know* I was drunk to do that." Asking questions of him: "You a one woman man, or you a *playa*?" "So that jacket, you in a gang? A Hell's Angel?" "You got condoms? It's okay if you don't."

He mumbled the answers that got her to laugh, not giving up real answers, though. Keeping her interested while getting her to go where he wanted. Straight west to Watertown was a risk now, thanks to the Kid Cops back there. Another memory of Nate screaming and burning flashed as he drifted again. He caught himself, snorted, sat up straighter.

Fawn, more of that laugh. "Don't fade out on me! Take a hit of ice. It'll help."

"I'll be fine. Enjoying a little downtime, need a couple of winks." He pointed out her side. "Take that road."

"What, the county road?"

"Yeah. We need to head South."

"You got a place?" She said it flirty, but tense. He wondered how many times she had been in this sort of situation before.

"I think I remember a spot."

After Fawn turned, Lafitte checked his sideview again. He'd caught a pair of headlights behind them, seemed to show up out of nowhere but then keep a steady distance after that. Sure enough, the headlights turned in behind them on the county road. He didn't think she had signaled anyone. Maybe the parking lot kids were curious. Didn't matter, as long as his strength came back in time.

Fawn's chatter stopped. Lafitte gave her a good stare. Without the posing, she was pretty average, someone you'd pass in the supermarket and not think much about. Maybe you'd notice because she was dressing to grab a man's attention in clothes tighter than what looked comfortable, but not so outrageous you'd dwell on it past the next aisle. It was her personality that turned the whole package on.

Lafitte said, "You ever thought of leaving this place? Maybe head to a bigger city, get a job there?"

She shrugged. "You mean to like to Sioux Falls? Why?"

"You're spending your night trying to get teenagers to like you, and you picked up a stranger who most likely stole a bike."

"You didn't steal that."

"You want me to have."

"Maybe I just like your accent. Southern, isn't it?"

"Which one of the boys did you have your eye on tonight? Wesley, I'll bet."

She sped up. Did a Jerry Springer head shake. "Fuck you, man. You don't know me. Could've been my brother, or a friend. What the fuck do you know?"

"He wasn't your brother."

"Fine, okay."

"I'm just saying, do you do it because you like the power you have over them, or because you're having a hard time finding men your own age around here?"

She backhanded his shoulder. Didn't hurt. "Fuck you! I'm not a slut. I told you that. I haven't made up my mind about you yet, anyway. And if that bothers you so much why did you even come with me?"

"Why do you think?"

She shrunk. "I thought you liked me some."

"If not?"

"Then I don't know. I like to get high. I guess you're some sort of killer, right? Going to leave me out in the woods." The words were sarcastic, sure, but she'd also sped up. Getting nervous.

"That's the problem with you small town girls. You're too trusting."

"Helped you out."

Lafitte smiled. He lifted his injured leg, pounded it on the floorboard. Fawn jumped. He said, "Just testing it. Feeling better."

GOOF KEPT bouncing around, telling Perry to close the gap or he would lose them. He hated the music. Old geezer rock. He asked, "Where's that Three Six Mafia CD I burned for you?"

Perry said, "Why do you listen to that? What do you get out of it?"

"They're badass, man. That's the way to live, like *Scarface*. You ain't pimpin', son. Bitches want to see the bling."

"You know I've got pussy anytime I want. You *know* that."

"Not the same quality as Three Six Mafia."

"How about your biker? You think he's hot shit and I'll bet he doesn't listen to *that*."

"But he went off with Fawn, too, man. No offense, dude, but that's like running your dick through a chainsaw. Don't care how bad he is. You know what I mean." Goof nodded at Perry's arm stretched on top of the steering wheel, scar tissue peeking out from under the sleeve.

Perry reached over and grabbed the front of his nephew's shirt, yanked him down so his cheek pressed against the bar where the dash should've been. Goof called him a motherfucker and an asshole and all the other shit kids said when they're scared. Held him there about a minute before saying, "Until you've had your turn with a woman bad as Fawn, stop playing baby gangsta, boyo."

"I don't know why I called you. I could've taken him down. Me and the guys."

"Yeah, sure." He let go of Goof and reached for the volume knob. Upped it. Zakk Wylde on guitar wailing while Ozzy did his thing. "Badass Goof to the rescue."

Goof rubbed the deep line across his cheek. "Don't call me that."

IF THE FUCKS behind them kept pace, Lafitte wouldn't have any time at all to make the switch. Maybe thirty seconds. Not enough. Fawn's leadfoot put them ahead but only by so much. Lafitte knew they were close, though. Been at it about the right number of miles. Now he just needed a way out.

Some hills were coming up. At the top of the first one, Lafitte said, "Shut off the lights."

"What?"

"Shut your lights off. It's okay."

She pushed in the headlights lever so that all they had was the dashboard glow. Really pitch black outside, Fawn leaning over the wheel, foot easing off the gas.

"No, keep up the speed."

"I can't see a damned thing."

"Do it. I can see."

He'd forced himself to see better at night. He had lived with thugs who thought it was the middle ages, ready to take out the leader or his enforcer and rise to the top. The road ahead was clear. Started to twist left.

"Left."

"I can't see—"

"Left, okay? You're not *that* fucking blind, are you?"

On the verge of tears. "I don't wear my glasses at the lot. I look terrible in them."

They would be in the ditch in five more seconds if she couldn't do this. Lafitte said, "Ease it to ten o'clock. You got that? Ten o'clock."

She pulled the wheel, did fine, drifting over the center line some but no one was coming. He talked her out of the curve, then told her to floor it when they were straight. He started looking for the best place to finish this.

He said, "Don't you have contacts?"

"No, just glasses."

"Why not contacts?"

"I don't know. I never thought about it. Easier to get up, pull my hair back into a rubber band, and wear the glasses to work."

"Where do you work?"

She hemmed and hawed. "There's a dollar store downtown. I'm a cashier. Not like it's my whole life, you know? Just money. I'll do better one day."

"Turn right here." Lafitte pointed to a narrow road separating two fields. Fawn turned.

"Awful deserted," she said. "If you want, I know a hotel about ten more minutes from here."

"This is fine."

"I mean, I didn't say anything wrong, did I?"

"No, Fawn. Not at all. I just need to take a piss."

He had her run past a few more fields then steer back towards the main road. They'd definitely lost the car trailing them, at least for a few extra minutes. Fawn parked at the corner of a field, left it running. "You go do what you need to."

Lafitte held out his hand. "Keys first."

"I don't think so."

"Keys first or I take them. That's your choice."

Fawn sulked a moment, finally putting the car in park and turning it off. She gave Lafitte the keys.

"Thanks. I feel better now." He got out, stepped about twenty feet away, and took a leak. Hoping Fawn would try to run away, make this a lot easier on him. He only wanted the car. Just needed the fucking car. Should've took it plain as day back in town, but thought this might get him further down the road. Was she trying to run? No. Fuck no. She wasn't leaving until she got her drugs or got fucked. Risking death, even, and Lafitte had played that up big time, but there she was, waiting in the car.

He zipped up and walked back over to the driver's side. Tapped on the window. She pushed the lever to slide it down. Nothing happened.

"I need the keys," she said.

"Just get out."

"Why? Get back in. I'll pay for the room. Come on, it'll be fun."

"Get out of the car." Lafitte reached for the handle.

Fawn flicked the locks. He took a step back, jiggled the keys in his hand.

She was crying then, a few quiet tears. Hands white-knuckling the wheel. "Hell no."

Had to be done. Lafitte stuck the key in the lock, turned, pulled the handle. She fought and scratched like a fucking wild turkey, screeched and tried to hold the door closed, but Lafitte flexed and the door swung open and Fawn followed with a squeal, losing grip on the door and rolling on the ground. Lafitte grabbed the back of her hair and she started shouting, trying to stomp his toes and kick his shins. He got her under control.

"I'm not going to hurt you," Lafitte said.

"You're hurting me now, you fucking pussy! Fucking faggot! Oh god oh god please please."

Fawn was on her knees, scalp in Lafitte's grip. He squatted beside her, watching the main road.

"I don't have any drugs. I'm not going to rape you. But I am leaving you here right now. Wait until I'm out of sight and then go find a phone, tell someone to come get you."

She was mad and scared, wheezing too much. "Why...why...did you do this...to me?"

Lafitte let go of her hair and stood. "I didn't have a choice. Look on the bright side, though. I could've taken your truck. Instead, everybody wins, okay? Think about it like that for a while."

He hopped into the wagon, cranked up, and spun his tires on the gravel getting out of there. Pinged Fawn with some of it, he was sure. He hoped she got back home okay. Maybe he'd drive by the parking lot again one night next time he was up that way, see if she was still there.

Yeah, who was he kidding? He would never see that town again.

PERRY KNEW as soon as the wagon's taillights went dark that the biker had spotted them and was going to turn off the main road into the dusty straightaways surrounding the corn fields. He just needed to figure out which one. Probably only a few minutes behind. He flicked the brights on over the hills and told Goof to keep a careful eye out for dust plumes.

"There! I got it!" Goof was poking his window like a madman. "Right there."

Just enough to point them in the right direction. Perry turned off. Too bad this guy knew someone was on his scent. Would've been funny to pull him off Fawn, their pants down round their ankles, probably start squirting piss when Perry put the empty gun to his head. They must have been closing fast, the clouds more concentrated as he turned again, the headlights blinded some by the dust.

Perry got lucky when he saw out of the corner of his eye some lights pop on suddenly in the dark, two squares up. He launched the car, shifted hard, made up ground. Took the turn hot but kept control. The lights caught someone standing at the edge of the field, waving her hands at him. Fawn. Face screwed up like a monster, mascara runny from tears. And then she dropped her hands, the fear melting to resignation. She knew the car. Perry hit the brakes and skidded to a stop. Fawn limped over to Perry's window, leaned down and rested her elbows on the lip after he rolled the glass down.

She looked across Perry. "Goof, if I didn't hate you so much, I'd hug you right now."

"Ew."

Fawn flipped him off.

Perry said, "What happened?"

"This dude got rough. I thought he was going to try something, so I was like, 'No way!' and jumped the hell out of there."

"You look beat up."

She huffed. "You would know."

"Hey, it was self-defense." Perry revved the motor. "But you deserve better than this. Let's go catch the fucker."

Evil little grin. "Now you're talking."

"Is he packing?"

"I didn't see one, but I didn't see much."

Goof said, "Uncle Perry's gun isn't loaded anyway."

"Would you shut up?" Perry held up his hand like he was going to bitchslap Goof. The kid flinched, then bowed up. "Do it! Come on, do it!"

Fawn said, "Save it for the real thing."

Perry took a breath, calmed down. "Get in."

Fawn walked around to Goof's side, shooed him into the backseat.

"No way, bitch, I've got shotgun."

Fawn shoved Goof hard. "Get the fuck back there!"

Goof fussed and cursed and climbed in the back, shoving old beer cans, spray paint cans, and hot rod mags onto the floorboard. Fawn dropped into the passenger seat.

"Still heading South?" Perry said.

"I think he's making a run to the interstate. He just didn't want to do it in Watertown."

"Got it. He won't outrun the 'Stang. Perry put his hand on Fawn's knee. "Are you alright?"

She covered her eyes with her hand for a moment, like she was about to cry. Then she sucked in a deep breath and said,

"Promise me that when we catch him, I get a little payback before you take him in."

Perry shifted into gear. "Done."

Fifteen

LUCKY COLLEEN. Three stitches beneath her right eye-brow, hardly noticeable. Some bruising all over, scrapes here and there. Bandages, salve. A couple of shots to calm her down and take the burn away. When the doctor came to tell her there was nothing he could do for Nate, she said, "I already fucking know that. Didn't they tell you I watched him burn up?"

The State Troopers went through the rigmarole of questions. What happened? Did he assault you? How did two off-duty deputies, both having a history with the subject, happen to end up at the same place at the same time? Oh yeah, she was fucked trying to explain it away, so she changed her answers each time. Pretended to have a concussion. They left her alone after awhile and she sat very still on her bed in the ER.

One nurse stopped by to ask if she would mind giving up the bed. "We've got an old lady with the flu coming in."

Colleen ended up in the waiting room picking at the band-age on her middle finger. The flu lady's old husband sat across the room, snoring while sitting up. A couple with a small baby, the husband holding a Ziploc full of ice to his busted nose. A really fat guy in a wheelchair, all alone, who kept making noises like he was going to vomit. A couple of Troopers lounged around near the door, probably to keep Colleen from leaving, but she wasn't willing to try them yet. Sheriff Tordsen found her there. He looked older than he ever had before, the face starting to slide. He wore his hat but not his uniform. Just jeans, boots, and a flannel shirt, like he didn't even stop to think before hopping into the car. After seeing him come in, Colleen looked down at her hand, kept picking. He sat beside her, didn't say anything for awhile.

Then, "Are you okay?"

Nothing.

"I'm sorry, honey. I can't feel as bad as you do right now, but you've got to believe I'm pretty damned close."

"Okay."

"I never expected something like this, though."

Colleen struck blood with her fingernail, pressed down hard. "Well, shit, Sheriff. Why not? We sure as hell did."

He didn't seem surprised. Just went *Hm* and let her stew.

She went on, "I mean, you could've at least been a tiny bit suspicious. You can still be buddies if he's in prison. I can't be friends with Nate in the grave."

Her voice quivered but she kept it together. The sheriff put his arm around her shoulder. She didn't want it there but she let him. Otherwise he'd just bother her more until she gave in, say nonsense like, "It's okay to grieve."

Grieve? Another way of saying "Fail".

Tordsen said, "Seems awful curious, you two out there running into Billy. It's a big county."

"Seems small sometimes."

"Yeah, sometimes it does, true. But you have to wonder when lightning strikes twice. Billy had stopped by the station before coming out to see me, and he talked to Nate for a few minutes. Then, barely an hour later, Billy comes after you both. What're the odds?"

Oh, that son of a bitch. "It's all a blur. Can I please go home? Maybe I'll remember it better tomorrow."

"You shouldn't sleep with a concussion, you know. How about you come stay with me and the missus tonight?"

She slumped, feeling tired but no way she'd sleep. "I'll make some coffee and get some friends to come over. I want to go home."

"Are you sure? All his stuff's there."

"I need his stuff around me. Feels better than nothing at all."

The sheriff hummed a few times, stretched his legs out. He watched Colleen's face. If he was waiting for her to break down, that wasn't going to hack it. The Sheriff's fault in the first place. All she and Nate had done was try to finish the job right. That's all. At least they had tried. Tordsen couldn't blame her for anything. He didn't deserve to.

The big guy in the wheelchair lurched again and hocked something into his mouth. He spit it on the floor. Colleen wrapped her hands around her stomach.

"Please, Sheriff. Take me home."

TORDSEN WALKED her inside the house she and Nate rented, a tiny old affair on a residential street, but fine until they were able to save up for one in the country. No, wait, no more of that. She was on her own.

The living room smelled like him. She couldn't explain it and she hadn't noticed it before, but he was all over. She had left the TV on when she left after his call. The sweats she had worn were tossed on the couch since she had taken them off the second they'd hung up. Asked if she wanted to have some fun chasing a wanted man. As soon as she heard who, like she was going to say no, right?

Her half-eaten bowl of ice cream, melted. Nate's new wireless Playstation controller on his recliner, a cheat book for some crazy sci-fi game she never paid any attention to. Some of their CDs stacked on the coffee table, stuff she'd brought in from the car after weeks of listening to the same things—Toby Keith, Nickelback, and of course Gretchen Wilson, which Colleen had listened to so much that the first one got scratched real bad and she had to buy a replacement. Nate knew how much his woman loved music. He'd bought her an MP3 player for her birthday a few months ago, and she'd already filled it up. Sometimes spent two hours straight looking for new tunes online.

Remembering the everyday stuff, the typical boring stuff. The times they were so comfortable being in the same house together that they didn't mind how boring it was in Pale Falls. Didn't feel the need to hit the cities. They didn't need to. They made up for it on the job and in the bedroom.

The sheriff stood right behind her, said, "How about I wait here until your friends make it over?"

Shook Colleen out of those cozy thoughts, brought her back to reality. She'd always hated that Playstation, but now no one would ever use it again anyway. What was she going to do?

She turned to Tordsen. "Why?"

He shoved his hands in his pockets, watched the ground. "I don't know."

"You think I'll hurt myself."

Tordsen's chin raised right quick. "Now wait a minute—"

"Think I'm not right in the head, like I'd be dumb enough to eat my gun, is that it?"

He held out his hands, pushing them, *calm down calm down.* "Look, I've lost people real close to me, so all I'm saying—"

Colleen stepped around Tordsen, walked to the door and swung it open hard. It slammed into the wall and shook the TV stand. "Leave, Sheriff. I've got a funeral to get ready for."

Tordsen took one of his famous deep breaths, slipped those hands right back into his pockets, and nodded. "You're right, you're right. Okay. But if you need us, give us a call."

"I won't need you."

"I understand, but you will later. And don't worry about work. It'll be there for you when you're ready."

Colleen thinking if she didn't need the money, she'd throw her shield at him right now. She stood, hand on door knob, looking back into the house, avoiding Tordsen's eyes.

Right before he stepped over the threshold, Tordsen said, "But you'd better remember something, missy."

She held her jaw tight.

Tordsen said, "I have to get ready for that same funeral."

He was out. She slammed the door. Shouted, *"Nate! God-damn you, Nate!"* over and over and cried and kicked the wall until she crumpled to the floor hugging her knees to her chest.

SHE DIDN'T CALL her friends. She didn't even call her Mom, in spite of several messages on the machine. One from Nate's mom. Sounded like they hadn't told her yet. What she did was sit for a while, mentally reliving the last year of her life. That night she met Nate in the middle of a slushy cornfield where two college students had been found decapitated. How Nate even told her later it was Lafitte who had encouraged him to talk to her. Ridiculous.

Tomorrow there would be more questions. Things about her story didn't add up, obviously. No matter how delicate the inter-rogation was, it would be too much. Fucking people would charge her with something even though she'd already lost more than she ever imagined. They'd talked about it, what if one of them was shot in the line of duty, that sort of thing, but she never thought she'd actually see it happen. The smell, the heat, the an-guish as he screamed. The flesh melting away. The smell. She pinched her nose. It was still there. That same sharp, charred—

"Enough! Enough! Enough!"

Up from the floor, moving fast. Most of their guns were lost in the fire, but she knew where Nate kept his most precious one. The back of the bedroom closet, under his shoeboxes full of pho-tos—the ones of ex-girlfriends he refused to throw out, said they were just good memories—in a heavier shoebox.

Colleen walked into the bedroom, got down on her knees and started digging through the mess on the closet floor, shirt and pants that had fallen off hangers, and summer clothes that had been kicked off after getting in from the shooting range or dirt track, left behind as October moved in nice and chilly. She dug, tossed the photo boxes over her shoulder. Time to burn those fuckers. The box was right where it always was, tied closed with an old shoe lace. Colleen untied the knot, lifted the lid. The pistol was wrapped in an oil-rag. She lifted it out, let the rag fall to the ground. Nate's grandfather's .45, which he'd used in Korea. Battle-tested and bruised, it was still a stellar piece of work. Made to withstand rain, mud, and incompetence. She smoothed her fingers down the side of it. She told herself, "I'm going to kill Billy Lafitte with this gun."

She noticed something else in the box, too, besides the two clips and box of ammo that were always there. A tiny maroon box, the kind jewelry stores used.

Oh no, he didn't. Did he?

Colleen took it, opened it. Dropped her hands to her lap. He'd bought her the fucking ring after all. A beauty—solitaire engagement ring. All the talk they'd had about "not enough cash right now" and "you deserve better", and look at what Nate had gone and done. She found the receipt and first three statements, smudged with gun oil, lining the bottom of the box. He had opened an account and was paying it off in installments. It was a third of a carat. More than she expected. She would've been happy with spray painted tin foil, she thought. No, that's a damned lie.

At least she was laughing, bringing the ring box closer to her face for a better look. He'd picked out a nice one, emerald cut, with a white-gold band.

"You asshole."

Her eyes watered, blurred the diamond. She wiped them with the back of her hand.

Fuck it. Not that it mattered before God or the State or anything. She took the ring out of the box and shoved it onto her finger. Perfect fit. Nate must've sneaked around and figured out her ring size. Sweet boy. A couple of minutes of admiring it, imagining how he would've proposed. Most likely on patrol. He would've rigged a fake call for her out to the river park or gun range, something romantic like that, and he would be in full uniform, too. Exactly.

Goddamned Billy Lafitte.

OUT IN THE GARAGE, Colleen tightened the last lug on the front right tire. She lowered the jack. She added a couple quarts of oil. Nate had left the car tireless in the front, hood up, trying to finish another upgrade but never quite getting there. It would run fine. It would suck gas and make a lot of noise, and the shifter felt loose, but this was what she had and it wasn't a bad choice at all. Another couple of years and Nate would've had his little hobby all pimped-out and ready for the track. It was a '74 Chevelle Laguna. Nate had restored the gold paintjob, found a replacement for the missing backseat, new steering wheel. The engine was mostly fine but needed some parts here and there, and Nate had gone after those first to make sure it would run before he tackled the rest. He told Colleen he'd bought the car from his uncle three years ago and was slowly bringing it back. She thought it was an eyesore, but after a while it grew on her. He'd taught her a few things, too. Colleen's dad had shown her how to change the oil and brake pads, but Nate went step-by-step through the engine restoration, the exhaust system, the transmission. Saved them some cash on maintenance. Helped buy things like, oh, engagement rings.

Colleen ran her thumb over the bottom of the ring again as she sat in the driver's seat and cranked her up. Caught instantly. Roared like it had been hibernating and was really damned hungry for some fucking pic-a-nic baskets. Barely enough gas to get out of town, though. She let it run while she went inside. Picked up the .45, a box of ammo, one of Nate's hunting knives, and a couple of cans of Starbucks DoubleShot, dropped them all into a plastic Wal-Mart bag.

She picked up the phone and called her Mom.

Took until the machine picked up, and Colleen waited while her mom figured out how to turn the thing off.

Her mom said, "Where have you been?"

"Mom, Nate's dead."

"Oh, god, no. No. Oh my god, Colleen, baby, I'm so sorry—"

"Mom, listen. I need to borrow your credit card."

Sixteen

DESIREE hadn't been fucked like that since…Jeeeeesus. Since last night? But better? She had come to think several years ago that marriage kind of dulled things and you had to ride the peaks and valleys, make your own joy when possible. When she was horny for whatever reason—some actor on TV, some song on the radio, some sweet memory of Franklin or that doctor she had been flirty with back in Washington or the men from college—she had grabbed Franklin and hoped he was up for it. Maybe less so for most of the past year, part of her payback, but even then she had needs.

These two days, though, this was something different. Desiree had never been a passive little kitten in bed, liked it on the hard side, but their lovemaking was still probably what any onlookers might call "average." Once she turned on her inner dominatrix, Franklin started working extra hard to please her. And, goddamn, she thought while stretching her arms over her head and pointing her toes right to the edge of the bed, he was succeeding.

Her "twenty minutes of pain" stretched to twice that, since something about Franklin not fighting back both enraged and titillated Desiree. She was *snarling* at him to toss it right back at her and she watched his skin rise where the whip struck. Not like she was out to hurt him, but even when she slapped the leather strap harder against his ass and thighs to get his attention, he cried out but never complained. Never even hinted at wanting it to stop.

What the hell was going on with him, anyway? Had he been too ashamed before to tell her this was what he liked in the bedroom? Worried she would think he was a freak or something? Was he suddenly snorting coke or having a mental breakdown?

Didn't seem like it. After the marathon foreplay or beating or whatever, he'd been hard as the fucking Washington monument. Desiree got on her knees and let him enter from behind. Nearly a half-hour later, she was aching and exhausted and he still hadn't come, but she had twice already and as the third washed over her and made her think she might have a stroke, Franklin finally let out a howl and she felt him go. It was hot. She thought about lava. She grabbed the sheets with her fists, her teeth. When he finally collapsed beside her on the bed, they caught their breaths and then just started laughing. He leaned over for a light kiss on the cheek, and she teared up some, snuggled against his chest, and they really talked. Like, a good talk, a real good one. About the sex, his surprise at seeing her all dommed out, her apologizing and him telling her there was no need. More laughing. Desiree telling him where she'd found the outfit, asked what else she should pick up there. Franklin said, "Surprise me." Then he said, "You feel like hitting that new restaurant tomorrow, the one you saw in the paper?" Yeah, a real good talk.

Her skin felt good. Her muscles ached down there but in a good way. The stretching led to humming. The sheets were twisted, the corners pulled off the mattress, their sweat and come spreading into wet oval stains, and she giggled when she rolled against the spots. Franklin had gotten up to take a piss. He'd been singing: "Give me that stuff, that funk, that sweet, that funky stuff." Made her laugh. When was the last time she'd heard that? Had to be at least ten years ago, or on the oldies shows—how can that be an oldie already? She felt too young.

Franklin segued into another one but she couldn't tell what it was over the sound of his stream. Talking a massive piss. Her man must've had an SUV tank for a bladder. Oh, that was dirty. Desiree was giggling so much by then that she almost didn't catch the ringtone on Franklin's work phone. Muffled. Probably in his pants, which came off and went flying out the bedroom door. Desiree sat up. Franklin obviously hadn't heard it. She slid out from the sheets and crawled across the carpet to the hall, dug the phone out of his pocket.

She didn't want the job butting in right now. The job was what got them in the hole they were still climbing out of. So maybe just one missed call? One nice evening without the "security of the nation" being in the palm of Franklin's hand?

Naked, sweat-slicked skin growing bumpy in the chilly room, phone in her palm while her husband in the bathroom now barked the "Bow Wow Wow" part from "Atomic Dog", his stream still going.

If she pretended she hadn't heard it, maybe that would work. He could buy that. She could pretend to be dozing off when he came back, conveniently waking when his body slid against hers under the sheet. That would be nice.

But if it was a *really* important call, missing it might have consequences. Desiree couldn't bear moving again, not so soon. Not until it was on the right way up.

"…Yippee yo yippee yay…"

Well…shit.

She could answer it, see if it was important or not. If so, pass it on to Franklin. If not, then say he wasn't feeling so well, something he ate, and he'd get back to them tomorrow, easy like that.

Or leave it alone. If it was important, they would call back.

She had a couple of more rings to decide. It sounded like Franklin was finishing up. If he heard it and got to it before she did, then the point was moot, evening was ruined, because even with a minor call, off he'd run to the office to pace around and ask tedious questions. He was much more impressive back in law school before he decided to go the government route, wanted a gun and a badge and some authority. Shit, if he'd gone for the money instead, then he would have even more authority, so it must've really been about the gun. Not that he was compensating for shortcomings. No indeed.

Caller ID said it was from a hotel in the Quarter she remembered passing almost every time they were down there. Always made the same joke to Franklin: "If I didn't already live here, I'd tell you take me there."

Why were they calling his work cell?

Desiree opened the phone, held it to her ear. "Hello?"

"Yes, could I speak to Agent Rome, please?"

"Well," she glanced over her shoulder at the bathroom door, then back at Franklin's pants. "He's not available at the moment. This is his wife. I could take a message."

The man on the other end stuttered before saying, "It really is urgent. It's about his guest."

"My husband has a guest?"

"Well…yes, the lady who's staying here under his protection. She's had an accident."

"I don't understand."

"Please, tell him it's very important. I need an ambulance."

"Because of his guest?"

Franklin's hand scared her as it descended before her eyes, gently lifted the cell out of her hand. She went slack, still staring at his pants as he took over.

"Rome here…" and walked out into the hallway, disappearing into the living room.

Desiree felt through his pants, found Franklin's boxers. She took a sniff. It was all her man. Nothing out of the ordinary, and after all these years, Desiree was sure she would know. But he couldn't deny something weird was going on. She checked them for dried come. Didn't see any. Motherfucker. Keeping some whore in that fancy hotel Desiree herself had never gotten a chance to even peek inside. That son of a bitch.

She imagined asking him, "Who's the woman? Who is she? So, sounds like a very special witness. Uh huh."

Whoever she was, she'd had an accident, the man said. That didn't sound so good. Put the hotel manager in a bad spot, sounded like. Serious, too. An ambulance?

Franklin wasn't long on the phone. Slapping it shut on his way back into the bedroom, Desiree still on the floor holding his shorts. He reached out for them. She handed them over and he slid them on.

"Sorry, baby. Emergency."

"What's going on?"

He knelt beside her, a tiny peck on the lips, grabbed his pants. "I can't tell you everything, but I've got a witness not doing so well."

"That was a hotel."

"Safest place I could think of."

He searched for his socks after kicking into his pants. Desiree grabbed his leg. "Let me come with you."

"I don't have time, baby."

"Who is she?"

Franklin looked down at her. Let a long moment pass, maybe thinking of something to say. You know, even if he was fucking Ginny Lafitte, it wasn't the end of the world. Just *tell* me, Desiree thought, and we can work it out. Hell, invite her to join us if that'll do it for you. As long as I know, you know? Just drop the secrecy.

She said, "Don't leave like this."

He sighed. Pulled his leg away from her grip and sat on the bed. "Baby, it's the job. I can't say no to an emergency."

"At a goddamned hotel around midnight?"

He gave up on his shoe, got down on his knees and scooted over to her like a much younger man. Settled his forehead against hers. "This isn't something to fight about. I can't tell you. All I can ask is that you trust me, okay? She's a witness. That's all. Ain't nobody but you for me, understand?"

Desiree liked him this close, liked feeling his heat. Wanted to believe him. Jesus, yes, she wanted to believe him. Problem was time. Time had built the wall. And no matter how hard she wished it to be gone instantly, the damn thing was going to need some jackhammers and dynamite. Secret midnight outings? Like a teaspoon trying to dig its way through.

She wanted to believe him anyway. She nodded. He kissed her cheek. Lingered. She turned her mouth to him. There it was.

One stick of dynamite, all in that kiss. But he broke it way too soon, slipped into sneakers instead of the dress blacks, didn't bother with buttoning the shirt, just grabbed a windbreaker and left like that, half-dressed and in a hurry. Desiree pushed herself up, couldn't decide where to go. Back to bed? Out into the living room to wait for Franklin?

He appeared in the doorway again. "Listen, I don't know how long this'll take. Get some sleep and I'll take the couch when I get back. Okay?"

Nothing to say. She crossed her arms. Nodded. Lips tight.

"Baby, please?"

She cleared her throat. "It's okay."

He blew her a kiss, and then he was gone.

Desiree waited a few minutes, not moving except in a slow three-sixty. Take the fucking couch? He didn't even do that when things were *really* bad between them. What, like the evidence of that woman wouldn't still be there the next morning?

It had taken her long enough to get most of what happened in Minnesota out of him. Months. Franklin was so loyal he would rather backhand his own wife than break confidentiality. Here he was starting all over again.

Desiree walked over to the bedside phone, called information for the hotel's number, then dialed it.

Once she had the same manager on the phone again, Desiree said, "Yes, my husband is on his way down, but he wanted me to email the right file to his partner's cell…I know, I know, but he's not answering. I think he accidentally turned it off after talking to you. All I need is the last name so I can boot up his files and send it along…no, not at all. Happens all the time. You shouldn't worry…Government wives, you know. Sworn to secrecy by proxy. Honest. Just the last name of the witness, because he told me but it's a hard one. Doesn't it sound French? Starts with 'L'?"

She fully expected him to say "Lafitte". Was prepared for it one hundred percent. When the manager said it, though, it still sent a chill through Desiree like ice cream hitting a bad tooth.

"Thank you." She hung up.

MCKEOWN was sleeping nice and hard. Really hard. When his cell phone beeped and buzzed on the bedside table, he took in a deep breath and surfaced from the dream he had already forgotten, and his cock was an iron beam. Oh man. And Alex's head was on his chest like it had always belonged there. Coming back to Alex's place had been the right move. It just moved right along, like they both knew the moment Alex stepped into the coffee shop that this was it. McKeown was a ball of nerves after talking to Rome, so he needed it more than he had first expected. So it took one more coffee, one stop at the liquor store for a bottle of South African wine, and only one short conversation that led to kisses, stripping, and Alex on his knees.

They must've both fallen asleep quickly. McKeown didn't remember dozing off. Just pillow talk that turned into a beach and the sound of waves, remembering bits of the dream, but once the cell phone went off, it seemed to McKeown that hardly any time had passed at all. They were tangled up in Alex's fine blue sheets, lights still on outside the bedroom door, a couple of candles in the room flickering, hardly melted at all since Alex had lit them.

The phone went again, reminding McKeown of why he was awake again in the first place. Shit. It didn't get to Alex, breathing deeply, way out there somewhere. The nightstand was within reach without having to jostle him, so McKeown took it. Checked the time first—11:47. So, yeah, only an hour of sleep. The ID showed the office calling, of course. Well now he had to get up. No choice. Couldn't risk Alex hearing this.

He opened the phone, whispered "Just a minute" into it, then hit MUTE while he slid out from under Alex, who couldn't help but blink his eyes open and lift his head.

McKeown said, "Need to pee."

"You're coming back, right?"

"Yeah, just a minute."

"Why do you have your phone?"

"I'll be right back."

McKeown couldn't find his underwear in the candlelight. Didn't have time to let his eyes adjust. He headed for the brightness of the hall, found the bathroom and locked it. Sat on the toilet. Felt like shit, but highly caffeinated shit. Like a triple-espresso headache. The lights in here were dim, fluorescent, but he still had to squint. Saw the phone in his hand. Almost forgot why he'd gotten up. How much of that wine did he drink?

He turned off the mute. "Agent McKeown here."

"Were you asleep?"

McKeown didn't recognize the voice. "Do I know you?"

"No, sir, I apologize. I talked with a woman who transferred me to you. I'm with the Minnesota Highway Patrol. Weren't you guys looking for a biker earlier today?"

McKeown sobered up. He'd had four glasses of wine. Too much coffee. The beach in his dreams was a combination of one he'd visited in North Carolina as a kid and some sci-fi movie he'd watched a few weeks ago. And he remembered in vivid detail everything he and Alex had done together that night. His dick was still fully erect.

"Still looking for him."

The Trooper said, "Well, we found the bike."

MCKEOWN DRESSED in the living room, left Alex in bed. He tried collecting his clothes quiet as a cat, but had banged into a couple of walls, rattled his belt buckle, and made a few floorboards creak. Still, Alex slept on.

The Trooper had said that some kids had tried to sneak the bike into one of their backyards. Kid's dad was up, heard a noise. All it took was a hard slap to get the full story. A man matching Lafitte's description had traded the motorcycle for an old station wagon, gone off with the older girl who always bought the kids cigarettes and beer. No word from her since then. An APB was out for the wagon, but McKeown wanted to talk to the kids himself, see if Lafitte had slipped and revealed anything that might help them out. Which meant he had to catch a plane out of Memphis pronto.

Was there any way to fuck this guy, the great guy, and then sneak out without feeling like dirt? Especially after lying to Alex about who he really was. When would McKeown be back in Memphis again anyway? It had been a temporary assignment, Rome pulling some strings without having to reveal the real reason for the transfer. Said it was a cold case, which meant that except for a couple of progress reports, everyone here left McKeown alone. He could imagine himself coming back for Alex, though. So, okay, maybe it wasn't so grim. McKeown could say he'd been called out of town on business, confidential client, etc. Lay the "FBI" stuff on him when the time was right. But not on the first night they'd slept together.

Shit timing no matter how you looked at it. The guy was going to take it the wrong way, period. All the reassurances in the world wouldn't keep the brain from equating "Important Business Trip at Midnight" to "Fuck and Run".

Then maybe don't say anything at all, slip out while Alex snored. He looked good like that, sheet only covering one leg and his crotch. McKeown wanted another look at his ass. A mental snapshot, thinking that's the last he'd ever see it in the flesh.

McKeown crossed his arms, holding his socks in one hand. Fuck.

ON HIS WAY BACK to the hotel to grab his stuff, McKeown had to concentrate hard to keep from welling up. Like he could just show up again at one of Alex's shows and not find the guy an ice cube. Maybe go in his black suit, flash the ID, get it out of the way immediately. All of that had to take a backseat to the manhunt, though. A personal beef now on the national stage. Real subtle, Rome. Absolutely low-key. Didn't matter. McKeown needed to get to Lafitte first. If he could do that, make the man understand that the Bureau would work out a good deal if he would wear a wire when facing Rome again, then McKeown was set. That was a careermaker, regardless of who had what photos.

The only reason he was on Rome's clown crew was because he'd screwed around with that lush. She'd said it was an "open marriage", and she came on strong. Maybe that was why he fell— she was as aggressive as a man, chasing her prey and pinning him down, no escape. Not like it would cost *her* a job or anything.

He'd stuck Alex's band's demo CD in, and was getting into it before remembering. He thought about throwing it out the window. Yeah, there you go. Good move, if you were sixteen. Keep it. Still a good night, at least for those few hours. He punched the FM button instead, the pop channel he'd found when he first rented the car, and listened to Christina Aguilera sing some racy lines in the style of a 1940s big band number. And she got away with it, too.

He pulled into a spot at the hotel. Fuck Rome. Fuck Alex. Fuck Lafitte. He wondered if the brass would let him have his choice of assignments. Thinking about living in NYC almost made him forget the taste of Alex. Almost.

Seventeen

SO MUCH TIME on the road, and Lafitte wasn't even out of South Dakota yet. He'd made one big fucking circle. And before much longer, he would need sleep. The road was getting to him. The rush of adrenaline from nearly being killed by Nate and Colleen, then carjacking Fawn after she helped him, was beginning to seep, leaving Lafitte like a deflated balloon.

If he had to stop, fine. Find a cheap hotel that would take cash and ask no questions, lose the car—leave the keys in, park it at a McDonald's or Taco John's. Find some clothes without getting noticed by security cameras, then hack off the hair and beard. By morning, he'd be unrecognizable, except to his family and Rome, probably. As long as it got him past the patrol cops.

He had to make Sioux Falls first, the biggest city for miles and miles out here in the middle of nowhere. Needed its hustle and bustle in order to get lost for as long as it took to sleep himself back to full-strength. Thought about fucking Star Trek, teleporters, or whatever the hell those nerds called them. Snap your fingers and you were there. Not yet. These days, it was either fly or grind, and he goddamn well couldn't fly anonymously.

The Interstate was dead straight and pitch dark. He wondered if Ben and Wesley had hidden the chopper away like he told them to, or if they went joyriding, called their friends, got noticed. With these goddamned kids, might as well assume the latter. Every overpass or exit ramp Lafitte slipped past without seeing lights flash in the rearview, that was a lucky one. Luck had a time-limit. And Sioux Falls was still nearly an hour South.

He ran his thumb across the cell phone. Steel God. Pretty much shot that dog dead. But the man left the door open, remember.

No, I can't, thought Lafitte. Not yet, anyway.

Why not call Ginny then? Hell, why not? Just call and *ask* what's going on.

Rome would love that. Lafitte laughed and played it out for the empty car. "Hey, honey? Yeah, it's me. So would you mind telling me what the commotion is down there?"

He laughed more and couldn't finish it out. Felt the hard bumps on the shoulder of the interstate and jerked the wheel left. Good thing the road was empty. Only sleep and deer to worry about. He realized that he might not get to see Ginny and the kids at all, even if he made it. Until right fucking then, he'd imagined slipping past whatever gates Rome had put up, but that didn't seem so easy anymore. He could barely get out of Minnesota without almost dying, so what were the chances of him driving a thousand miles without being seen?

Slim. None.

Why do it?

No answer from the little voice in his head. Come to think of it, Lafitte couldn't remember what that voice sounded like. No, he knew—it sounded like Drew. But he'd turned the volume so low on her voice, her face, that the only times she really broke through loud and clear was in dreams. When he had a Drew dream, Lafitte always woke up willing to stick a gun in his mouth if it would give him even just one more moment with her. But he remembered who he was, where he was, and that if he was too weak to kill Rome, he sure as hell couldn't pull the trigger on himself.

He'd thought about all that had happened back in Minnesota plenty out on the road. Why *hadn't* he killed Rome? Thought about it in bars, in tents, in bed while Kristal sucked his cock. The best answer he came up with, and it wasn't nearly good enough, was you couldn't kill a man for doing his job. It hadn't been personal. That's what it turned into later, apparently, thus this trip, but back then Lafitte would've checked off the same list as Rome: Suspect waves around a shotgun? Shoot without hesitation. Got an obvious number one suspect? Go after him harder than the law says you should. Evidence looking ambivalent? Follow your gut.

If Lafitte had shot Rome, he would've been killing himself.

No, not exactly. He would've been killing the cop he might have become if he weren't such a fucking scoundrel.

Every night before he closed his eyes, there they were. Photos of Drew on the slab, wounds cleaned by the medical examiner. Graham's shredded body, bleeding from everywhere. Rome's bloody face. Ultimately, they were all on Billy Lafitte's tab.

Hey, he was looking at them all right now, flashing by in stills, a slide show. Which meant he had closed his eyes.

Open.

The car was inches from the median ditch. Reflex, hard right. Red lights. A semi had pulled alongside while he dozed. Fucking wagon was going under the trailer. Hard left. Shit, might fishtail. Goddamned wagon was tail-heavy. Lafitte gripped tighter, eased the speed down. Gently. The car stopped feeling like it wanted to snap in two. He took in a deep breath and let the semi get out of the way before pulling onto the shoulder and throwing it into Park. Lafitte let his head loll against the headrest and took in massive breaths, let them out, in again. Held it. Then out.

He expected some survival instinct to take over and slap him awake and keep him one step ahead of whoever was looking for him. He thought about getting out of the car, pacing to get the energy flowing again. And suddenly he was outside. Didn't feel cold, but he was still shivering. He was actually watching himself pacing behind the car like it was on TV. A glance off to the right in the scrub brush. Ginny was standing there, not dressed for the cold. Baggy gym shorts, barefoot. A hoodie sweatshirt. She didn't look so good.

"Get in the car. You'll freeze to death," Lafitte said.

She shook her head. "I'll be fine. What are you doing?"

"I *was* coming to see you, but I guess you found me first."

Ginny's teeth chattered. Her sweatshirt was blood-stained. Lafitte remembered now. This was Ginny soon after they'd had Ham, when her hormones went nuts and she tried to kill herself. Couldn't handle the pressure of being a mother, and she hated getting so little sleep. She tried opening the vein in her left wrist with a corkscrew.

Lafitte asked, "Why is it you?"

"Oh Billy, You can't come see me, you know. Why even try?"

She had been in the hospital for a couple of days, evaluated, and then seemed to calm down. She took to Ham fine after that, didn't have any more episodes. The doctor slipped some info to Lafitte, though, even though he wasn't supposed to.

"She's afraid of you," the doc said. "Afraid of disappointing you. Maybe you said some things to her about how you wanted Ham to be brought up? Things she disagreed with you on?"

Well, yeah. But isn't that what it means to be married? You talk it all out. Lafitte had no idea that had bothered Ginny so much. After all, he was just excited to be a dad. His own father died when he was young, so now he had a chance to be someone else's dad and do it right.

What was with this guilt-trip shit, Ginny trying to push the responsibility for her gutless, heartbreaking little stunt off on him? Things changed between them after that. It was like Lafitte had to become two different people—the one Ginny saw at home, and the hardheaded bastard who worked the streets and got himself dirty. As long as those two roles were kept far apart, life was good. Once she got a peek at the other side, it started downhill again until she pushed him off on his own.

So she wanted to wash her hands of him? Fine. He had respected that. Until Rome got involved.

Lafitte stepped closer to Ginny, took her left arm and turned it over. Wrapped in gauze, small red spots. "What's Rome done to you?"

"Nothing."

"Really?"

She lifted her chin. "I'm more worried about what he's done to *you*."

Goddamn it, he hadn't even gotten out of the car. He'd fallen asleep and dreamed it all. Only realized that when he woke because someone was opening the car door he'd been leaning on. He caught himself midfall, wasn't fully focused yet. Then a couple pair of hands grabbed him by the jacket and threw him to the ground.

Voice like a kid: "Knock him out! Come on!"

"Shut up or get back in the car," from a man, much rougher but stinking of the Minnesota accent.

Lafitte felt the road press against his back. Someone was stepping over him, straddling him, while someone else held his arms. Knees were coming down, pinning his arms beneath them, an ass on his chest. Eyes back to normal. It was Fawn.

"Shit," he said.

She looked down at him with a wide evil grin, her crotch touching his neck, got his gag reflex going. He tried to buck her off, but he didn't have it in him.

Guy standing above Fawn was new. Bad customer, mullet, thick-lensed glasses. Would probably clean up into a nice Home Depot clerk if he was interested. But Lafitte knew his type. Not tough enough to make his own way in the meth trade. Plus that sparkly gold shit on his face, a huffer. Hopping around in Lafitte's peripheral vision was the little Goof kid from the parking lot. Doing some rap star poses and talking like a gangsta. Lafitte would've preferred the Troopers to these stooges.

"Thought you'd get away with it?" Fawn sounded like a third-string actress in a local play. "Oh no no no, you cocksucker."

"Wait, let me—"

"Fuck you!" She ground closer, his windpipe restricting. Felt like his face was full of blood, about to explode. Hoovered in air and tried not to black out. Fawn relaxed and took the pressure down a notch, tilted her head back, laughed deep and throaty.

Lafitte just concentrated on breathing, readying himself for one big push.

She said to the rough guy, "So, I get to have some fun first?"

"You're not going to fuck him, are you?"

Hands on her hips. "What if I did?"

"No fucking."

"Even if I let you in on it?"

"Jesus, Fawn." The guy shook his head.

"I'm just messing with you, Perry. Hurry up and do this before he bucks me off. I can feel it building up."

Lafitte heard a rattle and then a hiss off to the side. Couldn't see what it was. Almost ready to jump, but he had to do it right. This guy Perry didn't look like he was carrying anything gunlike, but Lafitte couldn't see both hands. Was he holding his left behind his back?

Perry looked towards the hissing. "You ready to do it?"

Goof's voice. "Ah-ight, you know whut Ah'm sayin? Let's KO this bitch."

Not good.

Lafitte lifted his knees, pushed his back up, straining against Fawn. She lifted an arm like she was on a mechanical bull, rocked her hips.

"Perry! We've got to hurry!"

Perry dropped to his knees and held Lafitte's head steady. Hands over his ears, seashell rushing all he heard. Fawn draped herself move heavily across Lafitte, scooting her ass down over his hips, her breasts hard against his chest. Shit. He thrashed his head, tried biting Perry's fingers. Perry gripped tighter, scraped the back of Lafitte's scalp against the asphalt.

Through the rush, Lafitte heard Fawn shout, "Goof, for fuck's sake, do it now!"

A couple seconds later, Lafitte watched this kid's face descend, hand outstretched holding a plastic bag. Goddamned thing smelled like…fumes. Spray paint. Made sense. Lafitte kept thrashing, feeling the burn on his scalp, probably tearing a massive gash back there. Goof held the lip of the bag over Lafitte's nose and mouth. He tried to hold his breath. One Mississippi…Two Mississippi…

"Fucker's not breathing it."

Fawn said, "Oh, he will."

She rose up, released the pressure off Lafitte, then sat down *hard* on his chest. Knocked the wind out of him, inflated the bag. Oh fuck, now his lungs were begging, and his body was going to take over and there was nothing he could do about it but take a nice, big breath.

The chemical odor made him want to puke. His lungs didn't give a shit and kept sucking sweet, sweet, golden air. Made him woozy.

"Is it working?" Goof's face too close, his nose too big.

"Get out of the way. Hang back a sec."

So tired already, the paint fumes didn't help. Like a visit to the dentist. Enough to numb, not enough to take him out.

Perry smiled. Bad teeth. One incisor longer and sharper than the others. Definitely not a dentist. "How you doing, Mr. Biker? Feeling good?"

Lafitte started talking without thinking. Couldn't understand what he said. Wait, did he say anything? Couldn't even remember. Where was Ginny? She was here a minute ago.

The bag descended again with a fresh blast of fumes. Stronger this time, but Lafitte didn't react as violently. All was cool, so cool.

Voices said things. Like a dream, he could make out words but not meaning. Stars above. Blurry people all around. Hard to keep his eyes open. Then a great weight was lifted from him and he was floating. Rising slowly, helped by invisible hands.

Being led. Not in the right direction. Opened his eyes. Towards an old Mustang, tricked out. Smelled rancid inside. Someone pulling his hands behind his back. He could only feel it vaguely. Heard a ripping noise, felt something sticky on his wrists. Tape?

Something pushing his head down, bending him towards the back of the Mustang. He reached a foot inside. Crunches, rattlings, cramped space. Like trying to fit a python into a coffee mug. Before he was in, sort of halfway, he heard, "Listen, one more thing."

Lafitte's head shook. Numb, it was like a bell being struck. But it knocked him damn near back into dreamland.

Where Ginny was waiting. She asked "Who's Kristal?"

EiGhteen

ROME FOUND GINNY in the hotel's dining room, all the lights dimmed and candles out except the one at her table. Someone had spread a towel on the floor in front of her chair. She was hunched over, holding herself tightly. As Rome approached, he saw the blood-stained dinner napkins wrapped around both her wrists. Like the manager said, "You should see her bathroom."

Savannah was the only reason they found her. The couple across the hall called to say there was a hysterical child screaming for a good ten minutes straight. The manager went to check on the situation, knocked over and over, hearing Savannah wailing. He finally used his master cardkey and found Ginny in the shower, conscious but fading, with her forearms gashed. Bloody handprints on the sink, mirror, toilet, shower curtain.

How had Rome missed it? Clear as day in her medicals, a hospitalization for "post partum depression", but the doc must've known the family pretty well to have kept a suicide attempt off the public record. Shit. Rome had wanted her afraid, yeah, but not *that* afraid.

He pulled out an empty chair and set it in front of her, very close. He sat down, reached for her arms, now draped in a thick hotel robe, gave them a rub from the shoulders down. Her hair was still damp. The manager had filled a glass with ice water for her, but it remained untouched on the table, sweating all over the linen.

"Ginny? I've got some paramedics on the way. How are you doing?"

She didn't look up. Took her a while to say, "I don't want to see him. I don't want him to see the kids. It's all my fault."

"Nothing's your fault."

"Yes, it's all on me. If I'd just stood by him back then instead of letting my parents talk me into the divorce."

"Hey, he is a bad guy. You did the right thing."

Ginny shook her head. "I can't face him. He won't understand. He won't forgive me."

Rome sat back. He'd been stoking her because he thought she was afraid of Lafitte, but maybe that wasn't it at all. She sounded ashamed.

He said, "There's nothing to forgive. Ginny, you're the good one here. He didn't deserve the second chance you gave him. Hell, probably didn't deserve the first. I'm telling you I'll get him in handcuffs on his knees and make him apologize to *you*."

She looked up, eyes like a scared bunny.

"We'll make sure he doesn't threaten you ever again."

"No, no, no! You don't get it." She shot up from the chair. Rome reached for her but she slipped out of his range and began circling the next table, hand trailing along the tablecloth. "He lost his job and I took away his kids. If I had stayed, he wouldn't have turned bad. I know he wouldn't. I took away his reason to live. That's why I called Graham. See? That was supposed to be his way back."

Rome said, "He killed Graham. Betrayed him."

Ginny giggled but her words were forceful. "I don't believe it, and I never will. That's what you've been saying from day one, and every time you say it, you sound like you're trying to convince yourself. You sound like an atheist on his deathbed."

"I'm sorry, but it's true."

She crept back in front of Rome and bent over at the waist, eye to eye. "Tell me again. Don't blink. Look at me."

"Ginny, please sit—"

"Look at me."

He did. Her face was pale, childlike, but lined with stress. Breath was like she'd had too much spearmint gum. Every pore shivering. Rome believed Lafitte was stone fucking guilty. Lack of evidence, solid alibis, and the confessions of the Detroit cell members they'd caught, none of it shook Rome's faith. In his mind, Lafitte was a slick talker, a quick thinker. He'd built himself an escape hatch. Maybe that girlfriend of his, Drew, could've changed Rome's mind, but she had to go and point a shotgun at him. What was he supposed to do? Let her shoot him? And since when did an innocent girl try to take on a whole ring of cops? Guilty, guilty, guilty.

"Billy is a traitor and a murderer." But he blinked. Goddamn it. Couldn't hold it back for ten more seconds. Or even five.

Ginny backed into her seat again. Slumped. "It's all my fault. Let Billy go and take me instead."

"I can't do that."

Ginny picked at the napkin on one wrist. "I don't want to help you anymore."

Some voices from the entryway, rustling. The ambulance had arrived. They came in fully packed, stretcher and everything. Rome stood, touched Ginny's shoulder.

"We'll talk later. Let these men help you."

She didn't respond.

Rome stepped out of the way as the EMTs started their cooing and sweet talk. The manager stood at the door, and Rome walked over to him.

"Where's her daughter?"

The manager said, "The head of housekeeping has her in the office."

Rome looked back at Ginny and the EMTs as they untied the make-do napkins to check her wounds. "I'll be back. If they want to move her, come find me."

The manager nodded. Rome headed out into the lobby. Very quiet, all of the noise from the Quarter oddly muted inside the hotel doors. The light had an old-fashioned quality, low and amber, an easy way to give that feeling of stepping into the past, even though out on the street all the neon and thumping bass made it obvious what century this really was. Rome thought about calling McKeown, seeing if he could dig up some more dirt on Ginny. He was not going to let her bring them so far and then cut the line like that. Hands on his hips. Pacing. Staring at the floor. Shit. Something about his way of handling things, he supposed. Could've been a softer touch. If Rome had known she felt this guilty, he would probably have built her up all this time instead of trying to wear her down.

Goddamn. In his head first, but then he said aloud, "God-*damn*."

"*Shhhh!*"

Rome searched out the noise, over his shoulder. Coming from the office behind the front desk.

"Excuse me?"

An older black woman's head peeked out from the office. Very short-haired, narrowed eyes looking over the top of big-framed glasses. "Watch your mouth, please. There's a child in here."

Rome walked over to the office. The lady's head disappeared. Very bright light spilt from the office, ruining the illusion. He stepped behind the front desk and over to the office door, leaned on the frame. He guessed this woman was the head of house-keeping. Reminded him of his aunts on his Dad's side—tough exterior but generous to a fault beneath it all. She sat in the manager's desk chair, rocking back and forth as Savannah played with a couple of dolls nearby on the floor, making up voices for both of them. The woman's nametag: Margherita.

"Beautiful name," Rome said.

She looked up. "My mother loved Italian stuff. But for a long time she thought you pronounced the "H" hard. Called me "Harry" all the time." A smile. "She figured it out about the time I was twelve. Too bad she never made it to Italy."

"What about you? Did it rub off?"

She shook her head, screwed up her mouth. "All that cheese makes my stomach hurt. Who are you, anyway?"

As soon as Rome had spoken, Savannah had stopped playing and crawled over to Margherita, hiding behind her leg. She watched Rome with one eye.

Rome said, "I'm with the FBI. Savannah's mom was a witness I was trying to keep safe. I need to ask baby girl here a few questions."

Margherita moved her hand to Savannah's head, stroked her hair. "Can't make her, but you can try, I guess. *Think* before you ask, understand?"

"I've done this before."

"All right. Guess I was just saying, that's all."

Woman would make a fine social worker, Rome thought. One question over the line, and she would shut him down, absolutely. Tread lightly, then. He knelt down, his knees cracking. He smiled at Savannah, still hiding, gripping Margherita's leg tighter.

"You remember me, sweetie, don't you?"

Savannah nodded.

"Can you tell me who I am?"

She shook her head.

Margherita patted Savannah's head. "You can talk to the man. It's okay, baby."

Savannah mumbled into her protector's leg, but Rome still made it out: "You're the man who makes Mommy cry."

The woman turned her face to Rome, narrowed her eyes. "Mm hm."

"I've been trying to help your mommy, sweetie. Did she tell you about Daddy?"

Another nod.

"What did she say?"

"Said Daddy is mad at her. I want to see Daddy."

"Your daddy's not here."

"Mommy said Daddy misses me but can't see us because she did a bad thing."

"Aw, sweetie, no. Your mommy didn't do anything. It was your daddy—" He caught himself. Thought, You can't tell a kid her dad's a nasty guy. He was surprised at how easy it had started out of his mouth, even.

Margherita said, "Mr. FBI means that Daddy had to go far away for now. You know how you're far away from home right now?"

The girl nodded. She had buried her face fully into Margherita's leg now. Rome was afraid she would start to cry. She mumbled into the leg again.

"What was that, sweetie?"

She lifted her face just enough to say, "Is Mommy still bleeding?"

"No, Mommy's just fine. You can see her real soon, okay?"

Rome rose to his feet again and said to Margherita, "Thank you." He stepped out of the office, back into the lobby. A couple stood at the desk. Tourists, early-thirties, white. The man wore a visor, a joke T-shirt making fun of the mayor. His wife, over-tanned, in a stretchy tank-top, skirt, and flip-flops.

The man said, "Excuse me, we've been standing here for, like, five minutes now."

Rome stopped. "So?"

"I'm sorry, what?"

"So, five minutes. Is that really a long time?"

The man did a slow-burn staredown. "I don't think that was necessary. Can I speak to your manager?"

Rome pulled his ID and flashed it. "Sorry about that. FBI. It's been a long night, and I didn't mean to take it out on you guys. Maybe you'd like to find another hotel tonight?"

The man blinked a lot. His wife gripped his arm tighter. He stumbled, finally got out, "Gee, wow, I didn't know. What's going on?"

That was when the EMTs wheeled Ginny's stretcher out into the lobby. The manager was going on and on as they ignored him, rolled her right outside.

Rome said, "Excuse me." He met the manager halfway.

"They say she has to go now. She's been taking pills, I think, and they say it's urgent."

Rome crossed his arms, uncrossed them, covered his mouth with his palm.

"I couldn't make them wait, not even one minute, to come get you. They said you can meet them at the hospital."

Rome sighed. "Okay, you did okay. Handle your guests here. Can you sacrifice Margherita for the rest of the night?"

The manager nodded, and Rome sent him to get her and Savannah. He watched as the ambulance lights flared and then moved off quickly. It wasn't even a matter of moving on to Plan B anymore. He was shaken to the bone.

Using the woman to lure Lafitte onto Rome's playing field, wow, that just struck him all the sudden as really fucking cowardly. Or how about putting together a covert team in order to help get some revenge on one guy? Some people abused their power by simply using the company jet for golf trips, but Rome wrote himself into an opera.

He took out his phone, dialed one of his local team members, sounded like he woke her up.

"We need a couple of people at the hospital to guard Mrs. Lafitte. I'm going to take her daughter up there, then call her parents, but let's get someone there to make sure no one can get to her."

It took a moment for the answer to come back, raw throated. "Which hospital?"

Rome gave her the details, told her to keep it quiet. "If someone asks, you say she came to me with info. I did *not* go to her, understand? We were conducting a private inquiry out of respect."

"Sir?"

"I thought I was clear, agent. It is a reasonable request. She just tried to kill herself, like, *again*. Our new priority right now is to get her healthy and happy."

"Fine, sure."

"Meet me there. You've got a half hour."

Rome hung up, turned to see that Margherita and Savannah were waiting for him, the child limp on the housekeeper's shoulder.

Yes, he would take them to the hospital. On the way he would call Mrs. Hoeck and explain. And then he would…yeah, that was the hard part. Instead of letting Lafitte cruise on down here at the boiling point, Rome would have to meet him on the road, somewhere the fucker wouldn't expect him. As soon as the FBI suits McKeown had out there on watch got Lafitte located, Rome would call off the dogs and do the rest of this on his own. But first, Ginny.

As he started for the car, Margherita and Savannah in tow, he remembered Desiree. Last time he saw her, she was on the floor, confused, begging him not to leave her alone. But he *had* to. She wouldn't understand. He had to do it in order to get back what he'd lost. Fucking Lafitte mentally castrated him. Man can't let something like that go.

Out the door, into the light crisp breeze that passed for cold weather down here these days. He'd have to call Desiree from the hospital, and he needed a story. Don't think of it as a lie. Just…a need to know sort of thing. As long as he came back alive and re-tooled, she would forgive him again.

And if he didn't come back this time?

Man, Desiree would be so pissed.

Nineteen

MCKEOWN'S PLANE flew into Sioux Falls, for god's sake, which then meant he had to stomach another hour and a half drive as a passenger with a Trooper who wouldn't shut up. Even when McKeown said he had some calls to make or some email to answer, the guy kept going. Mostly about how the meth business was giving the State Police more to do in these little farming towns. Otherwise, not much crime at all.

McKeown read it as a small timer trying to impress a Federal Agent. Like Deputy Nate before he went and got himself killed. Idiot. McKeown had really wanted to rent a car. Would've been nice, maybe an SUV, something to make him tower over the State patrol cars and also have some time to himself. Instead, the Troopers volunteered. Kind of surprising that South Dakota would let the Minnesota cops escort him, since most of the drive was on the Interstate running straight north and south through SD, but whatever the local politics was, McKeown didn't give a shit. All he wanted was to question the witnesses, find Lafitte, pitch the deal, and get back to Memphis.

Memphis. Took long enough to get out of there. Slept on the plane for two hours. Changed into his suit, but left off the tie. If the Minnesotans thought he wasn't formal enough, fuck them.

Let them put it in writing, then. It was now nearing dawn, the sky was an unfocused blue-gray that fucked with your vision. And his mind was back on Alex again. Pictured him barely covered by the sheet. Caused some tingling. Should have woken him, let him know *something* instead of just running away.

Did Alex even know McKeown was gone yet? Could still save this, explain it all, if Alex had slept right through and not noticed the absence. He risked a call. What was the worst that could happen?

It rang five times. Around the second ring, the Trooper said, "It's just another something to do. Not like they're bad kids or anything. Even the guys making it, some of them don't know any better."

"That's great. Could you wait a minute, please?"

The machine clicked on. Took forever for Alex's voice to start in, and McKeown knew it was bad news: "I'll call you back when I feel like it. And if this is Josh…don't bother."

McKeown thought about hanging up, but changed his mind. The *beep* went and he said, "Let me explain. Pick up the phone."

Nothing. McKeown could feel Alex hovering over the phone. Really feel it.

"I didn't want to wake you, but I'm calling now. Isn't that something? I'll be back as soon as I can."

More nothing.

"It was one of the best nights of my life."

Another *beep*, then the line went dead and clicked him off.

He lowered the phone to his lap, stared at the cell's wallpaper—the Starbucks logo. Didn't seem so funny anymore. The Trooper said, "I'm sorry. Trouble at home?"

McKeown was set to pull his FBI intimidation routine, either *You guys seem to take things pretty casually here, don't you?* or *That's confidential.* He couldn't really blame the guy, though. What was it like to be coming up fast on forty and realize the excitement you'd signed up for was only a fairy tale? With McKeown, it was almost the opposite—he's expected his share of reports and endless bureaucracy, but it turned out life in the FBI was more fun than not. At least until Rome showed up, and even then you had to admit that tracking down a dangerous wanted man was a thrill. It was just the boss who made it suck.

The radio squawked and Trooper Louwagie picked up, said, "Yeah?"

"You got the FBI with you?"

McKeown got his "casual" line ready again.

"Roger that," Louwagie said. "We're about an hour away."

"No need to hurry. The Deputy handled the questioning, so we let those folks go back to bed."

Wait, what? McKeown said, "Ask him which deputy? We didn't authorize any deputy to handle this."

Louwagie relayed it back. Got the answer: "But she said she would report it back to you and see if you had any follow-ups."

McKeown took the handset from Louwagie. "Why the hell would I fly up here if I'd already assigned someone to question them?"

The radio cop said, "I don't know how you people work. Look, we'll wake everyone back up if you need me to, but they won't be happy about it."

"Hold on." McKeown took his finger off the switch, took in a deep breath. Louwagie was trying not to pay attention, eyes straight ahead. McKeown clicked in again. "Okay, who was it? If it's not your fault, let me yell at her, then."

"She's already gone. But I know her pretty well. She's from Yellow Medicine, and she knew all about you, said you had been helping her boyfriend get in at the academy."

McKeown closed his eyes and thumped the handset against his forehead. It had to be a nightmare. Click. "Blonde, young, kind of stocky?"

"Well…"

"It's Colleen, isn't it? Yeah, I know her. Shit. Listen, can we radio her car, get her back to where you are?"

A long silence on the other end before, "That was kind of the weird thing, I guess. She wasn't in her squad. She was in this old hot rod. Said it was her boyfriend's. I've never met him."

"Not in uniform either?"

"Can't say she was, no. I was thinking you must have called her on short notice. I'm telling you, though. Shouldn't be hard to find her. She's a beauty."

"What, you think the Deputy is pretty, and that's supposed to help?"

"I meant the car."

Time for another deep breath. He cut a look at Louwagie, who said, "Need something?"

Eyes back to the road. "To be back in Memphis for a start." Click. "She didn't happen to head west instead of turning around and going home, did she?"

"How'd you know?"

A SOUTH DAKOTA TROOPER grabbed Colleen barely five minutes after the Chevelle's description was radioed out, as she was rolling along a county road south of Watertown. McKeown had Louwagie backtrack to meet up. They found the Chevelle and the Trooper's patrol car on the shoulder, Colleen handcuffed and in the backseat. McKeown said he wanted to talk to her alone, asked the Trooper to pull her out behind the squad.

Colleen didn't want to look anyone in the face, eyes down and her lips pouting, bundled tightly like whatever she was feeling would burst the seams of her denim jacket. McKeown had only met her once when first connecting with Nate, but in nearly every conversation after that, he could tell that Colleen was back there pulling the strings, feeding Nate questions, pushing her man to be more aggressive in dealing with the Feds. Good woman to have behind you, if you could stand it. McKeown saw the attraction—although she looked pretty plain in the face, pale, nothing special, and her body was more like an Olympic gymnast's in all the wrong, overmuscled ways, Colleen still radiated something special. Maybe it was confidence. Right now, it was rage.

McKeown sidled up beside her, mirrored how she was leaning against the car, crossed his arms. "Listen, I'm real sorry about Nate."

She snorted. "Yeah, okay. Everyone's *sorry* about Nate, but I'm the only one who's angry about it."

"Maybe that'll come later."

"By then it will be too late." Then she huffed, putting on a good show. "Guess you don't have to worry about him now. Out of your hair."

"Hey, that's not fair."

Colleen shook her head and finally lifted her face. "Are you telling me you guys didn't use him? Isn't that how you work? Use him and then toss what's left?"

McKeown had had enough. He thought of Alex saying the same exact thing. McKeown stood back up and reached for Colleen's cuffs, yanked the chain down hard. Got in her face. "What did I tell him to do? I told him to stay put. Don't go after Lafitte. We didn't want him to think we were onto him. So shove your attitude up your ass. I've only had three hours sleep."

The cuffs were biting into her skin but she bit her lip to keep from complaining. Good girl, thought McKeown. He loosened his grip.

She said, "How awful for you. Oh, and I watched my boyfriend burn to death in my car." Narrowed her eyes. "*So* sorry about that."

McKeown twisted the chain, watched Colleen's eyes go wide. "You're looking for revenge. I get it. It's not going to happen."

Her voice squeaked with pain when she said, "Fuck. Off."

McKeown let go, caught the Troopers trying to listen in. He flashed them his "annoyed agent" mask and they turned away, started mumbling back and forth. Jesus, they acted like children up here. A little respect, please?

He leaned close to her and said, "What did you get from the witness?"

"What? What witness?"

"How the hell do you think we found you? You went and talked to my witnesses. What, have you got a scanner in the car?"

Colleen lowered her chin, looked off. "You're crazy. Just let me go home." Her voice trailed away. Looked like she was about to cry.

"Come on, give this up. What are you doing here anyway? You had like three or four hours head start on me, but you're still dicking around the backroads. So what did they tell you to keep you nearby?"

"Can't say." She tightened her lips and closed her eyes.

"Damn it, Colleen—"

Louwagie yelled out, "You two doing all right back there? Can't we take this inside?"

McKeown ignored him. "Here are your options. Take me along to help you look, or I charge you with something really awful and send you off with our helpful State Police here to a really bad jail cell, and I promise I'll lose the paperwork until well after the funeral."

Colleen scratched her nose, then tried to rub her wrist. Jittery. McKeown wondered if she had taken diet pills or something before heading out. She said, "What happens if I help you?"

"You can go home once we're done."

"And Lafitte's going to jail? That's all?"

Well, fuck. Lie to her. Anything. Just lose the Keystone Cops already. "You want him. Rome wants him. As long as he answers my questions, I don't give a shit which one of you gets him first, understand?"

She didn't respond at first. A bit of a mouthbreather, McKeown thought. Out for revenge? These days? Hilarious. He was hoping she would calm down by the time they caught up with Lafitte. If not, well, he'd deal with it, especially if she was as hot to trot for the FBI as Nate was.

He pointed to the Troopers. "Them," and to himself, "Or me."

Colleen stared at the ground, lolled her head around. "My scalp itches."

"If you've got the info I think you have, those cuffs can come off."

It wasn't much of a grin, but it was better than what she'd shown him so far. She said, "Okay, I might know a thing or two."

TWenty

LAFITTE WOKE to Perry and Fawn shouting at each other. Opened his eyes, and he could make them out in the gray dawn light pulsing in slowly from the high window of what looked like a cinder-block basement. Then he realized he was seeing all of this through only one eye because the other wouldn't open. It hurt, sort of. He was still pretty out of it, the smell of left-over paint fumes blending with the backed-up sewage wafting from the drain on the floor beside him. It should make him want to puke, but he couldn't get up enough energy to gag.

Still alive, which was something, but not much. Fuck, kill him, that would be fine. He didn't mind dying. If it came too close, you fought it off, sure, but that was just instinct. When he really thought about it, dying itself wasn't the problem. It was the way he was in this basement. Helpless was worse than dead.

So, okay. Lafitte needed to string some thoughts together. He had a *mission,* goddamn it.

The argument between Fawn and Perry was mostly attitude and cursing in that weird Minnesotan cadence. Lafitte didn't bother digging into the actual words beneath the accent until Perry said, "—can't turn him over looking like that! There's no fucking reward for *that!*" Pointing at Lafitte with each *that.*

Fawn held a knife in one hand. Some bloody handprints on her jeans, blood on her shirt, fingers. Not good. She placed her free hand on her hip and waved that knife around. "Oh, no, yeah. Don't give me that shit. You knew what I wanted."

"Jesus, woman, maybe some cigarette burns, that's what I was thinking. Holy fuck, look at him!"

Made Lafitte wonder if he still had that eye after all. It was cool in the basement, but Lafitte was shivering, sweaty, and his skin stung. Especially his chest. Looked down to see he was bare-chested, hands pulled behind him. He tugged, felt rough wood against his back and arms. Tied to a beam, probably with wire. It wasn't giving way.

What worried Lafitte most was his chest, covered in blood, all gashed up like Fawn had tried to carve out his heart or something. Took in a deep breath—*hurt like a bastard*—to see if that gave him a better look. Almost like...letters. She'd carved some fucking letters into his skin. Hard to tell upside down and backwards and with one eye. First one could've been an "8", like a digital one...No, a "B", really boxy. Then an "A" Then there was another "B" and then a "Y". There was another word under the first. Puffed his stomach out. Looked like it bookended with "R"s. Another "A". He had it then. She'd carved "BABY" on top and "RAPER" beneath. "BABY RAPER."

Oh, that *bitch*.

She'd carved deep, too. Definitely going to leave scars.

Perry kept on, "We take him in now, shit, they'll throw us in with him. That's fucking assault!"

"No way! They'll think that shit's funny. Put his ass in jail with *that* on his chest, you know what's going to happen."

"Yeah, I'll know for sure. Because I'll see it in person from the next cell. This isn't some fucking TV show. Cops'll go after anything bad, and—" Stabbing his finger towards Lafitte. "—*that's* fucking bad."

Fawn crossed her arms, blade sticking up. "Just say we found him like that."

They wandered into another room and the conversation grew cloudy. A basement with rooms, the walls looking makeshift, homemade. Lafitte strained his neck looking around to get some idea of where the hell this was. He couldn't remember much about the night before. Knocked out, in a car, Goof staring at him in the back seat, then lights out again. Dragged across the ground. Down some stairs. Then it was a blur—face kicked, sides kicked, Fawn whispering dirty shit in his ear and then laughing because it pissed Perry off, Goof doing his gangsta routine and landing a few weak punches to Lafitte's gut. They had searched his pockets. Goof said, "Cash and a cell phone. No ID."

Perry said, "How much cash?"

Goof flipped through. "Like a hundred bucks."

Lying punk. More like four hundred. Goof slipped most of it into his shorts.

"Give me that."

Then another blackout.

After that, he remembered Fawn sitting on his lap for a long time, breath hot and close against his skin. Stinging. Lots of stinging. Grabbed one thing she said out of midair: "Should've just fucked me nice. Hell, I would've gladly handed over the car if you'd have done that."

In the corner of the basement, some cardboard boxes. Beer logos on them. A keg nearby. Maybe this was a bar. Plenty of empty bottles and cans. Black garbage bags overfull, stretched out in spots. A big freezer in the corner, white but stained, one like you'd see in someone's garage. So it wasn't a big bar, maybe one of those small town joints out in the middle of nowhere. Did Perry own the place? Did anyone else know Lafitte was down here?

He looked up. The post they'd tied him to was part of the stairs. If they'd only tied his hands, maybe he could inch himself up, get some leverage on the wire that way. He lifted his knees, put his feet together. His left ankle hurt, and that gash from the wreck was still throbbing, but not enough to make him stop. He breathed himself a rhythm then held a deep lungful. Started to push. Lafitte's back raked across the rough wood, splinters digging into the skin, and the cuts on his chest felt like they were reopening, ripping further. And then the fumes, goddamn, those paint fumes nauseating him. He collapsed to the floor and his stomach lurched and something was coming up.

Lafitte turned his head but not quickly enough as he spewed stomach acid and Doctor Pepper onto his beard, chest, and lap, all over the floor beside him. It got up in his sinuses and he gagged when he tried to pull in fresh air. Another round of hot slime up and out. It burned into the letters on his chest. He kept spitting, trying to keep his throat from clogging up. Zapped all his strength, and he couldn't afford to lose any more right now.

Perry and Fawn rushed back into the room, Fawn laughing while Perry panicked.

He said, "Oh, god, oh no. Jesus."

Fawn pinched her nose shut. "Ewwww. Guess that means no more fun with you. That's disgusting."

"Shit, we've got to clean this up."

"I thought we weren't turning him in now?"

"I still have to clean up Granddad's basement before he finds out, right? He'll be here by ten-thirty."

Fawn bitched it up some more, seemed to enjoy Perry acting like a pussy. She even told him, "You're acting like a pussy. Calm the fuck down."

Perry got in her face. "It's all your fault, and if anyone finds out, I'll pin it all on you."

She bumped his chest. "Wow, I'm scared. You try to threaten me, and you might wake up with your balls in your mouth. Or you might not wake up at all. You want me to call my dad again? Remember what he did to you last time?"

"Bring him on. Just a lucky sucker punch was all."

"It'll always be a sucker punch. That's all you ever deserve."

Perry retreated, paced. Lafitte guessed they'd sent Goof home. They probably weren't far from where he'd first encountered the whole fucking gang in the parking lot. Smooth move, Billy. Trade in your bike. Probably would've been easier to outrun cops on it than try to outthink them.

Fawn stood with her hip cocked out. Her cheeks were flushed, like she'd been hitting the booze hard, but she was wide awake, not slurring. Chick could hold her liquor.

Lafitte spit out some more, couldn't get the nasty stringy stuff off his lips. He croaked, "Please, help." Gagged again. "Don't...I didn't mean..."

"Shut up!" It was Fawn. "You deserved all of it, and you know why. You know what you did. Just lost your nerve was all. You were going to kill me."

"No, I swear...no. No killing." Thinking, what the fuck did he ever do to give her that idea? Liquored-up chick also had an active imagination. "No..."

Fawn rolled her eyes, then searched around the basement, found a half-empty bottle of Wild Turkey. She had the top off before Perry figured it out and tried to stop her, but he didn't grab her wrist until the bottle was already tipped over and raining down on Lafitte's chest.

Now, *that* woke his ass up. Like a nest full of wasps ripping into all those cuts at once. He let out a scream and choked himself again. More steaming acid erupted from his mouth and splashed down everywhere. Fawn let out a "*Son of a bitch!*" when it got on her sandals. Perry dragged her away by the arm. She fought him and was probably strong enough to break free, but he held tight. She whined.

Through the pain and adrenaline white noise, Lafitte remembered bar brawls the gang provoked, the way Steel God trained them to be so ferocious and give back tenfold what was brought against them that word spread far and fast. The only people who tried to take them on anymore were guys who had practiced, prepared, studied. No one-offs. The prize for taking down God's club was huge, a community pot that even brought enemies together for a common cause. And not one of those challengers *ever* took down the Steel Army. Why? Like God had told them: "You act weak, then you are weak. If you feel pain and can't laugh at it, go shoot yourself in the head and get it over with. This life ain't for you."

Lafitte would've loved a gun to his head right then. What a fucking failure.

He did his best to overcome the pain, swallow it down. Concentrate on these two morons. Listen. They might say something to save your life.

Perry was one loud motherfucker, but he didn't faze Fawn. Lafitte figured they used to date or something.

"Stop it, all right! Could you leave the guy alone? It's bad enough you've fucked us out of the reward already."

"Would you chill?" She was smiling. "Get him cleaned up so we can kill him. In a few days, we'll claim we found the body while we were out looking for a place to fuck. They won't care. He'll be half eaten by then and we still get the money, if there is any. I still don't think he's wanted or anything. Worth about ten cents."

Perry stuttered and puffed and fidgeted until he finally said, "Fine, we need that stuff. You know, you pour it on and it soaks up the puke."

"I don't know."

"It's like fucking wood chips or something. Shit. There's probably some down here. I know Granddad uses it for the drunks. Go get a bucket and water and...and towels. See if there are some towels up there."

"Fuck you. Why don't you get it?"

Perry shook his head. "I'm not leaving you alone with him anymore. Already enough to clean up."

Fawn didn't move.

"Hurry the fuck up, will you? For shit's sake, woman!"

She bared her teeth at him and growled, but stomped up the stairs hard enough to shake them, every tremble biting into Lafitte's back.

Perry yelled after her, "And get some pop! Like, Sprite." Then to Lafitte, "It'll help settle your stomach."

The door at the top of the stairs opened, then slammed loud. More shaking. More splinters digging deeper.

Lafitte cleared his throat as much as possible. The key was to keep the air moving in and out through your mouth. Don't even think of trying through your nose, a surefire path to retching. Cleared the thick from his throat and said, "Why? Why'd you let her do this to me?"

Perry. "Aw, man, shut up, okay?"

"Why'd you let her fuck me up…" Had to stop and swallow. It burned. "…if you wanted a reward so bad?"

The guy shrugged. "I had to drive the kid home. It's, like, twenty minutes there and back. I figured she'd tease you or something. Goddamn, I had no idea." He took another look at Lafitte and winced. "*No* idea."

Twenty minutes. There twenty and back twenty? Or is that the total? Lafitte couldn't ask or Perry would know what he was up to. Still, that gave Lafitte enough to draw the map in his head. If he could somehow get Perry to give him a break, some sympathy, anything before Fawn got back, well, okay.

"Man," Lafitte said. "My back is on fire, and I can't get all this…guh…shit out of my throat…" He let out a wet cough to make the point.

"Just shut up, okay? All I wanted was a reward. That's all. Fuck. *Fuck.* Don't talk to me." Pacing, pacing, erratic, like a lone ant on the bathroom tile.

"I know, I know, listen…you can still have it. I mean, there's a reward on me so big you wouldn't believe it. Probably set you up for a good long time."

"Yeah, right. I'm supposed to believe that?"

"Serious, man. I'm telling you…" The ropes of spit kept getting in the way, and Lafitte fought to not puke again. Get this asshole on board. Come on. "Keep that crazy bitch away from me and don't kill me yet. You got an internet connection?"

"Internet?"

"Do you?"

Perry nodded. "My stepmom does."

"Okay. Okay. I want you to look up 'Billy Lafitte'. L-A-F-I.. guh…um, T-T-E. Got it?"

"I need to write it down."

"Fuck writing! It's L-A-F-I-T-T-E. Easy fucking name, right? Come on. It's worth it."

More pacing, glancing up at the top of the stairs. Some noise overhead, footsteps on the floor of the bar. Fawn getting a move on.

Perry said, "It's, like, five in the morning. I can't go to my stepmom's right now. She would kill me."

"Then give her some of the reward...hold up...wait." He couldn't hold back anymore. The stream this time was thinner, but it burned ten times worse. He pushed out a mighty breath, let the mucus drip. "I'm telling you, I'm fucking famous, man. I'm a goddamn traitor to the country, and I'm worth a helluva lot more alive than dead. Would you wake her up for that?"

That just seemed to agitate Perry more. Jesus, and Lafitte had thought this was some sort of badass last night when they ambushed him. Guy was falling apart now, a total pushover.

"It's either that or wake up screaming from the nightmares."

Perry said, "Oh God, oh God, oh God. It was supposed to be easy."

"It still is."

Perry shook his head. "You don't know Fawn."

He rolled up his sleeve and bent over to show Lafitte his forearm, where the word "PUSSY" had been carved from the crook of his elbow to his wrist, scarred over, must've been a while.

"Holy shit, man. What did you do?"

"Slept with her niece. Thing is, I kept dating her a while after. That's fucked up, right?"

The door at the top of the stairs opened, banged into the wall, and heavy steps shook the stairs. Fawn again, humming some sort of pop hook you heard all over the radio in eight different songs. She came into view, looked over at Perry, who had yanked his sleeve back down.

"Here you go." She carried a tube of the vomit soaker-upper, a bucket full of water, and a couple of rolls of rough-looking paper towels. Held them out to Perry. "Just like you wanted. Get to work."

He reached over and took the tube. "You going to help?"

What a smile, a giant beaming, "Eat Shit" sort of smile. She set the rest on the floor and said, "You're the one who's scared of a little puke and blood."

"We don't have time."

"Okay, then let's just do this." She pulled up her shirt and pulled a pistol from her waistband. Lafitte pegged it—his own Glock. She had taken it from him while he was spaced. "Let's kill him already."

Perry made a sound like a wounded hawk when she whipped that gun out, and now he was easing towards her, hands wide and steady. "We can't kill him here. My Granddad's bar!"

"Shit, you keep telling me what we can't do. What the fuck *can* we do?"

Perry was now between her and Lafitte, so Lafitte couldn't see her reactions. Maybe she'd fire right through Perry, get them both at once.

"Look, babe—"

"Babe? You're fucking with me now?"

"Just, just, listen, okay?" Perry looked at his watch. "We've still got a few hours before we need him out of here. So we need to see how much he's really worth."

"You don't even know his fucking name!"

"No, he told me. Okay? I got him to tell me. Says he's wanted big time."

Fawn's head emerged from behind Perry. Lafitte played too sick to care. Her mouth was open, dumb look on her face while Perry kept on.

"We go look him up and see if it matches. Maybe they want him alive."

She said, "He's probably lying. You'd believe anything."

"Well, shit, if we know his name, we might be able to find a photo, too. Think about it."

Her head disappeared again. "How big is big time?"

"That's what I'm telling you we need to find out." Boy was almost whining at her now.

There was her head again. Pretty much blank, lost all its cartoon evilness. "Like, on the internet?"

"Like I've been *telling* you. We've got to hurry."

"Alright," Fawn said. "Just going to leave him here?"

"He can't go anywhere, and he's pretty fucked up. If you want, I can get him to huff some more gold."

Fawn stepped over to Lafitte, gun still raised, wrist flopped back but finger on the trigger. He looked up at her through his one opened eye, blurry and out of focus. The sour smell of the vomit seemed to hit them both at the same time as Lafitte gagged and Fawn wrinkled up her face.

She said, "Fuck the paint. I've always wanted to try this."

Took her gun arm back and swung, the frame smashing into his temple. Fraction of a blackout, sort of. Goddamn gun was mostly plastic anyway, but it still fucking hurt. A shockwave of pain starting at impact and spreading all over Lafitte's head and back again, rippling back and forth and in and out and it was dark and he wasn't conscious or unconscious either.

But he saw colors and for some reason had an image of Steel God's gang out on the open road, Kristal behind him on the hog, gripping his chest, while he hummed that same goddamned hook Fawn had been humming.

Before the stairs shook and vibrated against his back again, Lafitte was pretty sure he heard Fawn say, "That was cool."

TWenty-One

DESIREE MISSED her husband's call because she had fallen asleep at the desk in his office, where she'd looked up everything she could on Ginny Lafitte and whatever it was Franklin had gotten himself into. Once she saw a photo of Ginny, Desiree cooled a bit. Yeah, a pretty white woman, but kind of frail. Maybe Franklin liked the thrill of being able to lord some power over some weakling, but she was pretty damned sure a girl like that wasn't what got his cock up.

If she had to worry about anyone taking Franklin away from her, it was the other Lafitte—Billy.

Breaking through his passwords had been easy enough. Desiree knew his birthday, their anniversary, his favorite music, his mother's middle name, and about a hundred other likes and dislikes that popped up in the course of spending so many years together. Only took her six tries. But what she found…wow.

Mostly, she pieced it together through following the trail of his requested documents, expenses, and cell phone records. All this time that Franklin had been trying to redeem himself in her eyes, he'd also been looking for a way to flush out Lafitte. On his own, vigilante style.

"Well, I'll be fucked," she mumbled after getting through it all to find that he'd actually done it. Lafitte was already on the road, heading south, straight into Franklin's net.

But something must've gone wrong. If he was using the ex-wife as bait of some sort, and there had been an emergency involving her, then what?

Next thing Desiree knew, she was in a hotel lobby full of finely dressed people milling around, all carrying little plates full of *hors' doeurves*. Ginny Lafitte was there, too, tinier than Desiree expected, but that was her mind drawing the woman in the way she'd expect was least attractive to Franklin. It was Desiree's dream, so it was Desiree's rules.

"You're not messing around with my husband, are you?" Direct was usually best.

Ginny smiled politely. A shrinking violet, but no home-wrecker. "He loves you."

"Yes, I know."

"That's all. It's not about you or me. It's about my ex-husband."

Desiree sighed. "Just another case, though, wasn't it?"

The second she said it, she knew that wasn't true. Franklin had been wrong about Lafitte, but he couldn't accept that. He had to find *something* to pin on the guy. Should have been easy, right? Lafitte was like Pig-pen from *Peanuts*—walked around in a cloud of dirt. That's why Franklin came home so defeated, distant, violent. Whatever had made her husband excited about his job—the same thing that had him coming home to her grinning and joking like a teenager in love way back in the day. Desiree wished she could bring him back all on her own, but it struck her now just how unrealistic that was and how it seemed like neither one of them could fix this until Franklin had dealt with Lafitte. And goddamn it if that wouldn't put an end to him, too.

Dream Ginny lifted her glass of wine. "To Franklin."

Desiree wanted to snap the stem off the bitch's glass and stab her in the eye with it. Like getting to Lafitte by proxy through his wife. Anything to help Franklin so he would come home again.

She woke because she thought the phone had been ringing. Yawned herself awake and stared at the screen, a PDF of a court document she had opened but forgotten why, then felt the chill you feel when waking up in the middle of the night, hours before sunrise, knowing this wasn't normal. A few stretches later, she wandered downstairs, saw the blinking light on the answering machine, pressed the button.

Franklin. Not coming home. Emergency. Will let you know more in the morning.

"Oh, you fucking liar."

She immediately picked up the phone, dialed Franklin's cell. Straight to voicemail. Tried again. Same thing.

She threw the handset across the living room. It put a dent in the wall, bounced onto the hardwood floor. She almost started breaking more things, but she caught herself, sank into the love seat. Remember, it's going to be okay. She would talk him down later. He had the whole FBI behind him if he needed help.

Or did he? Wasn't he told to leave Lafitte alone? Who was working with him on this? Some young flunkies looking for a quick trip up the ladder?

Desiree remembered that young man who had called a few times over the past several weeks. What was his name? Ken? No, she never got a first name. It sounded Scottish or something. McKen?

She finally caught a glimpse of the time on the wall clock. 3:28 in the morning. Well, she wasn't going back to bed, so might as well put on some coffee and get to work.

THE CALLER ID wasn't helpful. The agent's phone number wasn't anywhere. Must be blocked. So it was back upstairs to Franklin's computer. Mc Something. Mc Something. Needed to check his email.

Once again, no problem with the password, and there she had it. A whole slew of them: MCKEOWN, JOSHUA. His go-to guy, obviously.

A couple of the shorter emails were tagged with "Sent via BlackBerry". Must be on that thing all the time, like Franklin with his cell. Maybe she could use that, then. No harm now. She hit COMPOSE and marked it "High Priority". Wrote, "Urgent, call me at home ASAP." Typed in the home phone number, wondered if maybe that was a mistake—he clearly had the number, so repeating it might seem weird to him. But if not, he might call the cell anyway (or he might still call it), so she left the number and added: "Cell's recharging, turned off."

SEND.

Desiree crossed her arms, swung the office chair left and right with her foot. Thinking, aren't these FBI guys on call all the time? Should only be a few minutes.

After a few minutes plus five or six more, plus dinking around on Franklin's spider solitaire, Desiree went downstairs to pack. She didn't know where she was going yet, but hoped to by sunrise. If this McKeown hadn't called back by then, she'd try one of the others on Franklin's contact list, or maybe ask for Franklin through the main office. Or why not just take her own cell phone and start out already before her husband made it too far away?

No, if it looked like she was way behind, she would book a flight and rent a car. Anything she could to keep him from marching straight into…into…whatever was going to happen.

A few changes of clothes. Some basic toiletries, make-up. Sneakers, just the one pair would do. She pulled on some jeans and a sweater. Her cell. Last but not least, the little .38 S&W Franklin had given to her. She'd shot it a few times at the range to make him happy, but she probably hadn't touched it once in the last few years. Except that one night, the time he hit her, when she opened the nightstand drawer and picked it up and thought terrible thoughts for a few minutes before slipping it into the back of the drawer and choosing that other option—to make his life a *living* hell.

This time, using it might save him. But she couldn't take it along on the plane, so…well, what the fuck was she thinking? Like being handed a washcloth and pointed towards a forest fire, and told, "Beat it out."

She sat on the bed, gun in her lap, and waited for the sun to come up.

TWenty-tWo

COLLEEN TOLD HERSELF he was a minor glitch.
That's all McKeown was. And chauffeuring him around alone
gave her more options than if he'd brought the troopers along.
Why did he do that, anyway? The one time she'd met the agent,
she sized him up as an empty suit, by-the-book, forever an un-
derling. She had wanted Nate to be more than that, which is why
she pushed him so hard to hold these guys to their promises, show
them his leadership potential.

But here he was in the passenger seat, even stopped to buy
them both some coffee at a gas station after getting rid of the
Troopers like they were fleas. Colleen could tell these guys wanted
to play escort, wanted to do something more than stop drunks on
Interstate, but McKeown just withered them. All it took was a
couple variations on "your service is appreciated, but any further
involvement would interfere with our goals. You don't want to
interfere, do you? We're all after the same thing here" to get those
folks in their cars and back on the road while Colleen and McKeown
headed back east. Yeah, this guy had some smooth moves. He'd
even gotten Nate's gun back from the troopers somehow. He had
handed it back to her like it was nothing, not even commenting

on how old and big it was. Almost as if the guy didn't even give a shit. How can you be a cop and not care about guns?

McKeown was right, too. Nate was dead because he'd been all puffed up by her encouraging him to shoot for better. McKeown shouldn't have smeared it in her face, though. It wasn't fair to die because you showed some initiative.

She told McKeown the kids with the bike had mentioned that their friend Goof—or maybe not really a friend, but just a guy they'd grown up with in town—had called his Uncle Perry not long after the biker left with Fawn, and they had gone off looking for the station wagon. And also that Perry didn't work much, wink wink, except that he was helping his grandfather with day-to-day chores around the bar in one of the little towns south of there, one pretty much only for the local farmers. Said it was a cinderblock bunker with a trailer next to it, called "No Gas Bar", since Perry's grandfather had written "No Gas" above the simple black and white "Bar" sign to let people know the pump out front didn't work.

Problem was that the kids hadn't actually been there. Only Goof, who wasn't around when Colleen was there. The dad of the guy who had traded the station wagon for the bike, he didn't know either, but was sure it was easy to find off Highway 75. Colleen had passed the turn once, only figuring it out by the time she made the Interstate in South Dakota, and was turning around when the Trooper nailed her.

This time, she was multi-tasking, trying to think of a way to get rid of McKeown after questioning Perry, if he was even there. It was a long shot, the only real lead either of them had, but maybe not much better than waiting on the Interstate around the South Dakota border and hoping Lafitte would choose fast over scenic.

Not like McKeown seemed to care much. She already saw it shaping up—him thinking he was in charge and Colleen just a driver who would do as she was told. Fuck. Not likely unless he had back-up. After the coffee, the ride had been too damned quiet anyway, the arrogance steaming off this guy as he flipped through a file folder and sighed a lot. Twice, though, he made calls, waited for the answering machine beep, and left messages that sounded much more personal than business-related.

Like, "Please pick up. I really can explain. I couldn't until now…come on. Don't be like this."

And, "Look, I'm sorry. Okay? I'm truly sorry. I promise I won't call again today, but think about it. I'll be back soon."

McKeown hung on the line after that, eyes skyward, bobbing his head, until Colleen heard the ending beep and McKeown closed his eyes, cleared his throat. He snapped his phone shut and stared out the window.

Well, the guy was hurting. Not as much as Colleen, but surely a hell of a lot more than her own damned Sheriff, it seemed, or her mother, and especially the Trooper. McKeown seemed to be a guy who understood: Pain could piss you off.

"Sounds like you're having some trouble," she said.

McKeown cut a glance at her, trying to intimidate, as usual. "None of your business."

"If that's the case, take the drama down a notch in my car."

"Look, just drive."

"I'm not your prisoner, so don't even. My fucking car, my fucking boyfriend who died trying to help *you* motherfuckers, so don't *even*."

"I didn't ask for Nate—"

"No, you didn't, but he was willing to help out anyway. Doesn't that count?"

McKeown sighed, waved his hand at her, and kept staring out the window. Another mile of quiet. Colleen didn't feel like bottling her voice any more, now that she'd started. "Was it coming here that pissed her off?"

"Pissed who off?"

"Whoever you were leaving a message."

He grinned, but it wasn't a fun one. "Yeah, it was getting up in the middle of the night and having to fly to Bum Fuck South Dakota without even saying good-bye. I'm sure that's why he's not talking to me."

"Him?"

McKeown bit his lip. Oh, yeah, Colleen could tell that wasn't supposed to slip out.

She said, "It's okay if you're gay."

"Goddamn, I *know*, all right? If I don't want to share my personal life with, with, you or anyone….let's stop talking. Forget what I said. You don't know me."

What, like, McKeown had the moral fucking high ground now? What a prick. And a fucking self-absorbed faggot. She said, "They wouldn't like it at the Bureau if they knew."

He turned to her. "I said to stop."

"If that's what's bugging you, though, tell me. Might as well. Or do I have to tell Agent Rome that your love life is causing you to fuck up on the job?"

Whatever he was about to say, he stopped. Then, "I don't appreciate that."

Colleen crossed her left hand over, stuck up the ring finger. "You see this?"

"An engagement ring?" McKeown took her fingers lightly in his. "It's beautiful. My God, I'm sorry."

"Even worse was I didn't find it until after he died. He had bought it already, but just hadn't asked yet. I'm thinking he had something special planned."

McKeown let go of her fingers. "That's sad. Really, I can't imagine how you feel."

Colleen put her hand back on the wheel. Admired the ring again. Very nice. Nate had done a good job picking it out. "Talk to me, then. Your boyfriend? Doesn't like your work?"

"Look, it's not what you think. I'm not *gay*, you know."

"Not to hear you or look at you. But that's only on TV anyway, isn't it?"

"I like both, I mean. Can't…never been able to choose one."

"You're bi."

He scrunched up his face. "That sounds so weird. I just like…both. Then I met this guy down in Memphis, and things were going really well. It was bad that I couldn't tell him who I really was. I thought, I don't know. He could use it against me, or he wouldn't like it, or someone would see."

"That sucks." Colleen had never known any fags before. At church, it had been drilled into her that God hated them, but she hadn't read enough Bible to know why. Those radio guys Nate liked were all anti-gay, but more politically than religiously. McKeown might have been a Fed prick, but pretty much like any other Fed prick.

"Last night was, like, our first time."

"Aw, really?" She thought it was gross.

He nodded, looked pretty torn up about it. "The call came in about Lafitte, and instead of waking him up and telling him the truth, I sneaked out. It was only on my way back to the hotel that I realized…you know, I should've…but it was too late."

"Shit. Too bad."

"He won't answer the fucking phone. You know, it wasn't like a one night stand, I didn't think. We'd been moving towards this for weeks, and he seemed pretty serious. Why didn't I wake him up? I'm kicking myself."

Colleen made sympathetic noise. She wondered if McKeown was the fuck-er or the fuck-ee, or if she'd learned about that all wrong and he was both.

"I must really love this job," he kept on. "Because right now I hate the fucking FBI but look at where I am. Right where they need me"

Right here, Colleen thought, would be a good time for McKeown to remember that he was talking with a woman who had lost her fiancé not even a full day ago and could give a shit about his trivial boy problems. But she was the one who started it, just looking for conversation. Anything to occupy her mind. Helped her think more clearly if there was more going on up there than watching herself shoot Lafitte down like she should've back at the scene. Or how Nate should've wriggled out of the car and rolled around on the ground to put the flames out. How she should've risked burns herself to go drag him out. Colleen would've preferred scars to this, hunting a man because it's the only thing she imagined might take the lump out of her throat.

She said, "How about this, though. If it means you could have a nice, no fear climb up the FBI ladder, why not choose girls? You know, get married. Maybe even find a kinky one who didn't mind that sort of thing. Wouldn't that be better?"

He gave her a lazy laugh. "You can't just...*fix* things like that. It's not a game."

"No, but if you want to be with a man and the FBI at the same time..."

"It's not about them. They'd be fine with it, I guess. I mean, maybe some of the guys would give you a hard time, and maybe it would close certain doors, like, unofficially—"

"Yeah, but you want them to stay open, right?"

He nodded, turned to her. "Best case scenario, sure. But it's social, not legal."

She sighed. "I *know*, listen. You're major pissed off right now and you've only known the guy two weeks. But if you're bi, find a girl who doesn't care. Right? You have to compromise."

McKeown turned back to his window. Quiet a long moment. Colleen thought they had maybe twenty something more miles to go. She didn't want him going right back into "prick" mode. Keep him talking.

"Marry a beard," she said.

"Excuse me?"

"Find a wife who wants health care, or a woman who needs a green card. Tell her she can fuck anyone she likes except you. Take her to parties, ceremonies, all that stuff. Tell her the free ride stops if she ever spills your secret."

"You must think I'm rich."

"No, only richer than her. That's all I'm saying."

McKeown tapped his cell phone's antenna on his bottom lip. "Sounds like you've thought about this a lot."

She grinned. "What? Are you trying to imply something?"

"Not at all, no. Just saying you've thought about it."

"It's common sense, Agent McKeown. You got a first name I can call you?"

HE WAS ABOUT to tell her when his cell phone buzzed to life again. Saved by the bell, so to speak. McKeown didn't realize exactly how much info he'd been revealing. On a roll. He glanced at the message on the screen. Another email from Rome. Same as before but with extra !!!s and an "URGENT".

McKeown wondered about that. Rome's cell phone still charging? At a computer but not near a landline? If he didn't find out now, then Rome would start with the threats again. Okay, fine. Call him, and don't tell him a goddamn thing unless he already knows.

He dialed the home number. Rome's wife picked up on the first ring. "Hello?"

That was weird. If Rome was emailing, he expected the man to be hanging over the phone, ready to pounce. "Um, this is Agent McKeown. Your husband asked to speak to me."

"No, I'm sorry about that. I'm the one who sent the messages. I'm sorry. Am I bothering you?"

She had a nice voice, very polite, personable. What the hell did she want? "You said it was urgent. Has something happened to Franklin?"

"Well, no. Not exactly."

The voice blinked out, fuzzed over, and he was only catching a couple of words. "Hello? Mrs. Rome? I…the signal. Hold on a minute." To Colleen, "Pull over and let me figure this out. I need a spot with good coverage."

"How would I know?"

"Look, just," McKeown gestured. What was so hard about this? "Pull off on the shoulder and stop when I tell you."

She slowed and eased off onto the narrow shoulder, McKeown watching his screen as the strength bars waned, then another popped up. Two. That was the best he could get, he supposed.

Middle of fucking nowhere. "Here's fine. Fine." Held his phone up to his ear as he climbed out of the car. "Mrs. Rome? Are you still there?"

"Can you hear me?"

"I can now. Hold on." He bent down and turned towards Colleen. "You leave, and I swear, you'll regret it more than that stunt you pulled earlier."

Her eyes went wide. Shit, was that too harsh? Remember: her boyfriend just died, man. Ease up. He added, "Please? I'm asking nice."

"You got it. We're partners now, buddy."

He grinned. Did hicks do sarcasm? "Great, we sure are."

Outside, he paced beside a corn field, empty now except for leftover pieces of stalks. Had to hold his fingers in his open ear to hear Mrs. Rome over the wind.

He said, "Now, what's happened to Franklin?"

"He said something came up with the case and he had to go out of town. But he didn't say where and I can't reach him."

Shit. It was McKeown who was out of the loop, not Rome. Pulled some sort of fake to the right. "I'm afraid I can't tell you anything. It's confidential."

"More like it's your dirty little secret."

"Excuse me?"

"I know what happened to Ginny Lafitte, so quit treating me like a Stepford wife. I need to find my husband before he kills that man or gets himself killed."

Son of a bitch. Some tractor trailers roared down the county road and blew wind and dirt all over McKeown. Like a vacuum cleaner sucking his brains out of his ears. Mrs. Rome was a smart one, which fucked up McKeown's plans royally. He wanted both of those assholes Rome and Lafitte alive and in jail while he got himself a permanent posting to the Memphis branch.

So how would she play this one? He tried, "Again, that's information I can't tell you."

"I'm guessing you ain't told your bosses either."

Oh yeah. Smart old bitch. McKeown would've liked that if she wasn't pissing in his sandbox.

She didn't stop. "He's been going behind my back about it, so I'm damned sure he's not on the level with the Bureau."

"I don't think this is a good time to talk."

"He's out there and he's looking. You're helping him. So maybe I should sic the dogs on both of you."

Fuck fuck fuck! "Okay, fine. Listen. I don't know where your husband is. He didn't tell me what he was doing or where he was going."

"Mm hm."

"I'm serious. I ignored your first page because I didn't want to tell him what *I'm* doing. I'm already trying to keep Lafitte from killing him."

"You know where Lafitte is?"

"Maybe, I don't know. I'm following a lead. Look, you said something happened to Ginny Lafitte?"

"That's right. Tried to kill herself. Franklin had put her up in a hotel here."

McKeown closed his eyes, let out a long breath. What he'd suspected had been right all along—Rome was cutting his right hand man off the case. "She okay?"

"I got some nurse friends at the hospital. They say she's fine. Crazy, though. Talks all soft and gentle but has crazy eyes."

"If he calls me, I'll call you, how about that? As long as you don't tell anyone else what's going on."

Nothing for a long moment. McKeown checked to see if there were still any strength bars. Then, "Mrs. Rome?"

She said, "How can I trust you?"

"I don't know. I can't trust your husband. How's that for something in common?"

"Okay. If he calls me first, I'll let you know. Help me keep him safe, understand?"

McKeown said some polite things and closed the phone and shook his head. He regretted letting Rome have so much power over him, especially now that he knew how expendable he was. It was all down to Lafitte. Whoever found him first.

He climbed back into the car, told Colleen they could keep looking for the bar.

"Who was that?"

He shrugged. "Business."

A couple of minutes passed quietly. Then Colleen turned to him and said, "How about a girl with a strap-on? That enough to keep you happy on the job?"

TWenty-three

AS SOON AS PERRY and Fawn's footsteps faded, Lafitte got to work. First thing he needed to do was stand the fuck up. After Fawn had hit him with the pistol, Lafitte had seen colors, felt the sting, his head ringing like a church bell, but he hadn't passed out completely. He got his marbles back quickly and pretended to be out cold for the spectators.

Then they left and he gritted his teeth. It amplified the pain in his head, but enough to keep him down. He pulled his elbows as far up the beam as he could, then brought his knees in, tried to squat.

That worked all right. It also reminded him he had a gash in his leg that was probably getting infected. And also that he was exhausted, high, and aching all over. Plus, he stunk like puke, paint, and sweat. Now he was mobile, able to crabwalk around the post, see what he was dealing with. Stairs to his right. The underside of the stairs on his left, thick with cobwebs littered with dead bugs. Nothing to grab hold of or use to cut the wire.

He felt as far as he could with his fingers, trying to find where they'd tied the wire on his wrists. Not really heavy, more like speaker wire, maybe. But they tied enough loops to make it really fucking hard to break free even on a good day.

Lafitte didn't even try. It obviously wasn't a good day.

He swiveled his head, checking the beam for a nail or something. Needed to slice through. Nothing. Took another trip around. Still nothing. Shit.

"SHIT!" He yelled, listened. No one was there to hear.

He bounced his back off the beam long enough to grate his arms up the wood. Not as bad as the splinters in his back, but still a painful trip. Felt good to take in a full breath, even one tinged with paint fumes. No clue when Perry and Fawn would be back. If they figured out he really was who he said he was, then maybe they'd hurry back and turn him in quickly. At least then he could get some medical attention, a good meal, and some sleep. Perhaps prison wouldn't be so bad. He was pretty well versed in hand-to-hand these days. Got trained by the cops and the bikers, so he was the full package. Yeah, he could do well behind bars—makes some deals, kill the right enemies, bribe the right guards. No one would turn him out. Maybe a target on his back from Hell's Angels or Mongols or Outlaws who knew he rode with Steel God, but then there would be those bikers who saw him as a hero for the same reason.

Unless Steel God had sent down the Word that Lafitte was *persona non grata*.

Then he was toast.

Worth the shot? Willing to see if the pen was the best place for a guy like him?

Lafitte looked around to see if he'd missed anything. Maybe a loose rock or broken bottle or anything he could reach with his feet. He tried running the wire back and forth over the corner of the beam, but the wire dug deeper into his wrists. No, he needed something to snap it, and fast.

He looked up again at where the post met the stairs above his head, the two boards meeting at an angle. Like a pair of scissors left open. If he could wedge the wire in there hard enough, that might do it. If he were a goddamned acrobat.

Could it be that hard? He tried gripping the beam with his fingers but couldn't reach. Maybe with his feet, like a monkey.

He reached one back there, bent his ankle, imagined trying to do that with both feet and no help from his hands. No go.

Hurry. Think. Blow the clouds out of your head.

The stairs themselves. Impossible to reach those. But if he could, yeah, that would give him what he needed to stretch and break the wire. Riiiight, and how about a good sharp knife, too? And while we're dreaming, maybe a nice hotel room with fluffy pillows and Pay Per View porn.

Okay, but what if you didn't have to walk up them, not necessarily? Use them for leverage. Think it out.

Lafitte lifted his boot and landed it on the edge of the third step. Tried the same with the other foot while he pushed his back against the beam. Okay, so there he was in midair, a lot of pressure on both ends of him. But it was a start. One foot then the other up to the fourth step. Made him more horizontal. That didn't feel good. A fall now would rip all holy hell out of his back. The pressure was building, getting to him. He put it all into his back and ass and tried scooting up the beam. Inching. Straining, teeth bared. Working. He was closing the space between the beam and stairs, too, having to crunch himself even more.

Ready to try another step. First attempt, his foot slipped and he nearly lost it. Fought to hold on and get his foot back on the steps. Aching, flailing, he finally got it to stick. He took some time, breathed some energy back into his limbs. Second attempt, he got his foot up on the next step. Stretching him hard now. Then the other foot. Slowly. All out of whack, feet higher than his head. Shit, could he give any more?

One more push.

It was all teeth and veins and muscles. The wire caught once and he had to inch it down off a jag of wood, get it over. The whole deal was feeling like a bad idea, but he was already this far up. Even more crunched. Only way to go now was to brace his knees and get his torso higher, try to move his wrists as high as his shoulders.

One of the wire loops snapped. Shit. Might be easier than he thought. He leaned forward as far as he could, abs tight, not happy. Lafitte remembered contortionists he'd seen on TV, could cram themselves into a small glass box. Some sort of yoga bullshit. Fuckers had to be mutants or something. Even with training, steroids, and some awful beatings that left him twisted all sorts of ways, this deal was rocketing up the All-Time-Bad list in Lafitte's head.

Even with one loop snapped, it felt like it was in the middle or something and wasn't loosening the overall bind. Lafitte yanked his wrist, stretch, stretch, nothing. So it was the wedge or nothing. One more time. He thrust up and felt raw scraping on his arms. Still half an inch off.

"Oh, *Jesus fucking Christ motherfuck!*"

The wire caught the wedge good and tight. Lafitte laughed. *Now what?*

He needed more…something. Needed to flex or pull or slice.

The stairs. The steps. Yeah, stretch across those. See if it would free up his arms. He lifted a boot, straightened his leg along the step until he hooked the steel toe around the edge of the next one. Good. Shit. It hurt but it worked. He could feel the muscles relaxing, giving him more options. Lifted the other boot. His body fought, wanted to sag, drop, give out. Lafitte fought back. Rigid as iron while reaching slowly, slowly, then wildly looking for a toehold once he was fully extended.

Got it.

Half-twisted across the steps, the wire cutting off circulation in his hands, Lafitte knew if this didn't work, he was at the mercy of gravity and those two hicks. His fingers were getting tight with all the blood, numbing. He pulled hard with his toes, sliding his body further along the steps, arms stretching behind him. His calves hung off the other side and he was able to scramble his boots back onto the steps.

Rise, damn it, rise!

It was circus freaklike, bowing his back, feeling dizzy and nauseous all over again but holding his breath and yanking the wire with everything he had in him. It was stuck firmly in the wedge now, and it wasn't giving an inch.

Until it snapped without warning. The slack in Lafitte's arms shocked him and he started to fall backwards. Turned just in time to catch his side on a step, reached across and grabbed two more for support, and he was free. Fingers tingled liked electricity was running through them. His mouth hung open, a thick rope of spit dripping five feet down to the floor below. Sure, he was free, but he had used up all his strength getting that way.

They're going to come back. They're going to come back with cops or Feds or some garbage bags, so get up. Get the fuck up. GET THE FUCK UP.

Lafitte crawled up the remaining stairs. He put his back to the door and pressed against it. It didn't give. He kept pressing, using the leverage to help him lift and stand on wobbly legs. He tried the knob. Locked. Didn't look like much to it, though. He twisted it left, slipped off.

Wrapped both hands around, took in a deep lungful of air and tried again.

Pop.

He opened the door and immediately fell down. Face first. Used his hands to brace himself but couldn't stop his momentum. His hands slapped linoleum and stung. Took a knock to his cheekbone but avoided another one to his nose and swollen eye.

A quick look around. A dark kitchen, cluttered. Lafitte made out the fryer, a sink, stack of plates. Some cardboard boxes. Took him a moment to remember what Perry had said to Fawn: Granddad's bar. Okay, that gave him something to go by. Can't be out too remote if it's a bar. Need people to make a bar work, right? And people meant cars.

Lafitte's head was clearing. Blood flowing better, yeah, yeah. Still not up for a game of hoops or anything. He rolled onto his back, sat up. Felt hammers on his body in places he didn't expect. Pulled his hands close to his good eye. Still swelled red with blood but getting better. The wire had cut his wrists, gave him a few burns, but nothing that wouldn't heal itself within a day or two.

Still, he knew escape was a lost cause on his own. Sitting up made him want to puke again. Everything was swimming, much worse than a marijuana buzz or the high he got slinging back a whole bottle of wine. All that fucking paint they made him huff, Jesus. He was weak and thirsty and hungry and sick. Best he could hope for was to thumb a ride, maybe convince someone he had been in a motorcycle wreck and needed a lift to the hospital. Of course they would ask questions, but he'd make shit up until he felt strong enough to jack the car. No time to waste on doctors. Lafitte needed to get South.

He reached over for the closest counter, used it to get himself on his feet. Waited for the muscles to straighten themselves out before he tried walking again. From up here, he could see through the service window out into the main bar, not all that much bigger than the kitchen. A dump. Cheap particleboard tables, mismatched chairs, a home-hammered plywood bar covered with what must've once been pieces of a dining room table. Not bad for a guy's home rec room, but as a business it reminded Lafitte of the daiquiri shops in New Orleans, most little more than a menu, a cheaply-built wooden counter, and a couple dozen frozen drink machines. Small investment, pays back a nice living.

He used the counter as a crutch, lurching along until he found the swinging door out into the front room. He eased through, using the wall on the other side to keep him standing, took it in.

The two small windows were covered with neon beer lights, so he couldn't see outside. Didn't know what time it was at first, then remembered Perry saying it was really early, just after dawn. Good ol' Perry, a fount of knowledge, that guy. Lafitte weaved through tables over to one window, panting by the time he hit the wall. Getting a view through the small spaces as best he could, but not really able to tell much—gravel parking lot, empty. Streetlamp. No signs of life, no other dwelling.

"Fuck."

He made it to the front door. Went ahead and opened it. Somewhere, the sun was rising, but Lafitte couldn't place where from. The icy morning air hurt his chest. The dim light was still too fucking bright. He squinted, ached, then wondered how far he could make it across the lot and through the black dirt of the soybean field across the street to the small speck of barn on the horizon. Shit, halfway across he would be winded.

But free.

He grunted. Closed the door.

He braced himself on the closest table, a wobbly one, and his arms wobbled, and he sat down in a chair. Took in a big breath through his nose, everything started to clear up more and more, making it more and more obvious how fucked he was. Like, for fuck's sake, the Sergeant-at-Arms for Steel God couldn't even walk across a parking lot at this point.

Make that *was* Sergeant, like, "not anymore". At least being in the gang was easier. Morally, maybe not, but it sure as hell beat *this*. He raised his head. *This*. Taken by surprise, beaten silly and humiliated, chased all over the country, probably heading into a trap anyway.

So, call him, then.

God had left him that lifeline, right? The man wouldn't have reminded Lafitte about Mom's number if he didn't mean it. Sure as shit he wouldn't.

But you call Steel God to bail you out, there's no turning back. There's no family reunion. You sell your soul to Steel God and be whoever the fuck he wants you to be.

Lafitte held his right hand in front of his swollen eye. Not even a flicker of light or shape. Would probably take a few days to heal. Hard to keep a car on the road one-eyed. He was starving. He was thirsty. He had a free bar to himself right then but didn't want any of the bottles behind it.

Look, if he'd left once, he could always do it again. Tell Steel God he was a One Percenter now, through and motherfucking through, then steal his bike while he slept. Why not? Lafitte had been hunted by worse and lived.

It was the best he could do. Lafitte headed behind the bar, the whole time feeling his empty stomach sink lower until he felt that he was in freefall. But his hands caught the edge, held him up. He kept on creeping closer to the telephone.

Picked it up, flipped the handset over and dialed the number from memory. Rang three times. Then, a woman who sounded like somebody's mom said, "Hello?"

"Is this…Mom?"

Quiet for a moment. Lafitte said, "Hey, still there?"

"Whose Mom are you looking for?"

Who the fuck was he supposed to ask for? Shit on that. Lafitte laughed low, coughed, said, "The Mother of God."

After another long pause, the woman said, "Tell me where you are, Billy."

The shock of her knowing his name didn't register until he was halfway through saying, "I don't know. Some dive bar out in the soybean fields. God, I don't know anything. They're going to get me soon."

"Billy," she did it again. "Is this the bar phone you're calling from?"

"Yeah, and they're coming back." Coughed, swallowed some bile. "Locked me…in the basement."

"I've got the number on Caller ID. You stay there, okay? Hang on."

The bar spun. No, Lafitte was spinning, standing still but spinning. "I don't know. I really don't know. Mom?"

She said more, but the phone was suddenly falling. He watched it clack against the floor. His knees went, and if he had-n't held onto the bar until the very last second, it would have been a much harder fall. As it was, it was hard enough.

MAYBE A MINUTE, maybe ten, maybe an hour later, the door of the bar opened and Lafitte heard it but couldn't see. Half dreaming, half comatose, felt like. Footsteps. Then the swinging door into the kitchen, followed by Perry's shrill *"Shit! Shiiiiit!"*

Quick steps, Fawn's, probably, also through the doors. Then a bunch of yelling he couldn't understand before more doors, more steps, then Fawn's loud voice saying, "Found him. And he's been busy."

Twenty-four

SO NOW the little prick had stopped answering his phone.

By the time Rome had reached McKeown's voicemail for the fifth time, he had the car up to eighty-five without realizing it as he sped north through Mississippi on I-55. He didn't want to tell anyone his plans until he reached St. Louis, where he would liaison with the local branch and explain whatever elaborate lie he'd dreamed up along the way. It hadn't come to him yet, but it would.

At the hospital, Mom and Pa Hoeck showed up within a couple of hours, accompanied by a big white son of a bitch Rome had seen around. Took him a minute. This was a big-time lawyer, one who'd been all over the New Orleans news, taking on the big controversial cases that always got appealed right up to the Supreme Court. And that's who the Hoecks had in their corner.

First thing out of his mouth: "Agent Rome, my clients are filing a lawsuit against you and the FBI for plenty of bad shit, and my first act as their counsel is to kick your ass out of their daughter's hospital room."

Like he would even dare. Really. A Federal Agent was bulletproof. "Man, I think you'd better cool your heels and think about who you're talking to. I'm here for Mrs. Lafitte's own good."

That started Ginny crying, her mom cradling her. The Dad so red in the face, you'd think he might stroke out or lash out, either or. Ginny telling her, "Billy's coming to get me. Oh God, I can't…I can't. Coming to get the kids!"

The lawyer took a few steps closer, careful not to touch Rome and get himself an assault charge. Leaned in and lowered his voice. "I know all about you. Spent the whole drive over talking to your superior. Agent Stoudemire did not sound pleased. So don't put on a show here. Your own agents are ready to escort you out of this building if you do."

That was that. Rome wagged a finger in the man's face, said, "You stay right here. I'll be right back." Then out into the hall, knowing full well he was done, no more plays from his high horse. Goddamn it. Just…just go, then. Get up there where the action was. Hands on. No time to lose. He had to get in his car and *get gone*.

So he did.

Desiree had tried to call his cell, but he hadn't thought of how to explain any of this. Jesus. What was the point of all the painstaking step-by-step rebuilding of a stronger, better plan when all of it could fly apart at the same time? Like right now?

He tried to keep it in, but he exploded with "*Shit!*" and punched the roof of the car with the fist in which his cell phone was curled, hurt his knuckles. He flipped the phone into the passenger seat, noticed the cracked screen. Another *Shit*.

Desiree had already broken through one layer of protection that night they got back together through rough sex, that sweet release from all the months of anger, and he let it slip that he was after Lafitte again. Bundled it into a convenient lie, sure, telling her that the Bureau had mandated his involvement, more like he was a consultant than anything else. She didn't buy it completely, though. Now that he thought about it more, he wondered if Desiree suspected him of having an affair with Ginny. The way he'd been sneaking around, made perfect sense unless you had more important fish to fry. Ginny, nervous little white girl. Probably cute, yeah, he could see that objectively. Nothing to write home about. Legs and ass had no shape at all. Plus, how she kept finding ways to bleed, that turned him off.

She hadn't even made decent bait. Rome blamed himself for that, mostly. He had pushed too hard, too focused on getting Lafitte to see what the pressure was doing to Ginny. She was all eggshell, and he was all hammer.

Without McKeown, Rome might as well be a lone vigilante anyway. That's all this was. A barroom brawl blown up to Super Bowl proportions. Lafitte hurt Rome, so Rome wanted to hurt him back, and someone had to win or lose. No more goddamn stalemate.

Rome gloried at the spectacle, remembering football broadcasts swelled with bombast and self-importance, computer graphics of robot warriors playing in stadiums ten times larger than the biggest he'd ever seen, all for a Sunday afternoon showdown between the Saints and the fucking Seahawks or some shit. Oh yeah, let Fox TV get hold of him and Lafitte. What could they make of that?

The phone went again, broke Rome's train of thought. He figured it was Dee again. Could be McKeown, though. Or another team member who had been in touch with McKeown. He reached for it, swerved over the center line but corrected while lifting the phone's screen so he could see.

Well, goddamn. It was Stoudemire. Fucking boss man calling from his own goddamn cell phone this goddamn early.

Beep. "Rome."

He started right in. "So how the hell did Ginny Lafitte end up in a New Orleans hospital after a suicide attempt in one of our hotels? You have anything to do with that?"

"The suicide attempt?"

"Don't bullshit me, Rome. It's all on you. Her mother's lawyer has already spilled the whole story. Your guy McKeown's off in South Dakota looking for a fucking biker, he said. Took one of our planes. But the cops up there are saying it might be Billy Lafitte. Does that sound about right?"

"I already told you plenty enough that I don't answer to you."

"You do now. We've heard from Washington. I'll forward you the email."

The morning chill numbed Rome's fingers. "Yeah, do that."

"As soon as I can reach McKeown, I'm reassigning him and bringing him home to make a statement. You'll need to make one, too. So come on in, get an attorney lined up, let's do this friendly, okay? We don't want anything to get out of hand, and you'll still come out the other end all right."

It was the sort of language you used on hostage-takers, not colleagues. "I'm all right now, Shane. I'll even forgive your little power trip or whatever this is right now." C'mon, find something. "I've got work to do, and if Lafitte has anything to do with this bike gang we're after, that's news to me."

A loud sigh from the boss. "Have you been shitting us the whole time? I mean, I tried to warn you sweetly, remember? Working Lafitte's *wife*? My God, man."

"Not my fault the man's got his hands in so many dirty deeds. We scratched the surface and saw what bubbled up."

"Come on in this morning, all right? Let's spin this to your advantage. Say what you just said, but on the record. It'll make sense. Then we can move on."

Yeah, Rome thought. *Exactly* what you'd say to a bona fide guilty hostage-taker: Hey, we're your pals. Ain't nothing going to happen to you. Scott free, I'm telling you. Trust us, man.

"I can't come in."

"No, don't say that. You'll come in, everything will be fine."

"I can't. I'm out of town. Let's do it next week."

Stoudemire covered the receiver, his muffled voice behind a shuffling noise. So he wasn't alone on this. Had some guys there coaching him. Fuck. Some serious business if they had to send in a whole team to help out.

He removed his hand and came back with, "Well, how about this? Tell me where you are, and I'll get you directions to the nearest police station. You can stay there until I reach you."

Rome smiled. The guy had no clue. And Rome wasn't going to help Stoudemire do his job either. "I'm busy. Next week,

Shane. This really sounds like a minor administrative thing to me. It can't wait until next week?"

Another exhalation. Stoudemire lowered his voice. "Jesus, Franklin, it's either this or a warrant. Please."

Rome pulled the phone away from his ear, turned it off. Stared straight ahead while pressing his thumb against the back panel, slid it open. He shook the battery onto the floorboard.

A fugitive. Been doing the best he could to stay within the law while still trying to bring in a motherfucker like Lafitte, reasoning that once he did that, the Bureau would understand, surely. Down the drain now. He was a goddamned fugitive.

No, not yet. He could still fix this. Put the phone back together, dial Stoudemire again, and save his ass. Yeah, explain it so these guys all understand. He wouldn't lose his job. At the worst, early retirement and the occasional "consultant" gigs to prop up his income. Don't throw away good people over a shit stain like Lafitte.

Rome pulled the car onto the shoulder, the barely-there daylight now giving him a dim but better view of the kudzu-covered ditches at roadside. He got out, went around the car, opened the passenger door and knelt. The battery had bounced under the seat. He clipped the battery packet back into the phone. Slid the cover on. They could probably pick up the signal from that alone. Or, hell, the Bureau probably had the things rigged with tracers that didn't even need batteries, so maybe he'd wasted his time. Didn't matter.

The whole thing gave him some sympathy for Lafitte. Made sense now why the man would rather take a runner instead of use his connections with the Sheriff's Department to get off lightly. At least that way Lafitte didn't owe anything to anyone.

Rome could understand that, absolutely.

How long before the Bureau cut off his phone? No chance. They would want to track him. Then how many calls could he make, get some plans in order, before they caught on? How far would his ID and title get him before the word got out nationwide?

How about Desiree?

He held the phone in his hand, stared at the blank screen, not quite ready to turn it on yet, knees starting to ache mightily down on the ground. Guess he could find his wife later. He only had one more shot at Lafitte.

So...what do you do?

By the time he'd left the phone in pieces strewn across the ditch twenty minutes later, he'd made two calls. And if Stoudemire or McKeown or whatever team of experts was looking for him figured out who he'd spoken with, it was game over.

Rome smiled as he got up to speed. Sang an old gospel song, "Won't we have a time, when we get over yonder..."

TWenty-five

FAWN PUNCHED Redial on the bar phone. Got a busy signal. Tried again. The same. She wouldn't dare show Perry anything but her tough bitch shell, but inside she was freaking. Turned out this asshole, Lafitte, hadn't been lying to Perry after all. He was a Grade A Federal Fugitive, worth a small fortune if brought in alive. Didn't say nothing about him being brought in dead. Considered to be one of the most dangerous criminals in the top ten. Possibly "in league with known terrorists".

She hadn't been scared of him while he was tied up in the basement, puking and sputtering. She even laughed when the mugshot came up on the screen along with the "Do Not Attempt to Apprehend" and "Use Extreme Caution" banners. Soon as they got back and found him passed out behind the bar with a phone nearby, her panic level shot up like a rocket. Who'd he call? Were a bunch of Al Qaedas on the way? And just how the fuck did he escape from the basement?

Perry being equally freaked didn't help at all. Pacing, staring at Lafitte, pacing more. Tripping over his own feet and his granddad's barstools. Rambling, "Aw, shit, aw, shit, *shit*. Not good. Not *good* at all."

"What? He's still out. Let's hurry, tie him up, get him to the police. They sure won't care about him being beat up, not with him being so wanted."

Perry spun to face her. Man, his eyes. Never seen them so crazy before, and she'd actually dropped some tabs with him once. This was, like, ten times that. He stabbed a finger back towards the bar, said, "But who did he call? Only guys someone like him is going to call are some bad characters." Every word like he was Al Fucking Pacino.

Fawn crossed her arms, shook her head. Made her way back over to Lafitte and toed him. Then a little harder. He shifted an inch or two but wasn't up for any hand to hand combat. She knelt beside him, wanted to touch him. Goddamn, she wished she could turn herself off sometimes. It was, you know, what she'd gotten used to. Craved the company of someone from outside that tiny-ass town more than the sex and drugs, really, just so she could tell her story different every time, watch as the guy listened, or pretended to listen, it didn't matter, and realize *he has no fucking idea.* Not one iota of who she really was. The locals, they already had her pegged. It was unavoidable in towns that size, even if you didn't know everyone personally, you still knew too much about them.

The dude who showed up at the burger stand morphed into the guy who stole her car, left her alone in a field. Had scared her bad. On her knees, thinking she was going to be raped, beaten, killed, and that it wasn't going to be at the hands of someone she knew, and it wasn't going to be a situation that made sense. She'd always thought she'd die from drunk driving or an overdose or some scorned farmer fuck buddy shoving her into machinery. At least she could understand that. A sad story, but not a fucking *spectacle.*

Shivers.

Fawn stood. Perry was pacing again, mumbling. Whatever she'd seen in him to start with had faded the first three days. Now he was pitiful, another bad stop on the merry-go-round of her life. Had to play nice because they always came around again.

"I'm going to call the cops. We'll say he broke in. You go find more wire and clean up all that shit downstairs."

"What if his friends get here first?"

"Well, fuck, I don't know. Hurry then."

That's when they both heard the car pulling up in the gravel lot, closer and closer, muscle car engine never going to sneak up on anyone. It burped off. Couple of squeaky doors opened, closed. Fawn pulled Lafitte's pistol, didn't even know if there was one in the chamber or not. Been a while since she'd been shooting with Dad. She crouched behind the bar, signaled Perry to hide, but he wasn't even looking her way. Frozen in the middle of the floor. Really obvious to anyone trying to look through the windows. Did they even lock the front door on their way in? So used to not bothering, even leaving the house unlocked at night, the way people had always lived out in the middle of nowhere.

Couple of voices, dampened, hard to understand. Then someone tried the doorknob. It jiggled but held fast. Goddamn good habit to get into, Fawn thought.

Then a knock. Loud. Looked like Perry had instinctually turned toward it but couldn't get up the nerve. Fawn willed him to hide or sneak into the back or *something* other than just standing there. Nerve was not the brightest idea right then.

Another knock. This time followed by, "Hello? Anyone in there?"

Perry opened his mouth and Fawn gave him a *Shhhhh* that she hoped they couldn't hear outside. It was so loud, though, how could anyone miss it? Loud like a movie soundtrack. Oh god, now she'd really fucked up.

More knocking. "Please, open the door. I'm with the FBI and I have a few questions for you."

Perry was moving before Fawn could react. He looked back at her, whispered, "That's a good thing, right?"

Going for the door. Not even taking a few seconds to think how the FBI just magically knew they'd caught Public Enemy Number Four. Yell at him, and whoever it was would know they were in there. Fawn stood and double-fisted the gun, aiming right

192 Anthony Neil Smith

for the back of Perry's head. Not her fault if he got in the way, was it? Steady, wait, get a grip.

Perry unlocked the door, opened it enough to stick his head out. Fawn imagined him pulling it back in, except it wouldn't be there, all hacked off by a machete or something. She closed one eye, cleared a path down the sight.

Then there was Perry's smiling face, right where it was supposed to be, telling her, "Hey, we're okay! They're real!"

He opened the door wider. Revealed a thin young guy holding up his ID standing beside a woman with big shoulders and tree trunk legs. No contest in a fight, even if Fawn fought dirty, she realized right quick. Hid the pistol in her waistband again, then said, "Looks like we've done your job for you."

COLLEEN LOOKED DOWN at Lafitte and grit her teeth because she actually felt bad for the guy, what these slack-jawed yokels had done to him. They denied it, of course. Said it was all self-defense. Fawn even showed them a bruise. A little one. Didn't compare to the deep *Baby Raper* cut into his chest.

It was the cop in her feeling sympathetic, so she squelched it, closed her eyes and saw Nate's burned corpse again. In the future, it would probably be a nightmare that kept coming back to haunt her. Right then and there, it was the only fucking motivator she had. Opened her eyes again and lost her breath a second. Slight, no one noticing. But the sight of Fawn and Perry standing over Lafitte acting as if they were heroes when all three of them should be linked up and taken in, it was enough to make her think the whole chase was pointless. She wasn't getting revenge, and these two losers weren't getting a reward. They didn't know that yet, though.

McKeown sat Fawn and Perry down, stared at them across one of the greasy tables, barely wiped from the night before, as they told him about this crazy biker threatening Fawn.

"He forced me into the station wagon, left his bike. I was *so* scared," she said, her best "rehearsing for the Oprah show" drama going on. "I thought for sure he was going to rape me and kill me, and God knows what else."

McKeown watched their eyes, said, "But how did Perry find you?"

"It was his nephew, one of the kids at the parking lot. He got suspicious and gave Perry a call. Thank God he drove fast."

"So, hold on. How'd you end up here, then?"

"That guy didn't know these roads, so I let him think I was going where he wanted. But instead I made it here, jumped out and tried to run. He caught me, but Perry made it just in time and hit him over the head. He was out cold, so we drug him inside."

Colleen didn't feel like sitting. She paced behind McKeown, kept watch on Lafitte, who was snoring. What the hicks were telling McKeown didn't match up with the scene on the ground. If they dragged him, he'd have dirt or gravel dust all over him. The only dust was on the soles of his boots. His wrists were circled with deep raw ruts, some bleeding. If these two hadn't roped him up, who had? And why had he been unwound from the restraints? Also, neither one explained why Lafitte was covered in puke or why he had gold paint flaked around his nostrils. Made sense for Perry, marked for life with his gold stain like a tattoo, and his brain worked at about the speed you'd expect from someone like that.

Colleen got down on her knees beside Lafitte's head, gently rolled it to the left. No blood on the back of his skull. A nasty bruise on his temple, though. *Hit him over the head*, yeah, right, my ass.

McKeown had figured it out without even having to see. Maybe he wasn't such an empty suit after all. But fuck yeah, she wanted one of those black suits. Wanted one of those ID wallets with her FBI card. Wasn't in the cards, though. Nate, now, that would've been sweet, living the Special Agent life vicariously. Like that movie with Brad Pitt and Angelina Jolie, but without the marital problems and the part where they tried to kill each other. Anyway, she was just thinking he was a better cop—and a lot better looking—without a tie.

McKeown twisted the knife. "When did he get sick, then? Before or after you drug him in here?"

They both tried to answer, tripped over each others' crap lies. Colleen gave up trying to guess. She called out, "Who carved this into his chest?"

Fawn looked over, condescending dipped chin leading. "He was like that before."

McKeown cut them off, said, "Also, how long's he been here? If he took you from the burger shack last night, and it's now past dawn…" Colleen wanted to giggle when she saw him pretending to count on his fingers. She held her lips tight. "So, why didn't you call someone?"

Perry cleared his throat. "Look, we can talk about all this later, can't we? The dude is out cold, but you'd better lock him up now. We'll follow you, whatever we need to do. I don't know if you're aware of the reward. I'd like to get that process started, too. You understand, right? Glad to answer all your questions, you know, just later."

They seemed so fidgety. Fawn kept looking at the clock hanging behind the bar. Perry had sweat circles under his arms, around his neck. What the hell were they scared of? Colleen was staring right at it, took another minute for it to gel. The phone, right there on the bar above Lafitte. Whatever had happened here, it looked like he'd at least gotten a shout out through to somewhere. These two knew. Someone was coming, and it sure as hell wasn't the police.

Colleen stretched up for the phone, took it, hit Redial. Got three whiny tones, then that bitchy robot voice: "The number you have dialed is no longer in service…"

Just like Lafitte to fuck up the one chance he had to call for help. Still, Perry and Fawn were really on edge. Could be they didn't know he had misdialed. Hell, even better if they didn't.

"Agent McKeown," Colleen said. "Could I have a word?"

He gave her a quick nod, apologized to the hicks and left his seat. He leaned across the bar, Colleen mirrored him, and they spoke directly into each others' ear. Her peripheral vision caught Fawn rubbing her hand on Perry's bouncing knee, her whispering up a storm, trying to calm him maybe. Or feed him what to tell McKeown.

"All lies," Colleen said.

"Oh, yeah, that's an easy one. You called me over here for that?"

"*No*, jackass. I'm not a meter maid, remember?"

"Hurry up."

"That's just it. Those two really want to hurry. I think Lafitte got loose and tried to call for help. But when I redialed, I got a disconnected number."

She waited, figured it would be enough.

Of course not. "And?"

She squinted at him like, *Are you dense?* "They don't know he messed up. They really think someone is coming. Get it? You give them a way out right now, something that sounds real enough, and they'll take off, I swear."

McKeown seemed not to register what she'd said for a moment, still staring straight ahead. Then he blinked. "Yeah, that's good. Tell them the Minneapolis office will send their reward or something, tell them I'll call ahead. Give them a phony slip of paper."

"They don't even need paper, I'll bet."

"We'll see. Come on."

They pushed off the bar and headed back over to the table. Fawn clamped her nails into Perry's thigh. His leg stopped bouncing. Colleen thought she heard Fawn hiss through her teeth, *Got it?*

"Again, let me say thank you." McKeown pulled a pen from his pocket as he looked back and forth between them, nods and eyes. "I'm going to contact our office in the Twin Cities and give them your info. They should be in touch tomorrow or the next day."

Fawn said, "Why not today?"

"You know how it is. If you owe the government, pay up now, sister. But if the government owes you, don't hold your breath. But I'll put in a good word, make sure this gets expedited."

Perry was smiling, twitchy, down with everything McKeown was saying. Fawn was the one Colleen worried about. She wasn't even looking at McKeown anymore. Arms crossed, lips shriveled like she'd sucked a lemon.

As they stood up, shook hands with the agent, Fawn said, "What happens to him now?"

"I'll need to make sure he's able to travel, then take him in. After that, I'm afraid we can't tell you. Confidentiality."

Perry reached to touch her back, but Fawn flinched away, started getting worked up. "You mean one of the most dangerous men in America's right here in this bar and all they send is you two? No back-up or SWAT team or anything? Not even a proper car."

McKeown shrugged. "This was pretty sudden. We had to improvise."

"No, I watch all those TV shows about real life detectives, and you *never* improvise. You always say it's never like we see on TV."

Now McKeown's palms were open, cautioning. "Hey, listen. Every case is different. As soon as you guys are on your way, all I've got to do is pull out my cell phone and we'll have a whole fleet here. The officer assisting me can restrain our suspect with handcuffs. But first, we want you out of harm's way. Go home and wait for a phone call. Then you'll know how much we appreciate your help."

Perry said, "Come on, baby."

Fawn stood her ground. "I'll bet if I stand across the street and wait, all we'd see is nothing. Something weird's going on."

Perry grabbed Fawn by the elbow, pulled her a couple of steps towards the door. "We'll deal with it later. We've got to go, remember?"

Fawn pulled away again. "You know, it's pretty convenient that the fucker makes a phone call and suddenly these two show up. Like, really, the FBI's going to send a preppie and a bull dyke over in a muscle car? You buying this?"

Colleen's muscles tightened all over. Bull dyke? This tubby white trash bitch wanted to talk shit about *her* like she herself was the Queen of the Fucking Nile?

She stepped up beside McKeown, hand on top of her holster, unsnapped with a fingernail, ready to go. "Ma'am, please, that's unnecessary. We all have our jobs to do, and it's time for you to leave the premises."

McKeown reached over like he was going to touch her arm, thought better of it, but sounding like a diplomat all the sudden. "Hold on, hold on, okay, so that's procedure, okay Miss? The deputy is going by the book, all right?"

All in the training. Why didn't Colleen think of that? She was making things worse all because this whale with too much blush and mascara was pissed off that she thought the officers who she had just lied to had now lied to her. Yeah, that was a good point. Colleen eased her hand away from the holster.

She said, "No need for escalation. Just a precaution. You're not the problem here."

Perry stood frozen between Fawn and the door. Colleen could nearly hear his thoughts, so obvious they were sweating through his pores—

Paint fumes and Beer and Panic and Ditch her and run.

So obvious, Colleen said it out loud before she realized. "Ditch her and run."

Perry, hands over his head like he'd heard an air raid siren. "Jesus, what?"

McKeown, palms out. "Wait, no one's telling anyone to run."

You could see it in Fawn's face. Darkening, brows furrowing, cheeks puffing with air. She reached under her shirt, her waistband.

Colleen reached too.

FAWN HAD BEEN fucked over enough for one day. One long horrible day. And it came to a head when she was sitting at that table in the bar next to Perry while these agents, if that's who they really were—damn, that chick sure didn't look like one to Fawn—whispered over the bar. Perry was ready to lose it. He wasn't breathing so good and he told her, "I want to puke."

She soothed him, rubbed his thigh, told him to stick with the story, except if they asked about the wrists or the shit on his chest. Say he was already like that. Stick to it like a chant. But don't let them go into the basement. What really got to her was that she was feeling sorry for Perry again. Right then, Fawn wanted nothing more than to go celebrate their reward. They would split it, sure, but why not put it together? Buy a great house, get their lives together instead of wallowing in meth and paint cans and all the boredom that kept her fucking and drinking like it was a marathon but not getting anywhere. Get the reward check, then go home and start over like the past five, six years had never happened.

But the more she watched Perry—skinny, haggard, gold-stained lip and oily hair, scared to the point of pissing his pants—the more she wanted to take the full reward for herself and move to the Cities. Or, hell, even farther. Didn't her high school friend Pat send her postcards from the beach in North Carolina one summer? The most beautiful place she'd ever seen. Maybe there. Fuck splitting the money. Fuck "fair". Fuck Perry.

What would she do when she got there?

Something different. Didn't matter. Even the crappiest job in Carolina was better than being rich out in the bean fields.

So how to ditch Perry then?

Simple. Go home, fuck the shit out of him, and leave with the check when he fell asleep. He wouldn't come looking for her. Too much work to even consider that. Plus, Fawn wouldn't leave a trail. By the time she felt like telling her parents where she'd run off to, Perry would've sunk back into his cheap life in his cheap trailer, huffing fumes and sometimes selling dope to get by another few weeks. Maybe there would be some regret, some righteous anger, even, or a tiny desire for revenge. Never enough to get him off the couch and on a plane. Just keep rubbing his leg until it's time to go.

Then the preppie fruit Special Agent—he thinks he's hiding it, but Fawn knew he was queer the first five minutes—came back over to tell them, pretty much, there wasn't going to be any reward today.

When then? Days? Weeks? Months? How long would she have to play nice with her ex, tied to her again like a brick on the ankle while she was trying to swim for shore.

And where was the proof anyway? Not to mention the back-up. These two miraculously show up to save the day? Not likely.

That's when Fawn stopped giving a shit anymore. No matter which direction she swam, which guy she rode, which plan she hatched, it was like she had a built-in Fail circuit ready to blow the very second things were looking up. Why? Wasn't she a good person? Like, no saint, but not bad. She treated people okay. So why?

She couldn't even speak her mind. She tried telling those people how she really felt, and all she got from the preppie was lies, and the butch chick wanted to draw a gun on her.

If there was no fucking reward and no fucking escape except for out that door with Perry…no, not an option. They had underestimated her. Same as Lafitte had underestimated her. The whole world kept on passing her by without a second glance. But there she was all the sudden, surprise, surprise! She would have Perry tie them up and then call the real cops, the real FBI, settle all this and get a real check dropped in her hand. Perry can have a third. Don't even give him the illusion of this being a fair split or that they had a chance to hook up again or any of it. Just a nice "It was fun, but I've got to go now."

How was she going to pull that off? Well, that was easy. The answer was right there in her waistband, courtesy of Lafitte.

She did this, she'd be a hero. No one could ever ignore Fawn again.

She grinned.

Exactly.

COLLEEN SHOT FAWN in the face. Fast, too. She'd barely freed the Glock from her pants when Colleen went into gear. Was already mid-recoil when she thought, What if it's not a gun? Right above Fawn's left eye, not quite dead center. The .45

slug exploded out the back of her head. Blood and brain sprayed across Perry's pants and shoes. He didn't stick around to gawk or puke, either. Colleen took a shot at him, too, but missed when he ducked and flung the door open and took off. Guy didn't even try for his Mustang. Just a flat-out run. She was aiming for him through the doorframe, but McKeown batted her arm down before she could squeeze the trigger. He was yelling at her, too. She hadn't even noticed.

"The fuck are you doing? Aw, fuck! Jesus Christ!"

Colleen was still in all ringing ears and the trance that went along with it. She'd never actually killed anyone before. Only dreamed about it. How did it feel?

Not so bad. The bitch deserved it. Made her less angry with Lafitte, too.

Then she thought, How would it have felt three days ago?

McKeown drew his own piece—took him long enough—and approached Fawn's crumpled body, kicked the loose Glock a few feet away, then crouched beside it. He took a deep breath, then stood. Didn't say anything for a minute. Colleen knew it was a real gun then.

She wouldn't need to defend herself. Cut and dry. Save an FBI agent's life and you're cool like that.

Saved his? Saved your own, how about it?

Colleen sniffed. Didn't matter. She and Nate used to tell each other before shifts, "Come home." Always "Come home." Didn't matter anymore if she came home. Maybe she didn't even want to. Never sleep in that bed again. As many different beds as possible. Wear that ring and tell any number of men in bars she was married, let them think what they wanted. Dispatch fuckers with guns and walk away, simplifying justice. Getting ahead of herself, though. One at a time.

McKeown was still staring at the gun, frozen in place. Colleen walked behind the bar. Lafitte had moved a bit. The gunshot must have broken through his haze. His head was turned, his arm stretched out. His breath was louder, steady.

Colleen still had her gun out. Never occurred to her to re-sheath it. Maybe Perry would come back blazing. Yeah, right. She pointed it at Lafitte, squinted down the sight. Noticed her hand wasn't shaking. Wavering like a skyscraper on a windy day. Dead center of the ear.

"Hey," McKeown said.

Colleen looked up.

"What are you doing?"

She kept the gun on Lafitte. "Nothing."

McKeown repeated, "Nothing," and stared off to the side. Hands on his hips. He shifted his weight, one knee to the other.

Colleen imagined it: one gunshot. McKeown would look shocked, go all speechless, then just tell her, "Go on, get out of here. I'll handle it." Because that's what happened to women in movies who made good on revenge. Except Farrah Fawcett, okay, but the others were given a free pass.

She glanced down at Lafitte one more time. Shit. He'd had a really fucking bad day. She laid her gun on the bar. "What now? Do we need to call somebody?"

McKeown shook his head. "Help me get him into a chair or something."

TWenty-six

RUN. Goddamn. Run, don't look back—fuck, why'd you look back? Just go.

Perry knew she was dead. He'd seen the back of her head burst like a melon. Even if he'd never seen it in real life before, it was close enough to the movies and he knew without a doubt. If they could just shoot Fawn like that, without warning or shouting or anything, then there was *no way* the yuppie and dyke were cops. No fucking way.

He was out the door and in the dust so fast, he didn't even stop when he stumbled on the asphalt and skinned his hands. Pebbles and glass and shit. He pumped double-time. Fuck. Left his car. Fuck. If they wanted him, they had their car. Fuck. It was no contest.

Cool air on his sweaty skin gave him goosebumps and cramped his stomach. He looked back again before heading into the ditch, tripping and hitting the dirt face first. If it were summer, he could hide in the stalks. But all around was open prairie, already harvested, black dirt churned up top. He was far enough down the rise that he couldn't see the bar anymore, even though it was a stone's throw. Across the street, train tracks ran parallel for a good fifty or so miles, he knew. The closest trees were a windbreak for a farm house. Maybe a mile away. Better than waiting for a train. He could do it. He could make it. Cut across the field, even if they did follow. They wouldn't dare drive out into the field, right?

Perry pushed himself to his knees, heard an engine whining from somewhere. Not the Chevelle. Something more…open. Hard to explain. He didn't have time to figure it out, more afraid than he'd ever been of anything in his life. Fuck, he wanted to huff right then and there. No, wanted his head clear. Only reason he'd started huffing in the first place was to control the nerves without having to go to a fucking doctor like he was some mental freak. He started coughing at even the thought of doctors, dentists. More than that, too. Spiders. Airplanes. Calling people on the phone. Public restrooms. He even got nervous thinking about sex, thinking he might blow too soon or disappoint with how small he was, and maybe that's why he'd felt comfortable with Fawn. She'd said he was just the right size. She'd stomp spiders in his trailer. She'd deal with bill collectors when they called. The things you take for granted until it's too late.

He'd caught a last glance as she fell. Her right eye stunned, wide, accusing. The rest all blood, hair, muck. Would he see that every night now? She'd be a ghost in dreams. She'd be dead no matter what. It's why he got nervous around corpses, too. One look at his grandma in her coffin, shrunk away to nothing, all waxy-like, and that's the only way he was ever able to remember her anymore.

The engine whine was louder. Motorcycle. Perry could make it out, a big hog. Like it was armored, all Mad Max-ed. Mounted by this monster, man, *biiig* guy. Wearing goggles but no helmet, just a bandana. Coal black hair like a mane shooting out the bottom. He wore a suede sportcoat, weird looking on him, like he was going to burst the seams out of the shoulders. Jeans were dark, looked new like he'd bought them at a Wal Mart twenty minutes ago. Boots were old, though, and dirty as shit.

Right behind him was a hot little number, helmeted, in chaps and a furry jacket. She rested her chin on the giant's shoulder, no doubt to keep the flying hair from slapping her in the face. Hugged him tight. Coming fast.

Perry's arms were up and waving before he thought much about it. He wandered into the middle of the road. At least with some company he didn't feel so vulnerable to the killers he'd escaped from. Let them come now. No *way* they'd kill him with an audience. Maybe they had a cell phone. Ring up the Troopers. He had his proof about Lafitte, and he had Fawn dead at the bar, probably still bleeding all over the carpet so much that the killers couldn't clean it up this fast. Even if there wasn't any reward money in it, Perry thought it was still worth it to turn it all over, no more vigilante bullshit. He was clean except for blood and worse spattered on his shirt and arms. No powder burns on his hands. For the first time in his life, he *wanted* the cops to question him, oh please please *please*.

Waving hard now. If the biker wanted around him, he'd have to swerve. Perry thinking, Give me a chance. Hell, I'd stop for you. The little voice in the back of his mind that coughed when he thought about airplanes said, No you wouldn't. Only reason you went after Lafitte was because you had the element of surprise.

Shit. What if these two were part of the same gang as the killers? What if Lafitte had an army of thugs coming to his rescue?

Did he still want them to stop?

His arms flagged some and he thought about waving the bike off and making a run for the farm house. Maybe they'd get the hint. Or maybe they had nothing to do with Lafitte but would still stop and chase him and beat him, rob him.

Perry felt like someone was tightening a noose around his neck. Hard time breathing. Like he was going to throw up. Coughed it away, coughed hard. The bike was right on him now and Perry couldn't make his feet move.

The bike eased to a stop in front of him. The engine wound down, off. The big man was staring, waiting. Perry noticed the girl was holding some sort of electronic thing, yellow, had a screen on it. Not an I-pod.

Perry sucked in air, rambled it all out. "I need a cell phone, please. I need to call the police. Someone...someone got shot. Please, call Nine One One. My grandpa's bar, back that way..." Took a few breaths while limply pointing behind him. "We've got a terrorist in there, but he's American, and his friends came to get him, said they were cops...shot...shot my...Fawn."

The big guy said, "What's a Fawn? Like Bambi?"

"No, no. She's...was...I dated her, and we're friends, but I think she's dead now. They shot her. God, they shot her." Perry couldn't stand up anymore. Sinking to his knees, feeling around until his fingertips touched the road. Fawn dead. Perry had run away. Had to live with that picture, the hole in her head. The open eyes. Fucking dead.

He said, "Please, a phone? Or just, I don't know. Just...God." Then he was crying and trying hard to stop by swallowing, but that hurt his throat and he cried more because he'd never been more scared. Scared of being scared. Waiting for that fucking Chevelle to show up again. Awful. Pussy. Should he say *fucking* and *pussy* right before he died? Maybe apologize to God for the bad things he'd done. He didn't know how. Didn't even know how bad he was compared to anyone else. The paint was bad, everyone said so. But he wasn't hurting people with it. He wasn't forcing it. He sold drugs to people who wanted them. Okay, that was bad. Sorry about the drugs. And sex before marriage. Still, he had loved her, so that couldn't be so bad. Just in case, Sorry about sleeping with Fawn. Because "sleeping with" is nicer than the word he shouldn't say before he died.

The big man told his girl to get off the bike, and she did, and then he did the same. Pulled a thin cell phone from his breast pocket, flipped it open. He looked down at Perry. "Got a couple bars. Wait, one keeps flickering. Still, one bar. Relax a minute, man. Keep it together."

Perry nodded, tried to stop his teeth from chattering by grinding them back and forth. He was cold, colder than he should have been, like it was snowing even though it wasn't. The girl, Jesus, tight jeans. He liked those jeans. Tight jeans and one of those cheap fur jackets, fake for sure. Perry thought Jamie Lee Curtis in *Trading Places,* but better looking in the face. Nicer hair. The girl calmed him down but got him hyped up too. Not now. Didn't need sex nerves on top of "gonna die" nerves. But it was okay. Guy had a phone. Guy was cool. The Chevelle hadn't shown up. Yeah, that was okay. Only thing he didn't like was the big revolver sticking out of the big guy's waistband. Perry got a glimpse when the wind whipped the coat open just enough. Guy caught it, buttoned it. No need to freak. That was common out here. Lots of people had guns. No problem.

Perry spoke up. "Please, Nine One One. Hurry."

Guy looked over at him like he'd forgotten Perry was there. Grinned all weird, face squinching like Santa Claus if he were a bouncer. The guy stared at his phone another moment before closing it, snugging it back into his pocket. He watched the girl then, still in her helmet, walking in a circle out in front of the bike out past Perry, who had to turn his head to see. His stomach had cramped up, paralyzed him. Couldn't keep them both in his field of sight without moving, and he didn't think he could move without shitting his pants.

After watching the girl a minute, the big guy said, "This it?"

The girl held out the little yellow gizmo. "Yeah, we're close."

Big guy turned to Perry. "Where's this bar?"

Perry shook his head. "Man, you've got to call the cops first. I'm not kidding. This is some bad shit."

The girl had walked farther ahead. She called out, "I see it. It's off the road, right past this rise. I'm pretty sure."

When she got back to where the big guy stood beside the bike, both looked down at Perry like he was a dog in a pen. That was a bad feeling, worse than the fake cops back at the bar. Couple of people examining you like it was their own private pet shop.

"You think?" she said.

Big guy grunted. Leaned his head left, right. That Santa Claus effect again. Perry had been too naughty.

He opened his mouth to beg but his jaw hurt. He said, "Please...please...just call Nine One One and leave me right here. Don't even give them your names. I'll never tell."

Big Guy ignored him, said to the girl, "FBI beat us to him?"

"Maybe. But he said there were only two." To Perry. "Only two, right?"

Perry nodded, even felt like a puppy. Nodded fast. "Please."

The big guy rested his hand on the gun lump under his jacket, sighed. Tapped his fingers one after the other. Sounded weird on the suede.

The girl said, "There's a farmhouse right there, and if the Feds are still at the bar..."

"I know. I can still do it."

He took a step towards Perry, who fell off his knees onto his ass then tried to scoot back, but the big guy leaned over and landed a hand on Perry's shoulder. Perry moaned because he felt sick inside and thought he'd choke if he tried to yell, and maybe these two would leave him alone if he looked more pathetic.

"Sorry, dude. Wish there were a better way."

The hand gripped the back of Perry's collar, lifted him like he was wet paper towels. His bowels finally went. He tried to pull away, but this guy, like some sort of wrestler. Pinned his arms, squeezed the fight out of him. Couldn't get any air to yell for help. The fake cops were real cops. Maybe they could hear him if he yelled, but he couldn't get enough air in, and then less and less each time until he was burning and sleepy. That's when a giant arm wrapped around his neck and made him gag, got in tight under his chin, another hand reaching across his face, digging into his cheek. And then a hard jerk. Fuck! Bones in his neck cracking.

Don't say fuck.

Sorry, God.

He was half numb down his left side. Worse than cold snow. Not all smooth the way the paint numbed him. This was just all bad. Big guy hugged Perry closer. Gripped tighter. Clawed his cheek again, and then—

Sorry. Sor. S.

STEEL GOD dragged the skinny dude's limp body to the side of the road, tossed it in the ditch, watched it flop once, roll, fling its arm out wide. Waited another minute. It didn't move anymore. Steel God checked himself, boot to shoulder, to make sure none of the guy's shit had leaked through or dripped out.

"I wonder," he said, mostly to himself. "How many people get away with killing up here? Not one car passed the whole time."

Kristal stood with crossed arms, the GPS locator tucked against her ribs. "He'll get found. We need to hurry."

Steel God picked some bugs off his beard. "You're right. It's why I brought you along."

"You brought me along because it was my idea."

If it wasn't a grin, it was close. "Okay. That's what you want to think. Maybe I was curious, you still wanting him after he slapped you around."

"It was just the one slap, and my pussy doesn't do my thinking for me."

"Who said anything about your pussy? I meant your heart, little lady."

Kristal turned her face away. "Can we hurry this up, please?"

Steel God stepped back over to the bike, smoothed his hand across the saddle. "Soon as you admit it."

She did that thing women do, shaking her head to let him know she's only saying something to shut him up. "It's what's best for the family, all of us. We need him."

Steel God pursed his lips and ran his tongue between them. The wind picked up. It whistled and brought with it the chug of a distant train that would be along soon enough. He looked back over at the body. It was hard to miss.

"Maybe so," he said. "That's what we're here to find out. How far ahead?"

"Not even a hundred yards."

"Let's walk the bike in, keep things quiet. At least we know what we're up against now."

Kristal said, "Yeah, real lucky running into that guy."

Steel God grunted as he took the chopper by the grips and pushed it towards the blip they'd been following ever since Mom called and gave them the coordinates after doing a reverse look-up on the number. Sure as hell sounded like Lafitte, she'd said, even if he didn't use the code.

They'd lost the first blip, the one for the bike. Steel God had a locator on all his guys' rides. None of them knew. He had decided it was worth tracking Billy awhile once Kristal admitted what she knew. Regardless of the girl's encouragement, Steel God would have gone after him anyway. Kristal spoke one hundred percent truth: they needed that motherfucking traitor Lafitte back like birds needed sky.

TWenty-seven

DESIREE sat in a window seat on her way to Denver, the lay-over where she would board a flight to Sioux Falls, which would land around twelve-thirty, six and a half hours after getting underway and costing her a goddamned fortune. Sun barely up, she hadn't slept except maybe a half hour on the flight, and shaken awake by turbulence, the doubt began. Under her breath, said, "What the hell am I doing?"

Still no peep from Franklin on her way to the airport, then the short wait before she had to turn her cell phone off. She would try again at every stop along the way. Hard to tell which was getting to her more—the anger or the fear. Once Franklin had come back from Minnesota, after the violent streak ebbed, she had thought the dangerous days were behind them. It was a promotion, after all. No one wanted the top dogs out there getting shot at by rogue terrorist cops. But what do you do when a top dog *wants* to get shot at?

Another bump. The sitcom on the overhead monitors blacked out for a second, then came back. This seat cost a fortune, Desiree thought again, and it's still third class. Typical. Like Franklin, given all his options laid out on fine linen and silver platters, he chooses the shittiest one. New Orleans? Post Katrina?

She didn't get it at first, thinking maybe he wanted to see some strippers and eat some gumbo. Then she warmed to the idea. It appeared Franklin's plan all along was to wait out his bosses, who were obviously looking for the nearest exits before the whole city sank into the Gulf. Fine with Desiree. The King of a sinking kingdom was still a King.

Glanced out the plane window as the engine cycled down, first hint of the initial descent into Denver. Shook her head. Why had she done it? Why act like a raging bitch instead of steering them towards a counselor or something? Like she could win just like that, all hardheaded and self-righteous. Shit. Too busy planning her own little strategy to see the one Franklin was cooking up under the FBI's nose.

Where the hell was he, anyway?

Would be a big waste, fly all that way only to discover Franklin was safe and sound at home, hidden away in a boardroom or drunk off his ass in the Quarter. In that case, it wasn't Franklin she was after. After speaking with McKeown, Desiree turned to her most valuable source of intel: other agents' wives. She's met enough of them along the way to realize they all had an understanding. Let the husbands play cloak and daggers "That's Classified" and "Need to Know Basis". You want to find out what's going on, ask a few wives, all of whom share the same fears and know what it's like to be in the dark, and you'll find enough to piece together the real story like a jigsaw puzzle. All you owed in return is the same honesty that was given to you.

That said, it took four calls to discover that McKeown had caught a plane for Sioux Falls in the middle of the night, and was last seen driving away with a local policewoman in an old sports car, most likely down a county road back into southwestern Minnesota. Desiree put it together, knew who they had found. The tricky part was finding where they had found him. She climbed aboard the plane still not sure, but was getting there, maybe, and hoping she'd make it before Franklin.

So impulsive. Probably all for nothing. But she felt pulled along, like it was instinct moving, like the Holy Ghost, like stepping in front of a bullet to save your husband.

The bullet was Lafitte, and always would be unless Desiree got to him first and did what none of these goddamned pretty boy agents couldn't do, didn't have the balls or the permission.

Desiree dinged the flight attendant, asked if she could get a gin and tonic.

"Ma'am, sorry, but we're not stocked like that for a morning flight."

Desiree sighed, patted the seat beside her and asked the attendant to sit for a second. The girl, white, maybe in her early twenties, with fire red hair pinned up to make her whole uniform look like it was for a sorority costume party, glanced up the aisle, then dropped the smile and sat.

Desiree whispered, "You got orange juice?"

"Yes we do."

"So how much would it take to get you to pour one of your own private stash of tiny vodka bottles into that orange juice for me, sweetie?"

The girl caught Dee's grin, looked into eyes that had spotted better liars than this little sky waitress before they'd even opened their mouths.

"Twenty bucks."

A nod. "Ten, and I won't bust you once we land."

THE STATE TROOPER lit Rome up somewhere south of Memphis. Rome had been on the road nearly six hours, stopping only for gas and coffee, keeping the speed up near eighty most of the way. When police lights flashed in the rearview, he thought:

1) It's going to be fine.

2) It's over right here.

The State Cop would either be a Dick or Groupie: ready to show how big his balls were, or eager as little Nate to please Mr. Special Agent Sir.

Rome pulled over. The squad slid in behind him. Sidelight hit the tag. Then hit the driver's sideview, wanting a look at the driver. Rome readied his ID. Ran his palm down his face and took in a deep breath.

Two Troopers in the car, both getting out, flanking the car. Not a good sign. Doing that slow gait Trooper walk. Rome lowered the window, got his grin ready, and crossed his fingers.

"Good morning, Officer."

The Trooper leaned in, pointed at the ID wallet on Rome's lap. "Mind if I take a look?"

Rome handed it over. The Trooper flipped it open, nodded, and handed it back. "Seeing if it was you, Agent Rome, that's all. How's the trip so far?"

Big smile now. Come on. "Probably better if I could fly."

The Trooper laughed, his partner laughed and Rome soaked it in. "I hear you, yeah. You'd think your bosses would loosen the purse strings, right? Don't they know how much gas costs?"

"Hey, they're the government. They're the ones making it rise."

Another round of jollies, and Rome settled down. This seemed to be going his way.

"Well, it's a good thing we ran across you like this. We heard from the D.A.'s office in Memphis, and they've asked that we escort you to the airport. Your chariot awaits."

The grin was real when Rome said, "Much obliged, gentlemen. Send my regards."

"Anytime." The Trooper reached out his hand. They shook. A few minutes later, Rome was hot on the trail of a Tennessee State Highway Patrol squad, lights and sirens full bore, Rome's emergency blinkers flashing, all because he'd happened to have a few drinks with an Assistant District Attorney from Memphis at a conference on Terrorism and the World Wide Web. That's why you had to play the social game. You never knew when you might need to borrow another state's Learjet.

That was answered prayer number one. Needed one more before time was up and he turned back into a pumpkin.

TWenty-eiGht

COLLEEN WAS AFRAID to move Lafitte. It already looked as if he was in a coma, so maybe trying to rouse him wasn't the best idea. But after a few more minutes of staring at Fawn's corpse, the way her fingers still curled as if clutching the gun that was now a few feet away where McKeown kicked it, the agent perked back up and said he wanted Lafitte sitting, feeling better, and talking, like, right fucking now.

First Colleen went down to the basement and found the wire, the puke, the blood. A torture chamber. Perry and Fawn weren't the patriotic do-gooders they made themselves out to be after all. The whole story had smelled bad anyway, and now Colleen knew why. Yeah, that was nice. She had the makings of a real detective after all. Always told Nate that if she was given a chance…but in Yellow Medicine County it was all farm kids and crankheads ratting each other out. No one had much of a chance to detect anything other than the office pool betting on who the next OD would be.

Upstairs, she told McKeown and he said, "Hm. That's good." Rubbed his hands together. Guy was shook up, like he hadn't been in a firefight before. Like he hadn't expected to ever be. Neither had Colleen, but she'd come close, and she'd seen enough movies, read enough novels and true crime books to take a deep breath and put it out of her head. Later. Deal with shock later. Deal with the situation here now.

"So, about calling someone," she said.

"Not right now." He waved her towards the bar. "Come on, help."

"Can't we wake him up where he is? I mean, they always say 'Don't move the victim'. See if he can move on his own."

McKeown shook his head, squeezed his eyes tight a moment. "No, no, we don't have *time*, remember? The quicker he's sitting up, the quicker I can get him talking and writing out a statement."

Colleen knelt beside Lafitte, lifted his forearm so McKeown could have a closer look. Shook it. Fingers pale and purple. "You want him to write? Look at his fucking hands! His wrists are bleeding, his fingers are bleeding. Jesus, you really don't know much besides what they taught you in class, and you're even fucking *that* up."

"Just...look...this is different. I need him to talk now."

"There'll be time later."

McKeown flung his arms wide, let out an exasperated breath and cluck and said, "No! There's no time. It's not what you think, all right? It's none of your business either, but can't you act like the fucking patrol cop you are and stop trying to be my partner?"

Colleen crossed her arms. "Real nice, cocksucker."

He stepped over to Lafitte, bent over and lifted under his shoulders. "Enough, come on. Shut up and help."

She took a step back, leaned against the bar. "Tell me why first."

McKeown gritted his teeth and groaned. He tried to drag Lafitte backwards, slipped after barely a foot. He dropped Lafitte, shook his hand wildly. "Mother*fuck!*"

"What?"

"Bent my fingernail back. Jesus." He tightened his left fingers around his right. Then took a look, shook them lighter the second time.

"You okay?"

Stood there breathing loudly through his nostrils, looked around at the tables.

"Maybe there," he pointed to one against the wall. "Let him sit up, see if it helps."

Colleen didn't move. Pushed her tongue into her bottom lip.

McKeown said, "Listen, I'm sorry, okay? I'm under a lot of pressure here, and I promise I'll tell you later. I'm sorry for what I said. Now...please?"

He reached under Lafitte's shoulders again and waited, looking up at her. Colleen looked the other way, thinking this guy had some other agenda. She didn't like it. Only two choices for her were to kill the son of a bitch or take him in and let him face justice. Whichever way, she wanted him conscious too, at least. Shooting a man in a coma wasn't going to make her feel any better. Letting McKeown play with the system wasn't going to do it, either.

"Pretty please, Colleen, I need your help."

What an asshole. She rolled her eyes and bounced her hip off the bar, unfolded her arms and stepped across Lafitte. "You take one arm, I'll take the other. And don't go too fast, in case—"

And then it all went loud.

THEY'D DECIDED THIS WAY: Steel God was to bust in the front door and shoot the first person who wasn't Lafitte. Then Kristal, who had already gotten a peek inside a side window, would follow and take out whoever was left.

Steel God was already hotheaded when he didn't see Lafitte's aqua-blue hog in the parking lot. "Little prick's done sold it, I'll bet. Take me up on it?"

"I want to hear it from him first."

"Good. We'll rescue him, and then I'll punch him in the gut until he tells us what he did with it."

At least there were two cars in the parking lot Kristal could choose from on their way out. Only one was worth the trouble—the Chevelle had been loved by someone, while the 'Stang was a waste of space. Could be one or the other was leftover by a drunk the night before, thus no keys. Kristal hoped not. It had never occurred to them that Lafitte's chopper wouldn't be wherever he was.

Kristal came back after squinting through the dirty shaded window and said, "Two of them, man and woman, standing over Billy. He doesn't even look awake."

Steel God winked and pulled out his revolver. "Ready?"

COLLEEN could've sworn the door had exploded even though she recovered her sight enough to see it had only been kicked all the way open, sunlight now full-strength. Then a giant blocked the light and pointed a gun towards McKeown, who had already dropped Lafitte's arm and was reaching for his piece. Lafitte was falling and Colleen was going with him, yelling at McKeown to duck.

A real explosion. Fire sparked out of the giant's gun and McKeown danced and shook, sounded like a large slap, his shirt suddenly all red around his stomach.

Colleen tried to keep Lafitte from going down too hard by proping her body against him, but it wasn't happening and she had to choose: let him go or let him fall on her. She let him go. She reached for her gun. Should never have put it back in her holster. Should never have helped McKeown drag Lafitte. Should never have left home.

She had only looked down a few seconds, trying to get a bearing on her hands and the gun before rising for a good shot, but it was long enough. There was another person. A girl, like a fucking teenager or something. Right in front of her, kicking a boot heel at her face.

Colleen raised her arm too late. Heel cracked into her cheek. Ripped that skin open like a peach. She scooted back, needed space. Needed cover. Couldn't decide. Need to get her fucking gun up.

By the time Colleen had it, the girl was kicking again. The hand. *Crack.* Nate's .45 went that-a-way across the floor.

Colleen, flat on her back, black boot on her chest connected up to painted-on jeans and a cheap fake-fur jacket. Young face with hair hanging around, framing a pale tough bitch, tough as Colleen. Not tougher, though. It hadn't been a fair fight. Girl held her pistol two-handed, steady.

"Fucking whore," Colleen said, holding her busted hand tight against her body.

The girl shrugged. "Better than being a dyke."

"Why does everyone keep saying that?"

But the girl had turned her attention to Lafitte, crumpled on the floor. Took him in sadly, droopy. Long sigh. She knew him. She cared about him. "He's over here. Come check him."

The giant answered, voice like a bear in a cave. "Shoot that cop and do it yourself."

"Not yet. Come on."

Colleen heard some groaning from McKeown. She lifted her head as far as she could, trying to remember where he fell. Got something that looked like his shoulder. Groaning. Hard breaths. Squeezed out, "*Sh-iiii-t.*"

Colleen said, "Hey, are you okay over there? Talk to me, McKeown. Come on."

The girl stamped her foot on Colleen and pointed the gun some more. "Shut up."

"Talk to me!"

She watched as the giant stepped over to McKeown, toed his side. Then knelt, took the agent's pistol, grumbled something Colleen couldn't hear. But McKeown nodded his head, tried to say yes, but his teeth chattered.

The giant stood, tucked the extra pistol into his belt, and walked over to where Lafitte lay. Knelt again. His knees cracked. Older than he seemed, maybe. Took his time getting down there. Breathed out "Jeeee-sus." Placed a hand on Lafitte's chest, the carving, then held his palm an inch or so above Lafitte's mouth.

"Out cold," he told the girl. "Weak breaths. Somebody fucked him up seriously. We need to hurry."

Colleen was thinking she'd take the girl on. All she needed

220 Anthony Neil Smith

was surprise and a big rush of adrenaline. The training was foolproof, right? Cops always had the upper hand. Even without guns. Most people didn't want to shoot cops. Only the ones that really knew what they were in for if they *didn't* shoot a cop, but that wasn't this girl. Problem was that this giant, he was the type. Colleen needed off this floor. Needed to break this chick's leg. Needed to maneuver around her, take the gun. Take out the giant, no warning or anything.

She had forgotten about her hand, though. Took a quick look. Bad swelling, purple and blue. Throbbing. Making her nauseous. She thought she was ready for anything. Holy shit, why this? Holy shit.

The girl was speaking to her again. "—the keys?"

Had zoned out. "What?"

"The fucking keys to the Chevelle? Or the Mustang? Either one. I need the fucking keys."

Oh, hell no. Not going to take Nate's car. No no no.

But maybe that would give her some room to move. Distraction.

"My pocket. Keys are in my jeans pocket."

The girl lifted her boot. Crouched over Colleen's legs, patted her pockets. Yeah, the keys were right there. Girl reached her fingers inside, trying to snug past the lip.

Bingo.

Colleen twisted hard, pinched the girl's hand in there. She collapsed, trying to jerk her hand out. Too late. Colleen had already locked the skank between her legs, grabbed at her gun arm and missed, kept trying. Fuck the pain fuck the pain fuck it fuck it fuck it.

The girl was swinging the arm, Colleen keeping that fucking gun away but she needed to control the limb. Girl shouting, "God! God, help!"

Didn't take her for the religious sort.

Something shifted, and Colleen got some leverage. Caught the girl's forearm and squeezed, all her strength, inched her way up to the wrist. Colleen's feet, beneath her, pushing her body up, the girl still down. Colleen got the wrist twisted pretty bad and was about to slam it against the edge of the nearest table when she knew something was wrong. Felt it, like a chill in the air. Only took a few seconds but was all slo-mo like chewing taffy at the State Fair. The giant rushing at her. Grabbing her broken hand, squeezing. She was shocked silent by the pain. Icy all over. Sucked in icy air. The man's fist rushing towards her face and Colleen swore it sounded just like a train right up until—

STEEL GOD didn't let Colleen drop to the ground after slamming his fist into her nose. Oh, yeah, broke that fucker. Kristal heard it pop. But after, Steel God wrapped his arms around the cop and eased her over against the wall, sitting up. She wasn't quite passed out, wasn't quite with us. She was whimpering, but more like she was throwing a weak tantrum. Blowing blood all over, having to breath through her mouth, gulping too much, she said a few times, "It's not fair. Goddamn it (gulp) …not…ah…fair."

"I know," Steel God told her. "I know."

"Why? Why is all this (gulp)…why…why me?"

"Wrong place, wrong time. You were outnumbered. That's the way it is sometimes. Don't beat yourself up over it."

Kristal couldn't believe it. Steel God actually liked this cop. Admired her or something. She knew he was like that, always attracted to strong women who knew how to take care of themselves, but this was an obvious lezzie farm girl playing at being a cop. Come on, right? The cunt got in a cheap shot, was all. Kristal *owned* that's bitch's ass.

Steel God turned to Kristal. "Get me some water, will you?"

"We don't have time."

"Yeah, we do. Go on and get some water."

"What about Billy?'

"Two fucking minutes, missy. Get water. *Now.*"

Kristal pushed off the ground. Shook her arm. Felt like the wrist had been spun up tight like a rubber band. Passed by the

FBI guy. He was on his back, hands covering the spreading red puddle on his gut, knees up but swaying back and forth. Every breath had a "Ck-ah" in it. She wasn't sure if he deserved that. Guy was trying to take Billy in, yeah, but that was his job. Wasn't his fault Billy was so smashed up. Maybe they hit these two a little hard.

Whatever. Only way to survive on the road—strike first.

Behind the bar, Kristal lifted a mug, then saw a small glass-front fridge under the bar stocked with beer cans, beer bottles, some energy drinks, diet pop, and bottled water. Fuck the mug. She put it down and opened the fridge, grabbed a brand name water.

She twisted the top off as she walked back to where Steel God and the cop were still talking, real low. The cop said something about "I deserve my revenge. It's not fair," and Steel God answered, "Wish it all worked like it does in movies." He was quiet a long moment. Laughed, said, "Shit, I haven't seen a movie in years. Not since *Star Wars Episode One*. Was so fucking excited to see that. Man. Yeah."

Kristal passed the water bottle down to Steel God. "Here."

He took it without thanks, poured some into his palm, and told the cop, "Hold still."

The cop nodded. Then Steel God splashed the water on the cop's face, eased his hand down under her nose, over her mouth. Wiped the blood away.

He said, "Again?"

The cop nodded again.

Once more, a palm full of water. Smoothing it across her face. Cleansing. Kristal even thought she looked slightly prettier. Not even afraid much, like she was all prepared in her heart, that Sunday School shit.

Steel God lifted the glass to the cop's lips and let her take a few swallows. Then he stood, placed the glass on a table.

"I won't mess up your face," he told her.

"Thank you." Sniff. Pointed with her head towards the FBI guy. "What about him?"

Steel God stared at the moaning agent a good minute. "He's a pussy. Deserves what he gets."

The cop thought about it a moment. Then, "Okay."

Steel God stood back from her about four feet, lifted his gun and aimed it dead center at the cop's chest.

Then there was a loud *Croak*. Bullfrog times ten. Kristal flinched, yelped, realized it wasn't the gun. Then a second time, sounded more like "*Don't. Wait.*"

Lafitte's voice, strained to the breaking point. She glanced down. He was holding up his left hand, trying to push himself onto his right elbow.

"Shit, it's Billy! Hold on!"

Kristal was beside him, kneeling, helping. Stunned by the shape he was in, just now getting a glimpse of "Baby Raper" newly scraped into his skin. It chilled Kristal. She got Lafitte sitting up. Steel God stayed where he was, gun still raised.

If Lafitte was conscious, it was barely. God knows how he knew what was going on. Kristal wasn't even sure if he was aware of her. He kept pushing, legs scrambling. Trying to stand. Kristal kept *shushing* and telling him to calm down, that everything was okay, but he acted as if she were stray furniture he'd gotten tangled in.

He said, "Don't shoo...don't shoot em."

Finally raising his eyes to Steel God. Said it again.

"Don't shoot them."

Like a staring contest.

Steel God. "Got to do something with them."

Lafitte shook his head. Eyes closed. "Don't kill them."

Steel God. A sigh. "I'm tired of doing favors for you, boy. How about 'Thanks for saving my life, Big G'? Some fucking gratitude?"

Lafitte coughed. He gripped Kristal hard. She wrapped her arms tight across his chest, shook violently along with his coughing. Choking. An unholy mess.

Cleared his throat. "Please...*don't*...kill them. I'll...anything you say. Anything. Just, please."

The girl cop on the floor moaned, said, "Fuck, get it over with. It's not fair."

That stopped Steel God cold. Bent his arm up, pointing the pistol towards the ceiling. "You're saying you want to die?'

"If I can be with Nate, it'll be okay. I did my best. He'll understand. I want to be with Nate."

"You sad, sorry little bitch." Steel God relaxed, gun back into his waistband. "Here I thought you was braver than shit, but I don't grant death wishes, honey."

He turned to Kristal, but she dropped her eyes to Lafitte's bruised face. Not going to look him in the eye. She got Lafitte back and that was all she gave a shit about. Getting pawned off to Richie Rich like trailer trash. Like a used blow-up doll. Fucker was going to pay. She wasn't going to let him spit on her, trample her. Never met a man like Lafitte before and she was damned sure going to chew his ass soon as he was better. Chew his ass so that he'd never even *think* about dissing her again. Next break-up would be on Kristal's terms.

Lafitte was still shaking. Breathing was raspy.

Kristal said, "We need to hurry."

Steel God said, "Okay." Jiggled the keys to the Chevelle. "Here's an idea."

TWenty-nine

ROME FELL ASLEEP on the flight from Memphis to Sioux Falls, right as the clusters of cities and towns faded into brown rectangles, farmland already harvested for the year. Like another world. Weird how even though these were giant tracts of Mother Nature, the perfect angles carved by roads made it look more unnatural than the sprawling suburbs of the metro areas, meandering without rhyme or reason. Fell asleep without even realizing—been up for so long, going full speed—and before he knew it the co-pilot was easing him awake, telling him to buckle up. An easy landing, the surroundings like some atomic waste-land, scarred prairie cut through by a stream blocked with a long dead tree trunk. One of the smallest airports he had ever seen.

He checked his watch. Jesus, past lunchtime already. They gave him coffee and a breakfast bar on the plane, just happened to have some in the galley. He was starving. Couldn't think about that right now.

Inside, out of the gates and down a people-mover to a ter-minal with a giant bronze statue of some flyboy who must've been important around here. Didn't have time to find out who—Lind-bergh? That didn't make sense. Didn't care. Rome instead looked around and found his ride. Middle-aged white guy in casual khakis, sweater, and a bomber jacket, rather than risk the full uniform in "enemy" territory. Striding over, pulling a hand from his pocket. They shook.

"Franklin, long time."

"Good to see you, Wyatt."

"Where's your bag?"

Rome grinned. "Like I said, not that kind of trip."

"But it *is* Lafitte, right?"

Nod. Wink.

Wyatt looked around like he was a bad spy. About the same age as Rome, got along well. Wyatt was a Lieutenant with the Minnesota Highway Patrol and had been in the know when Rome was working undercover for Homeland Security at the Indian casino in Pale Falls, and they'd shared some beers and conversations. Even a couple of fishing trips up to Wyatt's cabin on the lake around Alexandria.

He kept in touch after Rome was recalled to Washington, sided with his friend, in private at least, saying, "Fucking Lafitte. Wished the storm surge would've dragged him under the Gulf rather than washed his sorry ass up here."

It was a no-brainer, then, when Rome needed a step two after the plane ride. Wyatt didn't even question Rome when he said, "You can't tell a soul. We're talking Top Secret government stuff, buddy. Off the books."

Wyatt said, "Just so you know, the home office is on the lookout for you. Sent out a notice. Not quite an APB, but still, they *strongly* suggest that anyone who's had contact with you phone in pronto."

"You tempted?"

Wyatt shrugged. "Maybe to see what they're saying about you, if I thought they would tell me. But you Feds, I wouldn't even get a fruit basket for my trouble. Goddamn, I could've slept all night and never had a clue about all the shit going down. After your call, though, turned on the scanner and it was all over the place. Just be glad I had some pull. Locals were trying to keep it under wraps, even though they're denying it. Not much my folks can do overall. I was able to squeeze a few favors."

"Then what's the plan?"

"Well, I followed up what you said. Can't find your man. McKeown, right?"

"That's him." Traitorous son of a bitch. Rome thought he must be a magnet for betrayers. Surprised his wife still wanted him so bad, hadn't run off and had an affair. Maybe that was next. "Like a ghost."

"The woman he was with, we traced her back to something weird earlier. Some kids say a guy gave one of them a motorcycle, left with the town slut, sounds like. She buys the boys beer and cigarettes, a little older. You know. So the boy's dad calls the cops, and this Sheriff's deputy shows up, not even from the right county."

"This is Colleen Hartle, right? Yellow Medicine deputy."

"Yeah, yeah, that's her. She's not even in uniform, driving her boyfriend's souped-up Chevelle. Jesus, you heard about earlier—"

Rome nodded. "Bad news. Goddamn."

"She talked to the kid, got some details, and split. Our guys caught her on the highway and held her until McKeown got there. Then she and him took off together. Last we heard."

The terminal was big and echoing, a few handfuls of people waiting for arriving passengers or holding off going through the security checkpoint. He smelled something greasy. Pizza at the little food court off to his right. Tempting. Would probably make him puke, though. Maybe some beignets instead. Shit, they don't do beignets up here. The cold shocked Rome. Goddamn, only just now chilly in New Orleans, but up here was like a walk-in freezer. He'd forgotten all about that. Crossed his arms and hugged hard.

Rome said, "I'm guessing the local cops got riled when they heard she showed. Probably woke up George Tordsen."

Wyatt held up a thumb real close to his index finger. "Little bit."

"So how do we avoid the shitstorm, mister?"

Wyatt arched his back, rose a couple of inches. Placed his hand on his chest like he was offended. "Why, sir, it always comes back to good police work. Thing is, this one kid was off with his uncle or something, so no one could find him last night. One of the boys said this kid they call Goof was off chasing the biker. I figured that's just a crazy story, you know. Kid's putting on a show for his friends."

"Okay."

"As soon as his uncle dropped him off, we were there. No need driving all the way back home, right? Goof had to show up sooner or later. Too bad I didn't grab the uncle."

"Why didn't you?"

Shrug. "Like I said. Thought it was a fib."

Rome held his breath a second. "It wasn't?"

Wyatt turned on a floodlight smile. A *You Owe Me Big* smile. "Kid gave up the truth. We went down to check it out. Man, have I got a crime scene to show you."

Rome's breath caught. A real fucking lead. Fuck the FBI. He needed to piss. Badly.

"Come on. What do you know?"

"Oh, I'm going to tell you. Going to eek it out on the way. More fun like that. I mean, I figured you had been monitoring all this, which is why your call didn't seem so out of place at the time. But if your own people are desperately searching for you and McKeown, shit. All I ask is that you scratch my back. I made my people hold back just for you. If you're going back up the ladder, you'd better promise to take me with you, buddy."

Bladder so full he was dancing some. "Fine, yeah, I promise. Let me hit the head first."

Wasn't even two steps towards the restroom when he heard a woman call out, "Franklin!"

Not just any woman.

DESIREE had landed fifteen minutes earlier than scheduled. One of the advantages of flying into such an unappealing destination, she guessed. Well, that wasn't fair. Just the agitation and booze talking. After all, if it was called Sioux Falls, there had to at least be a waterfall and some Indians or some shit like that. Nothing out the window gave her much hope that she'd be sticking around to do any sightseeing, though. The vodka the flight attendant had sold her eased her regret. Hard to get too upset about missing much of the rest of the country when you lived in New Orleans.

The airport was nothing more than a glorified garage. Tiny piece of shit. Made it easier to find her way, certainly. The plan was to drive up into Minnesota with the wife of a guy Franklin had been close to up here. He'd talked about fishing with him. Wyatt Bullerman. Wife's name was Olivia, and more than happy to tell what she knew. Especially since Wyatt had been gone all night himself, off chasing down a phantom biker that led to a possible murder at a bar.

So all Desiree had to do was rent a car, program the navigator for Montevideo, Minnesota, and maybe stop for lunch somewhere along the way. If Franklin ever got his head out of his ass and called her, how would that go? "Oh, yes, baby. Just so happens I'm in Minnesota, too. I'm not kidding. No indeed, mister."

First, a nice long trip to the ladies' room. Goddamn flight was too bumpy to use the plane's stall, so she held on until they landed and practically scrambled for the restroom nearest the gate. Stopped cold by the CLOSED FOR CLEANING sign.

Duck into the men's room? Not like there was anyone here right now. Not that the men would mind. No, no, don't get noticed. Don't get arrested.

Beeline for the main terminal, where the restrooms were always larger anyway. Not hard to find at all, and that people-mover didn't hurt one bit.

About five minutes later, she stepped out of the restroom, about to turn towards the rental car desks, when she saw her motherfucking husband standing right there. Right there in the fucking airport terminal in the same clothes he'd put on right before leaving her high and dry the night before. Talking to some salt-and-pepper-haired white dude, looked like another cop to her. She had radar for cops after being married to one all this time.

He wasn't *on* the same plane, was he? Did she overlook him? No way. Not possible. Only twenty or so people on the flight in the first place.

Franklin held up a finger for his friend. Dee heard him say, "I've got to hit the head." And he turned her way.

Like, what the fuck was she supposed to do?

"Franklin!"

THE THREE OF THEM sat in Wyatt's squad as he drove them out of South Dakota and on towards the crime scene. Once Dee appeared out of thin air, she had to come along. No other way around it.

"You could've just told me. Thought we were done with all these secrets."

Franklin sat with his wife in the backseat. Wyatt kept looking in on them. For a couple that had been married for as long as these two, and who were angrier at each other than he'd ever seen except in movies or on *Dr. Phil*, there was still a spark. It raised the hair on his arms. He wished he and Olivia could recapture that. They had plenty at first. She had been divorced with a kid. He'd been married with two. Slept with her a good six months before his wife found out. Goddamned divorce nearly drove him to swallow his gun, but Olivia was there the entire time, talking him through, comforting him. Yeah, like it was meant to be. Add twelve years and things had stagnated some. But, Jesus, if Franklin and Desiree could keep the fire stoked, why not Liv and him?

Made a note: Got to ask Rome how he did it.

And, hell, maybe the four of them could go grab some steaks when this was said and done. Seemed natural. Wyatt was stunned when Franklin introduced them and Dee said, "Olivia's told me all about you." How'd she pull that off?

Franklin was cowed. Couldn't meet her eyes. Bumbled through an explanation.

Dee cut through that haze right quick: "Lafitte?"

Okay, maybe Wyatt didn't want his wife *that* sharp. A man needed a few things hidden in the gun safe, after all.

"OF COURSE it's Lafitte." Franklin finally looked up. Then out the window. Fields. More fields. Black, straw-covered, far as you could see to the pale gray sky on the horizon. "It's always been. You saw what he did to me. What's that fucking thing the shrink said? Closure? Think I can get closure while he's out there doing fuck knows what?"

Raising his voice, pissing Dee off more. If not for Wyatt, they'd probably keep shouting in each others' face and then pull over, run out into an empty field and fuck so loud that whatever hicks might be able to hear can listen as much as they fucking want to, because fucking Dee is the only thing that even came *close* to making him feel like a man again after getting beat down by that…that…fuck…that…goddamn it…*Lafitte*.

Dee said, "You don't yell at me, Franklin."

"I'm not yelling at *you*. I'm just yelling. Just fucking yelling." He slapped the cage separating front from back. "Right, Wyatt? Yelling is yelling, right?"

"Can't say I'm enjoying it, buddy."

"Well, then." One more slap. "Okay. I'm sorry."

Desiree leaned forward and said to Wyatt, "You said we're going to a bar?"

"Yes ma'am. The owner showed up this morning, and there's blood everywhere, plus some goo on the walls that could be brains, we think. From how it's all spaced out, we're talking several people."

"Oh, God," Desiree said. "That's where Agent McKeown was headed."

What? She knew a lot more than Rome had thought. Must have got in touch with McKeown on her own somehow. Maybe he had called looking for Rome. That changed things.

"You talked to McKeown?"

Dee nodded. "I was looking for you, so I tricked him into thinking he was calling you. He said he was following a lead. If Wyatt says he hooked up with that girl—"

"Okay, I know that. Fine. But you actually talked to him?"

"He was out on the country roads, couldn't get a signal. He told me to let you know he was following a lead."

Rome sighed through his nose. "Shit." Pissed at the kid, yeah, but scared for him, too. What the hell was he thinking going after Lafitte alone? To Wyatt, "What else?"

"Then there's the basement, where we think Lafitte was tied up. Puke and blood all over, plus some speaker wire that had been around his wrists, stretched and snapped. That's what this kid Goof told us, the one out with his uncle and the uncle's ex-girl-friend, the town slut I was talking about."

"Town slut?" Dee let that one out slow and loose.

"Sorry, just…well, she was. Bought cigarettes and booze for teenagers in exchange for oral sex once they'd gotten drunk."

"Okay, fine, got it."

"Not sure if we're right, but you've got to see this. We think Lafitte scaled a pole, then snapped the wire, then got out into the bar. Just unbelievable."

Franklin said, "But we've got no bodies, no DNA on the brains yet, no eyewitness, no security cameras, nothing."

Wyatt nodded. "On the nose."

Franklin turned to Desiree, all the shame on his face dried up. "See, baby? That's why I won't get over Lafitte until he's dead, cremated, and his ashes scattered during a tropical storm."

She eased back into the seat, snugged her ass in. "My worry is that he thinks the same thing about you."

Thirty

GODDAMN, Colleen thought. God.....DAMNitfuck
fuckfuck.

Should have killed him. Should have fucking killed him.
Why the fuck didn't she...?

The hardest thing was that she was grateful to be alive. She
hated herself for it. Lightweight. Not cop material. Not Fed material. Just another shitty *poseur*.

Took a breath through her nose, hard to do. All swelled up,
broken for sure. Throb, throb, throb. Wanted to put some pressure on it, but her hands were tied behind her, one fucking broken, felt two sizes too big. She was on her stomach, hog-tied on
the backseat of Perry's Mustang. On the floor beside her, McKeown was dying slowly, had to be. Gut shot, not taking it too well,
bleeding, coughing, weaker by the hour. Couldn't have been more
than an hour already. Didn't even know where the fuck she was.
Just knew that bitch in the fake fur coat drove them away from
the bar, never said a word while Colleen bucked and cursed in
back. Got someplace shady, got out, and that's the last she'd seen
of the girl and her giant. Not to mention the guns—Nate's .45,
McKeown's service pistol. Hell to pay for those.

Worse, the giant had somehow shoved Fawn and Perry into the trunk together. Colleen didn't even want to think about that right now. She was too busy working on keeping McKeown conscious, fighting, while she wrestled with the wire and duct tape around her ankles. Not even worth trying to free her wrists. Automatic lost cause.

"Hey, hey, you're still with me, right?"

He was moving like he had bad cramps. Taped up wrists and ankles, but without the embarrassing extra cord she had keeping her arms pulled taut, calves curled up. She was born a farm girl and knew this position far too well. Had done it to many an animal herself.

Should've killed him.

Because....*fuck*...like this, she wouldn't die for a long time. Pressure on her lungs after awhile would speed things up, but there was a good chance she could be here for days. McKeown would be dead by morning. The hicks in the trunk would start to rot, and then McKeown, and...Jesus.

She thought about trying to roll to the side or scoot up through the space between the front seats. Open the door with her teeth or something. But every rescue fantasy turned bad when she thought about getting stuck, hurting herself more, suffocating.

Embarrassing.

Nate went out without a fight. Just screamed like a girl while the fire fucked him over. Not quick, not on his own terms. That fucking high-pitched spine-shivering scream, it was there to stay. Every memory of Nate was tainted by that noise bullhorning out of his mouth instead of "I love you" and "You're the One, Sweetness."

Colleen didn't plan on going out helpless. She came damn close to getting taken down by a badass biker with some heavy-duty artillery. That would've rocked. That, man, was *it*. Never been more ready to get her wings. Then that fucking Lafitte...

She'd been holding her breath. Forgot. Let it out and coughed.

McKeown wasn't moving at all.

"Hey!"

Nothing.

She craned her neck as far as she could, close to his ear.

"*Hey!* Talk to me. Wake up up up up up! Come on, boy, stay with me!"

"I'm good," he said. "Please, don't talk anymore."

"We need to talk. Tell me a joke or something. Tell me your name."

"You know my name."

"Your *first* name. Like, I'm Colleen, you know. Or do all of you guys talk like you're on the *X Files*? Last names even for people you're fucking."

"No…damn it." Even sounded pissy while gutshot. What a tool. He finally said, "Josh."

"Good, okay, Josh. Tell me about that guy in Memphis."

McKeown rumbled low in his chest, like laughing with his mouth closed. "You want me to talk about him?" Took a few breaths. "Best night of my life, maybe. Or close enough. What happens the next day? I'm going to die. Let me do that on my own, okay?"

"You're not going to die."

"You think? Can you do surgery with, what, psychic powers or something?" Another breath. Cough. A bad cough. He tried to stop the cough halfway through and it hurt even worse, Colleen could tell. Him coughing and saying "Oh god, no, no" and jumping like he'd been struck with an electric wire. She laid her head down on the seat to take the strain off her neck and waited him out. Nothing she could do. Goddamn Lafitte. Thought he was doing her a *favor*? Trying to be the hero again? Like he ever really was in the first place. Stupid Sheriff ate up his story like it was chocolate pie.

McKeown eased back into a regular rhythm, in and out, in and out. She tried again.

"I'll have my legs free in a few minutes, I promise. I'll get free and go get help." No way. Not going to happen. The giant had done this plenty of times before, she could tell. He was experienced at killing and leaving for dead equally. Could be a caring man, like back at the bar when he washed her face, made her feel like she was a worthy adversary, some sort of chivalry. Vice versa, he could be a sadistic motherfucker, knowing damn well what leaving them in this car would mean. Not just the dying part, which wasn't so bad, but the helpless part. The terror. The time to think. Sit and think what it would've been like if they hadn't gone chasing Lafitte. If she had stayed at home after Tordsen brought her back. If she'd had a long cry and downed some heavy painkillers and slept until the funeral.

Sit and think about when someone would stumble across their bloated, wormy corpses, dinner for the foxes and deer.

If that man would've just pulled that trigger.

"Keep talking," Colleen said. Needed to keep her mind off it all, too. "This guy, what was his name again?"

"Please, come on."

"Tell me."

She didn't think he was going to. Nothing but steady breath from McKeown for a long while. Little coughs. Cleared his throat. Spit. But then, "Alex. He played in a band."

Pointless or not, hearing him talk got her working hard on freeing her ankles again. "Good. What sort of band?"

Thirty-One

FOR A FEW GLORIOUS, sensory-deprived, echoing seconds, Lafitte thought he was dead. Free. Pure. Floating. At peace. And then he realized he couldn't be dead because this felt too good to be Hell.

Once the pain returned all over his body and the cuts on his chest lit up like firecrackers, he even imagined he might prefer Hell after all. Jesus. Fawn and Perry put him through the ringer. He'd been run through it before by wannabe terrorists, thugs, his own colleagues, and even that fucking Homeland Security agent, but this one might have been the worst. He couldn't remember anything past breaking the wires and getting up those stairs. Dialing the number that had been burned into his memory. A blur of voices. Many blurs when his eyes would open a slit, not get what he was seeing, then going back into the haze.

Except right at the end, a dream or something maybe, where Steel God had returned like Jesus in all his glory with this giant fucking sword except it was a gun instead and it wasn't protruding forth from his angry mouth. Going to shoot Deputy Colleen in the face. Colleen. What the hell was she doing there? Colleen the Avenger? Some other guy on the floor nearby, shot but still kicking. Steel God was going to shoot her? What had she done that was so awful?

Whatever. Lafitte told him not to. Silly, doing that to her. She spared him back on that road earlier, so the least he could do, you know.

Kristal. Was she there? Sounded like her, felt like her. Held him so softly. Yeah, if Steel God was there, maybe she was too. But why? Not like God needed any help.

Lafitte wondered if he'd had a heart attack. Body can only take so much stress. He was warm all over, the hurt parts not hurting as bad as they should. Stung like he'd stepped on a hornet's nest, though. That smell, couldn't place it, like incense. And, what, a salty taste in his mouth, around his lips? Tried to lift his arm. He could, but it was heavy. Wet. Then suddenly it was free and cold and not so wet. Shocked him fully awake, eyes wide, staring at his hand. He was lying in a bathtub, steaming water right up to his chin.

Looked up. A small bathroom, florescent lights, wide mirror. It was a hotel bathroom. And sitting on the toilet lid beside him, knees wide, elbows on his lap, was Steel God, holding a cigarette.

"Here." God lifted the cig to Lafitte's mouth. Lafitte didn't smoke, shook his head. God kept it right there. "Not what you're thinking. It'll help."

Lafitte caught on. It was *right there*, so he toked. Coughed some but still liked it. Explained the odor, at least. He cleared his throat and tried talking. "Jesus, man, in a hotel room?"

"There's vents."

"Yeah, into the room next door. Don't you know how this works?"

God waited while Lafitte took another hit, then hit it himself.

Said, "Look, Billy, I'm not usually like this, but I'm starting to feel, like, unappreciated or something. You call for help, and all I've heard from you is bitching."

Lafitte looked around some more. His clothes in a pile by the tub, looked trashed. His body warbling under all that water, looked tattooed almost. Bad tats, bled all under the skin. Bruises and cuts. But nothing broken, nothing gushing. Just a bad day, that's all it was. Question was, could he have gotten through that day on his own?

"I'm sorry. Really, I don't mean to be an ass. Look at me, though."

"Oh, they took you to town." Steel God pointed at Lafitte's chest. "Looks like we've finally found a nickname for you."

Lafitte dropped his gaze to the scars. Once again, still there: "Baby Raper."

"Fucking hicks. Did you run into them?"

A nod. "We got the guy. Think that FBI agent killed the girl. Don't worry, though. We handled it okay."

"What are you talking about, FBI? You didn't kill that cop, right? I told you—"

Steel God grunted, waved the joint around. "She's alive. They're both alive. But, fuck, man, I couldn't let them *go*, right? We wouldn't have got this far if I had."

Lafitte sat up. "What happened? You hurt her? You didn't need to fucking hurt her or anybody. We've got enough to deal with already."

Steel God rose up, chest puffed, but Lafitte held his ground. Guy could smack him, he supposed. Probably the worst of it. God said, "You ain't dealt with *shit*. All you've done is get yourself caught by a couple country yokels near about put you in a coma. I told you, make that call, and you did. So how about stopping the goddamn lectures and get yourself in shape to ride?"

"The only fucking reason you've made it this far is that I have to lecture your ass on everything, remember? The whole fucking reason you took me in."

Steel God said, "Shiiii—" and then let it fade to a groan, looking round the room like he didn't know where to look. But it told Lafitte the man agreed with him.

Couple minutes went by. Lafitte sank back into the tub. "Seriously, though. Thanks." Decided not to mention that as soon as he was up to speed, he planned on taking off again. Still had some business down South. Still had a chance to get a better life back. Soon as Steel God figured out what was going on, Lafitte would be a marked man. Already heard it in his voice—this rescue demanded repayment in loyalty. No more vacations. Damn right Lafitte owed the man big time, but sometimes it ain't about that. God would just have to get by on his own.

Didn't want to think about Kristal yet either. He hoped she wasn't using this to get back in with him. Not going to let it happen.

The water, starting to cool now. There was a box of Epsom salt beside the sink. They'd actually stopped for Epsom salt. Nice. He closed his eyes again.

Steel God said, "Where's that fucking bike I gave you?"

KRISTAL HEARD the guys through the bathroom door as she stepped back into the hotel room, a bag of clothes from Target for Billy hanging from her wrist. Fresh jeans, boxer-briefs, package of gray T's, socks, and a couple of pullover sweaters. Complete overhaul. At least his boots and jacket had survived in half-decent shape.

It sounded like Billy was telling Steel God what happened to the bike. "Someone hit me. Couldn't take it out on the highway like that, and the cops knew what to look for."

"Yeah."

"The fuck was I supposed to do?"

"You'll have to get the next one on your own, then. I don't know. Fight a guy for it, one of those sons of bitches trying to pull a *coup* on me. Won't be as pretty as yours, though."

"Shit, man, it was turquoise. The only reason you gave it to me was you were embarrassed. People think you're a fag or something."

Steel God laughed and Billy laughed and they kept talking. Kristal shut the door. The guys went quiet.

"Just me," she shouted.

They started up again, but Kristal tuned them out, tossed her package on the bed, pulled out the undies she'd bought for herself. Cotton, skimpy, retro sixties patterns. Something to make herself feel comfortable, sexy, fresh. Something to show Billy once they had some alone time and she felt like letting him in again. Might as well be now. Jesus, aching for it. But he needed some punishment, and not just healing time. Once he healed, Kristal was thinking another two weeks.

She took out the folding knife Steel God had given her for protection, cut the tags off Billy's new clothes. Steel God had meant protection from all the rapists out there, but what went unsaid and understood was that he meant in his own gang, too. Maybe he was a utopian at heart, but thank God he was a fucking realist in his head.

After she tossed the tags, Kristal sat on the bed, reclined, knees together swaying back and forth. Not the best situation, but better than getting passed to the frat kid. She turned on the TV. Stared at the last channel Steel God had clicked on, a local Doppler radar, some AM radio noise on the background. Sounded like a farm report.

Kristal flipped around the channels. Landed on MTV. Rich kids with their own show, thinking people gave a shit about them. Pretty girl. Fake as hell. Eye make-up glowing almost. Kristal remembered what it was like. She'd been that type of girl back in the day, but one that could handle a knife.

As a teenager, she'd wanted more than anything to be on *American Idol*. She followed that and about a half dozen other reality shows that made her well-off spoiled daddy's girl life look, well, dull. Why couldn't she have the spotlight? Why couldn't she get on *Idol* (two failed auditions), or *Real World* (five applications, no response), or *Made* or *Top Model* or any of those? Wasn't she pretty? Wasn't she talented?

Not really. Cute, knew how to do make-up, average tits. Could sing in tune, but nothing you'd want to buy. Her acting skills only seemed to fool her dad. Even Mom saw through the bullshit.

Near the end of high school, she discovered that the best way to pretend life was a TV show was to hang out with the wiggers—

suburban white boys trying to be down with hip-hop—turning their weekends into rap videos, playing at pimps and hoes, the girls in bikinis and lingerie thinking it was all fun and games until they woke up with guys they would never fuck when sober, several hours pregnant with kids they couldn't afford to abort without telling their Lutheran parents, who wouldn't let them go through with that anyway.

Kristal was smart enough to stay out of that shit. Condoms only, baby. Boys that stupid, she just liked the façade, knowing it was all an act, and who had to face their doctor dads, hardasses all, come Sunday when he noticed some kid had puked in the old man's golf bag. Watch their tiny pricks shrink faster than if they'd jumped in the pool.

She also knew when to switch sides. Like, watching her wigger boyfriend try stepping up to a biker one night, pissed at the guy revving his motor while they were all trying to enjoy some CDs, right? Like, watching her boyfriend posture and pose until the biker just lit into the guy, dropped him with a right, then broke his nose with a boot stomp. Like, that was the coolest thing she'd ever seen in real life. And later that night, she sucked that biker's dick in exchange for a ride any-fucking-where but home. Even better than TV.

She unfolded the knife again, ran her thumb across the blade a few times. Shame she'd never gotten to use it. Or was that a good thing? Must've carried herself tough to ward off attackers. Didn't they even want to try? Fuck, at least a half-assed grope or something. Show me I'm *worth* the stabbing you'll get, prick.

Could be that with Billy and Steel God on her side, you had to be kidding, some guy willing to take a shot knowing all hell would eat him alive? Billy. Man, he was something.

The deal was that Billy hadn't laughed when she lied about going cold-turkey off crank. Nodded along when she made up that crap about community college and said, "I think you should. Really, what's stopping you? Get some loans, find a roommate."

"All down the line," she'd said at the time. "I'll know when it feels right."

Billy had grunted, shaken his head. "It'll never feel *right*. It'll always feel scary, so you've got to go with scary. Story of my life. I had a choice between what felt right and what felt scary, I went with scary and acted all macho. You, though, your scary is different. A lot better than mine ever was. Yours is the right thing to do."

"Easy to say."

"You ever want out, give the word and I'll drive you wherever, get you set up, tell the gang you left one night. They'd never need to know."

Sighed. And what the fuck would that get her but bored again? Sure, Dad would be thrilled to hear from her, send her as much cash as she needed, but who would she have to pretend to be in return?

Instead, she stuck around, fucked Billy a couple times a week, fucked another guy for a while until she realized that with him, she wanted to get high. With Billy, she wanted to smile and be herself. It was an easier choice than she first thought. What the other guy had been talking about that whole time, though, about overthrowing Steel God and Billy because they were too old, too careful, yeah. Maybe that was the other exit, the secret one. But keep Billy. Billy would make a great Steel God. Might even help them grow into a real family with a real place to belong. Fuck the infighting. She was so over it. The men made it one big pissing contest, and it sucked. But if Billy was in charge, and if Kristal was more than his old lady, you know, like how Hilary worked with Bill Clinton, right? That would be cool. Better than owing on student loans. Better than getting into a sorority. Better than living in a McMansion. A *fuck* of a lot better.

Steel God stepped out of the bathroom, closed the door behind him. Hands on his kidneys, stretching his back. The man looked tired. A tired giant. He turned to Kristal, didn't move.

"He's been through hell."

She nodded. "He'll be okay, right?"

"Oh, yeah. I'm pretty sure. But it's going to take time. The man failed. Shit, that's a tough thing to live down. We've got to convince him it's time to succeed at something else, then."

"He's going to want to run again."

God laughed. "Yeah, so? Convince him not to. That's up to you."

She'd talked the big man into the plan after Billy had told her about how sick the big man really was. While he was gone, Kristal had acted as if Billy wanted her to look after him, and that Richie Rich was just a smokescreen. She told God it was in the club's best interest to get him back, so they'd started making plans even before the call came, just in case. The whole plan was a way to get God off the road with dignity. Kristal was sure he couldn't be cured. Lung cancer, or some kind of cancer anyway. Make it look like an overthrow, Billy stepping up, but really giving Steel God what he deserved—going out in a hellish blaze. Show *that* to the gangster pricks, throw some Sun Tzu on their asses, and they'd wise up.

"I'm just saying," Kristal said, "he's going to want to keep running and I'm not sure if I *can* convince him. It's going to take something bigger. He likes me, I know that. But he doesn't love me. It's going to take love."

"If the man fell in love twice before, he can fall in love again. You can make him. It's an act of will not to love, and that's Billy's one problem. Thinks he's tough, and the bastard is really pretty tough, true, but whatever it was made him be a cop also made him take off on a whim to go after his wife. That's what'll work on him once he's on top. Use it."

"I don't know if I can."

"Shit, girl." Steel God smiled. "You got a pussy, you can do it. You're trying to do it to me right now."

She looked out the window, caught Steel God's smiling reflection. He was everywhere. You couldn't get anything past him. Yeah, she was trying to put him on. If he knew that, then what else? Like maybe how she didn't plan on letting the big man come back into the fold after a break. He was on his way out anyway. She didn't want any conflict, no. Just wanted Steel God to accept his fate and mellow out his last days in a nice prison infirmary bed while Billy Lafitte ruled with a steel rod and Kristal's voice in his ear.

Did he really know? Then why play along this far?

He said, "I'm going out for a cigar. Work some magic while I'm gone, will you? Be careful with that knife." Out the door.

Liar. Everyone knew he couldn't smoke anymore. He lit the things up and pretended. Kristal grinned in spite of herself. How could you not love the enormous son of a bitch?

Wasn't long before she heard splashing around in the bathroom. She turned off the TV, pulled her boots off, and scooted up the bed and leaned against the headboard. Legs crossed at the ankles. She thought about taking her jeans off and slipping into one of the new pairs of panties, but decided it was too much of a tease. No, he'd come out and she'd hypnotize him with her rust-colored toenails.

Took a while, as expected. He'd been beat to hell and back. Tough boy, but still. When Billy finally emerged, he had a towel wrapped around his waist, barely long enough for him, one whole thigh exposed. Another over his shoulders. Hair wet, hanging down limp over his eyes and neck, dripping on the carpet. He didn't see her at first. Taking baby steps, nice and gingerly. A gash on his shin, bruises everywhere. The words on his chest like a brand. Then he raised his head, saw her on the bed. Stone expression didn't change. Was he glad to see her? Not? Pissed? She had no clue.

"Thought that was you back there," he said.

She patted the bed beside her, pointed a big toe at him. "We need to talk."

He nodded, very slight. He took a couple of steps her way before coming to rest on the other bed. Arms bent, fists on the mattress. Legs at ninety degrees. Kristal could see his dick and balls now, the towel not hiding anything anymore. Thick but limp. She felt disappointed but told herself you couldn't read anything into it right then after what he'd been through. The scolding she was about to give him didn't feel right either, but now was the time, take it or leave it.

She said, "You really hurt me, you know."

He sighed, blew strands of hair out of his face. He said, "I need a haircut."

Thirty-two

YOU HAD your Sheriff's cars, your Highway Patrol cars, your local police cars, eight in all, five in the parking lot and three on the shoulder of the county road in front of the "Saloon of Blood", as Wyatt said a couple of deputies were calling it.

"No one told the fuckers that maybe they should stay out of the lot, you know. Tire tracks."

Rome said, "You never know until you're already there. But still, you'd expect one car instead of five."

They eased ahead of the first car in line on the shoulder, parked. All three of them climbed out, Rome not even bothering to stop Desiree. Too late for that. Let the cops play defensive line if they wanted.

Wyatt turned, held out a flat hand like *Stay Put*. "I'll go smooth this over. If anyone asks about the net out for you, I'll tell them it's a misunderstanding, all taken care of. But I don't think it'll come up unless some cowboy radios in."

Rome nodded. "Alright. Your show."

Wyatt walked off towards the bar, motioned at a couple of his men, one joining him for the walk and filling in some details. A few deputies and Patrol officers milled around outside, eyeing and ignoring the strangers at the same time, somehow.

"Not very friendly," Dee said. She crossed her arms against the chill.

"True. The funny thing is, they pride themselves on being nice. All I ever heard about was 'Minnesota Nice' the whole time I was here. But I only ever had *one* real friend around, and that was Wyatt."

"I hope that's what he is. Not setting up some elaborate trap. Jesus."

Dee took in the stark landscape, so different from the South this time of year. The leaves already gone from the trees. Sky gray, like it was about to snow. Like it was always about to snow. Brisk wind bit through her sweater. She hugged herself tighter, drew closer to Rome.

She whispered, "Didn't their mommas teach them not to stare?"

Rome took a look. Yeah, she was right. Just wide open staring. Hostile. The cold wind didn't help.

He said, "If you were to talk to them, they'd be perfect gentlemen. But you're right. They're not quite big on social graces."

A long minute. Nothing to say. Rome wondered why the hell it was taking Wyatt so long.

Dee said, "You think Lafitte was here? You think he did all this…this whatever?"

Hunched his shoulders. Did he think that? Everything Rome knew about Lafitte from their previous encounter, everything he'd learned from Ginny and the in-laws, from the research into Lafitte's life on the Coast, none of it told Rome the guy would get off on mass murder. The terrorist shit, that was about money and power. Misguided, but not in the same way as the assholes blowing themselves up on buses and in cafes. Joining up with a meth-dealing biker gang? Survival. As much as he hated to admit it, Rome didn't see Lafitte as the guy for this. Lafitte might smooth-talk and wound and maim to keep on swimming, but if he was going to leave a mess behind, he would have a damned fine reason for it.

"Feels wrong to you, too, right?"

Dee nodded. "Man must've stepped in some serious shit, then."

"Either that or we're way off the scent."

Wyatt reappeared in the doorway of the bar, held his arm high and waved them over.

"Ready?" Rome said.

Desiree shivered. "I'll tell you after I've seen it."

A LOT OF BLOOD, turning to jelly. Cops with cameras flashed the scene brighter than snow every few seconds, the bloodstains showing up black all over the floor. Couple of bullets lodged in the wall, little orange flags marking the holes. Looked like they had the owner of the bar off in the corner, sitting down with a uniform who was trying to ask questions while all the old man wanted to do was get a better view.

Dee held up. Rome was proud of that. Wondered why he'd tried to hide all his business from her anyway. After all, maybe she had as much interest in taking Lafitte out as he did—like getting rid of the "other woman", except it was this traitor cop, right? The faster Lafitte got caught, the faster Rome was on his way to fame and fortune. Fuck the FBI. Sell the rights instead. Now that this mess with the blood and all had happened, his little fantasy of facing down Lafitte mano-a-mano was fading fast. It would have to be handled through the legal system now. He was resigned to that. With Dee in his corner, though, that would be okay. He could still talk to her about it all. Still lay the fantasy out for her, hope she wasn't repulsed by it. Another step in the right direction for them both.

Then he could check into consulting jobs, corporate security, maybe take a fellowship at a think tank. If he dragged Lafitte in alive, the FBI would forgive him enough to let him leave on his own terms with good recommendations. Surely. And they could move the hell away from New Orleans. Jesus, every day there, you can smell the city rotting away. Drowning but laughing about it. They didn't want to face facts—Katrina had killed New Orleans, and what was left was a ghost.

Wyatt brought Rome over to talk with a rough-faced man wearing steel-framed glasses that must've been from the early eighties. All uniformed up, but wrinkled.

"This is Sheriff Hutchinson. Sheriff, Special Agent Franklin Rome. He's an expert, I guess, on the suspect."

Hutchinson looked Rome over like he was a zoo exhibit. Fucking rural pricks. "You mean the biker?"

"One of them. Billy Lafitte was involved with some half-assed terrorism cell last year, so we think. Before disappearing, he attacked Agent Rome, nearly killed him."

"I remember that." Hutchinson stuck out his hand. Rome shook it. "Yeah, that was awful shit. Awful shit. Right here in our own backyard. You never expect that."

Rome turned his head, surveyed the bar. "But this? How about this?"

"This, yeah. We hear Lafitte's in with bikers now. A couple of local yahoos got the idea they could take him down for that big reward your people are offering. Now there's no trace of anyone except this blood, those brains. It either belongs to the bikers or the locals. Still have to say I'm more used to seeing bikers murdering than I am terrorists. No one's safe anywhere anymore."

"What about the other agent who was looking for Lafitte?" Desiree had come up behind Rome without him realizing.

Hutchinson shrugged. "No idea, ma'am. No reports from anyone. Even if your agent is still on the road, I suppose he would have called in if things were alright, right? Until he does, we'll have to test the blood, see how much belongs to how many people."

Yeah, after fucking up the parking lot, *now* he wants to go all *CSI*. Great.

"Can I make an observation?" Rome asked.

Hutchinson rolled his bottom lip over his top, pulled it across his mustache. "My guest."

"You've got one obvious exit wound, one with brain matter. The rest of the blood is spotty, nothing life-threatening."

"That's damn fine detecting, sir." Dry like the humidity.

"What I'm saying *iiii*—" Drag it out more. Make his face

turn red. C'mon. "—*iiis* that you might have someone still alive. If not here, than maybe in the surrounding area."

Hutchinson raised two fingers to the bridge of his nose, pushed his glasses up. Squinched his eyes shut. "I don't know if you noticed on the way in, but, uh, it's kind of flat out there."

"Exactly. So all the little windbreaks can hide a lot of deer, and maybe hide a couple of incapacitated people, too, huh?"

Wyatt said, "Not a bad idea. We've got plenty of guys standing in the parking lot wasting taxpayer money. How about we send them around?"

Hutchinson opened his eyes again. Looked at Rome, blinked a lot. "What did you say your name was again?"

He pulled out his ID, held it open just long enough that anyone else would be pretty impressed, but not enough to read anything. "Call me Special Agent. Or even That Black Bastard Agent. But don't pull this tired act on me, please. That Sidney Poitier flick is, like, forty years old."

Snapped the ID closed, turned, and marched away. Let Wyatt deal with the territorial pissing. Until they came and carted Rome away, his jurisdiction was the whole fucking world.

Dee eased up beside him. "What was that all about?"

He waited until they were outside in the swirling wind again, shielding their eyes from the kicked-up dust. "I heard that Miss Colleen and her boyfriend were in a car wreck yesterday. They'd gone after Lafitte and apparently found him, got too rough."

"So?"

"Lafitte had a chance to kill that girl and he didn't take it. No fucking way he would pull that, I don't care how much trouble he's in. You can just feel it. The man's actually got a soul, tiny and shriveled up as it may be."

Dee finished the thought. "If they're not dead, then maybe he wanted them found."

"God, I hope so."

Another minute passed, and then Wyatt came out with the Sheriff. Wyatt had a bullhorn. He called all the bored uniforms over into a circle. Rome and Desiree stood on the outside of it listening to Wyatt send teams of two and three here and there, every clump of bushes where someone might hide a body or a motorcycle or a car. Not one word breathed about it being Rome's idea. Exactly the way he wanted it.

Thirty-three

COLLEEN WONDERED if she could die from muscle aches. Strains. Or if her limbs would reach maximum stress and spasm her to death. Getting close. She wanted to cry and scream, but she held on and kept McKeown talking.

Alex's band. Alex himself. His first night with another man. Gross, but it made him happy, kept him alive, and kept her mind off how fucked they both were.

It was getting harder to keep McKeown going. His blood, aw dude, she could smell it all together with their sweat. He was dying, and she had to sit here helpless and watch. She'd watched two people die already in the last two days. She'd killed one of them. The other one wouldn't have been dead if not for her. Like, the pain was too bad. Love sucked. If they'd just been fucking, it would've been different. If she'd given herself a few more years, party and fuck and forget them three days later. Go through a slew of men. Then maybe she wouldn't be sitting here in an abandoned car full of bodies, hog-tied, her chest hurting every time she remembered she wouldn't be able to tell Nate about it later. If there was a later. Or maybe she would get to tell him later, if later meant the afterlife. Unless shooting Fawn in the face counted as murder and she went to Hell, because there was no way Nate was in Hell.

She asked, "You still awake?"

McKeown murmured, sleep talking.

"*Hey*, fucking answer me, Josh. All right?" She leaned her head closer to his. "You. Need. To. Stay. Awake. And. Talk."

"God, please, it hurts."

"Hurting means you're alive, dumbass. Listen to me, you still like women at all? Or have you passed the point of no return?"

"What?"

"Still bi, or all fag?"

He took in a deep breath, started laughing. Or crying. No, it was laughing. Then he said, "Ow, ow, ouch."

Anything to keep it going. Take his mind off the pain. Off himself and his boyfriend, or whatever. Even if it creeped her out. "I'm just thinking, you know. I try to be pretty and people still think I'm a dyke. Can't be a butch dyke, though. I mean, I wear jeans all the time, but they're tight, and I have cool hair, even if I keep it pulled back for the job."

"You're a cutie, I can see that. A little boyish in build is all."

"I keep in shape. And at home, I have naughty clothes. Little silky things and thongs and shit, but that was just me and Nate. But, listen, I'm saying that the reason I'm asking about you is that I can look at girls and feel, like, they're *hot*, you know? Like *really hot*, and it makes me tingle but only because I wish I could be that hot."

"Didn't Nate think you were hot?"

"Of course he did." Colleen didn't want to think about Nate, but there it was, the both of them fresh from the shower, her in his uniform shirt, straddling him on the bed. Jesus. She was going to give herself a stroke if she kept this up.

She swallowed hard and said, "But maybe I might like being with a woman, you know. If I think they're hot, maybe pull some of this bi-curious stuff the college kids think is hot. I'm just saying."

He chuckled, trying to keep quiet. "I guess. I mean, don't think about it as cut and dry. If the *person* is sexy to you, man or woman, isn't that what's important?"

"You can't lie to yourself and make it happen."

"Sure you can. I did. Look…" McKeown pulled in air through his nose, whistling. He was fading again. Colleen had made him use up all his energy. Shit. Now he was just going to die even faster. She had to listen hard for his next words. "If you like the girl and she likes you, then do it. But if you don't feel like it and don't feel any regret at walking away, hey, there's your answer."

"Yeah, that's what I thought."

Quiet again. Colleen tried to shake thoughts of Nate, them playing dress-up together, posing naked with guns and taking photos, using the handcuffs out in the garage. That one time in the backyard when they thought no one could see, but then they caught the neighbor boy looking. Shake all that. Come on. You're not going out like that, so fucking sad. So goddamned…but she liked it. She liked it because those times made her happy and no matter how many dicks she could've had instead of settling for Nate's five-incher, she couldn't imagine any other man making her as happy, understanding who she really was the same as she did him. So why not lay your head down facing the back seat, stick your nose in there tight, close your eyes, and just let it all go? Think of Nate. Make a date with him on the other side. He's already vouched for you with St. Peter. Sometimes cops have to kill. That's all there is to it. Jesus forgives, and he forgives you both for shacking up before marriage and now you can be together for all eternity, and on and on and on—

"You weren't really thinking about being with another woman, were you?"

Colleen blinked, felt the pulsing of her muscles, straining in time with her heartbeat. "How come?"

"You were trying to connect with me, keep me going. That's sweet…shit." Talking between gritted teeth now. "I tell you what, though. If I had survived this, I would seriously quit the fucking FBI. Jesus, I always thought it would hurt a certain way, but not like *this*."

"Come on, Josh. Stay with me. Your body will keep fighting as long as you tell it to."

"…ah…I would've quit, though. Maybe I would've written a

book, or a screenplay, or...I don't know. It just seemed more fun than...ah...shhh...being a lawyer. But after Alex...I would've quit and gone back to him and gotten on my knees. He was going to be my Nate. Or at least one of them."

Colleen was crying now. Thrashing. Her broken hand was on fire. She wanted the fucking wire gone *now*. Not going to let this happen. No no no. "Shut up and breath, please, will you? Save your strength."

"No, listen..." cleared his throat. Voice cracked. "Here's what you tell my boss. Tell him I handed in my resignation, okay? That right before I died...sh, sh...I, ah, quit. Yeah...I found myself, so that's that. I quit. Okay? You'll tell him?"

Colleen pulled so hard she heard her snapped bones crunch together, gulped down a breath when the pain charged all over like electricity. Swallowed wrong. Choking. She coughed it out, drooled on the seat.

Got her rhythm back and said, "Josh? Don't leave me alone. Do it for me. Come on. Goddamn it! You asshole! Fucking fight already!"

If he was still breathing, she couldn't hear it. Couldn't tell a thing. He was still. She stopped fighting, listened. Still couldn't tell. Leaned her neck as far back as it would go, stretched, and got ready for one more fight.

And then she saw the shadow pass over the seat, grow larger. Someone outside the car from the other side. Voices, shouting, like, "Found them!" and "Over here!"

Behind her, someone trying to open the driver's side door. Locked.

A voice: "Locked. Get the slimjim."

Colleen shouted, "Just break the fucking window! Hurry! Fuck!"

She cranked her head around, but it was stiff and she couldn't even get it to her shoulder. Thinking, Please be cops, please be cops. Otherwise, it was going to be like that college party all over again, when those guys tried to rape her. Fucking farm boys figure out she's the only one alive in the car, then her trip into Hell starts earlier, hurts worse, and bleeds more than if she'd just suffocated in the Mustang. Not to mention that Fawn would be down there waiting for her, too.

She heard the thud and crack of a baton against the window. Then someone else saying, "No, you just put pressure in the middle like this—"

And a few quiet moments later, the glass shattered and rained down into the driver's seat. An arm scrambled for the lock.

Colleen was already shouting over and over, *"Get an ambulance! Officer down! Hurry! 911! Officer down! You've got to hurry!"*

The drivers seat flipped forward and a face appeared, topped by a State Trooper's hat. "Deputy Hartle? Agent McKeown?"

"Yes, for god's sakes, who the fuck else—he's been shot! He's dying! Come on!"

The Trooper grabbed the rope connecting Colleen's ankles to her wrists, sliced through with a pocket knife. Her feet collapsed hard against the side. Not responding. Needed circulation. "Oh shit. Oh Jesus. Oh shit."

The Trooper worked on her ankles. Wrist still bound, she still reached for McKeown's shoulders, tried to roll him towards her. Like wearing boxing gloves. Straightened her purple, numb fingers.

"Hey, come on. Wake up, please, wake up. For Alex. You can quit now, really. You really can."

Nothing. Got nothing.

The Trooper said, "Don't move him. You can't jostle him like that."

"Did you call the fucking ambulance yet?"

"My partner's already called them. On the way."

She kicked her feet. "Forget about me. Help McKeown. And get out an APB. Lafitte and two other suspects. Stole my car, a Gold Chevelle, seventy-four, all tricked out. And they've got our guns. Come on, call it!"

"Okay, calm down. It's okay. Calm down."

The Trooper backed out of the car, keyed his radio and called in the details she'd given. Colleen reached her finger up under

McKeown's nose. Didn't feel a thing. She couldn't tell if he'd stopped breathing or if it was just her sleeping fingers. She started to cry, but then swallowed and slid her top teeth on her bottoms and let a chill run through her. Better that way.

THE AMBULANCE beat Rome by only a few minutes. Colleen sat on the ground leaning against the Mustang while watching as the EMTs got to work on McKeown. Not dead after all, or at least they were trying to bring him back from the dead. They wouldn't tell her, but the way they hustled, it had to be good news, right?

Rome, bit fatter than last she'd seen him. Guess New Orleans can do that to you. He arrived with an older Trooper she'd never seen before and a good-looking fortysomethingish black woman. What, Rome's partner? Boss? The other two lagged back while Rome first checked on McKeown. Got yelled at by EMTs.

"He's my agent!"

"Just get back!"

"Give me an update or I'll arrest all of you! Obstruction or something."

The head EMT looked up. "Five minutes, okay?"

Rome nodded, stepped back, looked around and found Colleen, knees bent, cradling her broken hand, which had been crudely splinted by an EMT before she chased him towards McKeown. She'd refused to let them work on her busted nose, not until he was stable. She didn't say a word to Rome. Even felt some hate towards him. No clue why.

He stood above her, a foot or so back. "You okay?"

"Yeah." Clipped it.

"Sorry about Nate."

"Yeah."

"I was hoping to work with him."

"Sure."

They both listened to the chatter of the techs, watched them plug in IV lines, clean up the blood. Seemed like forever before they raised the stretcher and headed off to the ambulance. One of the techs shouted back, "We're taking him to meet the MedEvac chopper! Flying him to Sioux Falls! Surgery!"

And they were off. Rome didn't follow right away. Stared after the techs until McKeown was out of sight behind the doors. He said, "Lafitte was the one who let you live, right?"

Scoff. "If you can call it that."

"He hurt you?"

"I'm fine. Look, Billy was almost in a coma. You're right about him letting us live, but if he hadn't woken up..."

Rome waited for more. Let him wait. There wasn't anything else Colleen needed to say.

Rome scratched his knee. "Who shot McKeown?"

"Biker. He was seven feet tall."

"Steel God?"

Colleen shrugged. "Like Iron Man? I don't know. He didn't introduce himself."

"So, you saying Lafitte's not to blame for the murder back there, either?"

"Fuck." She laughed. Nose pounding, hand throbbing, swelling, and all her muscles cramping like hell, but laughing anyway. "Nobody's had time to check the truck yet. Couple of hicks that were looking to score off Billy. One tried to kill me. I killed her first."

"Jesus."

"Yeah. It's a clean shooting. Ask McKeown. If he lives."

"Your first?"

"So far."

Rome reached his hand down. Motioned his head up. She grabbed hold, pushed off the ground. Hands buzzing with a million pinpricks, deep purple. Awkward there for a moment. She still wavered between hugging him and punching him. Finally just let go. Stood still, both looking anywhere but at each other.

"You did all right, considering. Kept your head. Came out of it alive, helped us get the net out."

What, he going to make the same offer to her he made to Nate, now? The FBI really liked her "go getter" attitude? She said,

"I didn't have a choice, *sir*."

Rome huffed. Then, "Yeah you did. You and Nate both. Stupid ass kids. You know, the whole thing was ready to go, all on point. Had him where we wanted him. Aw, but you guys. Playing cops and robbers? Playing like some fucking movie? You want to be pissed at someone? Get a fucking mirror." He stabbed a finger at her. "Because this is all on you. Get it? They've got two more firearms because of you now. Think about that."

She pressed her lips together. Felt like her heart was in a cave.

"No excuse. Just no excuse."

Colleen mumbled, "Yessir. No excuse."

"Jesus." Hands on hips. Tiny steps left, right, circle. Then back in her face. "You want to be a great cop? Stop the vigilante shit and get with the program."

She had to stifle a laugh. Would've been sharp. Would've followed up with, Yes sir. Just like you. Bit her lip hard.

The biting did it. She could tell, like he was reading her mind. Rome was done with the blaming. Knocked the wind out of himself, hadn't he?

Rome shook his head and started away, trailing with, "We're heading to the hospital. You can come along."

"Thank you, sir."

He didn't look back.

"Sir?"

He stopped.

"Agent McKeown wanted me to tell you something."

"All right."

"He said to tell you to fuck off."

Absorbed it well—not a smile, not a grimace. Just…took it. Rome nodded. "Could've told me that to my face."

Kept walking. After another minute, she took a deep breath and followed like she'd been told to.

Thirty-four

SO KRISTAL SPILLED her big plan. Oh, yeah. Ambitious, wasn't she? Took her about fifteen minutes of bitching to get to it. All this about she wasn't anyone's *property* to trade around, and she would choose who she fucked and who she would ride with, and that this had to be a *real* relationship or she was done. And yes, for his information, she sure as hell fucked Richie Rich. Fucked him good and hard. He worked his ass off to please her, and got his tongue deep in there, and maybe Lafitte ought to think about that for awhile. Even with all that good fucking, she still wanted Billy more and more.

Lafitte played along and sounded sorry and sad in all the right places. Barely listening, trying to think of how to slip out, get a new vehicle, and keep on towards Mississippi. He'd run a few scenarios through his head—take the Chevelle, take the chopper, take a bus, carjack a dude, take Kristal and let her plan it, leave Kristal behind—but they all ended badly. That's what you got from Steel God. If he liked you, he'd cut you a break, even fight for you. If you screwed him over, well, Lafitte remembered Red Gator, only a few days ago, realizing that hammer was coming down and he was helpless to stop it.

He sat on the bed barely moving except to show Kristal he was pretending to listen. She eventually crawled onto his bed, which jostled his bruises and cuts, and snuggled up behind him, arms wrapped around, lips closer to his ear as she started in on "The Plan".

It sounded right, too. If he really had been thinking of knocking off God and taking over, Kristal was right about this being the best way. Also the sleaziest. Most cowardly. But definitely the smartest.

"And no one will question it. They'll forget eventually. Hardly even worth the fight, once they see what sort of leader you'd be. You, you're, like, a natural."

"How long's it going to take?"

"Soon as we're back, I'm thinking a month? A month sound okay? And since he'll be in on that part, it'll be pretty smooth."

Her hands on his skin were warm, sweaty, stung his "Baby Raper". Girl got a worried mind, like in those blues songs. Maybe Led Zep. Breath on his ear was fingernails on a chalkboard. Lafitte rotated his head, felt his neck grind, then the cracking sound, gave him some relief.

He told her, "Okay. Okay. I think it's best for the whole crew. But we can't just out and out betray him, make it obvious. I'm not going to do that."

"God, no, I'm with you." Lips touched his ear. "It's not about *power* or anything, but more, uh, what is it?"

"Security."

"Yeah, sure. Security."

"A little security sounds sweet to me right about now."

She squeezed him to her. He didn't cry out when the wounds she pressed bit into his nerves. It was okay. He was a thousand miles away already.

"Hey," she whispered. "I wasn't going to show you until later, but…" Kristal hopped off the bed, giggling. She bent across her bed and grabbed her package. Looked like the underwear all the college girls wore, with cartoons and colors and shit. She headed for the bathroom. "I'll model for you. Be right back."

Sure, that was okay. He was tired, hurt, and not at all feeling up to much, but she was a pretty little thing. And those toenails, painted a rusty red, goddamn, she knew what he liked.

WASN'T MORE THAN fifteen minutes later that Lafitte found Steel God lounging poolside. It was indoors, heated. Outside the window, gray shaded everything. Might even have seen a snowflake or two. Across the pool, a couple of kids splashed around while their grandparents reclined, the woman reading a magazine and the husband napping.

Lafitte started to sit down beside Steel God, had to hold the waistband of his jeans to keep them from sliding off. Kristal had bought the baggy kind. Thought it would make him look cooler. Couldn't wear his belt because of a bad bruise near his kidneys. Sucked in air as his muscles tightened in bad places.

Steel God said, "I dropped by a while ago, but heard some fine moaning from Kristal. Thought I'd better leave you to it. Something not working?"

"No, working fine. Just can't go for too long. My body can only take so much. Overran the cup pretty quickly."

Steel God laughed. Made the grandma look up. "Poor Kristal."

"There's always tomorrow night." Not that she'd complained. Was sweet like those hookers you see in movies, helping a guy through his first time.

They sat listening to the splashing water, the sharp echo of the kids play-screaming, running around the pool with water guns, slipping a couple times, then up and on the run again.

Lafitte wanted to tell Steel God that maybe he could ride with him a while longer, but not forever. Forget Kristal's plan, or even what he'd originally mapped out with the big man early on. It was tough to imagine what would happen to Kristal, though. Did his leaving mean handing her over to the boys in the gang? Would Steel God take her on? Lafitte didn't think so. She would probably have to start over, fight her way back to the top, pick the right horse to bet on. The leftover cop in Lafitte was hoping to think of a better option he could offer, but nothing came. It had been too long. The cop candle was close to burning itself out. Let Kristal take care of herself.

Lafitte cleared his throat, ready to throw the girl to the wolves, but Steel God spoke first.

"She tell you her grand plan?"

"Yeah. Mm-hm."

"That one, I'm telling you, too smart for her own good. She would've been good on *Survivor*."

"I've seen it a few times."

"Good stuff. Between Trump and that one, I learned a lot about all the political shit."

"Too smart for her own good, you say?"

"She could have anything she wants, so what does she want? To lead my gang. I don't get it. Maybe just thirsty for attention. Can you imagine her in law school? She'd make partner like that." He snapped his fingers. It echoed loud enough to shut up the kids for a few seconds.

Lafitte waited. Looked away. Then, "I told her she should try college."

"Nah, she won't. Girl's scared she won't be the best in the room. Scared of competition. That's a damn shame, because she doesn't understand that competition makes you sharper. Here, she knows she's three steps ahead of the other women, five steps ahead of the guys, and about a step ahead of you and me."

Lafitte grinned, turned back to God. "A whole step?"

The big man raised his eyebrows. "If it's any more, then you're in trouble."

The grandmother kept a close watch on Steel God from the corner of her eye. The big man turned, threw her a wink. The woman reached over and woke her husband.

God had known all along. Lafitte should've expected it. That's why he would suck as a gang leader. Kristal would rock, though. She'd learned from the best.

Steel God said, "It'll be your gang, you know. Your real family. I can teach you some, but the rest is your call. I won't give you any slack when we have to fight it out, though. You've got to win it on your own. Much as I want this to work, I can't trust some piece of shit fake to lead my people. You have to actually win."

"Wait, what do you mean?"

That big Steel God grin. "You'd better be the real deal. What's the point of coming to get you otherwise? Fuck, it's time. If someone's going to take over, it needs to be the one who doesn't want to. That's the only one who'll do it right."

"Oh, Jesus." Lafitte spread his knees and bent over, tried to keep it all down.

"What's that they say, 'Only Nixon could go to China'? Or Reagan taking it to the Soviets? Or Kirk to the Klingons."

"I never thought...I thought I'd be long gone before it got this far—"

"Goddamn, man, get yourself together." Steel God smacked Lafitte's shoulder, nearly sent him out of the chair, but that same hand gripped his shirt, held him up. "We either do it this way or I have to manufacture some other way to die. What, a bike wreck? No, man. You're it. You're the one going to kill me, and you're going to take care of the club."

Lafitte gripped the armrests of his chair, felt dizzy like he was in freefall.

Steel God kept going. "And if that little girl of yours thinks her plan worked the way she wanted, fine. I'd rather go out now than, you know..."

"I don't want it. I mean, I called you because I didn't have a choice, but I didn't know it was for this. I was going to take off again."

He watched as Steel God turned his face towards the pool and slumped deep down in his chair. "Ungrateful little ass."

"It's my wife, man."

"Your ex. Fucking ex. What do you expect, everything to go back to normal? You don't get normal anymore."

"Then stop me. I'm calling your bluff."

They sat quietly for another few minutes as the grandfather gathered the boys out of the pool, tossed towels on their backs, and ordered them back to the room. Big guy for an old man, like a former football player or something. Reminded Lafitte of his high school coach. The grandkids whined the whole way to the door until Grandma said they were going for pizza.

"See," Lafitte said. "It's like…I *know* it's a trap. Like, a bad one, too. But I can't help it. You've seen those fish swim upstream to spawn and die? There it is. You've got your blaze of glory all planned out, and I've got mine."

"Why? Why like that? Call it a second life or something. I'm offering you a full-blown resurrection."

"Aw, fuck no." Lafitte stood. Had to work at standing steady. One sway and he was in the pool. "That ain't nothing except being wanted twice as much for two different reasons. And, and, don't forget the whole gang gunning for me, like some 'King of the Mountain' shit. Look at me right now! That's what I get for even thinking about…"

He let that one go. Steel God didn't even have to finish the thought: *For even thinking about going back.*

Under his breath: "Fuck it."

Steel God grunted and pushed himself out of the chair. Slid behind Lafitte on his way to the door, said, "You want to run, I'll be the one who calls the Feds on you. And I'll find another guy to take over. Don't think you're special. You're just the best I know so far."

Left him standing there wobbly. Heavy bootsteps echoing on the tile. Each one like another brick on his tomb.

HE WAITED. Waited until Kristal had gone to pick up dinner at a nearby taco joint. Until Steel God said, "Got to drop one" and locked himself in the bathroom.

Lafitte picked up the phone, tried to decipher the instructions for an outside line. He punched the right button and then had to remember the number. Or had it been changed? But why? They were the ones who had called Tordsen in the first place. They *wanted* to be reached, right? Even if the FBI put them up to it.

The number floated back. They always do. Along with it came his old home number in Gulfport, the name of his kids' preschool, Ginny's favorite perfume, her dress size, Ham's favorite toys (the water guns, of course), Savannah's giggle while she watched *Sesame Street*.

Fuck.

Almost didn't dial the final two digits.

But how could he decide if he wanted to keep going or not unless he really *knew*?

He pressed the final two and listened to the ring. Maybe they wouldn't be home. Then it was easy. Keep motoring south. Keep going. Consequences be damned. Keep on.

"Hello?"

Lafitte cleared his throat. "Mrs. Hoeck?"

Took her an extra breath to say, "Yes, it is." Like he was a telemarketer or something.

"How is she? How are the kids?"

"Oh god." Yeah, she recognized the voice now. "Billy."

"How are they?"

He'd kept in touch with his ex-mother-in-law more than anyone else down there. Mrs. Hoeck was the only one willing to tell him the truth. She was Christian to the core, believed in forgiveness and all that. Even if it made her sick to do it, that's who she was. She always told him, "You're forgiven" like it chilled her blood and she had to let the Holy Ghost itself say those words for her because she damn well couldn't on her own.

The woman said, "We have your son and daughter. They are both well, but they miss their mother. Children shouldn't have to live like this."

"Like what?"

"Ginny sliced her wrists. She's alive, but maybe past the point…" She choked up. Took in a long breath. "She'll need psychiatric care for a long time."

Oh God. That's what it was all about? She'd turned suicidal again? "She's stronger than that. She was last time."

Under her breath, "Help me, Jesus." Then, "It's *you*. They want you, so they wanted to use *her*. They sent that, that, agent. He wants to put her away."

"That's not on me," Lafitte said, his voice upping a notch in volume. "He started it. I was clean."

"You've never been clean, son. Turn yourself in so Ginny and your children will know where you are at night."

"Doesn't matter. I want to see them. I want to tell them everything's going to be fine."

"It's not!" She had never raised her voice like that before. "You didn't even listen. You can't see Ginny. She's being hospitalized. She won't respond to anyone. She's staring off, babbling, that's what's left of her. All because the…the damned government wanted to use her as bait."

"But I can help—"

"And now I have to raise your children. Ham's own mother has disowned him, and it's a miracle she didn't hurt Savannah. Tried to kill herself with the child in the next room."

"No, wait."

"You can't help anymore. You should have done that a long time ago, Billy. You can repent. Take your punishment, whatever it may be, but your spirit will be clean. For once, you'll be clean."

Trying to thump her Bible on him? After what he'd seen? That trip with Graham, *that* was his shot at redemption. Tried to take the high road with some wannabe terrorists only to find out they had neither high nor low roads, just one straight and narrow path to Allah. Mrs. Hoeck could take her Jesus Saves crap and…

"Just…listen. The kids. I can't see…? No, you're right."

"If you turned yourself in, I would. I would bring your children to see you in jail, and you could explain to them how it's right for you to be there because you've done something wrong. You've done wrong and realized it. I would make sure they were in your life then, absolutely."

Lafitte felt goosebumps rise. "For real?"

"I give my word."

He sat on the bed. The softest bed he'd been on in a long time. A cheap chain hotel, and he was thinking this mattress was a luxury. Jail bed wouldn't be so soft. But he'd be someone's dad again. Sleeping bag out on the highway, wherever you happen to land, something romantic about that. Getting colder up here, and they'd either retreat to Steel God's cabins outside of Aberdeen, the three he'd built with his Dad's help a handful of years back, or they'd go way down to Mexico, live cheap on the beach until it was time to migrate back, following the birds.

Lafitte said, "Would I get to see Ginny?"

"Listen to me, son."

"It would be nice to, you know. I'm trying here."

"No, Billy, listen. It's all well and good. We're not going to make a deal. Do the smart thing here. The FBI tapped my phone because I told them I'm the one you would call. I've kept you on the line long enough for them to trace where you are."

He closed his eyes. "That's not fair."

"You called me, remember." Cold. The bitch never wavered—praying for you or cursing you, the bitch was ice.

"Shit." He hung up. Sat there. Said it again. "Shit."

The toilet flushed. The bathroom door opened almost simultaneously. Steel God's stink flooded the room. Lafitte coughed.

Steel God said, "Who you talking to?"

A grin. "My mother-in-law."

The big man's eyes went wide. "Shit."

"Yeah, shit."

"Ain't it weird how I put so much faith into such a stupid little prick like you?"

Couldn't say anything to that. Something Lafitte had wondered on and off himself.

He said, "So?"

"Gotta get. If Kristal's not here by the time we hit the parking lot, *adios.*"

Lafitte inhaled too much stink, coughed again and pulled his shirt collar over his nose. "What the hell, man?"

Steel God cupped his hands, tried to waft the current directly towards Lafitte. "You smelled ten times worse before I prettied you up in the bath."

"We have to wait for Kristal. We leave her, she'll spill everything she knows. That girl's not taking one for the team."

"Hot damn, that's officer thinking." Steel God turned to the wall-mounted mirror behind him, took a look. Got his face close, pulled down his bottom eyelids. "You going to be ready for this?"

"Ready for?"

"We have to get serious distance between us and here. You can handle it?"

Maybe not. Thought about seeing his kids again. Been so fucking long. Won't get to teach his son to hunt, but he could tell the kid about girls. About staying in school. Make some serious money and avoid law enforcement at all costs. Tell Savannah all her future dates needed to know her dad was, like, in the pen. Uh huh. Pull that one, some little teenage pecker will shrivel up. Or later, she might bring him a grandchild to look at one day.

And then see what happens if the Feds catch him and lock him up and waterboard him or whatever the hell they do anymore, and that self-righteous bitch Hoeck reneges on her promise. She wouldn't though.

But was he willing to risk it?

Lafitte figured he had less than ten minutes to choose.

Thirty-five

MUTED TV, half-strength lights, too cold, a local uniformed cop at the door. Rome sat waiting for word on McKeown. Wheeled directly into surgery, one of the doctors telling Rome he couldn't be optimistic beyond "We'll do our best." So they'd taken over a waiting room and were waiting, Wyatt out in the hall on the phone, Desiree off buying them both coffee, and Deputy Colleen huddled in a chair on the other side of the room, a magazine in her lap. But she hadn't turned the page in a half hour.

Rome checked his watch. Yeah, a half hour. Like an eye blink in doctor time, he guessed. When you're waiting, so much longer. He stood, paced a few steps, hands in his pockets. All coming to an end, it seemed. The whole chase, his whole reason for existing the last year and a half. Every non-Lafitte thought followed by one that brought him back onto center stage. What a shitty way to live. Dee had every goddamned right to be pissed enough to follow him across the country. And telling Colleen not to go all vigilante. That was it. The moment he could actually laugh at himself. Leave Lafitte to the pros. He had to take care of his wounded colleague first.

Walked across the floor to Colleen. She didn't look up. Breathing kind of funny because of the bandage across her nose

Rome had insisted she get once they got to the ER. Not ready to have her hand looked at yet, not until McKeown was out of danger.

"I was hard on you back there."

"Mm."

"And I am sorry about Nate. He was a good man."

She lifted her eyes. "Good cop."

"He was that."

Colleen plunked the magazine onto the empty seat next to her, leaned back, fingers fidgety on the armrests. "Thank you. I don't feel like talking."

"Sure, okay. No problem. Just, you know, I have an idea you could make Nate proud. Might take some time, but if you wanted to work towards joining up with the Bureau, especially after today—"

"I'll think about it later. Not now." Finally raised her eyes. "Do you have a cell phone I can borrow?"

He reached for his instinctively, remembered he got rid of it along the Interstate. Shook his head. "Not with me. I'm sure Wyatt would, once he's finished."

"Just want to call my mom. That's all."

"If you want, I can get someone to take you home anytime. We can get your statement in a couple of days. You've been through a lot."

She barely moved her lips. "I'm fine."

"Okay."

He turned as Desiree stepped into the room with two small cups of coffee. "The machine stuff was the best I could do—"

Wyatt was right behind her, saying "Excuse me" and brushing past, bumping her, Dee holidng the cups high and out as they sloshed.

Wyatt said, "We've got him. Here in town."

Rome looked at Dee. Her eyes wide, lips parted. He said, "Lafitte?"

"Yeah, and that biker he runs with. The police already have three unmarked cars in the lot. The Chevelle is still there, and so is the Harley."

"Are they going in?"

"Not yet. The biker's name is Steel God, and he's a madman. We think he'd make a break for it if we tried anything less than SWAT. I'm telling you, he's insane."

"No, that's not it." Colleen was speaking up. "He does what he has to, but he has a lot of respect, too. He washed my face after breaking my nose. Very impressed with how I fought."

"That's one cop. He had the advantage. This time he'll probably feel threatened and go out guns blazing."

"Well, yeah, but he's not going to be a coward about it. He'd rather charge your guys rather than hide behind hostages."

Rome sniffed. "It's not a bad profile, but you didn't get to spend that much time with him. You don't know his history."

"Don't need to."

"Yeah, you do. I know he spared your life and all—"

"Shut up! Would you just shut up?" She bolted from the chair, held her hand to her chest. "Such an arrogant asshole, Rome. You think you're the shit, all the time."

"I'm guessing you might have a dash of Stockholm Syndrome."

"I feel fine. Steel God didn't spare my life. Lafitte did. He's going to listen to Lafitte. So what you've got to do is talk to Lafitte first, if he's not still passed out."

More cops coming into the room. Wyatt leaning his ear to one of them, taking in the news, nodding, whispering orders.

Then he said, "How about we go on over, call the room, see if Lafitte will talk to us? If she's right, we can end this nice and calm."

Rome shook his head. "I'm not a negotiator."

"When it comes to him, you are."

Another look at Dee. She gave the slightest shrug, enough to telegraph *As long as it's over.*

Rome said, "Okay, make sure as many guests on their floor get out now. Get someone on the stairs."

"They're way ahead of you on strategy. All we need now is you talking this boy out."

They started for the door. Dee set the coffee onto a table, fell in beside Rome.

"Don't even say it," she said.

"Wasn't going to."

He was nearly in the hall when he realized Colleen wasn't with them. He whipped around. "Come on."

She took a step, then took it back. Said, "No, I'll stay with Josh." Not even "McKeown" anymore.

Rome told Wyatt and Desiree he'd meet them at the end of the hall, waited until they were out of earshot.

Then he waited some more. No need to even ask her. Just let the silence build and she'd start to fill it in.

Two minutes.

Colleen finally said, "I'm not coming. I don't care anymore."

"That's bullshit."

"No, really." Her lips squirmed like she had a bad taste in her mouth. "Fuck, it's, like, all I wanted was to fuck Lafitte over bad. Like, head shot bad, you know? It's his fault Nate's dead, and I don't care what you say, that's the way it is. So then that… that…*fucking bastard* saves my life? I was ready to die, man! So ready, wanting him to pull that trigger. I was waiting for angels to greet me, all that shit. If I couldn't get revenge, I just wanted to go be with Nate."

Louder and louder. Not wailing, but right on the edge. Rocking back and forth on the balls of her feet.

"And, and, and now Josh might die, and that's *my* fault. And, fuck, I killed that girl back there. Hardly had to think about it. Jesus." Couple of tears. She laid her palm on her cheek, left it there a long time before sniffing, brushing it away. "I just wanted to be a cop because it was, like, strong. I liked being strong. But I'm not anymore. I don't want to see anyone else die."

What do you do? Hug her? Shit. Rome clasped his hands in front of him, mimicking the pose he'd seen from his own superiors. Stare at the ground a moment before coming back with a checkmate smile.

Rome said, "How about I order you to go?"

"You can't." She sat down. "I'm going to quit anyway."

"So? How about this, then. I hold you as a material witness. You still get to come along, and after, I can let you stew in jail for a while."

Colleen touched her bandage. Poked at it. Squinted her eyes when the pain hit. Sniffed in real big and clamped her hand on the armrest again. "Do it. It's the only way I'm moving."

He watched her short fingernails grip the wood. Nothing some handcuffs and a taser couldn't fix. Seemed to work almost every time. But she'd gotten all buddy buddy with the boy. If it helped her feel better, after all she'd been through, then why bring her along anyway? At best, she'd be able to point out the biker. At worst...no, there was no worst. And best wasn't that great, really. Let her off the hook.

Rome let out a deep breath. "Fine. I don't care. Your life."

Her hands went slack. "Thank you."

"Your loss. Can't change your mind."

A slow shrinking, hand slipping between her knees. Face down. Feet one on top of the other. "I'll let you know if there's any news on Josh."

He stood there another half minute or so, finally saying "Yeah."

Down the hall he met up with Wyatt, Desiree, and a bunch of adrenalized cops. That was more like it. They trooped out into the mid-morning light. Hungry to go. Rome thought, This is what it means to be a cop.

Thirty-six

LAFITTE FOUND Steel God at the end of the hall, looking down at the parking lot through the window. The big man kept staring, said, "Think they're here."

"Is it safe to look?"

"Why not? They want to shoot me? Just like that?" He pointed to a sedan, unmarked but still obvious. "Got one. Him and a partner in the front seat. Probably going to hide until the cavalry arrives."

"Which means?"

"Time to go." Steel God smiled. Fucking smiled.

"If you see one, there's probably more on the other corners."

"Rather let them chase us than trap us." He turned and started down the hall. Someone had been peeking out their door, opened just a crack. Steel God smiled all his teeth at them. The door shut. Lafitte followed, still trying to decide. Run? Stick together?

Or get away safely, do the math later.

Still a hard choice, knowing what he knew about Ginny, the kids, his whole fucking life. Shouldn't be so hard. In the end, it came down to what would work best.

"Wait, wait." He stopped. Bent over, put his hands on his knees. His body still aching, cramping. "What if we split up?"

Steel God turned back. "For good?"

"No, like, for a day. If Kristal and I can somehow sneak out and take the car, then you can tromp out of here, lead them all on a wild goose chase. I don't know. Just…it'll give us time to make it back home."

"Our home?"

Lafitte nodded. He meant it. Like it or not, that's where he had to go. "Yeah."

A couple with a little boy came out of their room. They saw Lafitte and Steel God, stopped whispering, frozen.

Lafitte pointed down the hall behind them. "Stairs are that way."

The father put his arm around his wife, led her in front of him so his back was a shield to the two bikers. Another door opened further down the hall, businessman type, same scared look.

Lafitte said, "They're clearing the floor. We're out of time."

Steel God crossed his arms and stared after the fleeing people. Lafitte was wishing hard he didn't get any ideas about hostages.

Took a minute for the big man to say, "We stay together."

"It's a bad idea."

"We're past bad. I didn't come all this way to have to split up. And you're in no fucking shape to be alone."

"I'll have Kristal."

"Only until you slow her down. Then you got no one."

Lafitte couldn't argue with that. Goddamn it, this was all he had left, and it wasn't much.

"Okay," Lafitte said. "Okay. Okay."

"You okay?"

"Yeah."

Steel God clapped a hand on Lafitte's shoulder. "Keep watch at the window. Let me know if anyone else shows up before we get back."

"Going to get her?"

"Be right back." Wink.

He walked back to the room. Lafitte started for the end of the hall, nearly ran into a couple of teenage girls wearing the same

T-shirts, ST. JAMES HIGH SCHOOL VOLLEYBALL. Their
eyes went big. Moved over against the wall. Lafitte kept on,
flicked a thumb over his shoulder. "Stairs are back that way."

"**WE NEED TO GO,**" Steel God said as soon as he
stepped into the room. "Now."

Kristal had shoved Billy's old clothes into the shopping bag,
plus the leftover guns, the ones she'd taken from the cops at the
bar. She reached in and pulled one out. "Need this?"

Steel God crossed the room, took it. "You and Billy in the car.
I'll follow."

Kristal nodded. "I've been thinking, maybe we should split up?"

"No, we talked about that. I don't like it."

"But it's the best way. Split the focus, and you've got a better
chance—"

"I said no!" Thunder. Startled Kristal. He took a deep ragged
breath. Coughed, spit on the carpet.

Kristal stepped over beside him, laid her hand on his back.
"Look at you. This is hard enough already, but how are all three of
us going to make it out together like, you know, this fucked up?"

"We will."

"We *can't*." She rubbed. "I know what we've talked about,
and maybe it's time to switch gears. In a few days, after the heat
is off, we'll meet up."

He flexed her hand off his back, full height again. "Goddamn
it, look. You and me, we've got this plan, but I know you're going
to fuck me over."

"No, come on, never."

"Shut up. Fucking shut up already." Got a finger in her face.
"I said I *know*, not that I'm guessing. You hear me?"

Kristal's lips twisted. "Billy told."

"Fuck, I figured that shit out long before then. So if I get
caught, it's no biggie. I go to prison, I've got people on my side in

there, and before too much longer I'm either dead in the infirmary or dead in a fight. That's fine. But you, let's say Billy's not strong enough to make it. You'd drop him in a second."

She turned away. "You asshole. Piece of shit. I wouldn't."

"Or say they catch you." He closed in behind her. "Jesus, the things you'd tell them in exchange for a deal. I can't even begin to—"

"Fuck you! Never. Not even once."

Grabbed her shoulders, spun her around. Shut her up.

"I know what Billy sees in you. You're good at that, showing him innocence where he wants to see it most. But I've known you longer than that. You might be smart, but you're still the same manipulative selfish bitch who came crawling to me wanting to suck my cock, move right up the ladder your first night, remember?"

Her eyes were already down and right, hard. She nodded. "Mm."

"And what did I say?"

Her throat contracted. Thin cold lips.

"Answer me. What. Did. I. Say?"

"That I'd have to prove myself."

"Yeah."

"I've been doing that everyday. I finally got here to the top." Eyes back to his. "And you turn out to be a weak pussy. Fucking dying already."

His eyes. She hadn't seen them go sad like that in forever. He took a step away from her.

Kristal said, "It's time to split up. This is my call now."

Steel God shrunk. Just her imagination, maybe, but he shrunk a good three inches like magic, she could swear to it. He said, "I still make the call."

"No. Not anymore. If you want to keep on playing this game, you do what I say this time."

"I. Um." Cleared his throat. Gruffed it up. "There's a lot left in the tank, missy. I'm not called Steel for nothing."

Kristal laughed. The laugh of an actress on Broadway. High drama bitch. Withering. "Why do you think I stopped going after your cock? Like, I gained some fucking *respect* for you all the sudden? Jesus. Because you were limp, man. L-I-M-P. So I found the next best thing—the guy going to replace you."

"Hey—"

"Just been waiting you out, old man. My fucking granddad is tougher than you, and he's had three strokes."

Steel God backhanded her, split the skin at her temple. She bounced onto the bed.

"Only reason I never fucked you was because you weren't my type." Whatever had been vulnerable in his eyes had turned batshit insane. He said. "I don't have time for fucking games. Fucking double agent shit. The women in my bed, I tell you one thing, they're honest. If they're not when they get there, they are when they leave."

She smirked. "Want to bet?"

He didn't have an answer.

She said, "You *believed* them, didn't you? You had no idea what they were telling the other women."

Steel God's breaths were heavy, strained. Kristal touched where the skin had split. Stung. Pulled away two bloody fingers.

He said, "You want to play? Let's play. At least we'll finally get some truth out of you." Unbuckled his belt.

"Are you kidding? We don't have time!" Kristal said.

"Too late. We're shooting our way out anyway." Unbuttoned his pants. "It might hurt going in, but it'll only take a couple minutes."

The zipper came down and he pulled his dick out. Just like Kristal had heard. Every part of this guy was huge. Had to be nearly a foot soft, goddamned thick, and it was growing. A piece of the tip was gone because one of his earlier girls bit it off. Never heard from her again.

Steel God reached down, grabbed Kristal's shoulder and turned her over. She fought but the grip was intense. Flipped her onto her stomach, one hand pinned under, the other free but useless. Steel God laid a flat hand on her back, started working on her jeans with the other. Yanking. Tearing. Not getting anywhere.

She slipped her pinned hand lower every time the bed bounced. Steel God put his knee on her back and ripped both back pockets off her jeans with his hands, taking most of the denim with it.

That loosened up things big time. She got her hand deeper into the pocket. Around the knife.

Her jeans completely assless now. Steel God gave it a slap. Grunted.

"Girl needs a tan, I tell you."

She inched the knife from her pocket.

One of Steel God's fingers slipped inside her ass. Kristal cried out.

"Hey, sweetie, relax."

"No, please, I'm sorry, I'm sorry."

"Just relax and take it, okay? I'm going to let you move, just get on your knees."

"Please, I won't, I promise. Please, God, please, no."

His knee came off, but he grabbed her hair and yanked hard back. Felt her scalp stretching.

"I said *on your knees!*"

He threw Kristal onto the bed. She did like he asked, got on her knees. Got the knife out, too. Had to do it fast, fast, fast. Opened it.

Steel God grabbed her hips. His cock rubbed against her bare cheeks.

She pushed herself up, spun. A second there, Steel God backed off. What had she expected? Rage? Surprise? She got neither. The man's face was like Jesus paintings. Reached for her. She sliced his hand. Steel God flicked it back like he'd been snakebit. Kristal didn't wait. She drove into him, pushed him against the wall, stabbed into his crotch. Got one of his balls.

"Yes! Fuck yeah!" He said it with spit flying, blood from his hand getting all over Kristal as he pawed at her. She twisted the knife in his ball-sack. Pulled it out.

Steel God swung a knee into her gut. She gritted her teeth and felt the muslces spasm, tighten. She was going to fall down.

But first she grabbed Steel God's beard, wound it around her hand, brought him down with her. Freed the blade from his balls, aimed the next one for his neck.

Not exactly where she'd hoped. Damn thing went straight up under his jaw, behind his molars, the blade not long enough to slam into his soft palette. Fuck. She worked the blade back and forth in the hole. Back and forth. Making it bigger, making it work. Slicing all up under his jaw. Her fingers slick and red with him. Just kept working it. Steel God's hands slapped at her arms and at the blade. More. More.

He got hold of her but she slipped away, unplugged the knife from his jaw and held it ready to thrust again. Fucker still swiping with his hands. Slid down the wall. Too much blood in his mouth. He choked. Blood ran. He choked again. Got this steady throat-clearing rhythm going but it wasn't doing shit.

Kristal eased up the stance. Stared down at him. Felt behind her, ass skin cold, goose-bumped. She swallowed. Hated to see the old man like this. She stepped closer, above him. Weak arms slapping but she pushed them down. Grabbed his hair, pulled his head to the side.

"I'm sorry, God," she whispered. "Self-defense, you know."

Took the point of her knife and poked it against the jugular. Harder and harder until the skin sunk, pierced, and a pulsing stream started. She twisted the point clockwise, over and over and over and over and over…

Thirty-seven

WYATT PULLED his car behind the unmarked. Three Sioux Falls squads followed, then kept on past him, going to rendezvous with the other lookouts. Hotel guests had milled out into the parking lot, hanging around their cars and hoping for a good show. The cops were trying to round them up, get them across the street to a parking garage.

Rome climbed out, looked up at the floor where Lafitte was supposed to be. Thought he saw someone peeking out the window facing them. Then it was gone. Mind fuck? No, it was really him. Don't get excited. Do your job.

Lucky to even have the job. He called in to the Bureau on the way from the hospital, explained the situation and covered his ass concerning the cross-country trek. *Intelligence that demanded immediate attention. Could have compromised the Steel God investigation had it been broadcast.* The brass called off the net on Rome and instructed him to proceed with caution, allowing the local police to do their job and then taking Steel God, Lafitte, and their female associate into Federal custody later.

With pleasure.

He told Desiree, "Look, I've got to coordinate, get some guidelines set. Just stay in the car, please, babe?"

She hadn't even gotten out yet. One foot on the ground, ready to protest, but then she settled. Where else was she going to go, anyway? She nodded. Nice to be able to communicate with your wife like that, almost psychic. That's the sort of shit that made a marriage work.

She smiled and he smiled and he closed the door. The reflection of the hotel in the window as Dee turned her head away and Rome wanted to say…wanted to…but why? Sort of fatalistic, right? The urge to say "I love you" before a situation like this, but didn't that put you on track for the inevitable? Some sort of premonition overtakes you, so you need to say it *one more time*?

Dee looked back at him, probably not expecting him to still be there watching. Blinked a few times. He shrugged at her. She nodded. That was enough, right?

WYATT WAS just a driver at this point. Rome took him by the arm as he went to search out the local cop in charge. Said, "You stick with me, you get a piece of this, okay? As far as I know, they haven't done as much lawbreaking in South Dakota."

"Maybe not murder, but that gang of his—"

"We've got multiple murders, attempted murder, kidnapping, Jesus, you'll be running for office before long. Helped bring down a wanted terrorist and all that."

Wyatt slowed, almost got left behind. "Remember before, okay? Let's just take it step by step."

"You think I'm overstepping?"

Wyatt went "Hm" and crossed his arms. Stared down at the asphalt.

"What?"

"Hell, you know, I heard that conversation with your bosses. You think they're going to let you take credit for this, give you a big hug, no worries? As soon as he's in cuffs, I swear, they'll find a way to push you out."

Rome smiled. "I know. That's why you've got to shout louder than me, make it look like you deserve him first. My career depends on you beating me, right? And making it look like you talked sense into me."

"Didn't I just do that?"

"Sure, but let's do it again in front of the uniforms. You coming?"

DESIREE watched her husband and Wyatt through the windshield gathering with light snow. Slow, fluffy stuff. It would take another fifteen minutes to cloud the window enough to shade her from the scene outside. Wyatt crossing his arms. Rome acting like the ring leader. Dee thought, One car ride was all it took for his hard-on to come back.

Oh, that cocky strutting son of a bitch. Got his hog cornered, going to take it down with his teeth. Mirror opposite of ten months prior. And nothing she could do about it.

Had to be a trial now. Had to spend the next God-knows-how-many years prepping for that. She would have preferred Franklin putting a bullet in the man's head. Nice and clean. Claim self-defense. Don't claim anything at all. Walk away like it never happened. Maybe the best way to get her man back—let him do what he'd wanted to do rather than try to stop him.

More Lafitte. The fuck sort of relationship did that make?

She remembered sitting on her bed before flying up here. Cradling the gun Franklin had bought her. Wondering. Just wondering.

Desiree took in a deep breath through her nose. A gust of wind blew some of the snow off the windshield. Wyatt and Franklin were already moving on. Pretty soon they would have the whole place on lockdown. Then it was out of her hands.

She opened the glovebox. Found it on the first try. One thing she learned being married to an FBI man was that they always had a spare gun in the car. You never knew when it might come in handy. This one wasn't so big. She lifted it out of the glovebox. Fit her hand, too. She knew some guns. This one was a Sig Sauer 9MM. She checked the clip. Full, of course. Jacked a round into the chamber, then looked around. No one was paying her any attention. Cops couldn't even imagine what was going on in her head.

Hard to believe it herself.

Relax. Relax.

What are they going to do, really? All you need to say is that he threatened you, aimed a gun at you. If not a gun, then say he was reaching for one. For something.

Yeah. Sweet. They didn't know it yet, but Desiree was their Jack Ruby out of all this mess.

She slipped the gun into her jacket pocket, opened the car door and stepped out.

Thirty-eiGht

THE DOCTOR came into the waiting room, looked around, seemed startled to find no one but Colleen there ignoring the loud talk show on the TV. She'd turned it to that channel, turned up the volume, then ignored it. The noise broke her concentration. It kept her from thinking about much at all.

As for the doctor's expression, it wasn't a bright and happy smile.

He pointed at her. "You are…?"

Colleen stood from her chair. "A friend. Everyone else had to go catch the bad guys."

"There isn't any family here, correct?"

"No, it's just me now."

He coughed, kept it in his throat. "Just too much blood loss. We've done all we can do, but it's almost like he's not really fighting for it."

"Oh God." If he died, that was a third. Third one on her conscience.

"I'm very sorry." The doctor touched her shoulder. "You said friend, right? Not girlfriend?"

Colleen shook her head. "No, he wasn't…no. Just good friends."

The doctor crossed his arms. Quiet. Then, "Is there someone else I need to talk to about this?"

"I'll call Agent Rome's cell and let him know."

"Just let him know I need to talk to him, okay? Don't mention this."

She shook her head. "Yeah, right. Whatever."

"Um, look, he's awake thanks to the drugs, but fading. You want to talk to him?"

It was kind of creepy, she thought. The last person to see him alive, to talk to him? That was…wow. She didn't have that chance with Nate. What would she have said? What was the last thing they said to each other? Probably shouting about how to best take down Lafitte's bike.

"Oh, okay," Colleen said. "I want to."

THE OPERATING ROOM was quieter than she expected. Heart monitor still beeping, other beeps clashing with it, but not so bad. But McKeown, in the center of it all, was a lot bloodier than she expected, too. Didn't someone vacuum up the blood? Blood and tubes, IV's, medical tape, everything haphazard and stained.

They let her see him alone. At first Colleen thought he might be asleep, or, hell, passed on already. The closer she got, though, she caught his eyes. Watching from the time she'd opened the door and start slowly across the floor.

What's that they tell you when you're dealing with someone about to die? Stay positive. Joke around. Make them feel loved and warm and all that. Smile.

She didn't smile. She didn't say a word.

McKeown asked, his voice still holding a little volume, "Did you tell him I quit?"

Colleen nodded. "Well, no, not exactly. I told him you said for him to fuck off."

He grinned, blinked. "Ah, well. Okay, that's…okay."

"He seemed okay with it."

"Only because you said it. Me...no..." He cleared his throat. Looked pained. "Wouldn't put up with that from me."

Colleen teethed her bottom lip, looking around. Smelled like someone had splashed around a bottle of Scope. The breathing machine was making one long exhale, like it just gave and gave. It never expected anything in return.

She said, "You want me to call your mom or something? You want to talk to her?"

Grunt. Then, "To hear her cry? Sorry, but that's not the last thing I want to hear. Not...mm...like, not like she's already disappointed enough. Only son, no grandkids." He tried to smile. "Guess next they'll find the bi-porn in my apartment and put it all together. Wish I could see that."

"So. They told you, then? Like, they really *do* that?"

"You figure it out. They stopped working, asked if I wanted to talk to anyone. I didn't know who would still be here. I thought Rome, you know?"

"They've got Lafitte surrounded in a hotel."

McKeown lifted his head. "Really?"

"Sounds like a slam dunk."

Laid his head back down. "Cool. Okay, good for him. Shit, been chasing him long enough."

Colleen had a lump in her throat. Cleared it.

McKeown said. "I'm sorry about Nate. Really. He didn't deserve it."

"Yeah."

"Would've made a good agent."

"I don't mind him dying on the job, but he wasn't really. We were so fucking stupid." She closed her eyes. Felt like collapsing. Opened them again. "Dying by getting shot or whatever, that's fine. But burning like that—"

"Just so you know...death by getting shot isn't so great either."

Collen laughed. Caught herself, but then saw McKeown's face and kept it up. "At least it smells better."

McKeown stiffened, sharp breath, then held it a moment before letting the air go. "Shit." Turned back to Colleen. "Do me a favor?"

Like she could say no. Like anyone could deny a dying request, right? Fuck.

"Okay."

"Let me tell you first."

"Sure. But I'm sure I can."

"Listen…that guy I was talking about, Alex? I want him to know, okay? It was only one night, but he's thinking I ran out…he just needs to know."

"You've got his number?"

"Yeah, yeah. Um…goddamn it. I can't…you know how you put a number in your cell and can't remember it anymore?"

"All the time."

"I would've gotten it eventually." He was fading. Too much energy.

"Tell you what," she said. "How about I go tell him face to face? I've never been to Memphis."

"It's good. Good food. Lots of Elvis, though."

She crinkled her nose. "He's not so bad, I guess."

"I know, some of it." Another ragged breath.

Colleen tried to imagine watching Nate die like this instead. It wasn't any easier. Hell, you shouldn't have to think about that shit at this age. People are supposed to get old together before one dies in his sleep before the other one dies three weeks later from loneliness. It wasn't right watching young guys writhe like old-timers. Like her grandpa, cancer eating him up, couldn't concentrate on what she was talking about. She refused to visit him those last six months.

Why not Memphis? Why not? A new place, alone, take her mind off things. Not like she wanted to go back to work, have to hear all the sympathies and accept all the flowers and feel all the awkwardness as the people tried to coax her back to normalcy, but that would just remind her more. And at least it wouldn't be as cold down South.

"I'll go. You said he was in a band?"

"Named 'Poor Man's Fish'. I don't know, he explained it to me once. They play mostly at this little joint called Southern Corner. I love that place."

"Okay."

"I won't tell you what to say."

Colleen rubbed his arm. "I'll do better than I did with Rome."

"Thanks. You know. Thanks for everything."

"Well, you did keep me from getting arrested. I owed you."

"One more...um, one more thing?"

She didn't say anything because she pretty much knew. Curled her lips some, looked away.

McKeown said, "Would you stay with me? Until?"

She nodded. Stared at his arm, all tubed up. "Sure, Josh. No problem."

She stood there at his bedside. Seventy-three minutes.

Thirty-nine

TIME TO TRUCK on out of there.

Lafitte watched the Minnesota squad car pull in and knew something was up. Shouldn't be on South Dakota turf. Then that tall skinny black man he should've killed way back when stepped out.

"Fuck. Me."

He watched Rome scan the hotel walls, then felt heat like radar as the man zeroed right in on him. Lafitte jerked the curtain into place, peered through. Everyone was a blur. Rome saw him. No doubt. Rome saw him. Brought his big guns, too. Funny, but Lafitte had always thought Rome would want another face-to-face. Guess he'd given up on that. Rather face Lafitte in the box than out in the world.

Couldn't blame him.

Rome had turned to talk to a woman still seated in the car. Not a cop, at least not a uniform. A fine looking woman, too, skin like exotic coffee, just a touch of cream. Looked like she was in her forties, but those kickass forties, like a Demi Moore or Pam Grier. Wanted to get out of the car, but all Rome had to say was a couple seconds worth to get her to stay put. Shit, like it's his *wife* or something? Who brings his wife to a fucking siege?

Good to know, though. Lafitte mapped it out in his head—
if he made it out, that was the car he was heading for. Talk about
your rich fucking leverage.

Rome and the Trooper with him walked away, snow blurred.
Starting to fall heavier now. This time of year, nothing to worry
about. It would melt before it could gather. But it was building
up on the squad with the woman.

Yep. Time to truck on out of there.

Strange that Steel God and Kristal were still in the room. What,
was she packing? This wasn't a packing situation. Lucky to get out
with the clothes on your back. Lafitte walked down the hall,
knocked on the door. Kristal shouted out, "A second! Be right out!"

Lafitte didn't have one of the key cards. Knocked again.
"They're *out there*. Come on already."

"A fucking second!"

Lafitte huffed, balled his fists. Took a lot of energy. Had to
think about what he was about to do. Might have to wound a
few cops on the way out. Steel God would flat out kill them.
Lafitte couldn't say he was that far gone yet. He liked cops. Liked
being a cop. Was going to aim for their shoulders. Aim for the
chest on the ones wearing vests. Knock them down, stun them.
They'd be sore the next couple days, but alive.

Finally, the handle on the door dropped. Kristal slipped out,
barely opening it a crack, trying to bring it closed. Just her. No
Steel God. She carried the shopping bag. Wore God's blazer tied
around her waist. Jeans ripped to shit. Her fur jacket looked
stained. Hair a mess.

Goddamn it, Lafitte fucking *knew*, you know?

Reached out before she got the door closed, big hand pressing it open.

"No," she said. A hiss right after. He kept pushing. Too
weak to fight her. Both of her hands white-knuckled the handle,
blood all over her fingers. She said, "No, please, just...go, we've
got to go."

"What about Steel God?"

"He's sick, okay? He wants us to go. You don't need to see him like—"

Fuck the bitch. Arm strength fading, Lafitte leaned into the door, put his whole shoulder into one last effort.

Kristal yelped, fell inside. She hit the floor, bag emptying everywhere. Lafitte kept his balance, barely, swung the door behind him, slammed it shut.

Blinked a few times to make sure he was seeing it right.

Blood. Blood. Blood. Trails and pools and smears on the wall.

So much dark blood coating Steel God below the neck that Lafitte thought for a moment the man had been decapitated. Then he got it. Steel God, the way he'd never imagined him—mouth wide, eyes rolled back, killed by a woman with a little knife.

"Jesus."

Steadied himself against the wall.

Kristal pushed herself up. Already talking. He missed what she was saying, instead looking at the blood on her fingers, the ripped jeans where the blazer had slid out of the way. Fuck. Steel God had tried to…yeah. No. Only if she had…the only reason she would've…

"Are you listening to me? Please, Billy, you've got to listen." She was crying, but he didn't care. Tired of her fucking acts. Tired of her schemes.

He said, "Well, goddamn, you didn't have to…*fuck*…you didn't have to do *that!*"

"I didn't have a choice." Inching towards him, stooped. Bloody fingers outstretched.

"Were you actually that fucking stupid?"

Stopped the tears, but still had that achy whine going. "He, he, was going, going to rape me. So strong. I, I, it was all I could do. Oh god, *why?*"

"Yeah, really strong. Stronger than you. And you think he couldn't have gotten that knife away if he had wanted to?"

"But…he was…no, Billy. No." A little more clarity. Lafitte watched it dawn. "Shit. No, goddamn it. How could he?"

"Because of this right here. Because he didn't want to go out there and risk me getting killed. This way, we've got a distraction."

She shook her head. "No, it was…I had the better of him. I know I did."

"Shut up."

"Please Billy." She grabbed his shirt.

He wrenched her fingers off. "I said *shut up*."

Kristal sniffed up her tears and said, "Let's get going. We'll talk later."

Lafitte looked over her shoulder at Steel God. Face lifted to the ceiling. Nothing up beyond it for that man. No stars, no heavens. Off-white plaster, that was all.

"We've got to split up," Lafitte said.

"The fuck we do." Not sad anymore. Not doing her little soap opera drama. "He was the one we needed to split with. You and me, we're going together."

"Too late for that. We're surrounded. We go out two different directions, we've got a better chance. Same plan, just without…" Couldn't even look at him anymore. She did a number on the big man. Shit. That shit wasn't right, the last look the cops would get of him, all gutted over pussy rather than filled with a hundred .40 caliber slugs in a firefight. How the fuck could God have wanted this? But there he was, all laid out. Guess he figured he would drag them down on the road, so better push the endgame earlier than planned. "Fuck. *Fuck*. Oh, fuck."

"You think you can do it alone? You need me. You're still not strong enough yet."

"Doesn't matter. I've got an idea."

"Tell me."

"No way. You don't tell me yours either. One of us gets picked up, at least the other can't roll."

He'd thought of splitting up as soon as he saw Rome's woman in the squad car. Kristal could deal on her own. They would meet up later and head back at the gang's sanctuary. But…*shit*. God-damn Steel God. Couldn't think past the shootout. Like a perfect robbery right up until some asshole decides to go upstairs, wake the homeowner, and play thug. You shouldn't fuck up your meal ticket. But this girl didn't even stop to think about it. Maybe just wound the man, not castrate and slit his throat like a pig. She was like a bug zapper. Couldn't help but attract trouble.

Kristal stood straight. Eyes clear. That was fucking cold, girl not even caring if her act was convincing anymore. "If they catch me, you're going to suffer twice as bad. I'll make sure the word gets out that *you* betrayed him. You. Not me. Last time you did good hiding, but if they've got me, you'll be caught in less than a week. I fucking swear."

"Sure about that?"

Little lip curl, little eyelash batting. "Where are you going to go? Back to the gang? Back South to your *wifey*? Back to Minnesota? Where? Mexico? You can get to Mexico on your own? With every fucking biker and every fucking pig looking for you?"

"Damn, baby. C'mon." Shook his head. "I'm not trying to—"

"We go together. You're always going to be more valuable than me. So you either keep me free or I'll tell them whatever they want to know about you, and that'll also keep me free. You're a walking golden ticket."

Smart bitch. Too fucking smart. Damn, like, played everyone she'd ever known. Girl could fuck and connive her way to a Ph.D. if she wanted, but she'd rather hold expectations low. Lafitte thought it through.

He held up his palms and said, "Hold up, give me a minute here."

"Fuck that, we've got to go." She knelt and rebagged the stuff that had spilled. Adjusted the blazer to cover her ass again.

Lafitte stepped past her, sat on the bed that wasn't splashed with blood. Took another look over at Steel God. Each time the corpse looking worse and worse, the little details popping out. His face, what wasn't covered by the beard, was usually flushed red, on fire. Now it was just pale with broken blood vessels webbing across. Whatever dark and murderous soul had lived inside him, it must've added a lot of mass, because he seemed shrunken. An illusion maybe, but who was Steel God, really, if not a product of his own reputation?

Brought down by this woman crawling on the carpet, fighting to be in control. Fighting to be a badass. Like one of those plate-spinners. Five going at once.

"I'm going out alone."

She looked up. "Didn't you hear me just now?"

Lafitte stood. "Yep. Don't care. We're splitting up. Meet me at that truck stop, what was it, a Flying J? You know, the one where we stole the guy's wallet, bought breakfast, and then fucked in the bathroom. After that we'll head home. You bring any shit to our doorstep, I'll see it coming from far away. You got it?"

"I don't believe you."

"I swear." Held up his right hand. "Just like you wanted. I'm taking my place at the head of the pack."

"By getting rid of me?"

"Shit, baby, blow a few cops and you'll be on the street thumbing a ride by sundown."

She hung her head. Said *Fuck* over and over, whispered and sharp. Her hand still inside the shopping bag. Lafitte watched, had a good idea why.

She pushed off the floor and came up on her knees with Steel God's pistol. Tried to get her other hand wrapped around, too, but Lafitte had been waiting, already moving before she even realized. Boot connected with her hand. Gun flew. Lafitte kicked again. Put Kristal on her back. Fell on her like bricks, flipped her over, wrenched her arm up high, knee on her neck, just like the police had taught him.

She clenched her teeth. Not one sound.

Leaned close to her ear. "Good girl. Don't want to attract attention."

"You...like, were all weak."

"Just trying to catch my breath. How the fuck do you think I'm not already dead ten times over?"

"I don't know."

"Cop blood. That's what it is. Listen, I'm going to leave you here bound and gagged and shit. Tell whoever finds you whatever you want about me. Doesn't matter. I'm still gonna be fine."

"Please, Billy, please. Okay, I understand. We'll split up for now."

"Too late."

"Goddamn it, Billy! I'm trying to help you!"

Lafitte reached across her to pick up the gun. Held it by the barrel, wanted to knock her out. He slammed the handle across the back of her head.

She thrashed, "No, fuck, *no don't don't.*"

He hit her again. And again. Remembered Fawn trying the same trick with him in that basement. And again. How it didn't work. Never works like on TV. And again. Harder. Blood. Knee crushing her neck. And again. And again.

All the shit that had happened.

Fuckers torturing him in the basement.

Rome killing Drew, innocent as all the goddamned snow in Minnesota, then trying to say it was Lafitte's fault.

And again.

Yeah, self-righteous son of a bitch Rome setting him up. Using Ginny to do it. His fucking *kids*, for fuck's sake.

And again.

Nate and his girlfriend trying to kill him. Had to watch the kid die. Had Colleen on his trail wanting revenge. Saved her fucking life.

And again.

This bitch here trying to tie him up, squeeze his balls.

And fucking *again.*

Kristal stopped talking. She stopped thrashing. She stopped period.

And again.

Lafitte fell off her, against the wall. Her eyes, still open and glaring at him. Lips parted. Not at all like Drew's, which had been apologetic—sorry she had fucked up. So Sorry. Lafitte's hands shook. All he had to do was tie her up. Tie the girl up and go. That was all. What the *fuck?*

The gun, handle thick with Kristal's head goo, aimed towards his face. The whole time he'd been slamming her with it, the barrel was pointed right for him.

Turned his head to God's corpse. Voice strained, "Why do I keep getting so lucky?"

Forty

THE LIEUTENANT in charge at the hotel told Rome, "We've got some SWAT guys running point in the stairwell, but we're not ready for full coverage yet. There are still some people we want to get out. And we've heard it's getting loud up there, like our perps are arguing amongst themselves."

Rome looked at Wyatt.

Wyatt shook his head. "I'm only here as an observer."

Back to the Lieutenant. "Charge the door and toss in a flash-bang."

The Lieutenant frowned. "From what I've heard, Steel God eats flash-bangs for breakfast."

"But where's the proof? Throw in two, then. Just…" Rome waved his hands around, hoping they'd do something sensible. "Whatever. Just…*something*."

"We thought you were going to talk to him first."

"He already knows I'm here. I saw him looking out the window. By now, he's got some plan or something. Talking won't do shit. So…let's fucking *move*."

"We'll do what we can, sir." The Lieutenant turned to a Sergeant, started mumbling. Not even real words, Rome thought. Trying to get rid of him is all. Got this far, finally able to corner

Lafitte, no chance of escape, and all he can do is stand around with his thumb up his ass pretending to be leading these jokers. Maybe someone in some office had told them Rome was the one in charge, but these guys, always some excuse for moving slower than he wanted them to. Traffic. Bad communication. Still some guests in the hotel that needed to be moved. Didn't want to alert the media yet just in case these idiots saw themselves on TV and decided to up the ante. Like shit. Like it really could be pushed any higher. Come on.

Rome bundled himself tighter. The snow was still light, but blowing all around in the wind so that it was tough to see beyond about twenty feet. Rome glanced over his shoulder, barely saw Wyatt's car back there. Snow blanketing the windshield. No need for Desiree to sit there alone if she wasn't in any real danger.

Standing, waiting. Rome thought about what was next. If the Bureau forced him to resign, he could use what he knew to get some nice rec letters, move back East, get involved with corporate security. Yeah, real cloak and dagger shit. Those guys actually encourage you to skirt the rules. Shit, planning black ops, packing the latest arms, that was outright cool. Plus, traveling all over the world on private jets and having money practically thrown at you. Desiree deserved some perks like that. She'd been deprived long enough.

The Lieutenant was saying something and Rome latched on when he heard "Problem."

Whipped his head around. "Excuse me?"

"We think a handful of new people have gotten inside. I don't know, they slipped past somehow."

"And they're not contained?"

"Well…" Shrug. "If they missed the initial call for evacuation and just got back from whatever they were doing, you know, we can try calling rooms that didn't answer the first time. But if everyone else would just stay in their rooms—"

Rome said, "Fucking hotel walls are paper thin, man! Shots'll go right through."

"My people are extremely well-trained."

"So what? So's Lafitte. That biker ain't bad either. Charge the room already and get this over with before they take it out into the hall or lobby. Then we're really fucked."

The Lieutenant's face was red. Lips moving. He wanted to, Rome could tell. Wanted to tell him where to go. Wanted to take him down. Copper's dream, getting one over on a Fed.

Then again, that would be Mr. Lieutenant's ass.

He swallowed hard, said, "The protection of the public comes first. Nobody charges anything until we figure out if this can be *peacefully* resolved...sir."

Rome shook his head, made some ticked noises. Like, yeah, the party line conquers all. "All right, all right." Signaled surrender. "Come get me when you grow some balls."

He left Wyatt behind to run point while he trotted back to the squad car. Snow coming down even more, getting in his eyes and melting. Blinked clear. Getting his hair all wet, too. Not at all the scene he'd imagined. If these lame-ass cops didn't screw the pooch on this one, he'd gladly settle for another go in the interrogation room. Break Lafitte down bit by bit. Not even about Q&A anymore. Well beyond that. Just a nice steady drip of humiliation.

Rome shook the thought away on reaching the car. Looked in the passenger window. Dee wasn't there.

Checked the back. Maybe she was napping.

No. The car was clean.

Maybe someone asked her to move. Maybe she needed a bathroom break.

He searched around, found the closest uniform about thirty feet away. Called him over.

"Did you notice if my wife left that vehicle recently?"

Blank stare.

"Tall woman, in her forties, wearing...ah...the hell was she wearing...like a, a,—"

"Jacket?"

"Yeah, it was purple."

Nothing. "Was she....um..."

"Black. Yes. Goddamn it."

The uniform showed his teeth, sheepish, said, "Sorry."

Rome pointed. "Use your radio, please. Ask if anyone else has seen her."

The uniform spoke into the handset on his shoulder while Rome searched the ground outside the car. Not much snow sticking because of the wind, but enough to get a path started. He followed five feet before losing the trail. Frantic. Don't think it, don't think it.

Caught the trail again between parked cars, heading towards the hotel.

Not if she was going to the bathroom, surely. Dee would know better.

No, no, no.

He rushed over to Wyatt, grabbed him, said, "Do you carry a spare piece in your car?"

"What? Slow down."

"A *gun*, man. Do you have a spare in the car?"

"Well, yeah. I mean, shotgun's in the trunk."

"Not there, like, up front. A back-up, just in case."

The Lieutenant was paying full attention now. Wyatt steered Rome away, whispered, "Keep it down, for fuck's sake. Jesus."

"Show me."

"Don't you already have—"

"Please. Show me."

Wyatt didn't move for a moment. Rome took a step in the direction of the car. "Come on."

Wyatt took a deep breath. "It's in the glove box."

Not another thought. Rome started hard for the hotel, Wyatt shouting behind him, chasing.

Shit. Shit. Shit. Baby going to get herself killed. No, no, no, no.

The Lieutenant spoke into his radio: "Hey, hey, we need to subdue Agent Rome. Middle-aged, African-American. You have a go to taze. Repeat, a *go* to taze."

Forty-One

A KILLER.

All the time he'd spent trying to avoid recognizing that's what he was, even when he'd fucked up and helped his partner in Gulfport kill that banger they couldn't pin shit on, then in Detroit, those wannabe gangsters—that one was self-defense—but then what he'd had in mind for Agent Rome when he broke into the man's home…still, he didn't go through with it. He was pretty sure he was weened off the bloodlust by then.

Even as an enforcer for Steel God, he tried real hard, and most of the time he was able to maim or intimidate instead of outright kill. Only killed when the other guy was really gunning for him. This whole trip, going *out of his goddamned way* to make sure innocents didn't get taken out in the crossfire, and look where he ended up.

Killed a biker slut in a motel room. He'd already disarmed her, could've easily overpowered her, tied her up. But Lafitte had really wanted her to shut up. For the love of God, why wouldn't she shut up?

Asked himself again as he leaned close to the bathroom mirror, focused on his bruised face, the dark circles under his eyes. He'd used the entire little bottle of hotel shampoo to get the blood off. Letting the hot water run over his hands now. Not hot enough. Not for what he wanted to feel.

Lafitte couldn't imagine leaving Kristal like she was, so he'd dragged her over to Steel God, arranged then so God had his arm wrapped around her, cuddled close. It wouldn't fool anyone, what with the trail of blood Lafitte had left, but it was fitting. Like a photo of an ancient tomb in *National Geographic*. A Father guiding his daughter into the underworld. Or close enough.

The blood was as bloody as usual, and Lafitte had gone through every washcloth and towel, tossed them on the floor, wondered how the maids would've reacted if they had happened on something like this. Like, could've at least left one or two clean ones, you pig.

He was ready. Splashed steaming water on his face to shock himself higher. Adrenalized.

Pistols, two of them, loaded and ready.

Kristal's little knife, cleaned to a shine, ready.

One more look in the mirror, not even wanting to look back at the bodies. Nodded to his reflection. All right, then.

Out into the hallway. Quiet. He hoped they were all cleared out already. If not, he hoped to pull this off without any stray bullets. Not even about trying to be a nice guy anymore. Just wanting to keep the numbers down—no need to keep adding bodies to the list of charges.

Best shot at an exit was the elevator, maybe. SWAT would have the stairwells covered. The lobby was out. Like a pit of poisonous snakes, almost for sure. But the second floor? Third? Maybe he could jump from there.

Any better ideas?

He punched the down button and waited. Only three floors above them. Four below. He put his ear to the elevator door. Sounded like it was coming up. Maybe they'd filled the car with cops. Lafitte hopped in place, sucked in air. Shit, this was *fun*, man. If you're going out hard, this is the way to go. Having a grand old time.

The elevator dinged.

Lafitte slung the guns up towards the doors. Waited.

When they slid open, it was one guy, hands up, in the back corner. Jeans, tight polo shirt, gray hair, buzzed. The grandfather from the pool, the one who looked like a coach.

"Whoa, partner. Hold on a minute, now. I want to talk to you."

Cute. Not an official negotiator, though. Lafitte could already count that off. In fact, he was pretty sure the phone started ringing in his room while he was waiting for the elevator.

Lafitte said, "Get out of there."

The guy stood stock still and the door began to close. Lafitte stepped up, held the door back with his boot. "I said *GET. THE FUCK. OUT!*"

"All right, all right. This is your call. Whatever you say, buddy."

What was he thinking? Some sort of hero trying to do what the police couldn't?

This coach or whoever eased out of the elevator, hands behind his head. Facing Lafitte, who was headed back. Shit. Didn't want two fucking flanks.

"I'm going to get in the next elevator. You're going to come with me."

Coach said, "Boy, I just came up to see if we could find some common ground. I understand what you're feeling. My own son's got twenty years to serve for manslaughter, and I know what it's like thinking there's no other option."

Lafitte didn't answer. Steady on the guy. Kept himself in shape. Fucking ripped, man. Shirt was tucked in. Only place he could hide a gun would be his ankle.

"You a cop?" Lafitte asked.

Coach shook his head. "I'm just a man. Like you."

"Fed?"

"Listen, I'm nothing. They called me, told me what was up, and…I don't know. Maybe it was Jesus. I think it was. Jesus spoke to me, said, 'Go talk to the man. He doesn't really want to cause any problems.' So here I am."

He was a hero all right. Shit. Only reason to take him along on the elevator was to keep him from running and telling SWAT where he was. Let him preach all he wanted. As long as he didn't sing to the folks in the uniforms.

Lafitte waved the gun. "Press the down button."

Coach didn't move. "No sir. I'm here under the Lord's protection. We're not going anywhere."

"Hit the goddamn button or I shoot you in the knee."

Coach raised his chin, stood straighter. "The Lord is my shepherd."

Lafitte let out a breath. Losing time, losing time. Losing the element of surprise. He stomped over, punched the button with the tip of his gun.

"When we get on, get quiet. You want to talk, whisper."

"I said we're not going anywhere." Coach took a bold step forward, hands still behind his head.

Lafitte stumbled back three feet. Still off-balance. "Shit!"

The hero took his chance. Tucked in and charged, tackled Lafitte in the middle, pinned his arms up. The wind left him.

Coach took hold of Lafitte's wrists while straddling him. Lafitte bucked, yanked his arms every which way. Coach shouted, "I've got him! I've got him!"

Bucked again. Threw Coach to the side. Lafitte got his knee up between him and Coach. Pushed as hard as he could. Broke that guy's grip, Jesus, like a vice. Scrambled back. Coach was up on one knee plotting another charge.

No fucking way. Just, no.

Lafitte closed his eyes, raised both guns, and fired.

OUTSIDE the radios squawked, "Shots fired! Shots fired!"

Rome raised his head, still shaky from the taze. "Oh, Desiree."

The Lieutenant was on the ball now, yelling into his radio, "Are we ready to go in? Can we?"

The answer came back. "Negative. Negative. Need ten more minutes."

The Lieutenant glanced down at Rome, cuffed and seated on the curb. "We didn't send enough people inside. Those guys are sitting ducks."

Rome said, "If my wife…if she's…not okay—"

Cut him off with a quick *Shhp* and then, "Don't make us use the pepper spray."

COACH WAS DEAD or dying, maybe dying—wheezing up a gusher—but Lafitte didn't have time to care. The stairwell door opened and a single SWAT was drawing down. Lafitte was running for it, already anticipating, firing both fists. Bulls-Eye. The SWAT went down. Lafitte knew he had to hurry, since the body armor had plenty of padding and the guy would be up in a moment. Lafitte got there into the stairwell, looked up, down. Fuckers hadn't even had time to set up yet. Why the hell would you only send up one guy?

Lafitte stomped down hard on the SWAT's chest. Bones cracked. The SWAT grit his teeth and bent his fingers into claws. All armored up, full on pads and helmet. Lafitte could barely get a handle on the guy. Going to have to take him out. He reached down and got the AR-15 before the SWAT could get his breath back. Then he bent over, shoved his pistol under the SWAT's chinstrap, and pulled the trigger. His facemask splattered red. His body spasmed once good and hard before going limp.

Lafitte gritted his teeth, sucked air in and out, stared at the body. Fucking *made* him do it, man. Not a fair choice. And no time to think about it. Lafitte wanted his vest. He set the semi-auto down, set the smaller pistol down, and shoved the big one in his waistband as he got on his knees and started working on the Velcro straps. Not much time. Once word of those shots hit the airwaves, they'd be coming all quick like.

He had the left side undone when from the landing one floor below he heard:

"Lafitte!"

A woman's voice.

"Hands up!"

He lifted his hands. Glanced over his shoulder.

It was the good-looking black woman he'd seen Rome talking to outside. Had herself a nice compact nine, it looked like. One hand on the railing, one with the gun.

He took a chance. "Mrs. Rome?"

"Don't talk to me."

"Come on, let me know if I'm right, at least."

Took a moment. She took one step up. "Eyes ahead. You don't look at me."

"You're going to shoot a man in the back?"

"I'm a woman and this ain't the OK Corral."

Fuck, fuck, fuck, *think*. Well, maybe push off, fall down the steps onto her? That would surprise her. But she might still get a shot off. Take a jump to the right, use the stairs going up as cover, at least long enough to take higher ground. But higher ground won't help get him out of here.

Or risk it all, grab the gun in his belt, and see what happens.

She kept talking. "You took him away from me for so long. He changed. And as soon as I think we've gotten past you, here you come again."

"I didn't even know he was looking—"

"Of course he was looking. Every goddamned day he was looking. He was going to lose everything, even me." She cleared her throat. "I can't lose him again, not to you or the government, or his own nightmares, whatever. He's mine, you hear me? Mother fucker, you don't want it in your back, you'd better stand up slowly, keep those hands up, and turn around."

Lafitte rose to his feet. Didn't turn around just yet. Too far away from the AR-15. No, had to go with the gun in reach. He said, "You're really going to kill me to keep him from getting involved again? You love him that much?"

"You don't know anything."

"Fuck, you heard he was using my ex-wife and kids as fucking bait? And you tell me I don't know anything?"

"I don't care. I've heard what you've done, made that bitch stone crazy."

Lafitte felt his guts rumble. "That's not on me."

"I don't care. I'm not a judge. I'm just doing what someone else should've done a long goddamn time ago. Turn around."

Guts on fire. Guts going apeshit.

Lafitte grinned. Couldn't help himself. Okay, this was it. The whole ball game. Three seconds left on the clock, the Hail Mary pass.

He said, "All right. Let's get this over with. I've got a gang to lead."

His hand twitched, and he dove for the gun as soon as he started turning.

ROME HEARD the next two shots. Weak, like firecrackers set off underwater, but he flinched anyway. This time the radio squawks were unintelligible, frantic, and the remaining cops didn't wait for orders. They just moved, moved, moved, shouting, "Go! Go! Go!" Right past Rome, ignoring him, guns drawn, into the lobby. Rome tried to imagine what was going on, who was alive, who was dead, and on which side his wife ended up. Jesus.

Mouth dry, gaping. Couldn't call for her. Couldn't turn around to look at the hotel and the advancing line of cops.

More shots. Three of them.

Rome looked up at the sky, blinking snowflakes away, as if it might have an answer for him. Yeah, right. Nothing but gray, cold, and endless.

AcknowleDGments

Thanks to Brandy,
who likes everything except the endings. All my love.

To Victor and Sean-—
for listening, for the advice, for the utter audacity,
and for the next round of golf. The next decade of
Crimedoggedness will bark louder than the first.

To Allan Guthrie, the teller of unvarnished truth—
stings when it's bad, but he sends you out to keep fighting
round after round until you win, goddamnit!

To Ben, Alison, and Narco (Lisa)—
giving me a stage for the story I wanted to tell,
and for helping make it even rowdier
and more profane (thus, better).

Born and raised on the Mississippi Gulf Coast, **ANTHONY NEIL SMITH** now lives on the frozen prairies of rural Minnesota, where he teaches at Southwest Minnesota State University. He's the author of *Yellow Medicine, Psychosomatic* and *The Drummer.* He's also the editor of the online noir fiction zine Plots With Guns.